House of Savera

ASHRAF JAFRI

authorHOUSE®

AuthorHouse™
1663 Liberty Drive
Bloomington, IN 47403
www.authorhouse.com
Phone: 1-800-839-8640

This book is a work of fiction. Places, events, and situations in this story are purely fictional. Any resemblance to actual persons, living or dead, is coincidental.

Published by AuthorHouse 9/18/2012

ISBN: 978-1-4772-6400-3 (sc)
ISBN: 978-1-4772-6399-0 (hc)
ISBN: 978-1-4772-6401-0 (e)

Library of Congress Control Number: 2012915827

Any people depicted in stock imagery provided by Thinkstock are models, and such images are being used for illustrative purposes only. Certain stock imagery © Thinkstock.

This book is printed on acid-free paper.

Because of the dynamic nature of the Internet, any web addresses or links contained in this book may have changed since publication and may no longer be valid. The views expressed in this work are solely those of the author and do not necessarily reflect the views of the publisher, and the publisher hereby disclaims any responsibility for them.

To my loving wife Tecla whose help and encouragement
made it possible for me to write the book; and to
her creativity for providing fitting title.

To my children, Dani and Fabia for their positive suggestions and
lessons that allowed me to use my computer as my writing tool.

To my daughter Fabia, for her assistance in finding
and restoring lost pages and taking the time to teach
me how to save and retrieve my written work.

To my close friends, thank you for reading my work and
providing positive and encouraging words along the way.

Chapter 1

Sybille Tells Her Story

Peter Goes to Russia

My father, Peter Savera, was born in Spain into a wealthy socialist family. His father, Carlos Savera, and his grandfather, Juan Savera, were the founders of a local socialist party. The family developed a very close relationship with the Russian political bosses of the Soviet party. This relationship was associated with many advantages for the Savera family.

My father, when he was around five years old, loved airplanes. When his father returned from trips to Russia, he brought home model planes for Peter. His interest kept on building throughout more trips and more models. They tell me that when he was a teenager, he asked his grandfather to help him get into the Soviet aeronautical institute. His grandfather promised to try to get him into the academy. "But you must start learning Russian and study hard to pass your high school exams," he said.

Peter promised to do what his grandpa, Juan Savera, wanted him to do. Peter asked him, "Who is going to teach me Russian, Grandpa?"

"Don't worry. Next Saturday, there will be a teacher here at four p.m. sharp, and you will start your lessons. Your teacher does not speak much Spanish, so you will have to work hard."

Peter said, "Grandpa, thank you, thank you. I love you." He kissed his grandfather. Peter went to tell his father and his mother the news; they were happy for him.

Months passed, and Peter was progressing well in his written and spoken Russian. Peter was able to carry on a fairly decent conversation

1

in Russian. Juan Savera was successful in getting his grandson admitted to the Russian aeronautical academy.

Three months after Peter Savera demonstrated his ability to meet all the conditions imposed by the academy, Peter's Spanish passport arrived, fully endorsed for an extended period of stay in Russia. The whole family was delighted by Peter's admission to the aeronautical academy. Plans were underway for Peter to fly to Moscow and from there to the Soviet Aeronautical Academy near Moscow. The plane, a three-engine Russian academy plane, was arriving in two days; a farewell dinner was planned for Peter's friends and immediate family members. The Russian ambassador and socialist party members were also invited.

Peter's mother and grandmother were preparing his luggage. His suitcases were packed with woolen garments, underwear, and socks; they wanted to protect Peter from the Russian cold. Grandmother had knitted woolen gloves for Peter. The world of Peter Savera was going to change drastically; he had never lived away from home and luxury. Peter was excited but at the same time a bit apprehensive. He went to his mother and confided in her about his fears. She told him, "My Peter, we love you more than you think. I know you will succeed and bring honor to your grandpa, who is giving you a dinner fit for a prince."

The day of farewell arrived. The ornate dining room had experienced elaborate dinners before, but this dinner was filled with pride and love. All the members of the Savera family were dressed in their formal clothing; the mothers, aunts, and cousins were dressed in their finest silks.

The guests started to arrive. First Peter's friends and then the relatives were received by Peter and his very close childhood friend Arthur de Cordoba. All the ladies were received by Peter's mother and grandmother.

The arrival of dignitaries was announced by a uniformed guard, who was posted for such occasions.

The socialist party members arrived and were received by Peter's father. When the Russian ambassador Sergei Chernoff arrived, Grandfather Juan Savera went to receive him; they greeted each other. Carlos Savera brought his son, Peter. Grandpa Savera introduced them, saying, "Your Excellency, you know my son Carlos, but you never met my grandson, who with your blessing has been admitted to the academy."

"Of course I know Carlos," replied the ambassador. "We have traveled together a few times to Russia. Your son is a splendid man. And let me see our future aeronautical engineer. What a handsome man, Juan. Be careful: our Russian beauties will steal him."

They continued toward the dining room, where Grandfather Savera introduced Sergei to beautifully dressed ladies. The ladies were delighted with the ambassador's wit and charm when he spoke in perfect Spanish with a slight Russian accent. Sergei Chernoff delighted the ladies by making small talk. Everyone took their appointed seats, and dinner was served. All the waiters were busy bringing Spanish and Russian dishes. The guests enjoyed the dinner; pomegranate and orange juices along with Spanish wines were at the table. Dessert consisted of rice pudding, cakes, and pastries. Champagne was poured. Grandfather stood up from his chair and lifted his glass to welcome and thank the ambassador for his assistance. The two friends started to tell stories about their past adventures. It was getting late, and at last Grandfather Savera and the ambassador stood up to shake hands with others, signaling that it was time to go. The Russian ambassador gave Peter a big hug, kissed him, and wished him good luck at the aeronautical institute in Russia. Cars were waiting outside. Grandfather, Carlos, and Peter walked the ambassador to his car, and the guests left.

After the other guests left, friends and family members stayed overnight to see off Peter the next morning. Everyone enjoyed partying until midnight, when Grandma ordered them to go to sleep. All went to their sleeping places, but you could hear whispers and quiet giggling in the youths' quarter. Morning came. The plane was to arrive at the airport at seven-thirty a.m., and boarding time was eight a.m. Peter arrived at the airport with his parents and Arthur. The car brought the family to the reception area; Peter helped his father and mother to out of the car and into the office. The plane touched down, the airport authorities cleared all necessary paperwork, and the porters took the luggage to the plane. In the meantime, the crew of the plane came inside and met the passenger, young Peter Savera. The captain shook hands with Peter's father, and his father and mother hugged and kissed their son and wished him good luck. Peter said good-bye again to his friends and left with the captain of the plane. The plane took off exactly at eight a.m.

Peter Graduates from the Academy

During Peter's stay at the academy, he was allowed to come home every six months. In the beginning, he wrote home every week. He complained about the cold and wrote about how he bundled up to keep warm. He and his roommate went together to some of the school's functions in the clubhouse. On weekends, there were dances. He had been a good dancer even in his high school years; many girls always wanted to dance with him. He had learned flamenco dancing and showed off his skill every now and then when he wanted to impress the girls.

As the winter of his final year came to an end, his letters were more cheerful. It seemed he did not have much spare time to write anymore; either he was busy with his studies or was more involved in extracurricular activities. In his last letter, he sounded very happy and upbeat; he mentioned that the academy had offered him an assistant professor's job after his graduation.

Peter wrote his mother a separate note. The note read, "Dear Mama, I want to tell you that I have been dating a beautiful girl. She is charming, has good manners, and comes from a good family. She is my professor's daughter. She will be graduating from medical school next year. Her name is Anna.

"I am coming home on the fourth of April. Anna will be coming with me. Her father has approved Anna's coming to our house, and she will stay in a separate room under your supervision. Her father has written to Grandpa about me and how my studies impressed Professor Dmitri Yevchenco. He knows Grandpa. He told me that whenever Juan Savera visited Moscow, they spent few nights together. Anyway, Mama, please tell Papa only when you find him in a good mood. I do not want to upset him."

A letter arrived shortly thereafter from Professor Yevchenco. It was addressed to Grandpa, and after lunch he told Peter's parents what the professor had written. He gave Peter's mother a photograph of Anna, the daughter of Professor Yevchenco, and said, "Carlos and Maria, your son has graduated at the top of his class. His final paper on the stability of the Mig fighter jet was considered a breakthrough in aircraft design. This innovation has helped the Mikoyan design team tremendously." The professor also mentioned Peter's interest in his daughter, Anna, and said, "If it is all right with you, Anna, my daughter wants to visit your family. It appears they cannot live without each other, so congratulations are in order. I am looking forward to attending their wedding in June with my friend Juan Savera."

The whole family was happy because Grandfather Savera approved of the relationship. Peter's father and mother were so proud of their son's achieving high honors in the academy, which resulted in his appointment as assistant professor.

The next day, the ambassador called and invited the Savera family to celebrate Peter's success. In a week's time, the mailman brought a copy of the Soviet newspaper *Pravda* with a picture of Peter and an article describing his achievement and an award he had been granted by the Soviet Union. Another column described Peter's engagement to Anna Yevchenco, the only daughter of Professor Dmitri Yevchenco and his wife, Katharina.

ANNA'S FATHER ANNOUNCES THE ENGAGEMENT

Mr. and Mrs. Carlos were disappointed in their son for not confiding in them before the newspaper *Pravda* published news of the engagement.

Time was passing at an amazing speed. Grandfather called a meeting, saying, "Peter is arriving at the end of next week. I believe it is a Friday at noon. I want the family to arrange a reception in honor of Peter and Anna. There will need to be some sort of decoration outside and in almost all living areas, including the dining area. Flowers will decorate the entrance and formal sitting areas. Grandpa Savera told his son Carlos, "You and your boys will arrange a reception party at the airport. Make sure good-quality motorcars are available and serviced in advance of their arrival."

Everyone busied themselves with preparing the grounds, cleaning, polishing, and decorating. The remainder of the week passed quickly. Grandfather was finally taking a break, sitting in his reclining chair and smoking a Cuban cigar, when Carlos and his wife approached. "Come, Carlos and Maria. We seldom have time to talk to each other. Sit down, both of you. How are the arrangements going?"

Carlos said, "Father, there is something disturbing us. Because it is a very delicate matter, we want to ask your advice."

Juan sat up in his chair and asked Carlos, "What happened? I thought everything was going smoothly."

"Father, you remember, you told us that Dmitri, Anna's father, has announced Peter and Anna's engagement. The announcement should have come first from us. It is a little embarrassing."

"Yes, I know. When I saw the announcement, I was surprised, and as a matter of fact, I was a bit annoyed. I understand how all of us feel, so I called him through the embassy. You know, Carlos and Maria, he apologized and said he had gotten carried away. Perhaps he misunderstood," Carlos's father continued. "His suggestion is that you take care of announcing his wedding plans. Peter and Anna, it appears, have already decided to get married in June. I think Dmitri is right: we should wait for them to arrive and then carefully and diplomatically suggest to both we announce their wedding will take place on the fourteenth of June. What do you think, Carlos and Maria?"

Both Maria and Carlos agreed with Grandfather's plan. Carlos said, "Father, that means we have less than two months left."

Grandpa agreed and said; "Oh, of course, Carlos. Peter has been offered an assistant professor's job at a most prestigious institution, and he has to be in the academy on the seventh of August. He does not have too much time between getting married, honeymooning, and learning to be a professor. Dmitri would like for the newlyweds to spend some time with him and his wife. Carlos, my son, do not forget Dmitri that loves Peter, and he is going to be his boss."

"Yes, Father, you are right. You are absolutely right." Both husband and wife agreed with the old man.

Juan Savera continued, "Now, Carlos and my dear Maria, you have a big job ahead of you. I suggest you hire a professional team to organize this important wedding, and you must start now."

Anna and Peter arrived at the House of Savera. The announcement of the wedding was being prepared carefully and diplomatically. Grandfather did not want any conflict in the affair, knowing Dmitri's temperament. Just before the announcement, Dmitri called and told Grandpa, "Juan, don't forget to mention that the wedding will be organized by us here in Moscow. Here in Russia, the girl's parents organize the wedding. Peter and Anna will be at your airport at four p.m., and you will have a whole day to discuss the plans with them. I have already spoken with them. I personally will make sure that this wedding will be most elegant in our city. We live very close to Moscow."

Everything was ready to receive the engaged couple, who were just about to land at the airport. It seemed that whole Savera clan had filled the airport's reception area. Just few minutes before landing, the Russian ambassador and his entourage arrived to show Russian solidarity with Dmitri Yevchenco. Grandpa Savera and Peter's parents received the ambassador and his party with grace and courtesy. The arrival of the flight was announced on the intercom. The ambassador and the family stepped out to the receiving area, which was reserved for dignitaries only. The airport car brought the two passengers, and the crowd cheered. As Peter and Anna came to the podium, the ambassador handed them a bouquet of roses. Peter approached his mother and father and kissed and hugged them. He introduced Anna to his parents and grandparents. He approached the ambassador and presented Anna to him; she kissed him in the Russian style.

After all the formalities were complete, Peter introduced Anna to his cousins and friends. The family members were requested to proceed to the waiting limousine. Before approaching the limousine, Juan Savera and Peter's parents thanked the ambassador and his party for graciously receiving the engaged couple. Anna kissed the ambassador and gave him a letter from her father. The ambassador kissed and hugged Anna and whispered in her ear, "You are my daughter during your stay here. Now don't forget that."

They all headed to their respective limousines. The ambassador and his party went to their residences, and the Savera family members headed to the family mansion. The airport reception area was now empty.

Chapter 2

ANNA AND PETER'S WEDDING

The Savera mansion was decorated with family banners. Those family members who could not go to the airport, along with servants and extra hired help, came to receive the couple at the portico of the mansion. As the cars came to a stop and Peter and Anna stepped out of the limousine, they were showered with rose petals. Women and children started to sing in Spanish. The atmosphere was filled with joy and happiness.

It was still early. Peter led Anna to his room. Peter's mother and grandmother arrived in the room and, taking Anna's hand, told Peter, "No, no, Peter. Anna cannot stay in this room. She will stay in a room very close to ours."

It was snack time. Juices, milk, tea, and coffee, along with pastries, were served for Peter and Anna in their respective rooms. Peter invited his old friends, and Anna was visited by the ambassador's wife and daughters. The young girls of the Savera family joined Anna and her visitors. When the friends and visitors had left, both Anna and Peter were allowed to rest for an hour or so. After they refreshed themselves and dressed casually, they were invited for dinner. The parents, grandparents, and immediate family members sat together at a big table. After lunch was over, Peter was asked to come to the family room, where Grandfather and Peter's parents were already sitting, and the men smoking their Havana cigars. Peter was asked to sit near Grandfather.

"Sit down. You must be tired," Grandpa said.

"No, Grandpa, I am not—I am really good." Grandpa and Peter's parents asked about his stay in Russia and about his relationship with his future father-in-law. Peter suddenly remembered that Anna's father had given him a letter addressed to Juan Savera. "Grandpa, I have to go upstairs and get the letter for you." Peter returned and handed over the letter to Grandpa, who opened the letter and started to read silently.

"Peter, did you discuss anything with Dmitri about your wedding plans?" Grandpa asked.

Peter replied, "Yes, he brought up the topic with Anna and me. Anna and her father told me that in Russia, the wedding is held at the girl's parents' house."

"What did you tell them?" Peter's mother asked.

"Ma, what could I say? If that is the custom, how could I object, especially given that I have to work under him in Moscow?"

Everyone was silent; they did not know what to say. Finally, Grandfather Juan broke the silence. "I believe that the decision to have the wedding was already made between Dmitri, Anna, and Peter. We must call Anna and tell her that we have agreed to make an announcement within this week. The only thing remaining is to decide the date for a meeting with Anna and Ambassador Chernoff."

Carlos Savera, seeming irritated, asked, "Father, why Ambassador Chernoff?"

"I will tell you why. The ambassador is Anna's guardian while she is in Spain, as authorized by Dmitri. Isn't that right, Peter?"

Carlos agreed with his father. "Yes, you are right, Papa. He told Anna that right in front of me at the airport. All right, Father, that answers my question," Carlos told his father.

The next day, Ambassador Chernoff came for lunch at the invitation of the Savera family. The lunch was attended by all the Savera family elders, Anna, Peter, Ambassador Chernoff and Mrs. Chernoff, who asked Anna to be seated next to them; Peter sat between his father and mother. When lunch was over, the waiters were asked to fill each guest's glass.

Grandfather, who sat at the head of the table, stood up, and everyone was silent. "I welcome Anna in our home. She is a beautiful and elegant young lady. We welcome His Excellency, the ambassador, and Madame Chernoff to our home. We all have agreed that the wedding announcement will be made on coming Tuesday, and the date of the wedding will be June 14."

Everyone cheered. Grandpa lifted his glass, and the ambassador got up and proposed a toast. "Congratulations to all, and long live the union of Russia and Spain."

Peter kissed his father, mother, and grandfather. He then approached the ambassador's wife and kissed her and then the ambassador, who represented Anna's father. Finally, he kissed Anna gently. Everyone cheered. Ambassador Chernoff requested that Anna spend the weekend with him and his wife.

"Uncle Chernoff, I am going to Miss Anna," said Peter.

Mrs. Chernoff got up and hugged him. "Peter, you can visit Anna anytime. She will be at our house."

Anna came to kiss Peter and said, "I am going to miss you too, so come and visit. Uncle and Aunty Chernoff will be happy to see you."

Anna prepared her small suitcases and came down. They were all waiting to say farewell to Anna and the Chernoff family. "Oh, Juan, you know that Dmitri wants Anna to be in Moscow early next week," Grandpa said. "He is sending a plane to pick her up on Tuesday at ten a.m."

"Yes, he did say so in his letter. He also mentioned that there is not much time left to prepare for the wedding. We do need her."

Everyone cheered and complained that her stay was too short. Peter took Anna's hand, Aunty Chernoff took her arm, and they approached the waiting car. Anna gave a big hug to Peter and stepped into the car. They left the Savera family, waving good-bye. Peter could not wait to go and see Anna at the ambassador's residence. He drove there in his red MG around five p.m., as he had promised Anna. When he arrived, Anna was waiting with Natasha, the ambassador's daughter. As soon as she saw Peter arriving, she opened the gate of the compound and came out to meet him. Peter, instead of getting out of the car immediately, took Anna for a short ride around the neighborhood.

Peter stayed for dinner at the Chernoff family's home. There was Russian music playing in the background. The three young people played a game, laughed, and had fun. Ambassador Chernoff and his wife enjoyed seeing Natasha, Anna, and Peter so happy; they had not experienced such spontaneous joy in their house for some time. While Peter was there enjoying himself, Dmitri, Anna's father, called his friend Chernoff. The ambassador talked a while to Dmitri and then called for Anna and Peter. Chernoff gave the receiver to Anna.

ANNA GOES BACK TO MOSCOW

Anna was happy to talk to her father. "Oh, Papa, I missed you. Thank you for calling. We are so happy. Peter is here, and his family was very, very nice. Yes, Papa, we know that you are sending a plane on Tuesday at ten am, don't worry, Papa, I will be ready for the plane. Do you want to say hello to Peter?" She handed over the receiver to Peter.

"Good evening, Uncle Dmitri. I am sad she is leaving tomorrow without me. Yes, yes, I know, and I understand. Good-bye, Uncle." Peter gave the receiver to Anna.

"Papa, I will miss him too."

Dmitri tried to tell Anna, "Listen, my dear daughter, when you are here, I assure you that you can talk to Peter every day whenever you want. I will get a separate line for you."

Anna thanked her father and said good night. By this time, she was full of tears. Peter and Mrs. Chernoff came to console her. Peter wiped her tears, and everything was okay again. It was getting late, so Peter said good night to the family and led Anna outside. The driver brought the car right under the portico, where Peter said good night and told Anna that he would see her tomorrow. Peter left, and Natasha Chernoff took Anna inside.

Anna arrived at the Savera family house the next day accompanied by Natasha, Mrs. Chernoff, and Ambassador Chernoff. Peter was up front along with the family. Grandpa Savera asked the ambassador and family to join him inside, but the ambassador declined because of other engagements. Anna was happy to be in Peter's arms, and Peter took her upstairs, giving the excuse that she had to get ready for tomorrow's flight. All the young girls at the house flocked around Anna and Peter. Some were trying to teach Anna Spanish, and some were trying to learn Russian words. At bedtime, Peter's mother and grandmother arrived, sent the girls to bed, and left Peter and Anna alone to say good night. After five minutes, the ladies came in and took Anna to her room; she held Peter's hand until she reached her door.

Tuesday arrived, and the house was full of relatives. Breakfast was served, but Anna could not eat; she drank hot milk with fine Spanish biscuits as Peter sat next to her. When the car arrived, Anna asked Peter if everything was loaded into it. He replied, "Yes, darling, there is a big bundle of my love just beside your seat."

Everyone around them laughed and marveled at the intensity of their love. She kissed Peter's grandparents and parents. Peter helped her to step inside and then sat next to her; all the others followed in separate cars. Anna held Peter's arm tightly. They arrived at the reception area just as Anna's plane landed. A small transport picked up the luggage, and Anna went through the formalities. Ambassador Chernoff and his family came to say farewell to Anna. Anna was asked to step into the mini-transport, but she was holding Peter and did not want to leave, so Peter, his arms around her, led her to the transport. She sat there covering her face for a moment and then waved good-bye to all. She climbed into the plane, waving once again. The plane taxied to the runway and took off. Everyone was consoling Peter. Natasha, who had become fond of Anna and Peter, was silently crying at the sight of Peter's sadness. Natasha went to Peter and kissed him good-bye. "Please come and see us," she requested. The ambassador put his big hand on Peter's head with a fatherly touch and said, "Good-bye, son." They stepped into their car and left.

Chapter 3

PETER AND ANNA'S WEDDING

Soon after Anna left, Grandfather called a family meeting. He started by saying, "As you know, the wedding and reception are going to be held in a foreign land. This is a first for our family, and it requires a different approach. We want to make a guest list including everyone near and dear to us; however, Dmitri Yevchenco can arrange accommodation only for sixty people. Does anyone have a suggestion for how this should be managed?"

Carlos Savera stood up and suggested, "Father, there should be three lists: one of the essential people, such as very close relatives; the second of nonessential guests; and the third of essential help."

Peter interrupted his father. "Papa, in that case we should make the first and the third list first; these two lists will give us a clear picture of how many members we will select from the second list."

Grandpa immediately spoke. "Well done, my children. Carlos and Peter, you have solved a problem that was troubling me all night."

Peter's mother asked Peter, "What happens if the immediate family list, when combined with the third list, turns out to be fifty?"

Peter said, "Mama, that means we can only have ten people from the second list."

"What happens if there are twenty people on the second list?" his mother asked again.

Grandfather answered, "In that case, Maria, all twenty names will be placed in a basket, and ten names will be drawn from the basket. I do want our family and friends to think that we are doing the best given the situation. I wish we could take a lot more."

Everyone cheered Peter, his father, and his grandfather for having solved a difficult problem in one sitting. Grandpa asked two women and two men to prepare the list within two days. He also told them that he had no idea about Russian wedding customs. He suggested that two ladies who were fluent in the Russian language get together with Catherine Chernoff, the ambassador's wife, who would be delighted to take part in the preparations. "I will make arrangements for air passage to Moscow. Dmitri has promised to help. Peter, you, I understand, talk to Anna every night. You find out few things from her and her mother." Peter nodded. Grandfather dispersed the meeting and asked everyone to meet two days later at the same time and place.

Two days later, the second meeting was held. The guest list committee presented the three lists to Grandfather. He announced, "The first list has thirty guests and the third list seven. Therefore, the second list can have twenty-seven guests only. The second list had thirty-two guests, so we have to prepare ballots for thirty-two names and drop them in a jar …" Grandpa had not finished his sentence before Peter stood up and presented a jar filled with thirty-two names. "My son, you all have done your homework well. I congratulate the team. Now is the time to draw five names out of the jar. I give this honor to Grandma Savera, so please come forward." Grandma pulled out the names of the five guests who could not be invited, and everyone was satisfied with the selection.

Grandfather said, "Thank you, my dear. Now, ladies, have you any information about Russian wedding ceremonies and our responsibilities? What are we supposed to do?"

Maria answered, "As far as we have learned, we have to order roughly ten bouquets of flowers and presents for the parents, and of course an expensive gift for the bride. We have to share the expense of the air passage arranged by Dmitri Yevchenco; we were told that a donation of five thousand rubles towards the convention hall would be much appreciated. We understand that the bride's parents are going to invite all the guests to attend the Bolshoi ballet. When Anna told Peter that her father had been successful in convincing Bolshoi authorities to present Tchaikovsky's *Swan Lake* ballet for the guests, Peter asked Anna whether a Spanish flamenco dancer would be appreciated by Russian guests. According to Peter, she almost jumped with joy when she heard the suggestion. Anna told me that her father, her mother, and many of her friends loved flamenco dancing. Maria's committee suggested we take our best flamenco dancing team from Spain; this will give a Spanish flavor to the wedding reception and please many guests. Their presentation in Russia will bring tourists to Spain and will be a response to the Bolshoi Theater presentation."

Grandfather, Father, and all present at the meeting were delighted with the idea of having flamenco dancers at the wedding reception. They planned a family meeting to discuss the prospect of attending a family function in a foreign land with a different culture.

WEDDING PREPARATIONS

Grandfather appointed a team of six guests to instruct the rest in Russian etiquette and every day, simple spoken Russian. All the family members came to attend the dinner. A separate table was set close by for the hired help who would be attending the wedding. Peter's father thanked everyone, especially Grandfather; he praised his father for bringing order and helping to manage all aspects of the wedding plan. He proposed a toast to his father, his mother, and his wife for assisting in planning, and he praised his son Peter for his calm and mature approach. The guests all applauded and raised their glasses. After dinner was over, the groups separated and classes began; they worked till late at night and went away satisfied.

Time passed quickly. Grandpa spoke regularly with his friend Dmitri in Moscow, learning about Russian wedding customs and discussing logistical matters, including the travel visas that would be required of all guests except Peter, who had his own Russian passport.

Peter advised everyone to take light but warm clothing, saying that the nights could be cool even during the summer. The Savera mansion was humming with activity. New clothes were coming in, tailors visited for both ladies and men, packages were being readied, and gifts were being packaged in gold and silver papers with the insignia of the Savera house. Everything was checked twice over. Carlos Savera was in charge of all legal documents as well as passports, visas, and airplane tickets. Carlos had assigned Nicola Barman, who had been in service with Savera house for about ten years and had traveled to France, Germany and Russia with him on business, as his assistant.

On the eighth of June, the weather was hot in Spain. Grandfather asked Carlos and Peter to get all groups together once again for lunch the next day. Grandpa looked anxious and wanted to know if everyone was ready. It was only a week before the wedding.

When Grandpa arrived in the dining room the next day, everyone stood up and cheered his entrance. He raised his hand to thank them and sat down next to Grandma Alana. Grandfather asked Carlos and Peter, "Are you ready?"

Carlos and Peter both responded, "Yes, sir."

The other family members assured Grandfather that all necessary purchases had been taken care of and that everyone would be at the airport on time for the scheduled flight. When lunch was over, Grandfather, Carlos, Peter, and the ladies went to the family room, where they had champagne and Grandpa had one of his favorite Cuban cigars. For the first time in weeks, grandpa, son, and grandson were relaxing together. Dmitri had answered all the questions that Grandfather had asked. Dmitri Yevchenco confirmed that all passengers on the list would have reserved seats in the big transport, that a bouquet of flowers would be ready when the Savera entourage landed at a military base, and that all visas and paperwork would be delivered to Savera house two days before the flight.

THE WEDDING PARTY LEAVES FOR MOSCOW

The day that everyone had been waiting for finally came. Savera mansion was a hub of extreme activity starting at six in the morning. Men, women, and children all looked beautiful and aristocratic. They all came down to the dining area in groups because there were only twenty chairs at the table.

Limousines for parents, grandparents, and other senior family members arrived first. After the elders were gone, two big coaches came to pick up the rest of passengers, and well wishers followed in their own transports. There were many who came to say good-bye, and there were photographers from the Spanish press and Russian photographers from the Russian embassy. At seven a.m., a gray military transport from the Russian air force landed, and everyone cheered. The mini-transport picked up passengers from lists number two and number three, and a limousine transported the number-one list. All the luggage and accessories were already loaded in the plane. Ambassador Chernoff arrived and met Grandpa, Carlos, and Peter. He embraced Peter, kissed him, and wished him good luck. Very discreetly, he handed Peter a small package tied with a red ribbon and embossed with the Russian symbol of a hammer and sickle. Everyone boarded the plane, and it took off exactly at ten a.m.

The transport plane arrived at a military base close to the city the next day. There was a lineup of long, black Russian cars and big transport buses at the reception area. The reception area was filled with well-dressed civilians in black suits and ties. There were military brass, colonels, commanders, and generals—a very impressive gathering of important people. This was an indication of Dmitri Yevchenco's importance in the Soviet hierarchy.

Minibuses brought the elite of the Savera family. All the men were dressed in navy blue suits with red ties, and the women were looking very elegant. The first one to jump forward and hug Peter Savera was Anna Yevchenco, the bride to be; her tears of joy made her mother wipe her eyes a few times. Father Dmitri was proud to see the Savera family, especially Peter; he hugged and kissed both his daughter and Peter at the same time. Savera service men brought rose bouquets. Peter gave the biggest and the best to Anna, and he gave other bouquets to his future parents-in-law. Greetings and bouquets were exchanged all around. Dmitri Yevchenco introduced the Savera parents and grandparents to the colonels and generals.

When the formalities were over, the guests were directed to their limousines. Father Dmitri and Katharina sat with Grandpa Savera, his son, and their wives. Anna sat with Peter and two of her friends. Peter had his best man with him, and he sat next to Anna's friend Arianna. They were very young. Peter's best man was tall and handsome, and Anna's friends were giggling and enjoying just being there.

Limousines stopped at a large old mansion and dropped off the Savera elders and immediate family members. They were guided by Nicola Barman, along with a Russian guide, to their respective rooms, where their luggage was already waiting. Grandfather Carlos, along with Nicola Barman, toured the accommodation area and found all the facilities satisfactory. In the meantime, Peter and Anna's party was heading to Anna's place, where they enjoyed delicious food and drinks. Later in the evening, Anna and her friends accompanied Peter and his best man, Joseph Garerra; they were dropped off at the residence where Peter's grandpa and father were staying. There were still two days remaining for the wedding, and for Peter and Anna those days were dedicated to relaxing and having fun; however, it was a different story for the family, who would be overseeing every detail concerning the clothes, the gifts, and the official wedding at the registry office.

THE WEDDING

In Russia, there are no churches to get married in; it is all civil marriage. Grandpa, Carlos, and Nicola paid a visit to the registry office to find out what their family's role in the ceremony would be. The Savera team also visited the banquet hall again even though Anna and her mother had already taken them to the banquet hall to examine and agree upon the seating arrangements. At four-thirty p.m. on the wedding day, all the limousines lined up outside the guest mansion. Carlos had been told that the Savera family's limousines would not move until the bride's limousines arrived, because the groom's party would follow the bride's party. The groom's party waited for the bride's limousine to go ahead of the groom's. The long line of black shining limousines was an impressive sight.

The limousine carrying Anna, Peter, and the parents, stopped at the registry office. The parents stepped out first, followed by bride and groom, as well as the best man. Anna and Peter took each other's hands immediately and entered the big door. The bride was dressed in a beautiful wedding gown and holding a magnificent bouquet of roses.

Dmitri, beside Anna, and Carlos, on Peter's side, guided the couple to a podium decorated with red roses. Registry officials were ready with their books and official seals to mark the signed papers. The Soviet flag was hanging in the middle of the glass-domed building. By this time, the hall was filled with guests and dignitaries. The ceremony was over in a short time. Well-dressed waiters and waitresses poured champagne for all the guests. When the ceremony was over, Dmitri proposed a toast in Russian, and Carlos proposed a toast in Spanish. Everyone drank and cheered. Peter and Anna kissed and sat down in the special seats provided for them.

The time of the reception was approaching, and the limousines returned to pick up their passengers. Peter went with Anna in Dmitri's car, and the Savera family went to the guesthouse for a little rest before the banquet. Everyone at the guesthouse was informed by the chief of staff, Nicola Barman, that the transports would be at the gate at five-thirty p.m. Nicola and her assistant went to help Grandpa and Carlos Savera get ready for the reception, and a housekeeper named Rosita went to help the ladies. They all were ready on time. The guests were transported to the Soviet peoples' hall. The impressive building with its onion domes was decorated outside; the two flags of the Soviet Union and Spain were flying side by side and were illuminated from the top of the building. Dmitri, Katharina, Ambassador Chernoff, his lovely wife, and their beautiful daughter Natasha were at the reception area. Also present were handsome decorated military officers and air force officers in their blue uniforms; these pilots were specially selected because of their achievements during wars and civil life. Peter and Dmitri were very much attached to the air force test pilots, who were involved in testing recently introduced innovations in jet fighter technology. Some of these test pilots personally knew Peter, and of course Professor Yevchenco was head of the department. Dmitri introduced them to Grandfather and Carlos, who were conversant in Russian. While they were enjoying the company of the elite of the armed forces, Peter and Anna arrived in their convertible Mercedes. Bouquets of flowers were handed over to both Anna and Peter. Everyone behind the guest of honor and other dignitaries started cheering and burst out singing Russian folk songs. At the same time, the famous Russia army choir and band started to play and sing.

FLAMENCO DANCERS ENTERTAIN THE AUDIENCE

Bride and groom were again escorted by their parents. As they entered the hall, all guests rose and started singing. Bride and groom were seated in chairs decorated in red velvets. All the head-table guests took their seats. The tables were set for dinner; the champagne glasses were filled with fine Russian champagne. The guests started to toast and drank more while asking the married couple to kiss; the kissing was requested repeatedly. An announcement was made for the guests to move to the entertainment wing of this mirrored palace. It was ornate. Walls and ceiling were artistically decorated in gold leaf and green paint. Crystal chandeliers were hanging from the ceiling every twenty feet or so, brilliant and huge. These fixtures made the place absolutely spectacular. The program of activity was at every table; under the entertainment section were listed military choir singing at eight p.m. and traditional Spanish flamenco dancing at nine p.m.

All the guests from the dining hall slowly started to move to the Lenin entertainment center. The specially invited guests were guided by the ushers to their specific seats; the bride and groom were seated in the middle of the front row. The military officers were already behind the stage curtain. At exactly eight p.m., the choir singers appeared. As they were lining up, everyone cheered until they formed a group. Then the cheering stopped, and the band started to play a very famous song. The voices were so powerful and the music so nice that everyone was clapping and tapping their toes. More songs followed, each better than the last. When the music stopped, all the guests stood up and cheered. The singers and band members cheered back. The curtain closed, and it was time for refreshment. The tables had been set and were dressed with coffee, pastry, baklava, fruit, and more champagne. There were waiters who spoke both Russian and Spanish, and they were serving whatever the guests wanted.

Around nine, the guests were asked to take their seats. The dancers were heard organizing behind the stage curtain. The curtain opened, and the guests saw a tall man in typical black hat and boots, standing in a toreador style beside a woman dressed in an embroidered scarf with large round earrings. As the curtain opened, the guitar player started to play. Clapping and toe tapping began; the voices of singers followed the lead singer, and the public went wild. The posture of the man was impressive, and his lady partner's performance was equally astounding. The singing and dancing continued with guests shouting, "Bravo! Bravo!"

Many, including Anna and Peter, stood up and started dancing. Peter's parents, Carlos and Catherine, joined in, and Dmitri and Katharina could not resist joining their daughter. Nobody had ever seen this kind of enthusiasm amongst the young and among senior members of the armed forces in public. As Anna had predicted, the show was wildly successful.

The show was over at ten p.m. It was time for a cold drink. Flamenco dancing was hard work, and cold champagne was just fine. At the end of the show, the curtain opened, and cheers and "bravo" filled the mirrored palace. By eleven p.m., the palace was empty and everyone was taken to their quarters.

Dinner was held at the Dmitri mansion. The house was decorated inside and outside. Guests were still in the drawing room. Grandfather had ordered gifts for the bride and groom. Gifts also arrived for the parents of Anna and Peter; both opened their packages. Each had a deed of ownership to a condominium in Majorca, facing the ocean. This was a pleasant surprise to everyone, including Dmitri and Katharina; everyone got up and congratulated Anna and Peter. Anna's mother said to Dmitri, "Now we can visit Anna when she is in Spain." Dmitri and Katharina did not want to open their presents, giving the excuse that it was dinnertime.

They all left the drawing room. Toasts were offered to the married couple and to the in-laws on both sides; a special toast was given to Grandfather Juan Savera for his understanding, guidance, and patience. This time, everyone gave Grandpa a standing ovation.

Then Grandfather got up, and everyone fell silent. He said, "Here is to my friend Dmitri, who so graciously agreed and disagreed with me on many occasions but who amicably compromised and always did best for Anna and Peter. I thank Katharina for her patience." One could see that Dmitri, Grandpa, and others were filled with emotions. Finally, Grandfather thanked everyone for making these days a memory he would cherish. Dmitri, Katharine, Anna, and others came to shake his hand and kiss him.

When dinner was over, Grandfather was emotionally exhausted, so Peter, Anna, Carlos, and his wife said good-bye to all and accompanied Grandpa to their waiting car, which took them back to the guesthouse.

The next morning after breakfast, Nicola Barman came to remind Grandfather and Carlos about the ballet program that Dmitri had planned for the evening. All the guests from the previous night were invited, and the ambassador and his family were to be guests of honor, along with Anna, Peter, and Peter's parents. Unfortunately, the ambassador and his family had left Moscow the previous night for an important engagement.

Dmitri, Katharina, Peter, and Anna came to the guesthouse for an informal lunch. After lunch, Anna and Peter's families asked where they wanted to go for their honeymoon. "Majorca!" they both shouted.

Dmitri was surprised. "I thought you wanted to go to the Black Sea resort." Peter and Anna both laughingly replied, "Papa, we did not know we were going to get the Majorca resort."

Dmitri lovingly responded, "All right, my children, you can go to Majorca. When are you leaving?"

Peter asked his father, "Papa, is the apartment ready for us to spend two weeks there? Is it furnished?"

Carlos assured them that the place was a turnkey operation; even personalized toothbrushes were ready. Anna and Peter were so delighted that they jumped and rushed to kiss Grandpa and the whole Savera family. They both thanked Dmitri and Katharina for allowing them to go to Majorca.

Dmitri got up and told the family, "The Savera clan is scheduled to fly the day after tomorrow, early in the morning, according to the present plan. Now, if you children want to save time and money, you can fly with them."

Anna gleefully shouted, "Yes, Papa, we can be ready tomorrow morning. Right, Peter?"

Peter agreed. Katharina reminded all of them to attend the Bolshoi ballet, her favorite show. It was a happy gathering that gave a great joy to the Savera house. They all departed and promised to meet that evening.

All the guests who were present at the reception were to attend the ballet. Slowly, the guests started to arrive at the magnificent opera house. What a brilliant, shining, superb, and delicately balanced piece of architecture it was. Every seat was designed for the greatest comfort with art and workmanship that were second to none. The bride and groom were the guests of honor, surrounded by their parents and grandparents. The curtain opened very slowly. A violin played very slowly, as if to follow the curtain opening; suddenly, when the curtain was just about to open completely, the whole orchestra came alive. The music came to a crescendo, finished with a bang, and suddenly stopped for one second. As the curtain opened completely, the music came up softly, and the guests saw beautiful swans moving in a circle gently and gracefully with the music. The whole scene created a dream world. The show continued with great cheering and appreciation. When the show was over, there were many curtain calls before finally the curtain closed for good. The guests left through a private exit and stepped into waiting limousines. The grandparents and Anna and Peter thanked Katharina for a magnificent evening. They all were driven to their individual residences.

The next morning after breakfast, Nicola Barman came to the Savera table and reminded Grandpa about a scheduled Moscow city tour. He told them that a tourist bus would come to pick them up at ten-thirty a.m. He also gave a personal message to Juan Savera from Professor Dmitri Yevchenco saying that, unfortunately, the professor would not be able to accompany him. A luxury bus arrived at ten-thirty and all the Savera family and accompanying guests climbed up. The bus went around to the city's important tourist attractions. Grandpa was so comfortable in his seat that he dozed off.

The bus stopped for lunch at a fancy restaurant before returning the family to their guesthouse at three p.m. The bus journey seemed to tire out almost everyone except the young lovers. They all went to their quarters, including the newlyweds. Nicola had already arranged the necessary traveling papers.

Everyone woke up early for their flight the next morning, and breakfast was served in two shifts. Grandpa and his son Carlos and their wives were served in their rooms. Peter and Anna asked to have their breakfast in their room as well. Dmitri and Katharina arrived to pick up their daughter and Peter; since the newlyweds would be going away along with the Savera family, Dmitri and Katharina wanted some time with them alone before their takeoff.

SAVERA WEDDING PARTY RETURNS HOME

All the Savera family members, including their wedding guests, arrived on time to the embarking area. Anna and Peter were surrounded by their parents. Katharina was in tears, and Dmitri was trying to fight his tears. They announced that the plane was ready for takeoff at ten-thirty a.m. Mini-transports was waiting to take Anna and Peter to the plane. They were the last passengers to climb up into the giant plane. The plane took off and disappeared.

Dmitri and Katharina felt lonely. Their friends knew that Dmitri and Katharina were sad to see their only child go away, so Dmitri's childhood friend Alex brought other friends to distract and amuse them. They all sat in the drawing room, and drinks were served. They started to talk about the old days when they were in high school.

Alex told an old story, "Do you remember, Dmitri, when a grizzly bear came running toward you? I was so scared. Luckily, your father was a good shot; he shot the grizzly when it was maybe a meter away. You remember you dirtied your pants?" Katharina and the others could not help laughing.

"I just peed in my pants. I was really afraid! And since that day, I have admired my father a lot." You could see that the mood in the room was a lot better and happier. Alex got up and hugged both Dmitri and Katharina. They all said good night and left. Dmitri and Katharina finally went to sleep.

PETER AND ANNA GO ON THEIR HONEYMOON

Peter and Anna landed at ten a.m. It was a beautiful day, and news of the newlyweds' arrival in Madrid spread through the media. Savera family members and friends of the family started to gather at the airport.

The VIP lounge was packed with members of the international and local press. Very few had seen the beautiful Anna Chernoff, the daughter of famous, decorated aviation expert in the Soviet Union, Dmitri Yevchenco. The press room was filled with flowers and welcome signs in Russian, Spanish, and English, all paid for by airport authorities and international press corps. There were at least six photographers. The flight arrived a little early, and the crowed surged toward the reception area hoping to get a glimpse of the bride. Finally, the minibuses arrived with the special guests, Anna and Peter. The airport manager came forward, extended his hand to Anna, and guided her down to the podium. Peter followed, guided by his father. Peter and Anna were looking for Grandpa but could not see him. Grandfather Savera and Grandmother were not there.

Peter and Anna were concerned, and they asked Peter's father, "Papa, where is Grandpa? Is he all right?"

Carlos assured them that Grandfather was all right. "Well, what happened may be that he was too anxious knowing that both of you were coming. He was worried—he tossed and turned all night. I heard him go to the bathroom many times. He just did not sleep enough, so we advised your grandma and grandpa to stay home. We knew there will be a big crowd and it will not be good for them. Peter, don't forget he is over eighty years old."

Anna squeezed Peter's hand and tried to tell her father-in-law, "It is sad—my papa is about the same age as Grandpa Savera, and my mama is not so well either."

While they were talking, the airport manager took both Peter and Anna, saying, "We have to go to the press room where the press and camera people are waiting."

As they entered the crowded room, everyone stood up and cheered. Both Anna and Peter were seated at the welcome table. Anna looked around and said to the airport manager, "Lovely … gracias."

The airport manager addressed the crowd. "Good morning and welcome to Madrid International. I would like you to meet our lovely Anna Maria Yevchenco, who now is Anna Maria Savera, the bride of Peter Savera." Both Peter and Anna stood up, and cameras were taking lot of pictures.

The provost of the press corps requested of both the bride and groom, "I would appreciate it if my colleagues could ask a few questions." Peter told him to go ahead. The press asked many questions, the last to Anna. "How do you like Spain?" Somebody translated the question into Russian.

"So far, it is beautiful. I can tell you more when I have seen more."

At this time Carlos, the groom's father, stood up and thanked the press and the airport management for arranging the press room and providing all the facilities to welcome the guests with beautiful flowers. Peter's father and mother, along with the airport manager, guided the honeymooners to their waiting cars. Peter's friend had brought his convertible MG with the top down; it was a nice surprise for Peter and Anna. They both got into the MG, and Peter started the car and took off; both screamed with pleasure as Anna's hair started to fly in the wind. Peter, instead of going home, took off towards town, where he knew he would meet more friends at the ice cream parlor. Anna spontaneously kissed him and said, "Peter, my darling, I just love it." They were having such fun that Peter forgot about going home and didn't realize that his parents must be worried about him.

Peter's father and others, including his grandfather, were so worried that they sent search parties in different places, notified the police, and called many places, including the ice cream parlor. The owner of the parlor came out and told Peter, "Shame on you. Your grandpa and parents are almost having a heart attack because they think you perhaps had an accident. Both of you just arrived from Moscow and did not go home for two hours. Please get out and go home."

Peter got into his car and rushed home with Anna. He arrived to find his parents and grandparents waiting outside with the police commissioner. As both of them got out, they rushed to Grandpa, asking for his forgiveness. His grandmother and mother hugged them. Grandfather was so upset that his son Carlos took him upstairs. Everyone wanted to forget the whole thing. A late lunch was served. Grandpa proposed a toast to welcome the newlyweds and continued, "Children, I love you more than you think, but today you gave us such a fright. Please do not play with our fragile lives again."

Peter and Anna got up together to ask forgiveness from the family. They apologized for their stupid and reckless behavior and promised it would never be repeated. Both Anna and Peter went around the table to kiss and hug parents and grandparents. Grandpa looked at Peter and said, "Everyone forgives you. Let us eat and drink—but no alcohol for you."

The lunch was over shortly. Anna and Peter spoke with Peter's parents to again ask for forgiveness. Carlos tried to explain. "My son, your mother and I know you. When you were in high school, you did the same thing not once but many times. We were always under stress, and we always hid your absence from your grandpa in order not to upset him. Today you were with Anna, who is under the guardianship of your grandpa and is the daughter of his dear friend Dmitri, and that is where you broke Grandpa's heart. It was very irresponsible."

Both Anna and Peter were crying. Anna especially was ashamed to be part of this. As they were crying, Grandfather walked in; he saw them crying, Peter on Carlos's shoulder and Anna in her mother-in-law's arms. He knew exactly what was happening; he calmed them and reminded them that Nick was on his way to brief them about tomorrow's journey.

He took Anna and Peter in his arms and said, "I will just advise you. I promise you it will be the last time, so listen carefully." He spoke in Russian so that both Anna and Peter could understand and live by this rule. "When you have a precious commodity on your hands that belongs to someone, you must act responsibly. Promise to enjoy Majorca and be responsible."

He kissed them. Just at that time, Nick appeared; he greeted both parents and grandparents and excused himself for interrupting. Peter's father told Nick to go to the drawing room.

"Before we go and listen to Nick, could we ask you for a favor, Papa?" asked Peter.

His father said, "Yes, go ahead."

"When we go to the airport tomorrow, we would like to leave quietly in the early morning without telling anyone." Grandfather and Peter's father both agreed with their decision. Nick gave Anna and Peter all the necessary papers and written instructions.

The next morning was a lovely morning; the sun was just coming out to spread good morning throughout when Nick arrived just after seven. Anna and Peter were waiting for him. Nick had already collected the luggage, and when they arrived at the airport, he cleared them through and got them into the minibus. The plane was already there. The door opened, and both Peter and Anna went in. The plane started to taxi, and soon it took off.

Honeymoon Paradise Majorca

Peter and Anna were so tired because of their embarrassment and shame that they went straight to sleep on the plane. They arrived at

Casa Majorca resort barely two hours later. At their condominium, their housekeeper, Ramos, greeted them, introduced him, and escorted them inside. Anna was enchanted with the décor and the environment. She told Peter, "I think this is so beautiful that we will forget all yesterday's trouble. And please, Peter, let us have fun and just be responsible." The lobby was painted turquoise and orange, and there was an air of tropical paradise. The lights and hanging lamps were in art deco style, with brilliant Tiffany colors. Ramos accompanied them to the elevator. Peter pointed out to Anna the brass decorations on the elevator gate. They went to the second floor, where their apartment was. The housekeeper opened the mahogany door. Anna entered first, and she was delighted with the sunlight coming in. The living room had marble floors, and the walls were painted and decorated in aqua blue and pastel orange. Windows ran from floor to ceiling, giving the newlyweds a lovely view of the gardens in front and of the green-blue ocean on the side. The living room was furnished tastefully, with color-coordinated curtains, towels, and bed covers, and both were excited.

Peter told Anna, "What you see is a good reflection of the capitalistic world, where money can buy you luxury and more. Let us go and see the bedroom." It was furnished with a large bed and a reclining leather armchair. There was a stereophonic sound system that was connected to a radio.

Peter and Anna realized suddenly that Ramos was still there. Peter gave him some money and told him, "We will call you when we need you." Ramos showed him a call button in the small dining area and left. Anna and Peter lay down on the big bed and tested it for its firmness. They went to the miniature kitchen area and found the refrigerator filled with all sorts of drinks, milk, cheeses, and pastries.

Anna asked Peter, "Don't you think we should call your parents and thank them for this wonderful gift they gave us? It is heavenly. I have never even dreamed about something like this. I want to bring Papa and Mama here on their holidays."

Peter said, "Don't rush. Yes, we will call them, but let us explore more, Anna. We haven't even gone to our balcony yet, and this is our first day. Let's go."

The view from the balcony was breathtaking. Anna was impressed by the ocean and its many sailboats. The building's huge swimming pool appeared to almost be touching the ocean. The ocean was a bluish green, and the breeze from the ocean was hypnotic. It seemed to tell them to go to bed.

When Peter rang for Ramos, he was there like a genie. Peter asked him to bring lunch. Ramos gave them the menu of the day, and both ordered. In the meantime, they refreshed themselves, and by the time they sat down at the table, lunch had arrived on two big trays. A pretty young European girl accompanied Ramos with the other tray. Anna asked her if she could speak Russian, and she said yes in Russian. "It is wonderful! Now I can communicate in Russian." Anna said. "They even have someone I can talk freely with in my language.

Peter said, "Anna, what about me? I have been speaking your language all along."

"Yes, I know, but talking girl-to-girl is a different thing." Anna learned that the girl's name was Lisa. They started to talk while Ramos set the table. When the table was set, Ramos looked at Peter for instructions. Peter told him to go and take the girl too. They left. Both Anna and Peter were hungry, so they started to eat. After washing up, they changed into their new sleepwear and slipped into bed. It was almost three p.m. Then the telephone rang, and Peter rushed to pick it up. The operator said it was Mr. Juan Savera.

Peter answered, "Grandpa, Anna and I were just talking about calling you and Papa Dmitri. It is so nice to hear your voice. Grandpa, this place is so wonderful. Anna is so excited and thankful to you and papa. I am, too, Grandpa. We were also worried about your health. Just one minute Grandpa. Anna cannot wait to talk to you. Here she is."

"Grandpapa, you are a genius. You and Carlos Papa have made us so proud of you. Thank you, Grandpa, again. And can I call my papa, Grandpa?"

"Sure, my Anna, go ahead."

Before Grandpa hung up, Peter asked him to kiss Grandma, Papa, and Mama and thank them for him and Anna both. Anna asked Peter again to telephone her father. He picked up the receiver and asked the operator to call Moscow, 889-8819. The operator asked Peter to wait for the ring and reminded him that it was ten p.m. in Moscow.

Anna said, "Don't worry; Papa goes to bed late. I am sure he has his friends there." The phone rang, and Anna said, "Papa, it is me, Anna. It is so nice to hear your voice, Papa. How are you? We missed you and Mama."

Dmitri was happy to hear his daughter's voice; he told his wife to go pick up the phone in the bedroom. They talked and talked. Dmitri could tell by the tone of her voice that Anna was happy. Dmitri also talked to Peter, and Peter told him, "Anna and I would love for both of you to spend your next vacation here in Majorca."

Anna's mother was crying with happiness, and Dmitri was excited to hear Anna's happy voice. When the conversation was over, Anna felt emotional, and her big eyes filled with tears. She fell into Peter's arms. Anna and Peter were awoken by the doorbell. Peter went to check and found Ramos apologizing for the disturbance.

"Excuse me, sir. I just wanted to find out if you needed dinner tonight."

Peter said, "Wait a minute, Ramos." He went to ask Anna. "Anna, darling, Ramos wants to know if you want dinner because it is getting late."

"Peter, I am not hungry. I just want to lie in your arms. Come."

Peter went and told Ramos, "No, we do not need dinner, thanks." And Ramos went away, the Russian girl Lisa behind him. Peter closed and locked the door. Lisa told Ramos that newlyweds don't eat food; they need love.

The next morning, Peter and Anna got up early and helped themselves to juice and fruits and then called Ramos to bring breakfast. Breakfast came, and Anna was glad to see Lisa and started to chat with her. Lisa was serving them toast, jam and cheese, coffee, and tea while chatting. Lisa asked Anna quietly, "How was last night?" with a little smile.

"Oh, Lisa, it was wonderful," Anna answered laughingly. They finished breakfast. Lisa and Peter asked Anna to show where the massage facilities were located. She told them to get ready and ring the bell for her to escort them. Lisa left, and both changed into shorts and light shirts and rang Lisa up. Lisa took them downstairs and showed them both men's and ladies facilities for massage, shower, and sauna. Lisa suggested to Anna that after her massage and shower she ask for a pedicure and manicure.

Peter went off with a masseur, and Anna was left with Lisa. She asked Lisa, "And who is going to give me a massage?"

Lisa said, "Don't worry; I am."

Anna could not believe that this young Russian girl was capable of doing so many things. Anna liked Lisa and was delighted to be with her. It did not take too long for Peter to finish with both his massage and shower. He was waiting for Anna to be free so that they could visit the sauna together. This was the first time either Anna or Peter had had such a luxury in life. After the sauna they felt so relaxed that all their aches and pains disappeared. They went to their apartment and just flopped on their reclining chairs. They looked at each other, and Peter asked Anna, "Are we in paradise?"

Anna replied, "Peter, I just love it."

Lisa asked Anna "Did you like the massage, shower, and sauna?"

Anna said, "Oh, Lisa, it was heavenly."

Anna and Peter asked Lisa, "Where is this fabulous dining room we have heard about?"

Lisa took Anna's hand and led them to the dining room area. As they entered the room, Anna said, "Peter, look how many nice young people like us are here, and listen to the soft music in the background. Lisa, thank you."

Lisa said, "Good night, and enjoy your evening."

Soon a waiter appeared with a nicely designed large menu. They ordered the menu du jour and some red wine, enjoyed the lunch and the environment, and left. As they were leaving, a nice, tall young man and a beautiful woman with dark hair and green eyes approached them. "Hello, my name is Estefan, and this is my wife, Nazareth. Forgive me, but if I am not mistaken, you are Peter Savera."

"I am Peter, and this is my wife, Anna."

Estefan realized that Peter did not recognize him. "Maybe you will remember that we were students together in our first year of college at St. Joseph."

"Oh! Now I remember. We use to call you Este. I remember you were selected to represent Spain in the Olympics. Excuse me, Estefan, but my wife is trying to learn Spanish. I have to translate into Russian for now."

They continued talking, and Estefan said to Peter, "Peter, you and your wife are a celebrity. You and Anna were in every newspaper last week. That's how I recognized you. We all have changed. Actually, my wife, Nazareth, recognized both of you, and I told her that I was sure you were the Peter who was in my college."

They spoke for a while and promised to meet again. Peter asked, "I know you play tennis. Do you want to play doubles tomorrow?"

Estefan and his wife both were happy and said, "Let us do that at ten a.m., because later it gets too hot." Peter and Anna were both happy to find an old classmate of Peter's.

Anna and Peter got up earlier the next day. It was a little cloudy but still warm. A cool breeze was gently blowing from the north when they went down to the dining room and met Estefan and Nazareth, already ready for breakfast. They were happy to see each other, and they ordered their breakfast. Nazareth and Estefan ordered porridge, fresh fruits, and orange juice, while Peter and Anna ordered eggs and toast with orange marmalade. They finished their breakfast and promised to meet at the tennis court at ten.

All four of them were dressed in their white tennis outfits, and each had a racket. It was already warm, but the ocean breeze made the weather pleasant. The couples practiced for a while. Peter and Anna had not played for some time and had not realized that Estefan and Nazareth were Olympic-level players.

Estefan asked Anna to start serving. She served well, but Nazareth's return was powerful. When it was Estefan's turn to serve, his service passed Peter's court like a bullet. Anna and Peter were left standing looking at each other. Peter shouted, "Estefan, I don't think we can play. You are both too good."

Nazareth came to the net and told Anna, "Estefan was showing off. We will play few games and then we can go. What do you think?"

Peter said, "As long as you don't clobber us, sure, let us enjoy a soft game."

They played for a while, and the sun started to heat up the cool breeze, so they decided to stop. They all decided to go for a shower and sauna. They were enjoying each other's company, joking and laughing.

They spent the next few days' together, swimming, getting massages, going to movies, and eating lunches and dinners. On their last day in Majorca, Peter, Anna, Estefan, and Nazareth spent the whole day together and said good-bye in the evening. Peter and Anna arrived in their apartment and immediately called Carlos. They told him that their stay had been short but wonderful and now they were ready to come home.

Chapter 4
ANNA AND PETER GO HOME

Peter's father sounded sad. He said, "Peter, I am glad you will be here soon."

Peter asked his father whether Grandpa was okay. Carlos changed the subject and told Peter that all the arrangements for their coming home were complete. They should be at the airport tomorrow at seven a.m. Peter's father said good night and hung up. Peter knew that Grandpa was not well; they were sad to learn that.

"Anna, you know, Grandpa is going to be seventy-seven this year." They started to get ready in anticipation of tomorrow's flight. They went to sleep early and woke up at six a.m. when Ramon knocked at the door. He told them that he would bring breakfast in half an hour, leaving enough time for them to get ready. Anna and Peter got ready and had their breakfast in good time. Peter was still thinking of Grandpa. The car came and took them to the airport. It was a beautiful morning with a gentle breeze, and the sun was just coming up. They were on time for the flight and took off without fanfare. Going home was not so pleasant; the thought that something might happen to Grandpa while they were away in Russia was depressing.

Peter was silent. Anna knew what was going on in Peter's mind; she came close to Peter and hugged him. He was sad to think about his father and mother, who would have to live with Grandpa's condition. Peter had no idea what was wrong with him except that his father had once told him that Grandpa's heart was weak. They suddenly realized that their plane was descending. They gathered their thoughts and prepared themselves to disembark.

GRANDPA SAVERA IS SICK

They were received at the terminal by Nicola, Peter's father's assistant. Nicola was in a somber mood. Peter asked, "Nicola, please tell me what is going on."

"Peter, your grandpa is very, very sick." Peter and Anna started to feel sick. Anna held Peter's hand and wiped his eyes. When they got home, they realized that there was an unusual silence at the Savera house. They entered the house. Peter's mother hugged both Anna and Peter and started to cry.

"Ma, let us go to see Grandpa."

"Peter, your grandpa is in a coma. It is awful to see him in this condition."

GRANDPA RECOVERS

They all went in the room where Grandpa was lying. The whole family was around his big bed, some praying and some just sitting. Peter came close to him and whispered in his ear, "Grandpa, I am Peter. I love you; please open your eyes." To everyone's surprise, Grandpa opened his eyes. Everyone quietly cheered and felt thankful for Peter and Anna's homecoming and Peter's whispering in Grandpa's ear. Peter's father and mother hugged and kissed both Anna and Peter with great admiration. Peter's mother asked him, "Peter, what did you whisper in your grandpa's ear?"

"Ma, I just told him, 'I am Peter and I love you.'"

His mother hugged him again and said, "My son, you must be an angel bringing Grandpa to life." Everyone, including Anna, was impressed by this miraculous happening.

Carlos helped Grandpa to sit up, supporting his back with soft cushions. Grandpa cleared his throat and asked for a glass of water. Someone brought a glass of water. Grandpa drank slowly until he finished the whole glass. Then he looked all around him and asked Carlos, "Why is everyone here, and what happened to me?"

Carlos told him, "Father, you made all of us cry. You have been in a coma for almost two days."

Juan Savera looked puzzled and then asked for Peter and Anna. They came and put their arms around Grandpa. He wanted to know all about their time in Majorca and when they were leaving for Moscow.

"Grandpa, we cannot leave you in this condition," Peter replied.

"What condition? I was just tired, and I guess just dozed off." Everyone laughed, and Grandpa smiled too. He continued, "Peter and Anna, come here and listen carefully. Dmitri called before I went to sleep and told me that he was sending a plane on Sunday. What is the day today?" Peter told him it was Thursday. Grandpa told Anna and Peter that they must leave on Sunday, and they agreed. Peter's mother brought a tray with soup and dessert, and Grandpa ate his favorite chicken soup and rice pudding. He began to feel more energetic. He saw that Peter and Anna were still sitting near him and asked Anna to call her father and confirm that they would depart as scheduled on Sunday.

As the hours passed, Juan Savera was getting his strength back. His personal physician arrived just as Grandpa finished his meal. The doctor was happy to see him. They joked a bit, and the doctor found Juan in good spirits. As a matter of fact, the doctor said, "I think the coma condition gave Juan a much-needed rest. It is amazing how nature saved him from a disaster, I think."

The doctor checked his blood pressure and vital signs and declared Juan Savera a fit man. The entire household was jubilant, and a sigh of relief was in the air.

Anna called her father in Moscow and told Dmitri, "Papa, when we came back to the Savera house from Majorca, we found everyone in Grandpa Savera's room, gathered around his big bed. We were afraid to ask anyone what was happening. Peter's father realized our dilemma, and Carlos came and whispered in Peter's ear, 'Your grandpa has been in a coma for two days.' Peter went down and whispered something in Grandpa's ear, and believe it or not, Grandpa opened his eyes. Is it not a miracle?"

"Anna, I think your Peter is really a special gift to us."

Dmitri and Katharina were happy that the children were coming home. On Sunday, Peter and Anna said good-bye to all, especially to Grandpa, and left for the airport. The plane took off on time. Dmitri and Katharina were at the airport to bring Peter and Anna home. It was getting colder as fall set in; leaves were turning all colors, and there was a chill in the air. Dmitri's house was happy again. Guests were coming in and cousins were visiting; life was good. Dmitri and Peter left to go to the aeronautical institute, and life became very busy.

THE SECRET PROJECT

Three years passed by. Peter was working on a special military project; this project was very important, and things were progressing well. Dmitri combined forces with Peter in scrutinizing theoretical work and recording the results of prolonged testing. One night, both Peter and Dmitri worked till two in the morning. Katharina and Anna called the institute, and Dmitri picked up the phone. Dmitri and Peter were laughing and so happy that Katharina could not understand their behavior.

Finally, Dmitri sobered up, took a deep breath, and said, "Katharina and Anna, listen. Peter, with my support, has been working on this secret air force project for almost two years. After many trials and tests, the final test results have just come in, and we have succeeded. That is why we are so happy and celebrating. Don't mention anything to anyone. We are coming home now."

When Peter and Dmitri reached home, their wives were waiting with great expectations. They all danced, and Katharina and Anna brought coffee to sober the men up. Katharina wanted to know more about the project, but Dmitri put his finger on her lips so she would not ask any more questions.

Anna came forward and declared, "Okay, Papa and my darling Peter, we have some good news for you too. We are going to have a baby—I am pregnant."

That was a little too much happiness for such a short time, but they were drunk with good news all around. Dmitri wanted to get champagne, but Anna said, "Papa and Peter please go to bed. It has been an emotional roller coaster." They hugged and kissed and went to sleep.

They all got up late, although Anna and Katharina were up a little earlier, and Anna prepared breakfast. She made a Spanish omelet for Peter and simple eggs for Dmitri, along with toast and coffee. This was not an ordinary morning. Dmitri and Peter got up and suddenly realized what had happened last night—or was it this morning? Dmitri looked at the clock and saw that it was already ten a.m. He rushed to call his boss and gave him the good news about the success of project "Hawk." He told General Ustinov that the conclusive results had arrived that morning at two. General Ustinov congratulated Dmitri and told him to relax, that he would arrange the next meeting tomorrow at ten a.m. "You and Peter are prepared with the necessary documents to support the results."

At the meeting the next morning, Peter and Dmitri presented all the test results, supporting documents, and conclusions of the project. The general and his technical experts left, promising to get back to Dmitri. Months passed. One day, General Ustinov called and requested that both Peter and Dmitri attend a meeting organized by the scientific committee representing the Central Award Council.

The council chairman addressed all the recipients of the annual award ceremony. "The chairman praises the top winners, Peter Savera and Dmitri Yevchenco, for their work in the field of aviation related to Soviet air defense. Their work constitutes a big step in our efforts to achieve superiority in this field."

Dmitri and Peter were asked to stand up while everyone, including the council members, applauded. Both were elated. The council announced that the awards presentation would take place in the Lenin Achievement Hall at Sochi, a Black Sea resort, on the last Saturday in June. Everyone stood up and applauded the council. The results of the top awards were published in the national *Gazette* and international aviation magazines. Western papers could only speculate as to the mode and type of innovation; some said it had something to do with stealth technology, and others thought it was related to a new type of wing made with titanium skin. Peter Savera and Dmitri Yevchenco were on cloud nine.

Chapter 5

THE BIRTH OF BABY SYBILLE

Peter and Dmitri's work was published in a Soviet aeronautical prestigious gazette, without disclosing the finer points of the innovation, as well as the application of the discovery in future Mikoyan designs. The European magazine *International Aviation* immediately came up with speculations regarding the new discovery. Soviet aviators were filled with pride and waited for the day they could roam the sky fearlessly, without any impunity. The British magazine *Flight* came close when they wrote about aircraft stability. Whenever Peter and Dmitri read these aviation magazines, they enjoyed them and had fun.

One night Peter could not sleep. He was restless and daydreaming. He was lying on his back, gazing at the airplane models hanging from the bedroom ceiling, and wondering who made him reach these unusual, never-imagined heights. He looked at Anna, angel-like and totally dedicated. He did not remember anyone loving him so much, and now he was going to be a father. Suddenly, a strange feeling came over him, He drifted into sleep and dreamed he was flying a Mig 17 and was being chased by an American Corsair fighter. Peter could not pull out from a dive and hit the swamp. He woke up, screaming. Anna woke up, frightened. She hugged him and consoled him. Soon, morning came and breakfast was served.

Katharina asked Anna, "I heard Peter screaming. Was it a bad dream?"

Anna replied, "Ma, Peter dreams a lot, and he really had a terrible dream this time."

Time was flying. Anna's pregnancy was progressing well. The day arrived when Dmitri, Peter, and Katharina took Anna to the hospital, and a beautiful baby girl was born. Peter held his baby in his arms, while Anna looked at Peter's face with joy. Dmitri and Katharina took their turn holding the baby and felt extremely proud and thankful. Anna and the baby came home and found the baby's room fit for a princess. They sat down at the dinner table to discuss the name for the baby. Finally, they settled on Sybille Katharina Savera.

As soon as Baby Sybille was able to sit, Katharina took the baby in her lap while sitting down in front of the piano. She played simple tunes and sang at the same time.

The summer after Baby Sybille arrived, an invitation from Grandma and Grandpa Juan Savera came, inviting the whole Yevchenco family, including the baby, to visit the Savera family in Spain.

"We are dying to see Baby Sybille. Please come," Juan Savera said to Dmitri on the telephone. "I am sending you tickets for the whole family. You and your family will take an Air Canada flight on Friday at ten a.m. You just go to Air Canada counter at the airport at eight a.m. or before, and they will take care of the family. Hope to see you soon. Good-bye."

Dmitri told his wife and then Anna and Peter about the invitation. They were all in favor of going to Madrid. Dmitri called Juan and told him that they would be there.

DMITRI'S FAMILY ARRIVES IN MADRID

Dmitri, Katharina, Peter, and Anna with the baby were received joyfully by the Savera family. The women and girls of the Savera family had prepared the baby's room with balloons and ribbons. Everyone loved the baby and took turns feeding, changing, and holding her. Grandpa told everyone they were enjoying the presence of several generations in the room. Baby Sybille was already making sounds as if she were singing. When Katharina heard that she told Dmitri, "Dmitri, did you hear that? My training is working. And you said little babies cannot learn to sing that early."

After one month had passed, Katharina and her family wanted to go home. Dmitri reminded Katharina, "We are leaving in two days, so relax." Peter told his father and grandfather about the project that he and Dmitri worked on. Peter asked his father-in-law to tell his family about the award-winning project, but Dmitri did not want to divulge any classified information.

Dmitri sat between Carlos and Juan and said, "Peter and I have been working on a project that was initially conceived and designed by him. The more he worked at it, the more I saw it's potential. When I looked at the model, I realized he had discovered something really important that must be reported to my boss, General Ustinov. I told him not to tell or bring anyone else. He came to our aviation lab alone, knowing the importance of the find. Peter showed him the concept, the application, and the importance of the project. The general's jaw dropped; he grabbed Dmitri's arm and said, 'Is it what I think it is?' When we continued to study the impact of Peter's find, it turned out to be so important that the defense ministry immediately declared the project classified. General Ustinov ordered a meeting with special agents. He ordered that in order to keep the project under cover, the general wanted me to be the only other person to work with Peter Savera. The general set a time and date for the meeting without telling anyone; people attending the meeting would be informed about it at the last minute for security reasons." Dmitri suddenly stopped talking and told Carlos and Juan, "Maybe I have already said too much."

No one said a word. Carlos and Grandpa hugged Peter and told him, "We are so proud of you, my son." Carlos and Grandpa hugged Dmitri and thanked him for taking care of Peter. Grandpa Savera asked Dmitri, "You know, Sybille is our first grandchild. You and your family's coming here has made our house a place of joy and happiness. When you leave us next week, our house will not be the same. Come, Dmitri. See for yourself."

Juan took Dmitri by his hand and showed him how happy the children were. Dmitri said, "Juan, look—Sybille is the center point all the children are singing and dancing around her. I see what you mean."

Dmitri continued, "Juan, what we will do? When we go back to Moscow, give us one month to unwind and next month, you bring your family to enjoy our company. You must understand. Peter and I are heavily involved in our classified project, but you will have Katharina, Anna, and Sybille. When Peter and I are busy, Anna will drive you to show Moscow's highlights. Sybille will keep you busy—she loves to sing and Grandma Katharina's music lessons start every day at eight in the morning till nine a.m. don't worry; Anna is a great host. She will look after you and your wife.

Juan was happy and thanked Dmitri for this arrangement.

Katharina believed that children at this tender age learned and remembered subconsciously almost anything they saw or heard. "If you want to be a good parent, do good things, say good things, and play music and sing. This training provides a child with an excellent foundation for succeeding in future life," she said.

Dmitri's family and Peter returned to Moscow. Their life got much busier. Their holiday in Spain had taken away precious time from their tight schedule in the lab.

ANNA IS EXPECTING AGAIN

One evening, Dmitri and Peter arrived from the office and had just sat down in the living room when Sybille, who now was five years old, came running and sat down in Grandma's lap. Katharina and Anna, hand in hand, with radiant faces and big smiles, came to the living room and announced, "We have some good news. We are going to have another baby." Dmitri and Peter both jumped from their chairs and came to hug and kiss both Anna and Katharina.

Dmitri asked, "Did you see the doctor?"

Anna answered, "We went to the hospital and we saw your obstetrician friend. He was nice. We told him the purpose of our visit and said we did not want Papa or Peter to know until we were sure. He understood and took us to his office. There he examined me and told us that I am more than a month pregnant. We were very happy; we came running home to give you the good news."

Months passed, and Anna gave birth to a healthy, handsome, big boy. They named him Joseph. The house was full of joy fun and love. Dmitri began thinking of retirement. He was only fifty-eight years old, but he thought, *in couple of years, Joseph will be two. Even if I am semi-retired, it will be so much fun to play with Joseph and teach him about flying and many other things.*

Life continued. Joseph was now almost twelve, Grandpa was semi-retired, and Sybille was celebrating her seventeenth birthday. She graduated from the Soviet academy of music. She was a junior member of the Music Worker's Association and therefore was allowed to take part in various music-related contests and competitions. Her first award-winning performance was singing in the opera *Madame Butterfly* in Kiev. Her performance was so good that she won a Soviet national classical music award. All the family went to her first performance. Peter and Dmitri could not believe that she was a real opera singer and winner of the coveted Soviet national classical music award.

Grandma Katharina said, "I don't know why both of you are surprised. I have been teaching her music since she was six months s old. I knew that she was going to be a star. Did you see how Joseph has been playing piano? Do not tell me that the talent is not genetic. Joseph's talent is divided between his love for airplanes and music. I am sure it will be hard for him to achieve perfection in either subject. Even though everyone was surprised to see Sybille win so big at her age. We both knew her potential."

Peter and Dmitri had almost finished their third project related to aviation. The Politburo and the Ministry of Science and Technology never had so many innovations in such a short time. Dmitri received a special package from the award council, inviting Peter Savera, Dmitri Yevchenco, and the family to receive another achievement award at the Lenin Achievement Hall at Sochi

One day Dmitri told Katharina, Peter, and Anna, "It is amazing. I do not think I have ever had so much pleasure as I do with Joseph and Sybille. I know I loved Anna a lot, but I never had enough time to enjoy her. My life was on the edge of a sword; one wrong move and you were gone. The stress and tension were so great that they did not allow real living." He held his head in his big hands and cried quietly. Katharina came and held his head near her body, and Anna kissed his balding head.

Anna said to Peter, "You have been very quiet. How are you, my miracle worker?"

Peter told her, "Anna, Papa Dmitri is right. When you don't have time, you have enough health, strength, and will to do too many things at once. When you have time and will, you don't have strength, and you don't have health; everything in your body is wearing out. There is one consolation: children. Their being with us makes us feel so good that we forget the winters of life. When I see my children giving so much happiness and pleasure to the family, it really gives me a sense of pride and joy."

Chapter 6

DMITRI'S FAMILY ARRIVES IN SOCHI RESORT

Dmitri had told everyone in the house that a limousine would be at the door at seven-thirty the following morning to take them to the award center. The next morning, they all got up early and were ready at the outside door with the luggage when the car arrived. Sybille was looking after her brother. The limousine dropped them off in the portico area of the Sochi resort. It was a lovely area with flowers and even palms trees swinging in the breeze. Hotel housekeepers took care of the luggage and guided them to their apartment on the second floor.

Anna and Katharina liked their apartment, which had two bedrooms, a kitchenette, and two bathrooms. Anna liked the room in the corner with big windows, and Krista took the smaller room. The hotel appeared to be fairly new. After washing their hands and faces, they went down to the restaurant. Everything was on the house. Dmitri and Peter announced that the food was excellent, and Sybille had a drink made with pomegranate and apple juice. The chef came out and introduced himself and asked Dmitri if they had enjoyed the service. He thanked Dmitri's family and wished them good luck. Dmitri walked with the family outside in the garden; there was a pleasant smell of tropical flowers. Katharina and Anna went to their rooms, and Peter and Dmitri followed. Dmitri played some simple games he had invented with the children and showed them some tricks; Joseph always climbed up Grandpa's back and wanted him to gallop like a horse.

The air seemed to put them to sleep early. Next morning, they all got up early. Grandma looked after Sybille's clothing and hair and cleaned her face with a cream. Dmitri and Peter got ready. Katharina asked Anna, "Are you ready to go down?"

Anna told her, "Ma, you go down with Sybille and get a nice table. I will be there soon." Dmitri and Peter left with Katharina, Sybille holding Grandpa's hand. They went down to the dining room. They sat down, and Peter watched the stairs for Anna and Joseph, hoping they would come soon.

Chapter 7

A BIG EXPLOSION SHAKES THE BUILDING

The hotel alarm went off. There was chaos in the place; dust made it impossible to see anything. Dmitri told Katharina to stay still with Sybille. He and Peter were panicking. They went to the front door, where a military commander told them to stay inside.

Dmitri knew the explosion was from a bomb. The commander told him that the bomb blast was so powerful that a corner of the building had disappeared. In the meantime, air force and military commandos arrived, and ambulances and fire engines roared in. The place was a war zone. Both Peter and Dmitri were crying. General Spinoff appeared. When he saw both Peter and Dmitri crying, he knew that Anna and little Joseph were missing. The general took both of them to the dining room, where he found Sybille and Katharina. They were screaming and crying and were in bad shape. General Spinoff took them through the back door, where his car was parked. He told the driver to take them home. He gave the family his sympathies and told them he would come to the house as soon as he could to deliver news and figure out the next steps. He hugged them all, kissed Sybille, and told her to be brave for her grandma and grandpa and take care of her dad. The next morning, the newspapers carried not only the pictures of the disaster but also the story of the two famous Soviet inventors who were on their way to receive awards for their achievement and service to the nation. General Spinoff called Dmitri and told him that the government had set up a special committee to investigate the terrorist act. The general thought that the explosion might have been the work of a group in Chechnya.

When Dmitri's friends heard, they came over to share the family's sorrow and dilute the sadness. The family received telephone calls and cables from all over the world.

The Savera family was devastated. Peter's father, mother, and grandfather booked flights to Moscow immediately, saying, "We would like to be there with you, to share your and our grief, if you have no objection."

Dmitri and Peter brought the Savera family home from the airport the next day. They all sat in the living room. Sybille and Katharina came down, crying, to join them. Dmitri said with tears in his eyes, "Juan, I have to tell you that things were unusually good. Peter's and my work on project 'Hawk' turned out to be perfect; most scientists only dream of such glory. We were gifted with Joseph, our grandson. I cannot imagine how long we are going to suffer now that he is gone." Dmitri started to cry. He took out his handkerchief and buried his face in it, continuing, "It breaks my heart, and not only mine. Look at my Katharina and my beautiful Sybille—they have not stopped crying since the tragedy. I cry for my Peter. He does not cry, he does not talk, and he does not eat. He blames the Hawk project that stole his love and his precious Joseph." Sybille came to her father and stood behind him with her hands on his shoulders to show her love and understanding.

The next day, Peter's father and grandfather took Peter in the living room. Grandpa said, "We know you have experienced a very big trauma, and I suggest you may develop a serious psychological problem if you continue to stay here. We don't want you to get real sick. For you, the logical thing is to go away and resign your job. Dmitri and the general will understand."

Peter finally spoke. "What you think, Papa?"

Carlos said, "Grandpa is right. You have to come with us to Spain to change your environment. We all will be there, as your friends, your mother, and your grandmother can bring normalcy to your life."

Peter then asked, "What about my Sybille?"

Grandpa turned to Peter. "Peter, just think. Your father- and mother-in-law's lives are shattered right now. They need your daughter. If you take Sybille away from them, they will be alone, and loneliness does not allow you to forget the trauma easily. Sybille can be a healer for them, so let her be here with them. We can all visit them once a month."

Peter thanked Grandpa for being so considerate. "Grandpa, everything you said makes sense and is logical. Now the question is how to deal with this situation. Who is going to tell Papa Dmitri and convince him?"

Carlos said, "Don't worry, my son. We will. Dad is a refined negotiator and a compassionate one."

Grandpa Savera and Carlos went to Dmitri, and Juan Savera said to him, "Dmitri, you are right; Peter seems to be in a depression. It is important that we save Peter from getting into a severe depression. It may help if we take Peter away from here and Sybille stays with you for now. You need her support. We will come and visit you. Since you are retired, you, Katharina, and Sybille can visit us too, and it should not be a problem. If you agree, we all can sit down, and you can explain the situation and announce the final decision."

Dmitri thought for a while and said to Juan, "Probably you are right. Peter is in a depression, and you are correct to suggest that he should go away with you. My friend Juan, I will like to go away too. Every time we look around, we see Joseph and Anna."

They had a meeting. Dmitri told Katharina, Sybille, and Peter, "Your grandpa Savera has very carefully taken care of everything. The decision is, Peter goes with his father to Spain and Sybille stays with us. Every now and then, they visit us and we visit them."

Everything worked out according to the Savera plan. Sybille hugged her father and promised him, "I will call you every day, and please let me know how you are doing. Papa, I love you." They all wished everyone good luck before they left for Spain.

Sybille kept herself and her grandma busy. She called her music director and said, "I will like you to start booking concerts for me again; I feel strong now." Charles was happy to have her back. He said he would send her the latest operatic program and let her decide which program she wanted.

Sybille and her grandma started to work and practiced every day. This work was good for everyone, though it was certainly a big challenge after what they had gone through. Sybille moved between Moscow and Madrid, always taking her grandparents with her. Sybille's appearance at the Madrid opera house just fitted into her schedule; she was going to be in Madrid for her eighteenth birthday, where her father had planned a birthday party for her.

Sybille and her grandparents arrived at the Savera house a few days before her birthday. Peter and his mother picked them up at the airport. It was a happy occasion for all. Peter looked alive again, and Dmitri and Katharina were delighted to see a big change in Peter.

The atmosphere at the Savera house was happy. There were close relatives and some that Sybille never met. Peter's mother brought a young, slender woman and introduced her to Sybille as Isabel Savera. "Thank you, Grandmamma. Isabelle, it is a pleasure to meet another Savera."

Isabel told her, "I was always anxious to meet you. My husband is your cousin. We have been married for three years, and he told me about the recent happenings. My husband and I would like you to come for dinner tomorrow night."

Sybille looked at Grandma for approval. "Go, Sybille. You will enjoy her company and that of your cousin Oskar. Isabel is a linguist, she is the best cook I know, and she is full of fun and surprises."

Her cousin and Isabel came to pick Sybille up at about five p.m. the next day in their blue Audi. Sybille said, "Thank you for inviting me. I have spent a lot of time with older Savera members, but this is the first time I am with cousins of my own age. What a delightful difference."

Oskar asked Sybille to stay with them for couple of nights. Isabel told Oskar, "Oh, darling, can we do that? We can go dancing, singing."

"Isabel, if you take care of her during the day, I will take care of you at night."

Isabel looked at him. "What? I meant entertaining!" They all laughed.

Sybille meets GG

They arrived at a very modern house, recently built. Everything was of the latest style in the kitchen, the bathroom, and the decorations. Oskar told Sybille they had moved in last year. Sybille realized that she had been accustomed to living in older houses furnished with antique furniture.

She said, "Looking at your young people's living style makes me want to have modern things. I am glad you have shown me the style of young; I had forgotten how young people live today."

Isabel invited Sybille to the family room. She was surprised to hear someone say, "Hello, my name is GG."

Sybille looked around to find out who was talking. At last, Isabel introduced GG, her parrot, to Sybille, and told GG, "GG, look, this is Sybille, my cousin. Can you say her name? Repeat after me, Mama Sybille, Mama Sybille."

GG said in a sweet singing voice, "Sybille, Sybille, and Sybille." Sybille was enchanted. Then somebody else behind the curtain said, "Who is there?" and repeated himself many times.

Isabel said, "Topo, come here, and meet Sybille. She is my cousin."

Topo came out and jumped on Isabelle's shoulder. Sybille could not believe these parrots were talking like humans. Oskar came in and told Sybille, "It is unbelievable, isn't it?"

Isabel called GG and Topo, "Come here, both of you." They came and sat on a high table with a colorful cover. Isabelle asked them, "What would you like to sing?"

She gave a small candy to each, and they said, "Thank you, Mama." Isabel sat at the piano and started to play "La Cucaracha." Topo and GG started to sing in perfect unison. Sybille could not stop laughing; she told Isabel and Oskar that she had not laughed like this for a long time. Isabel stopped playing the piano. Sybille clapped and said thank you to GG and Topo. It was dinnertime.

Sybille liked the food, dessert, and drinks, and the setting of the table was modern and exquisite. After dinner, they sat down in the living room. She found the modern furniture was not only streamlined but also more comfortable than the antique furniture she was used to. Sybille was so enchanted with the talking parrots that she could not resist asking Oskar and Isabel, "Tell me, where you got these birds?"

Isabel said, "We got these gray African parrots in South Africa. We were on a safari holiday there, and the owner of the safari expedition, a young man our age named Errol Flint, became a good friend of Oskar. You know, it seems where ever Oskar goes, he meets people who like him, and if Oskar likes them too, they become good friends. After the safari was over, he took us to see Cape Town and other places of interest. The night before we were to leave, he invited us for dinner. A handsome and polite young man came to pick us up from our hotel. We arrived at his house, and his lovely and graceful wife received us at the entrance. As we entered the house, the décor and furniture gave an impression of being in a safari environment. There were two gray talking parrots sitting on a perch made to look like branches of a tree. The parrots greeted us and introduced themselves, and I could not stop laughing. I was so taken by these birds that I had to have some. I asked him how we could buy some talking parrots. Errol said we wouldn't have time to shop for parrots before leaving, and he and his wife agreed to sell us theirs and arrange all the export paperwork. We enjoyed every minute of their hospitality. At the end of the night, Errol kissed me, and they hugged both of us. Errol drove us to our hotel, and we brought our parrot's home safe and sound."

Sybille was impressed with their safari trip and by their bringing home two parrots. Isabel said to Sybille, "I know what is going through your mind: how can I have a parrot to take home?"

Sybille agreed, "Isabel, you are so smart. I love you." It was getting late. Sybille asked, "How long do these birds live?"

Isabel told her, "I think they have a long life like us, but I am really not sure. You know what? I have a book on gray parrots I will give you to read."

Oskar and Isabel took Sybille home at the end of the evening. Sybille said, "I forgot to ask you—a week from today I have a concert. Would you like to come?"

They told her that it would be their pleasure to see their cousin perform. Sybille thanked them for such a nice evening. On Sybille's birthday, she came down for breakfast and found her father sitting near her Russian grandparents. They all seemed to be in a much better mood than before. Sybille's father came and embraced his daughter. He looked more cheerful. She said to her, "Grandpa Savera is such a remarkable man. His logical thinking, along with his fairness in making decisions, made such a difference. It has not only saved us from depression but also brought smiles to our faces."

By five p.m., lots of relatives, including her favorite cousins Isabelle and Oskar, were there. The dining table was nicely decorated with flowers, and balloons of various colors hung everywhere. Isabel, Katharina, her grandmother, and others came to Sybille's room. She was dressed in emerald green with matching jewelry and shoes, but she was crying. Isabel came and whispered in her ear that she had a present for her. "Can you guess what it could be?"

Chapter 8

SYBILLE'S SURPRISE GIFT

Isabel took her arm and helped her to get up from the chair. She directed Sybille to the dining table and made her sit in the middle chair. Everyone rushed to the table. The big rectangular cake with eighteen burning candles arrived and was placed in front of Sybille. Katharina was at the piano playing "Happy Birthday." Everybody started to sing along, and they all shouted, "Make a wish and blow out the candles." Sybille did, and they all clapped. A photographer from Savera Corporation was taking pictures. A table in the corner of the room was filling up with many gift packages. Sybille went around kissing and hugging all the elders.

Her father was with a lovely, elegant lady dressed in a simple white dress with a blue bolero. Peter introduced her to Sybille, "Sybille, I want you to meet Andrea, a close friend of mine."

Andrea told her, "I have heard a lot about you. You have achieved a lot at your young age."

Sybille replied, "It is a real pleasure to meet you. My father is lucky to have a friend like you. Papa, I hope you can bring Andrea to my concert next week. I will get you tickets."

Her father said, "That would be nice. I am sure Andrea will like it." Andrea kissed Sybille, and Peter took Andrea off to introduce her to other people. Isabel and Oskar came and wished Sybille a happy birthday.

Isabel told her, "Sybille, we have a special gift for you, and we hope you like it. You have to come with us to your room to see it." The gift was in a special box with little windows and a little door. Isabel opened the door, and Miss GG stepped out. Sybille could not believe it; she loved GG. She said, "Isabel, you are an angel. Believe me, Oskar; this GG is going to bring lot of happiness too many. Oskar and Isabel, thank you so much. But wait a minute—poor Topo is going to be alone now. He will miss her."

Oskar told her, "Topo is not going to miss. He was jealous of her, and they were always fighting. We saw how much you liked GG, and we thought this would be a unique gift for your birthday."

Isabel told GG to say hello to her new mama. "Hello, Mama, Sybille, Sybille, Sybille," the bird sang. At that point Isabel gave a small candy to Sybille, indicating that she should give it to GG. Sybille understood that every time GG did something good, she should get a reward.

Isabel sat down with Sybille and gave her a book on caring for African Gray parrots. Isabel had made notes for Sybille explaining what to do and what not to do about the bird. Isabel said, "The most important thing is to give love, and the bird wants her living quarters clean. She will love to be groomed whenever you or your grandma has time. Sybille, we have to go."

Oskar said, "What about the concert tickets?"

Sybille said, "Oh yes, one second please." She went to her briefcase and gave them the tickets.

Days passed. Sybille spent mornings practicing her singing with her grandma Katharina at the piano as GG perched on top of the piano. Every time Sybille sang a high note, GG covered her ears with her wings. Eventually, GG got so used to Sybille's singing and Grandma's piano that she could whistle the tunes Grandma played. When Katharina told this to Dmitri, he could not believe it. Dmitri came to see Katharina playing, and GG flew over and sat right on top of piano. Katharina said, "Dmitri, go sit on that chair." She started to play "La Cucaracha," and GG started to sing. Dmitri was laughing himself silly. Katharina stopped playing, and GG also stopped singing.

Dmitri asked Sybille, "I wonder if GG can learn to talk Russian."

Sybille answered, "Grandpa, she learned English when she was in South Africa, and now that she is here in Spain she is learning Spanish. I suppose she can learn Russian, Grandpa. It is like teaching a child, though; you have to speak with her every day."

Dmitri was happy to have a teacher's job. He started to like GG; he told Katharina that the little parrot was very interesting.

On the day of Sybille's concert, she asked Katharina and Dmitri whether they were going to attend. Both Katharina and Dmitri said, "Sybille, we are tired. Meeting so many new people was too much for us. We are so tired that we will go to our room and sleep a little."

Sybille agreed with them. She told them that Charles Bronfman, her music director, would pick her up early before the show. Sybille had already given two tickets to her father. She returned from the concert late and went to bed.

The next day, Oskar and Isabel came for lunch and brought a bundle of newspapers. Every paper had her picture on the front page, praising her performance, and one paper, *Madrid National*, reported that Sybille should be awarded a medal of honor by the Spanish president to bring Spain in the international forum. All the papers were amazed to see a young, slim, and beautiful opera diva. Oskar and Isabel were sorry to see Sybille so tired. They discussed her health, but as usual, she said that it would pass. They were glad to see each other. Isabel thanked Sybille for inviting them to her concert. Isabel said, "Sybille, you are remarkable. You are so young and on top of the opera singers' chart. By the way, how is GG doing?" Sybille told her that she was enjoying the Savera house as much as Sybille enjoyed her being there.

"My grandma is teaching her some Russian baby songs," Sybille said. "GG is always at the piano when Grandma and I are practicing. GG loves music a lot, and she is always asking for a treat." Sybille showed Isabel her weekly program for feeding and grooming GG.

Isabel said to Sybille, "Don't give her too many candies. Of course, whenever you ask her to do something, like singing or making funny sounds, she expects a reward. But if she volunteers to do it, she does not expect a reward, so don't give her one. Sybille, can we see GG now? I miss her."

Sybille took Oskar and Isabel to her room, where her grandparents were sitting. She introduced her grandma Katharina and grandpa Dmitri to Isabel. Katharina came forward and embraced Isabel, thanking her for giving Sybille a bundle of joy.

"GG is giving Dmitri and all of us so much pleasure and work. Isabel, you know, when I am singing and playing piano, she leaves her little house and flies to sit on my piano. We sing, and she moves her head with the rhythm. When she gets tired, she flies back to her house and falls asleep. She is remarkable."

Dmitri came up to Oskar and asked him, "You think GG can learn to speak Russian?"

Oskar told Dmitri that she had to be taught, just like a child. Dmitri was happy. Oskar asked them if they were ready for lunch.

Sybille said, "I think we are all hungry. I came late from my concert—there were photographers and reporters, and our music director and conductor kept me busy with them."

Isabel asked her, "So where and when is your next appearance?"

"Isabel, we are playing in Zurich. I can ask them to send you a program." Sybille continued, "If you come to Moscow, we can be together for at least a month touring Europe, just before the cold winter sets in."

Isabel said, "Oh Sybille, I would love to, although I am going to miss my darling husband."

They went together to lunch. The table was ready, and Oskar and Sybille kissed their aunties and grandparents. Peter came alone and sat next to his daughter. He told her that Andrea had enjoyed the concert very much. "She still cannot believe that you have reached the status of a diva in your field, and she asked me to thank you for the opera tickets."

Peter said, "Isabel was telling me that you have gotten a talking parrot for your birthday. Are you going to take GG to Moscow?"

Sybille replied, "Yes, Papa, she will be a good companion for Grandma and Grandpa while I am on my opera tour. You should see how Grandma is teaching her. She can already sing the main tunes of the arias from *Carmen* and *Madame Butterfly*. Can you imagine how much fun both have? You know, Grandpa wants to teach GG to speak Russian. Papa, GG is giving us our lives back. I could not imagine leaving my grandparents alone before, but now I can."

Peter asked, "Sybille, when is your flight? If I am not mistaken, you leave the day after tomorrow. What about GG? I think she needs export papers."

Sybille told him that Isabel had already arranged everything. Isabel and Oskar were listening to Peter's concern; Isabel assured Peter that Uncle Carlos's office had done all that. As lunch was coming to an end, Grandma Savera gave a fur bag to Sybille. She told her, "This fur bag will match your fur coat and will keep GG warm." Sybille thanked her.

Oskar and Isabel came to say good-bye and exchange phone numbers. When they were ready to leave, Sybille went with them to the main door. She thanked them again for the gift of GG, and they kissed and hugged and promised to keep in touch. Many relatives and friends said good-bye to Sybille and her grandparents. Their flight was leaving the next morning. Almost everyone went to rest in their rooms. Dmitri and Katharina went to their room as well to do a final packing of their belongings.

Sybille was left alone in her room, talking to GG. "Do you miss Topo and Isabel?"

GG said, "I miss Mama, no Topo. Sybille, Sybille is my mama. I like you, Mama."

Sybille knew GG wanted a candy. "Show me how a dog barks and how an ambulance cries." The parrot imitated a dog perfectly and then made an ambulance sound. Sybil's little cousins were playing close to Sybille's room. They came running in the room and saw GG sitting near Sybille.

They all asked, "Did the parrot make that sound?" At this point, GG was barking like a dog. The children burst out laughing. Then GG again made the ambulance sound, and the girls went silly laughing. Sybille told GG to go to her house. She said, "Okay, Mama." Sybille told the children that GG was tired and needed to sleep.

Only very close relatives were invited to dinner that evening; all grandparents from both sides were there. Peter and his friend Andrea came. Sybille was glad to see Andrea again. Andrea talked to her about GG and asked her about her future concerts. Sybille told her that she had signed contracts with Russian and French recording studios that would keep her very busy. She had been reluctant before to leave her grandparents alone while she was away on recording appointments, but now that they had their little friend, GG, they would not be alone.

Everyone got up early in the morning to catch their seven-thirty flight. Grandpa Savera came down to say good-bye to his friends Dmitri and Katharina. Dmitri told Juan, "My friend Juan, you saved us from psychological breakdown. Staying with you and your family has given us hope and strength. Now we are ready to face new challenges. Your Peter appears to be doing well, and we are both glad that he has a nice friend. Our precious Sybille is fine with her new friend GG; she will play a big role in our happiness. Juan, can you see how the supreme programmer almost destroys you, and how he picks you up from so low to a new high?"

DMITRI, KATHARINA, SYBILLE, AND GG RETURN TO MOSCOW

Dmitri, Katharina, and Sybille hugged, kissed, and said good-bye to all. Peter came again to kiss his daughter and said that he would miss her a lot. They left for the airport.

When Sybille and her grandparents arrived home in Moscow, they were tired. They settled down for snacks and coffee. Sybille realized she had almost forgotten about GG; the bird had not received water or food for three hours. Sybille immediately got up and opened the door of GG's little house. The parrot was unhappy. Sybille told GG, "I am sorry—I did not take care of you."

Katharina brought GG food and put some in her bowl, and Sybille gave her a candy. GG said, "Thank you, Mama." Sybille said, "Grandma, I am worried about GG. Could you play 'How Much Is That Doggy in the Window'? If she sings, that means she did not suffer too much."

Katharina started playing. Immediately, GG jumped on top of the piano. Katharina continued to play, and GG started to sing and barks like a dog, exactly at the point where she was supposed to. Dmitri and Sybille started to clap: GG was okay. Sybille picked up GG and kissed her. GG said, "Thank you, Mama." Sybille asked GG to thank Grandma for playing piano. She said, "Thank you, Gama." Grandma picked GG up and kissed her.

The family developed a routine. Every morning, Dmitri got up early, brought GG's little house to the table, and opened her door. Dmitri was trying to train her to say "good morning" in Russian, but she was having a hard time following Dmitri, maybe because of his Russian accent. In the meantime, Katharina and Sybille came down, and GG jumped on Sybille's shoulder saying, "Good morning, Mama," and "Good morning, Gramma."

They just loved the way GG talked. Dmitri kept trying to teach GG basic Russian greetings, but GG changed the subject, saying, "Grandpa Candy."

Dmitri realized that it was boring for GG to learn spoken language. He suggested that Katharina play a Russian jingle slowly. Katharina started a very lively tune, Katharina and Dmitri both started to sing, and they could not believe their ears. GG was moving her head and started to sing. Sybille came out running from her room and saw three of them enjoying themselves. This had been her objective exactly. Sybille was more at peace now because she was leaving on her concert tour early the next morning with her music director and conductor. After a few lively songs, Katharina told Dmitri, "Let GG go to her little house and rest. No candies—she has to have her food."

Sybille left for Zurich, where she had to appear in three opera concerts. Sybille would also be appearing in Budapest and finally in London. The tour would take her at least two months.

During this period, Dmitri and Katharina were busy taking care of GG. They were on a first-name basis with her. She came out every morning from her little house and called, "Dmitri, Dmitri. " Sybille called home every night to hear about her grandparents and about her GG.

When Sybille came home from her tour, she was anxious to see how the family had been during her first absence. She arrived around eight p.m. As she entered the house, her grandparents told her that they had missed her. In the meantime, GG flew from her house and landed on Sybille's shoulder, crying out, "Mama." Sybille was happy to know that after a long absence, GG still remembered her.

More time passed, and after many more concerts, she had an appointment with a Spanish recording studio. It was getting cold in Moscow. She flew to Madrid and went to her father's house. She had informed her father earlier about the recording trip. Everyone was delighted to know that she would be coming to Savera house. She was almost twenty-three years old and lovely.

Sybille had an idea for producing a children's album. The songs would be sung by Sybille and GG and would be lively, simple tunes. These tunes would to be catchy and would be in three languages: Spanish, English, and Russian. When she was still in Moscow, she placed a call to Charles Bronfman, her music director, and told him about her idea.

He told her, "As far as singing children's songs with lively tunes, I could definitely prepare lots of material for you. But as for arranging the music to have a bird singing with you, I can tell you it is not easy. Are you are sure about this bird? By the way, what kind of a bird you have?"

Sybille told him GG was an African Gray parrot. Charles said, "Oh Sybille, you might have a chance. Can she sing now? Is she able to sing in three languages?"

Sybille told him, "Her name is GG. Presently, GG is with my Russian grandparents and is learning very lively Russian songs. When she was in Spain in my cousin's house, she was learning Spanish tunes and songs like 'La Cucaracha.' The reason I think the children's record will be an international hit is that every time we had children visiting us at my father's house, GG was a big success. She sang, and she made funny sounds, like imitating a barking dog. She can whistle many tunes, too. Charles, when I am on a tour with you, my grandparents are teaching her happy Russian tunes. My grandma is a concert pianist; she plays while GG, Grandpa, and Grandma all sing."

Charles said, "Now I am convinced you have a million-dollar idea.

You could make a lot of money, provided we come up with rhythmic and catchy songs and tunes that GG can sing. I wish we could record a video—that would be a bigger hit. There is a condition, though: I must see and hear GG before I start to work on it."

Sybille agreed. She said, "Charles, I have a condition too: that you will be my sole partner in the venture and that this recording will mainly belong to me, under the recording label 'Sibelius Recordings.' I really don't know too much about contracts, but Grandfather Savera knows. I will talk to him first."

Charles said, "I suppose you will be in Madrid in two days. I could be there, too. Can you bring GG with you? If she passes the test, we will go forward with our recording program. It should be all right, Sybille, but please do not discuss anything about a children's music recording, especially about a duet with a bird."

There was a problem for Sybille. She thought, *if I take GG with me, my grandparents will be alone.* She called her father in Spain again and asked him, "Papa, when I come to you, I don't want to leave my grandparents alone here. Can I bring them too? Maybe we can stay in Majorca."

Her father said, "Don't worry, Sybille; we will deal with that when you are here."

She rushed to tell her grandparents to pack and get ready to go to Madrid. They were surprised, but happy to go to a warmer climate.

Sybille and her grandparents were picked up at the airport by Peter and his friend Andrea. During dinner, she told her father her plan of making a children's record and probably a video. She asked her grandpa, Carlos Savera, about making the contracts. Carlos Savera applauded Sybille for her excellent ideas and told her that if GG cooperated, she would make a lot of money.

Grandpa Savera told Sybille, "I would like to talk to your music director about the business arrangement." Sybille told him that Charles Bronfman would be at the Savera house that afternoon around five.

Charles Bronfman came exactly on time. They met in his office on the ground floor. Charles was happy to meet Mr. Savera; he was impressed the way he explained and covered all the aspects of the recording industry. He also prepared a contract between "Sibelius Recording" and the recording company.

While Charles and Grandpa Savera were still in the office, Sybille went to pick up GG's house and brought her in the office. GG opened the door and jumped into Sybille's lap. Sybille had a small candy for her. She introduced her to Grandpa Savera. "I am GG, Grandpa. Where is Dmitri, Mama?"

Sybille, knowing the two-grandpa confusion, told GG, "You can call him Carlos." The parrot started to repeat "Carlos, Carlos." Sybille slipped a little candy into GG's foot and then asked the bird to sing with her. She started with "How Much Is the Doggy," which GG immediately picked up and started to sing in perfect rhythm and harmony. Charles started another catchy tune, and Sybille began singing and looked at GG. They all started to sing. Grandpa Savera and Charles could not believe how little GG's voice was so beautiful, clear, and in tune. Charles told Sybille, "Your GG passes all the tests. Mr. Savera, what do you think?"

"I have to tell both of you; I have never seen or heard any bird sing so clearly with such diction. Congratulations, Sybille, you have got a gold mine." GG raised her head and said, "Thank you, Grandpa."

Everything was agreed. A program was to be laid out by Charles, selected by the recording company, of a series of easy, rhythmic songs appropriate for children. Charles said good-bye to Carlos Savera and Sybille, saying to Sybille, "I will see you tomorrow. We have to practice for Thursday's performance."

Sybille's concert tour in Spain turned out to be a success. Sybille, her grandparents, and GG left for Moscow after the end of her concert tour. Charles Bronfman, in the meantime, had contacted a French recording company. Sybille and Charles had done business with them before and were impressed with their studio. They were known to be reputable and were well-connected in the entertainment market circuit. Before making an appointment with them, Charles called Sybille in Moscow and spoke with her about making an appointment with them. Sybille agreed and told him to go ahead and make the appointment.

Charles looked at his concert tour program and found out that Sybille would be singing in Paris in three weeks' time, he called Sybille and told her that her performance was scheduled on Sunday night. "I thought Monday at three p.m. would be perfect for our meeting, so I called and talked to David Jardin, the president of Paris Recordings. Charles and David agreed to meet for lunch at one-thirty." He advised Sybille to bring warmer clothing as the temperature is supposed to drop.

A few days before leaving for Paris, Sybille called Charles and asked him if they should take GG. Charles thought it was too early for that. He said, "Before we expose GG, we have to discuss whether they like the idea." When Sybille was ready to fly to Paris, she told her grandparents about the idea of making a record with GG. "Grandma, it is important that you train GG and practice. I don't want her to make any mistakes. We have an appointment tomorrow to see the president of the recording company. When we are back, I will let you know when we have to take GG for a demonstration. Both of you will be with us, and Grandma, you will be the piano player."

When Sybille returned to her grandparents' house, she told them the good news. "The record company in Paris has agreed to an audition. That means they want GG and me to sing children's songs with Grandma on piano. We are going to meet them in two weeks."

Dmitri told Sybille and Katharina, "That means we have to follow the program in three languages, as Charles Bronfman has said."

GG STARTS A SINGING CAREER

Sybille said, "Yes, you are right, Grandpa. Charles is sending the package. It will include Russian songs and the music sheets to go with the songs. He told me that you and Grandma have provided the basic information about those songs. According to him, he had a Russian composer and his teenage daughter help him to complete the package. The Spanish songs and music program were provided by Isabella Savera, my cousin in Madrid. The English songs and music package will be provided by Charles himself. As far as the audition is concerned, GG and I will need to learn two songs from each language."

Her grandpa Dmitri said, "I am sure you and GG can learn two songs from the Russian package. Actually, she knows more than two songs in each language now. The only thing is that you have to practice together, and Sybille, you have to spend at least two hours singing in each language with GG."

A package from Charles was delivered later that morning. Katharina was curious to know the details about the music. She opened the package and called to Dmitri and Sybille, "Come and see what Charles has sent." They got together and spread all the music sheets out; the song sheets were arranged with sheet music. Three packages were studied; Dmitri and Katharina recognized almost all the Russian songs, and their music was only slightly modified from the versions they knew. Sybille recognized the English and Spanish sheets. There was a note from Charles saying that he would arrive in Moscow in two days to go over the package and work with Katharina.

When Charles arrived, he started to explain his methodology, which was intended to create lively and enjoyable music. He sat at the piano and started to play two Russian tunes. As GG heard the music, she flew in and sat on top of the piano. She listened carefully and then suddenly started to whistle the tune perfectly. Dmitri ran into the room and got few candies as a reward for GG's singing. Sybille came in and started to sing Russian and then Spanish and, finally, English. GG continued whistling and singing freely without hesitation. Charles stopped playing, and everybody was cheering GG. Sybille, Dmitri, and Charles all agreed that she was almost ready for the audition. Sybille gave her a candy, and GG said, "Thank you, Mama."

Katharina, Dmitri, and Sybille worked with GG every afternoon. It was tiring for everyone, and it was is amazing that every afternoon when Katharina started playing a song, no matter what language or which melody, GG flew in from Sybille's room and landed on top of the piano to blend her voice with the tune in perfect harmony.

Sybille was asked by Isabel how GG was doing. She replied, "I don't know, Isabel. She is crazy about the music. You would think she has a musical gene. She never gets bored. Mind you, she does get tired after, let us say, about four songs. But when she is tired, she just takes off and goes to her house."

The tenth day of practice was a dress rehearsal; Katharina, Sybille, and GG were going to perform exactly as they would in the Paris studio. They would perform the show over the phone for Charles exactly at one p.m.

Dmitri had organized three packages of sheet music, lyrics, and timing instructions. The first two songs were to be in Russian, and Dmitri placed the first package in front of Katharina, even though she and Sybille knew all the music for all six songs. At exactly one p.m., Katharina started to play, and both GG and Sybille started to sing. They finished the entire program in about twelve minutes. Sybille was so happy, she picked up GG and kissed her, and then she kissed her grandpa and grandma. The telephone rang, and Charles congratulated everyone and told Sybille to give a candy to GG from him. They were pleasantly surprised that GG sang so well; she blended her voice with Sybille's and with Katharina's piano in perfect unison.

Katharina, Dmitri, and Sybille were getting ready to fly to Paris next morning. GG went to her little house and went to sleep. Sybille covered her house, and they all went to bed and got up early again to go to the airport. Charles had called earlier and promised to pick them up at the airport and take them to their hotel. They arrived at the hotel, went for dinner, and went to sleep. Sybille took GG out, caressed her, and sang her a lullaby. She could see that GG was ready to sleep. It had been a long trip for her, and Sybille sensed that tomorrow was going to be a challenge.

After breakfast of pancakes and croissants and of GG's favorite cereals, Fruit Loops, they were ready for the studio. They were received by the president, David Jardin. Katharina and Dmitri stayed in the studio lounge. Sybille and Charles went with David, signing legal documents and agreements.

In the meantime, the studio was filling up with technicians and other experts in the trade. Recording manager Robert Como escorted Sybille's group to a recording room and introduced Silvia Boson, who was in charge of the French and East European market, and Cesar Romero, who was responsible for the West European and North American markets. They all sat down.

Robert explained, "There will be three recordings. The first performance will not be recorded—we call it the 'feel-good session.' The next session will be recorded and played back for you and our marketing experts, and then we will sit down and evaluate all aspects of the presentation. I must point out that Silvia and Robert are specialists in the field of children's entertainment. They have marketed millions of records, books, and video recordings. So let us go and prepare for the presentation."

The recording room had a piano, and Charles had brought his violin. Just before the session, President Jardin came and took his seat outside the recording room. The buzzer went off and a red board reading "Silence" started flashing. Inside the recording room, Charles was playing violin and conducting. Russian songs were first in the presentation, followed by Spanish, and the presentation ended with English songs. Katharina was at the piano; Dmitri was there to see that music sheets and papers were in the right places. GG was sitting on the piano, and Sybille was next to Katharina. Charles signaled Katharina to start playing. Sybille and GG started to sing, and the violin blended in beautifully. They stopped for ten seconds after the first song and then played the rest of their repertoire. There was pin-drop silence, and then suddenly the whole studio burst into applause and cheers. David Jardin came in the recording room and said, "Oh, what a performance." He looked at GG and told Sybille, "I think your GG needs a solo recording. She is amazing."

Sybille thanked him and introduced David to GG, requesting of him, "David, give this candy to GG and tell her she was good." David gave GG the candy, and she thanked him. The crowd assembled at the studio could not believe how GG could sing. Sybille and her group, the recording manager, and the two marketing specialists went to the president's office. David came in and introduced his sound expert, Andrea Assisi. David Jardin spoke first. "Let me congratulate all of you and GG for giving a superb performance. Let me ask you, Silvia, what do you think of the presentation? Mind you, this was only the first try."

Sylvia was quite impressed. "If we went in the market with exactly this presentation, I know we could sell at least one million copies. I have only one worry. There are only six songs in this package, and the market is used to at least ten songs on a disc."

"What about you Cesar?"

"I agree with Silvia as far as the number of songs is concerned. However, there is an important item missing, and that is a percussion instrument. Piano and violin definitely provide lovely tunes, but you know they are a little too refined for children. The addition of an instrument that provides beat is essential so that children of any age can enjoy the recording more."

Charles jumped to his feet and said, "I knew there was something missing, but I could not put my finger on it. You are so right, Cesar. This collection with a drumbeat will have added spice, and it could become number one on the charts the way we have the arrangement now. It appeals to all the young at heart. You saw the audience outside the recording studio. There was momentarily a pin-drop silence after the performance, an indication of stunning effect. It has international flavor, it has unique voice combination and rhythm, and it has international fame figure Sybille and new phenomenon GG."

They all agreed. David suggested, "It is now lunchtime. We have our dining room here, so we can break up and go for lunch. After lunch and some rest, I will like to get together at two p.m. and reprogram our very interesting project."

While Katharina and Sybille were preparing lunch for GG, they saw that she needed a rest. GG enjoyed her lunch. She was very thirsty. Sybille took her to her little house, where GG drank from a tiny bowl of water. Sybille put a little blanket over her house.

After lunch, Sybille, Katharina, and Dmitri lay down on comfortable reclining chairs, resting for an hour. Charles was resting in the president's office. At two, they all came down to David Jardin's office. David asked, "Is there any other comment about the recording project? I am going to name this project 'GG project.'"

Charles said, "Now, it would appear that we need a percussion player. Who would be suitable, and how soon we can get one to practice? Is it possible we could include that in today's demo recording and see what the impact is?"

David told them, "I have already arranged a percussionist, and he will be here now."

As they were talking, a young man appeared with a small drum. David suggested that Sybille's party go with Rolland into the recording room and practice. As the music started, GG and Sybille started to sing, listening to the drum beat. GG was moving her head to the beat, and the music became lot more interesting. GG started to dance, and Dmitri joined in. David arrived, and the music stopped. All agreed that, the drum made a big difference. They practiced till four p.m. and promised to David that they would be there the following day at nine a.m. He told David, "We must complete the recordings by noon; we have our flight booked at one p.m."

David wanted to have a meeting in his office. Sybille took the lead and said, "Thank you for giving me the opportunity to talk and tell you that Charles and I are heavily involved in performances throughout Europe. Our company is on top of the charts, and I have recording contracts with major companies. GG recording is a small venture for us and not a major production."

David got up and said, "I have gone through your career and found that you are a well-known personality and a very busy person. I have a solution, if you agree. Here in our studio, we have access to a complete orchestra, and we will be able to take care of organizing the musical part for these six songs. The only favor from you and Charles I want is that you give us four more songs of the same caliber as these ones. When we are—that is, our orchestra is—confident of finalizing the instrumental part, Sybille and Charles, I personally will call you, and then your party can come, just for the day. Then, I assure you, we will complete not only the audio recording but also, simultaneously, the video recording. Sybille, please listen to me. I am doing all this work for one reason: this project has become our passion, and my people are talking about it all the time. One of my marketing geniuses told me—I am not exaggerating—that this recording will put a smile on every child's face. You cannot have a better compliment than that. We will not only make a fortune but also bring fame to us, you, and GG. You have worked hard along with your grandparents, and you deserve this success. We will not charge any expenses. Sybille, our marketing people are just waiting to launch this project internationally. They think because of GG, they can sell even in the Eastern world. Do you know what that means? I can imagine. Just wait and see."

Sybille and Charles agreed to the basic concept. Sybille told them, "We will go back and develop three more songs, one for each language and one solo by GG."

David was delighted with Sybille's decision. Everyone cheered, and Charles said to David, "We would appreciate if you could send this agreement in writing to us. We guarantee you will have the promised songs in three weeks or less."

David agreed, everyone shook hands, and David kissed the ladies. Later, he drove Sybille's party to the airport.

Chapter 9
GG SINGS SOLO

Sybille and Katharina, along with Charles, found another Russian song that was more delightful than the previous ones. Sybille called Isabel and asked her if she could look for one more Spanish children's song. Isabel sent her three songs and told her to select the best one. Charles found an Irish song that would qualify for recording. In about four days, he made minor changes in the music, writing a banjo and bongo drums into the Irish song and adding a touch of accordion to the Russian. Charles accepted Sybille's choice and went over the music with her. As far as the solo for GG was concerned, she developed an unbeatable rendition of Dean Martin's "Pizza Pie." In few days, Charles finalized the tunes and sent them to Katharina.

Katharina, Dmitri, Sybille, and GG started to practice every afternoon; GG enjoyed the work. During this time, David Jardin sent the papers, as per his promise. Charles called Sybille and told her about the papers from David. Sybille suggested that the papers must immediately be forwarded to Grandpa Carlos. Charles promised to send the papers on the same day.

The following Monday, Sybille played all four songs on the phone to Charles. He said, "I think we are ready to go to Paris for recording." Sybille agreed and called David to give him the news.

PARIS STUDIO PRODUCES GG AND SYBILLE SONG RECORDINGS

David asked Sybille, "Do you think you can all come the day after tomorrow? We will need the music sheets tomorrow."

Sybille told him, "I will send them now." They flew to Paris as scheduled. After freshening up, the whole team met in David's office. He told them that his orchestra had been practicing for the past two days and had made some minor changes to Charles's arrangement. They listened to the new arrangement.

Charles told David, "David, I must say, your people have done a great job. It is rhythmic and pleasant. And now let us see how GG and Sybille do with their singing."

They all went to the recording room, which was set up with a ten-piece orchestra. Sybille did not know how GG would behave with so many musicians around. She took the cover off GG's little house, hoping the parrot would not be afraid. GG came out of her house and flew directly to her usual place on top of the piano. The big red silence sign was flashing. Katharina was not on piano; she was sitting near Dmitri, and the orchestra was totally manned by David's musicians. Sybille was sitting near the pianist. Everyone was watching cautiously, not knowing what GG would do next. The orchestra started, and GG began to sing the first song. Sybille sighed with relief and caught up with GG. They finished all five songs without a hitch. David started to clap, as did the orchestra and the marketing staff.

David approached Charles and Sybille, kissed them, and shook their hands, saying, "I think we did it. Sybille, give me a candy. I want to thank GG."

Sybille said, "Thank you, David." David invited his management team and Sybille's group to his office for a final briefing. They all gathered in his office, and he started his briefing. "I think the time has come to go back to the recording room for taping and recording all the songs in two sittings today. You see, our video department has already tuned and organized lighting fit for recording video; therefore, the video recording will be done simultaneously. At present it is noon. We should start recording at twelve-fifteen, record five songs in the first session, break for lunch, and come back for the next four recordings at two. The last solo song performed by GG is very important, and I am a little bit apprehensive. I hope GG comes through. As long as Sybille is sitting near her, I think she will be all right. This will be a big achievement if we are able to record GG solo."

Sybille got up and told David, "I am pretty sure GG will be all right. I have talked to her, and I will reward her with candy a little before her solo."

At almost twelve-fifteen, the big red silence sign started to flash. Sybille was sitting close to GG. The recording of the first five songs went very well. Sybille picked up GG, kissed her little beak, and gave her a piece of her favorite candy. GG said, "Thank you, Mama."

Sybille's group left with GG in her house. Everyone went to the dining room. After dessert and coffee, they went to rest. Sybille covered GG's house.

At two p.m., the recording room was ready for the next four songs. The music director signaled the musicians to start, and they played song after song. David Jardin was overjoyed. He said, "I have never produced a single episode with such ease and such anxiety. Thanks to the music director and the staff for their dedication. I must say, the presence of a little bird has motivated all of us to do our best. I have a feeling that the next solo by GG will also go smoothly. Everyone take a ten-minute break and come back to complete this unbelievable video and LP."

After the break, they all took their seats, and GG came out and went to her place on the piano. The red silence sign was flashing. The music started, and GG began singing. She was fabulous: her voice was crystal clear, and her diction was unbelievable. She completed the song and stopped as the music stopped. Sybille picked GG up and put her in her little house.

Suddenly, she realized the importance of GG. She took Charles aside and told him, "After the video and record go on worldwide sale, I am afraid for GG. She will become a hot property. I want to talk to David and ask him to call an insurance agency to insure GG for at least ten million dollars."

Charles agreed with her. They said to David, "We would like to see you in your office. It is rather urgent."

They sat down, and Sybille asked David if he had a reliable insurance agent. He replied, "Yes, I do, and I was going to call him to insure our work today."

Sybille told David, "I am ashamed to say that GG has no insurance. We would like her to be insured for at least ten million dollars."

David jumped from his chair. "Yes, my dear Sybille that would be a disaster. By next month, GG will be known everywhere. I will call our agent right now." David came back to Sybille and assured her, "The agency is faxing a form for you to complete. The agent will cover GG as soon as you fill out the basic form, giving him details about the owner of the property. My agent is sending a package related to the coverage."

She thought for a moment and asked Charles, "Do you think I should call my grandfather Savera about the insurance? He knows a lot about it." Charles agreed. Sybille asked David if she could call her grandpa Savera in Madrid. David took her to his office, and there she made a call and explained the situation.

Her grandfather told her, "Don't do anything. I have all the information here with me; we will take care of everything." David called the insurance agent and told him to drop the insurance coverage.

Sybille and her grandparents came home. She called her grandpa in Madrid, and he confirmed that GG was fully insured for one million US dollars. Sybille told Carlos Savera all about what had happened at the recording studio. Grandpa was delighted and told Sybille that his lawyers would look at the contract. "You have to be very careful when a product reaches a million dollars in worth or more," he said. "There is a lot of temptation in the market to copy. You have to watch your junior partners, who have a tendency to find all kinds of excuses to keep more money. It is a strange thing with men: the more they make, the more they cheat. Don't worry; we will apply the full force of international law and will protect your work." Sybille was happy that she had called her grandpa Carlos; she knew he dealt in international business all the time.

Chapter 10

GG AND SYBILLE GO ON A PROMOTION TOUR

Sybille and her family were relieved to be home. This trip had been fairly trying and emotional for them all. They had enough time to relax and think about new projects. Charles called to remind Sybille about her upcoming trip to Japan, where the Tokyo cultural committee had invited her to perform as the main character in *Madame Butterfly*.

Sybille had forgotten about the performance. She asked Charles, "When would you like to start rehearsal? Maybe two weeks before the performance? I have done *Madame Butterfly* many times in the past."

Charles agreed and said, "I have many offers and invitations coming in. I know you are busy with the video and record coming out next month, Sybille. I don't want to overbook you and later regret it." They agreed that after the Tokyo appearance he would hold off on opera bookings. The marketing of the GG project would take extensive travel but earn ten to twenty times as much as opera appearances, although the latter was more prestigious. The records and videos were released with much fanfare and huge international publicity. David Jardin shrewdly convinced the international publicity bureau to accept a 1 percent commission on sales, rather than a fixed price. He invited the bureau chiefs in Eastern and Western Europe and demonstrated both the video and the record. They were blown away by Sylvia and GG's performance and accepted without a hitch.

It was just before Christmas, and radio stations and TV stations were playing small samples of the video and the record songs. The big hit was the solo of GG. The public could not believe that a parrot could sing like a professional singer. The recording company's telephone was jammed with orders of thousands of records, and big orders were coming in for video cassettes. The recording company was raking in big money, and the timing was perfect. David was in contact with Sybille and Carlos Savera every day and night, giving them details of the impact of their project throughout Europe and South and North America.

David told Carlos Savera that he was running out of both products. "I could never have imagined that we would sell 1.2 million videos and records in eighteen days."

Sybille called her grandfather in Madrid and tried to understand how and when the money would be transferred to her bank account. He told her, "Our Company will open an account in the name of Savera Sybille Entertainment. The profits from the sale of your videos and records will be deposited into that account. The reason I am doing this is to minimize income tax. Don't forget your profit margin: after paying off David Jardin's production costs, your music director's share of the profits, other expenses, commissions, and marketing costs have to be accounted for. It is a complicated accounting process; you know our Savera Corporation is very much familiar with the international business and tax laws. Sybille, my dear, when I told your father about your venture, he was so happy. He told me he wishes your mother were here to see you and experience your success. Sybille, soon you, as a single person, young and beautiful, will be our first millionaire."

Sybille started to cry And said, "Grandpa, thank you for saying such nice things. Give my love to Papa and mother Andrea. Good day, Grandpa." She ran to her grandparents and told them what Carlos had said about her being a young millionaire. They were happy and gave GG a candy to unwrap. Sybille asked GG if she would like to sing solo. She repeated, "Yes, Mama, solo."

Sybille wondered, "Grandma, do you really think she knows what she is saying?"

"Yes, Mama," GG said. Grandma Katharina and Dmitri were ready to sing and play piano. GG jumped up and sat on the piano. Katharina started to play "How Much Is That Doggy in the Window," and GG belted out the song with full force. They all clapped. Sybille picked GG up and kissed her, and GG was happy.

Sybille put a call through to Isabel in Madrid. She gave her all the news of the success of the record and video. "Isabel, your GG is going to change lives of many people. My Russian grandparents are overjoyed. Grandpa and Papa are all in a pleasant state of shock. Isabel, it all started from you and your GG."

Isabel told Sybille, "Sybille, it is your singing talent and your ability to train GG that made this possible. You programmed and dreamed this venture by yourself. I have to say, you are solely responsible for this international fame and fortune. Don't let anyone take that away from you."

Sybille told her, "Isabel, you are one of a kind. I love you. Kiss Oskar for me. By the way, if you need some fun and travel, come with me to promote the VCR and records in Hong Kong and Tokyo."

Isabel told Sybille, "I would love to do that. You see, I am four months pregnant."

Sybille was surprisingly happy. She told her, "Isabel, what a pleasant surprise. Congratulations! Tell Oskar to call me just about one week before delivery, so that I can plan to be with you. It will be the first Savera baby's birth I will witness."

Isabel told her. "I would love that. Oskar will be delighted. The other day, he was thinking about you. He told me that Sybille is a person who brings pleasure and puts smiles on people's faces."

They said good-bye and good luck to each other.

Weeks passed by until it was time for Sybille to go to Tokyo to promote her record. She was accompanied by David Jardin's marketing team. They were invited by the Sonya, a giant in record and VCR distribution throughout the Southeast Asian markets. Sybille and the marketing team members were amazed to see what a difference it made when they saw and heard the real characters behind the performance.

They moved from Tokyo to Hong Kong, where there was a bigger reception. Sybille was always overprotective of GG; she had requested special security for GG during her travel through Asia. Sybille and GG's appearances were previously arranged to appear in live shows on stage, radio, and television. All entertainment media were filled with Sybille and GG's performances. Children were enchanted with GG, and they were pushing their parents and grandparents to buy the records and VCR tapes. It was amazing to see how the entertainment market worked, giving pleasure to young and old and big profits to the entertainers. Everyone won.

Sybille and her party left for Paris. They had a meeting with David Jardin and his marketing team and discussed the next marketing strategy before the end of the holiday season. When Sybille left for Moscow, she was happy but tired, and she slept during the plane ride.

Dmitri and Katharina had missed Sybille and GG. The telephone rang, and Katharina answered. It was Oskar, her cousin, from his home in Madrid. Katharina called Sybille. She said, "Hello? Oh Oskar, how is Isabel?"

Oskar was crying. "We lost the baby. Isabel is doing well, but she is sad. She needs you."

Sybille was sad. Katharina said, "Good morning. We missed you."

Sybille told her grandmother about her cousin losing the baby. "It was her husband. Maybe I have to go to Madrid. She needs me." GG started to sing, "Good morning, good morning." Everyone was sad.

Katharina told Sybille, "Your grandpa felt very alone. The house was too quiet without GG and you."

Sybille sat down with both of them and tried to tell them, "Listen, both of you. When GG goes for more recordings, I have to go with her. Grandpa, what happened to all your friends? You don't go to your club or your aviation association, where both of you had such fun-loving friends and associates. I think it is my fault. I kept you for me, because I was lonely. Grandpa, let us go to the club on this coming Saturday and renew your bonds and friendships. Both of you will enjoy dancing, joking, and having political discussions. But you have to promise me that you will not get drunk; I have no respect for drunken people. Grandpa, promise me." Sybille hugged both of them, and finally Dmitri promised her that he would not drink. Saturday came, and they went to the club. When Dmitri's friends and acquaintances saw him, they rushed towards him and Katharina and hugged them. His friends led them to their table and ordered drinks for them.

Dmitri told them, "Doctor does not want me to have alcohol, no vodka please." Dmitri looked at Sybille and winked at her. Dmitri's friends knew about Dmitri and Katharina flying to Paris with their fantastic singing bird, and they also knew about the record's international publicity and sales. His friends told him about the stories they had read about Sybille in local and international newspapers. They complimented Sybille on her international fame and fortune. The secretary of the club came to the table and welcomed Dmitri and his family. He congratulated Sybille for bringing fame to her family and Russia, and he told Sybille, "I understand you have brought so much happiness to children all over the world. I wonder if you could arrange a show for Russian children to bring happiness to them."

The secretary sat down, and after discussion, they agreed to have a concert on next Saturday at eight p.m. More people came to the table. They talked, they joked, and everyone was happy; eventually, it was getting late, so they left.

GG SINGS AT A CHILDREN'S CHARITY

The next week, the social club organized an advertising campaign throughout the city. There were posters hanging all over, advertising Sybille and GG's concert for children. Saturday came, and crowds of parents and children were gathering in the people's auditorium. Katharina, Dmitri, Sybille, and GG were behind the huge curtain. As the curtain opened, GG flew from her little house to her favorite spot at the top of piano. Katharina started to play the Soviet national anthem, and Sybille and GG started to sing along. There was pin-drop silence for a moment when the song was over. Then the crowd went wild. Children were clapping and laughing. When GG started to sing solo, the children could not believe what they heard. The crowd was so moved that they demanded five curtain calls. The secretary came to the microphone and thanked Sybille, GG, and Comrades Dmitri and Katharina. All the crowed clapped and started to shout, "GG, GG."

Charles Bronfman called and reminded Sybille about her performance in Paris the next weekend. "We will meet at the airport. You will be arriving from Moscow, and I will be flying from Budapest. My flight arrives at six p.m., and you will be there at five forty-five. I think that will work out nicely."

Sybille agreed with Charles's assessment and suggested that they eat dinner at the airport before going to their hotel. Charles agreed and reminded her to phone if there was any change in the plan.

The time soon came for Sybille to say good-bye to her grandparents, and she kissed GG. She arrived at the airport and met Charles. After dinner, they went to a hotel near the university. She was very tired and went to sleep almost immediately. The next morning, Charles picked her up and took her to the university concert hall to start their practice and rehearsal. There were clear skies, with not a single cloud. Sybille got hold of the university arts and entertainment program. She showed it to Charles and asked him if they could go to the art gallery, having read that the artist who was running the art gallery was Norman Rockville Jr. Charles told her, "Look at the time. Let us go to eat first, and then we can go to the art gallery."

SYBILLE MEETS HER FATHER AND STEPMOTHER IN PARIS

Sybille's father and stepmother came to Paris to attend Sybille's show. When she met him in the lobby of the hotel they were all staying at, her father looked at her and said, "Sybille, you look tired. Let us sit down in the lounge. I have already checked both of us in. Just go and sign in and tell the clerk to send the luggage into the rooms. Make sure they know what belongs to you and which are ours."

After the formalities, the three sat down and ordered drinks. Sybille was thirsty and wanted a nice, cold fruit juice. Her father and stepmother ordered wine. "Sybille, you look strange. Is there something that you are not telling us?" asked Peter.

"Oh, Papa, I have fallen in love." Andrea and Peter looked at her as if they thought she was joking. "Papa, if you meet my Norman, you will just love him. He is one of a kind."

"Sybille, now I really believe you have fallen in love. I have never seen you like this before. When I first saw you entering the hotel, you looked so sad and lost."

Sybille replied, "Papa, you have no idea. When Norman dropped me off at the airport terminal and left, I was actually crying because I felt so alone. It was so good to see you."

SYBILLE TELLS HER FATHER THAT SHE HAS FALLEN IN LOVE

Peter asked, "What is his last name? Where does he come from? I am anxious to know. So you love him so much. What about him? Does he love you enough to marry you?" Her father now really believed that his daughter had finally found someone to be happy with.

"Papa, his name is Norman Rockville Junior." Sybille was watching her stepmother's and father's faces.

"Sybille, my baby, do not tell me he is the son of the famous artist."

Sybille started to laugh, and said, "Papa, no. He is the grandson of Norman Rockville, the famous artist."

Peter and Andrea started to laugh. "My dear Sybille that is the best news you could have given us."

"Papa, you know what is more important? He is remarkably successful in the field of art, and he is recognized as the authority on art deco. The university has elected him to do the charity art show. His paintings are of a similar style as Salvatore Dali's, but he is just more refined."

Andrea and Peter Savera were so happy, they hugged each other. "I am so proud of you," Peter said. "You have achieved so much in spite of losing your beautiful mother and your precious brother. Bravo, my lovely Sybille."

After hearing about her mother, she started to cry. Her stepmother and father took her in their arms and took her to the dining room.

The family enjoyed their dinner, and they lingered in the dining room for a while. Her father said, "Sybille, my dear, we have been following your career. You are at the top."

Sybille said, "You know, Papa, we have not seen much of each other for some time. That is why I sent you tickets for this concert so we could see each other and enjoy each other's company. It was the best opportunity, and I am enjoying your company so much. Yes, Mother, Papa has written so many nice things about you how you take care of him and how you personally cook for him. I am so proud of my father. Since leaving Russia and coming back to Spain, he has achieved a lot. To become director of civil aviation in Spain is a big affair."

Sybille meets Norman Jr.

Andrea asked her, "How and where did you meet Norman?"

Sybille started to laugh, "You would not believe how smart my programmer—you may call it God. As I told you before, the university in Paris is planning to build an addition to the main building to create an art and music faculty. In order to generate funds, they have invited many artists, and I was invited to appear in two operas. At the same time, Norman R. Junior was invited to exhibit his art in the same building. We have never met each other before. However, I saw Norman's name in the arts section. When I arrived at my hotel and tried to unlock my carrying case, which the porter had brought up, I could not open it. I looked at the name tag and saw that it read 'Mr. Norman R. Junior.' I called the desk and told them they had sent me the wrong luggage. The manager came to the phone and apologized profusely and said that Mr. Rockville had also just called and said the same thing. He had apologized to Mr. Rockville and told him the hotel would send a porter to exchange the luggage, but Mr. Rockville insisted on doing it himself.

"Soon there was a knock on the door, and there was Mr. Rockville. 'Good evening, Miss Savera. I am the new porter, and here is your luggage,' he said. I laughed because now I knew who he was and said, 'Good evening, Mr. Rockville. Here is yours. I can understand how they made a mistake. These suitcases are identical. And you are a charming porter.' Papa, from that moment on, I was in love. He asked me when he should come to take me to dinner, saying the hotel manager would be paying the bill to apologize for the mistake. Papa, I could not refuse, even though I had prior arrangement to have dinner with my music director and conductor. Mother, what do you think of that? Can't you see how this match is made in heaven?

"We had a delightful dinner, and everything he said and did just tickle me pink. He invited me to his art show; I went with my music conductor, Charles Bronfman. We entered the gallery, and we were amazed to see the caliber and refinement of the art. I looked around for him and saw him in the middle of the room, surrounded by beautiful young people. We started to look around, and I fell in love with one picture, a watercolor, so I called the sales girl and bought it. As we were about to leave, he saw us and came running to apologize for not noticing us before. He asked us if we liked something, and I told him, 'Yes, I did, and I bought it while you were surrounded by your admirers.' In the meantime, Charles excused himself and left us alone. Norman showed me some of his masterpieces.

"We talked, and I invited him to my concert. He said, 'I cannot come, but I wish I could. You see, my cousin is getting married on Saturday, and I must fly tomorrow.' I was disappointed, but we made up for it by spending the night together. His flight was leaving when your flight arrived, so we took a taxi, and I told him about our meeting here at the hotel. He left to catch his flight to Montreal. Just before kissing me good-bye, he asked me if I would join him in Montreal to be with him at the wedding. I said yes without thinking."

Norman Rockville Jr. leaves for Montreal

"So what do you think, Papa? Is it not fantastic?" Sybille continued, "Last night we had enough time to talk about his past. He told me that at an early age, both his parents died. His mother's sister took care of him. Her son was about his age. When one is young, the wounds heal faster. Especially when you have a loving aunt and uncle, and your cousin for a childhood friend, the pain runs away. Pain does not like love. While we were talking, he suddenly jumped and said, 'Oh, how stupid of me. There was something bothering me. It was like I was remembering a dream; your face was so familiar. The other day when I came to exchange luggage, I was sure that I knew you, but did not know how. Now I just realized that everywhere I go, I see you on TV, on magazine covers, and on the front pages of newspapers. I would never have dreamed that a world-famous diva would be my friend—and not only that, but that I would fall in love, and she will like that.' He wanted to know about my singing a duet with an African parrot. He had read in the newspapers about my becoming the youngest millionaire on her own initiative. Papa, we talked almost all night. We woke up when the hotel called. We rushed to change, and here I am, and he is in Montreal."

Sybille had to leave her father and stepmother earlier to get ready for the show. Peter and Andrea went to see Sybille's performance in *Madame Butterfly*. Andrea later told Peter that it was beautiful but sad. The next morning, Sybille took an early flight to Montreal. She wanted to be with Norman Rockville Junior, and Andrea and Peter went back to Madrid

Chapter 11

Dr. Norman Schoulz goes on sabbatical to Rangoon

Dr. Schoulz looked at the background data he had about his father. He then went thoroughly through his family history and, after a careful search, deduced that none of the members of recent generations had any indication of blindness or glaucoma. However, he discovered that in many cases, early infections of the eyes in the tropics appeared to manifest themselves in cataracts or glaucoma. He remembered that his grandfather used to be a visiting professor at Rangoon University. Burma was a colony of British Empire at one time; the environment was harsh, with lots of rain and heat and large populations of mosquitoes, flies, and other insects. When Grandpa Schoulz was in Rangoon, his son Karl was only sixteen years old. There was no air conditioning and no electric fans, only manually operated large fans made of mats hung from the ceiling on large hooks. A cord, which was covered with a bright cotton casing and had a large fringe, was tied to the middle of the flat mat. When the large mat was pulled back and forth, it provided air circulation and a cooling effect. A young boy servant in the house pulled the fan assembly during the afternoon when it got very hot. The doors of the house were always closed during times of high heat. In the morning and evening, the doors were always opening and closing, which made it difficult to keep insects and flies out. The family slept inside fine white screening material hung from the four posts of their beds, which kept out insects and mosquitoes.

Karl Schoulz was an active young man who played outside with the servant boys. It was hard to avoid flies during the hot summer. They came in and landed on food and everything else. Karl was fond of candies and sweet stuff. Flies and insects also liked sweets, so they loved to go around him. His mother made him wash his hands and face all the time. Every time Karl injured himself playing, the wounds would take a long time to heal, even though his mother treated them with Mercurochrome or iodine.

One day, Karl's mother noticed that his eyes were red. Karl kept on rubbing his eyes, and he had some white stuff sticking to the corner of his eyes. When he got up next morning, his mother saw that his eyes were swollen.

It was eight in the morning. Karl's father, Dr. Norman Schoulz, who was known by his first name, Dr. Norman, came down to have his breakfast. He saw Krista, his wife, crying while cleaning Karl's face with hot water into which she had dissolved a small amount of boric acid.

Dr. Norman Schoulz and Krista were on a sabbatical and were fulfilling their desire to spend winters in a tropical climate. Krista had a fair amount of time since the cook and other servants looked after the house chores. Krista treated servants and their families. She took great pleasure in helping people. Dr. Norman Schoulz was more interested in searching for new or traditional herbs, dealing with homeopathic and herbal medical practice. He was interested in preparing a catalog of plants with known medicinal properties. He spent a lot of time meeting Chinese and Indian homeopathic and allopathic doctors. They organized field trips; their findings created a lot of interest, and stories were published in the Rangoon newspaper about the group's exploits and activities.

When Dr. Norman looked at his son Karl's eyes, he sent a note with his house servant to Professor Peter Fog explaining the situation. It took about a half hour before a horse-drawn carriage came up to the portico.

Norman and Krista went to the front door to receive Professor Fog, and they all went into the living room. Krista asked Karl to come and meet the professor. Karl had a white handkerchief in his hand, which he used often to dry his watery eyes.

"Good morning," Professor Peter Fog greeted Karl. "Come closer. Let me look what is happening here." The professor opened Karl's eyelid while fixing his monocle to his right eye. Professor Fog looked at Krista and Norman. "I have to tell you, Krista, don't worry. I will send my compounder at one p.m., and he will clean and dress both eyes. He will use Argyrols, and I promise Karl will be playing outside after five days. However, in the meantime, he must rest away from the sun. Krista, I must insist you keep him inside the mosquito net and maybe give him a pair of sunglasses."

"But Peter, there is no sun today. It is the rainy season," Krista protested.

Dr. Norman asked how dangerous the infection was.

"Well, it is like infection anywhere. Once we kill the microbes, I hope he will be okay. He is still young." Professor Peter Fog took out his pocket watch, which was attached with a chain to his white jacket. "Oh, I must be off," he told Norman and Krista. "Our university has experts in every field from India, Singapore, and Europe; we can deal with almost any tropical disease. Have a good day." He put his hand on Karl's shoulder and said, "Good boy." Just before he left, he said to Krista, "Why don't you and Norman come and have a coffee with us tonight? We just received a brand new parcel of Java coffee. Elsa, my wife, prepares a delicious mixture of buffalo cream and coffee." He turned around and, waving his hand, left. They could hear his carriage wheels crushing the gravel and picking up speed.

Dr. Norman Schoulz, Karl, and Krista headed toward the kitchen and sat down at the dining table, which was set with place mats made from fine bamboo and dark brown cord. Their service girl brought coffee and tea pots. Krista took coffee but never tea. On the other hand, Dr. Norman did not drink coffee. Karl was not fussy; he could drink anything as long as it was sweet. He drank milk, coffee, or tea, depending on his mood. Karl loved the cook's special breakfast bread, butter, and marmalade that had real orange pieces, as made for the household of Queen Victoria. The jar read "By appointment to the queen." Every luxury thing seemed to be made in England. English muffins, chocolate, toffee—even the napkins had Queen Victoria's coronation picture. England had captured the market. It was colonial rule.

Karl wanted chocolate milk, so his mother asked Neeta, the kitchen maid, to warm the milk in the copper pot that was tinned to avoid copper poisoning. Neeta took out a chocolate pouch and emptied it in the pot. Krista asked her to keep a watch take the milk off the heat as soon as it began to boil, fill the ceramic mug, and bring it to the table. Neeta brought the chocolate milk, placed it in front of Karl, and warned him that the milk was hot. Karl took his toast, which his mother had prepared as way he liked it, and dunked it in the hot chocolate. He ate it with pleasure. Soon, his eyes started to bother him, and he noticed there were flies around. Neeta had a small fan in her hand and tried to shoo away the flies from Karl's face. Karl used a handkerchief to remove the water or tears running down his cheek. He was getting tired, so he went to his mosquito-draped bed and hid his face and eyes with a pillow.

Dr. Norman came by to see how he was doing. "Karl, I am going to speak to some others at the medical facility. I must go now as I have to attend a meeting at eleven." He called for Krista, and when she was standing beside him, he said, "Krista, don't we have sunglasses? Can you find them and give them to Karl? The light seems to bother his eyes." Krista started off for the sunglasses, and Norman turned around and said, "Listen, I have to go now."

He shook Krista's hand and extended his hand to Karl through the netting. The carriage was ready and waiting for him, so he left. Krista brought a pair of sunglasses and went to give them to Karl, but she found that he was fast asleep.

It took about two weeks before Karl's eyes cleared up. "Tomorrow is Monday," Krista said, "I will prepare a bathtub, and we will add some salt, like Professor Fog told us. You will feel good, and I want you to go to school. You will be playing soon, believe me, Karl." Krista had to go and leave instructions for Khan Zama, the cook, who was preparing the menu for a small lunch and a nice dinner to be seated at six-thirty p.m. Krista entered the kitchen, where Khan Zama was waiting for her. He got up from the chair when Krista entered and said, "Good morning, mum sahib."

"Good morning, Khan Zama," Krista replied.

"How is Karl babe?" Khan asked.

"He is much better, and I think he will be going to school Monday." Krista told Khan Zama not to give him too many toffees or chocolates, as they were not good for his eyes. Khan Zama agreed with her.

Professor Peter Fog had collected some swab samples from both of Karl's eyes when they were in a swollen condition. He put each in a labeled Petri dish and took the dishes to the medical lab, where he left them in the hands of Dr. Rama Swami, who was a microbiologist specializing in tropical diseases. He was a graduate of the Tropical Institute in Antwerp, Belgium. The Petri dishes were placed in the incubator and removed after twelve hours for microscopic examination. The examination indicated the presence of microbes that caused inflammation and redness. Dr. Rama Swami prepared a report for Professor Fog.

Dr. Norman Schoulz's family leaves Rangoon

Karl was soon back to normal, going to school, playing, and enjoying life. It was almost two years later that the family left Burma on a Thursday afternoon. The carriage was loaded up, and everybody was inside. Khan Zama had already told Professor Norman that he would be riding on the coach, sitting near the driver. All the family's servants and friends were standing nearby to say good-bye.

They were heading toward the Rangoon seaport, where Canard Line was running a midsize seaworthy ship called *Majesty*. There was a waiting room, well lit with a high ceiling and large windows all around. It was a bit cold, and the sky was turning orange-reddish in the west. Karl came running to tell his father and mother that the red sky meant they were in for good weather. There were thirty-seven passengers all together, including about ten English, German, and Indian teenagers, some students from the university, and some faculty members. Everyone looked happy and well dressed.

A ship's purser appeared at the entrance and announced the departure time. There were two desks, one for the customs department of the Burmese government and the other for the Canard Line representative. The purser requested everyone to submit customs papers to the government representative and present travel tickets and documents to the Canard Line representative. Everyone embarked in a very civil manner. Khan Zama came to say good-bye to Professor Norman, Mrs. Schoulz, and Karl. He went with the coach back to the house, where the new visiting professor's family was about to move in.

The *Majesty* blew her whistle and was dragged into deeper waters by a tugboat. Professor Norman and his family arrived in London after twenty-two days at sea and were received by university representatives. All their traveling arrangements had been made by an organization called Varsity Exchange. They stayed at the university guesthouse and in ten days were to leave for Montreal, Canada, where Professor Norman Schoulz was had a university appointment in the department of biological herbal medicine.

This department was sponsored by an international pharmaceutical company. Their interest was to take control of the research results in order to manufacture herbal medicine and carry out field trials before distributing the medicines to doctors and pharmacies. Their priority was to establish and promote medicines that used plant products. They were already using painkiller extracts from willow tree bark, which yielded large profits.

Professor Norman Schoulz was famous for his book called *Collection of New Uses of Herbal Medicine*. His use of herbal formulas had been very successful in removing gallbladder stones. The family settled down in Montreal in Westmount, a highly desirable location close to everything, including Dr. Norman's laboratory. Karl had graduated from high school and entered first year in his father's old university. In the meantime, after three years of research, Dr. Norman's presentations and discussion papers were being published in *Nature's Bounty* and other naturopathic medical journals. Soon after, his research produced remarkable formulas and medicines for blood pressure, blood thinners, and anti-infection formulations. The company that sponsored his department, International Pharmaceutical Corporation (IPC), was flourishing under recently appointed chairman Dr. Heber. He and Dr. Norman Schoulz were colleagues who studied together and traveled together to faraway places in search of useful herbs. They shared many patents.

The corporation had a high regard for Dr. Schoulz, and the facilities provided to him were even better and convenient now because his friend and long-time partner had become the chairman of the corporation. Professor Norman was beginning to tire easily as his sixty-fifth birthday approached. The company representative told him that he had one last trip to make to the Brazilian rain forest and gave him one month to prepare for the journey.

The chairman invited Professor Norman and Krista to dinner at his house. He told Norm, "I am going to send my personal car to pick you up. I know you want to retire. I promise you, this will be your last trip, and it's just for one month. You will have a team of six well-balanced PhDs. They will need your direction and guidance. They will give you every mental and physical comfort, and you will be back before the rains."

The chairman's car arrived to pick up Norman and Krista, and it took them to his residence for a private dinner. The driver brought them back by ten p.m. Krista pleaded with her husband not to take this assignment to go to Brazil, but Norman was unable to say no. Krista told him that she did not have a good feeling about this trip, but Professor Norman had already said yes to the chairman. They retired for the night, and Krista did not sleep well. She heard Norman getting up four times to go to the bathroom.

NORMAN GOES ON A FIELD TRIP TO BRAZIL

The time came for Professor Norman to leave for Brazil. Three limousines arrived at the house to carry the entourage to the airport, and they helped Dr. Norman to get into the car. Krista and Karl came out to say good-bye as the limousines left. Krista started to cry silently, tears running down her cheeks. Karl took her inside. His eyes were filling with tears also; he had never seen his mother so distraught.

"Ma," Karl said, "Dad loves these trips. And the company is providing him so many experts, including an MD and a well-trained nurse to look after him."

Krista told Karl, "You know, this is the first time I feel a nervous wreck."

"Ma, it is just one month," Karl said, "And the company has provided planes, cars, and comfort at the rain forest site. Everything will be okay."

They made tea and coffee and went to rest. While his father was gone, Karl completed his master's degree. His professor congratulated him on his work on mathematical discoveries. The dean of the department was so impressed with his paper that he offered Karl a substantial grant to do his graduate work under Dr. David Cider, who was a renowned scholar in the subject. He was a professor at a university in Berlin and had written two books on the philosophy of mathematics.

The month passed, and Karl's father returned from the Brazilian rain forest tour, bringing very unusual plants. He had learned a few new things from the leaders of the local tribe. He kept himself busy with his cataloging, describing their properties and uses in detail.

UNIVERSITY LABORATORY SENDS DR. NORMAN SCHOULZ HOME

Dr. Jim Stewart and a nurse brought Norman Schoulz to his house. It was eleven a.m., and Karl was in school when the doorbell rang. Krista came running down and was shocked to see her husband. "Norman, Norman, why have these people brought you home?" She could not hide her emotion.

The doctor came in holding Norman's right arm and addressed Krista. "Mrs. Schoulz, I am Dr. Muller. We rushed to see Professor Norman because his secretary came and said that he was sweating and burning with fever."

"Don't worry, Mrs. Schoulz. It is just too much work and no play," Norman lovingly told her as he held her hand.

Krista said, "Norman, you are still burning with fever."

Dr. Muller told Krista that the nurse would stay with him. She assured Krista that she would stay until his condition stabilized. The temperature was coming down, but he needed rest. They took him to the guest room on the ground floor, and Krista, with the help of the nurse, dressed Norman to rest in bed. When Norman was tucked in, Krista took the doctor and nurse to the living room and started to ask all kinds of questions: why, how, and when? The doctor assured Krista that tropical medicine experts from the clinic had already taken samples from his mouth and were making cultures to find out what kind of microbe was affecting him. They had taken blood and urine samples and were trying to contact the Atlanta Disease Control Center for help because he had been to the Brazilian rain forest just three months ago.

Krista and the nurse went in to see Norman. As soon as they entered, he opened his eyes and asked for cold water. The nurse brought a glass of water. As soon as he drank the water, he went to sleep again. Dr. Muller told Krista, "Do not worry, Mrs. Schoulz. Norman will be all right. I will say good night, but the nurse will stay."

She said good-bye to the doctor. Around three o'clock, Karl walked in. "Ma, what is happening? Where is Daddy? Why is this nurse here?"

She started to cry and told him what had happened. He rushed to go and see his father, but Krista told him not to wake him, as he had just gone to sleep. Karl sat down on the sofa and held his face in his hands, silently crying. Krista sat down near him and put her arms around Karl and started to cry too. The nurse joined them and was shaken to see the love and emotion.

"Karl, remember when he was going to Brazil? I had a strong, very negative feeling. I knew this long trip for a man nearly seventy years old was not good."

Karl replied "Yes, Ma, I remember, but he wanted to go so much."

Krista said, "Come have some coffee and cake I made for you." They sat silently, not saying a word. Krista told Karl, "If your father, in the future, wants to go on a jungle trip, promise me you will be on my side to deny him."

Professor Norman slept, and his department sent twenty-four-hour nursing care. They assisted him with all his physical needs. The next morning, he woke up early and stayed in bed. His mind was roving; he knew that his fever was perhaps either due to a parasite he caught in Brazil or to dengue fever from Burma. He convinced himself that it could not be a serious matter. After about the fifth day of illness, he had more strength and pep. He went upstairs with Krista to send the nurse away. At the same time, Dr. Muller rang the bell, and the nurse answered the door and guided the doctor indoors. Dr.Norman Schoulz, was about to take a shower, asked Krista to go downstairs and meet the Doctor.

Dr. Muller said, "Good morning, Mrs. Schulz. I have good news. Atlanta has confirmed the professor has dengue fever. In anticipation of the result, I had already put him on the right medication."

"I see," Krista replied. "You see, Dr. Muller, my husband had already diagnosed his own condition, and that is why he agreed to take the medication. What I don't understand is that he was on preventive medication before he left for Burma and Brazil."

"It must have been his immunity that went down because of high stress and the extreme climate," Dr. Muller said. "Let's us hope he improves his immunity and gets his strength back."

Dr. Norman came downstairs and thanked Dr. Muller. He said, "I think I can survive now. You don't need to come to see me here. I will come to the office on Monday, and I would suggest you do a few more blood and urine tests."

The doctor and nurse left, and Krista, with a sigh of relief, sat down with Norman and asked the housekeeper to make coffee and bring small pieces of pecan pie. Krista told him how afraid she had been when Norman came home with the doctor and nurse. That night they sat down for dinner together, and Norman started to tell stories of life in the Brazilian rain forest. He told them that the environment was so bad that one biochemist could not stand it and returned home. Karl was happy to see his father back to normal. It was getting late, and Krista kissed Karl good night and went with Norman to their bedroom.

KARL SCHOULZ TELLS HIS FATHER ABOUT HIS EYE PROBLEM

The next morning, they all met at breakfast. Karl came to his father with his coffee cup, and they started to talk. Norman asked, "Karl, my son, how is your work on the math project coming?"

Karl sat down near his father and looked at him. "Dad, I seem to be having problems with my right eye."

Norman sat up on his recliner and told Karl to come closer. Norman looked at his eye and opened the lid wider. "You seem to have some kind of infection. There are those white particles again, just like in Burma, when I took you to the university, and they found your eyes were highly infected."

Karl interrupted his father. "Dad, there is one more thing. When I close my left eye, the right one seems to have poor vision. I can read but not as clearly."

Norman was now concerned. Karl was only thirty-one years old. Granted, he was doing a lot of reading, but that should not impair his vision. He told Karl to get ready to go to the university medical center to see Dr. Martin, the glaucoma specialist. They arrived at Dr. Martin's eye research institute. Norman introduced Karl and explained the situation. He told him that the eye infection in Burma had been terrible, and he had not been treated with antibiotics. It had taken more than ten days for his eyes to get back to normal.

"Did you use any medication?" Dr. Martin asked.

"Oh, yes, there was this Dr. Rama Swami. He gave Argyrols liquid drops to be used twice daily."

"Professor Norman," Dr. Martin said, "Argyrol is not used anymore. Actually, it is withdrawn from the market. It has been declared poisonous."

Karl got very nervous. "So what should we do?" he asked Dr. Martin.

"Karl, take a deep breath. I will tell you that right now we will do an eye exam. I will personally check your cornea and your eye pressure, and finally we will do a field test. These tests will determine our response." So Karl went in the testing area. It took about an hour to complete the tests. Dr. Martin laid down the results in front of Professor Norman.

"So, what is the conclusion?" Professor Norman addressed Dr. Martin. "Dean, what is happening? Is there a problem?"

Dr. Martin reported that the pressure in Karl's right eye was higher than in his right, and that generally indicated trouble. His field results indicated that he had the beginning of glaucoma, although it was very slight. Dr. Martin continued, "There are a few types of glaucoma. The fluid that fills the eye is constantly replenished. In other words, new fluid is supplied to keep the eye active. The old fluid exits through a duct, and a pressure balance is maintained. Now, since the exit canal is blocked, the new fluid keeps coming, building pressure inside the eye. When that happens, the optical nerve bundle comes under pressure, and some nerves are liable to be damaged. When the nerve or nerves get damaged, the optic nerves that are providing image information to the brain stop sending images, and that is where you have darkness and no vision. The field test indicates and enhances those areas. This is serious."

Professor Norman was anxious to find out about corrective action. "So what is the next? Step we have to take?"

"With immediate effect, I will prescribe three types of eye drops, which I will mark. Number one and number two are designed to be used during the day. Take number one in the morning, say, around eight o'clock, and number two around ten o'clock. Repeat the doses again after six hours. Number three you will use before going to bed. Try to use only one drop at a time, and follow the directions provided with the packages."

Professor Norman was surprised that there was not enough research done on glaucoma to determine its causes and prescribe a definite cure or even predict who would be affected and at what age.

"Yes, yes, Norman, I agree. There is a lot of basic information in the books." Dr. Martin was himself frustrated with the poor fund-raising for research on glaucoma. Karl, whose field of interest was mathematics, which required lots of reading and writing, was quite afraid.

Dr. Martin assured Karl that recent innovations in surgical procedure had improved the chances of stopping the disease. Karl said, "Is that the only thing that can be done, stopping the advancement of the disease and not reversing the process?"

"Karl, no that is the bad aspect of this disease. The optic nerves die, and you cannot revive them," Dr. Martin said. "I wish somebody could come up with some plan to work on regeneration and activation of optical nerves."

Karl picked up the eye drops and thanked Dr. Martin, and they left. Karl was driving, and his father asked him if he had any problems with driving at night. Karl replied, "Dad, I did not even feel anything unusual when I was reading or driving; only recently I started to feel a slight change when I looked out of the corner of my eye."

They arrived home, where Krista was waiting anxiously. She opened the door and asked, "What took you so long? I started to worry. Since we arrived from Rangoon, I haven't had any rest; I'm always on pins and needles."

Karl stopped her in the middle of her concern. "I have some eye problems. Dr. Martin—he is Dad's old friend—did a thorough examination and prescribed these eye drops." He showed her the three small eye drop bottles. Karl tried to pacify her. He and his dad had already planned what they were going to tell her.

It was about dinnertime. The housekeeper had set the table and served some of the South Indian dishes that the family had learned to enjoy. Krista, during her stay in Rangoon, had prepared a hand-written recipe book for Indian dishes. They had become Norman's and Karl's favorites. Norman liked some Indian spices like turmeric and cumin. Their favorite dessert was rice pudding with cardamom, pistachio, and rosewater. They left the table, and Norman said to his son, "Karl, come and sit near me. Let us read the newspaper instead of doing university work."

Krista said, "I like that; it has been so long since we have sat down and had tea and coffee together." Krista was relaxed and dozed off beside her husband as he held her hand.

KARL GETS A FULL PROFESSOR'S JOB

As the months passed, Karl did his graduate work and published his thesis, titled "Micro philosophy of Mathematics." It received citations and admiration from the United Kingdom, Germany, the United States, and Canada. He received invitations from different universities, including Madras in India, to lecture whenever he wished. Krista and Norman were delighted and decided to celebrate at the Hilton downtown. Norman asked some of his staff to help Karl and his group to organize a gathering. It took place on a Friday night under the light of the August moon. Karl had invited Ingrid Borden. She was a student of botany in the agriculture department. She was doing graduate work on the feeding systems of plants and worked on different species of flowering plants, both tropical and Canadian. She wanted to study plants with fragrances; she was interested in the chemistry of scents and their relationship with reproductive behavior—the birds and the bees.

Ingrid and Karl had been going out for three years. She liked Karl, and now Karl's star was rising. The recent publication of his research papers and response to his philosophical approach to mathematics had opened a new window for graduate students in the world. His faculty members and the dean of his department encouraged him to continue and expand his philosophical horizon. Ingrid was enchanted to read Karl's work in scientific publications. The celebration at Hilton was a moment of joy for everyone.

Ingrid, Krista, and Norman got into Karl's car after the party ended, and they dropped off Ingrid first at her residence. Krista and Norman started to talk about Ingrid. They liked her a lot. She had a bright, rosy complexion, with blonde hair and greenish eyes. Her manners were regal, serene, and gentle.

What Karl liked most about her was her simplicity. At the celebration party, she danced with Norman and Karl. Karl danced with his mother. They waltzed, boogie-woogied, and did the polka. It was fun and introduced Ingrid to Karl's family as a sort of prelude to an engagement. Norman and Krista could not contain their happiness. Karl, his mother, and his father arrived home. Norman was happy but exhausted, and they all went to bed. Karl did not tell anyone other than his father about his eye problem. He knew it was of no use to discuss his problem. He had been searching the library for information about glaucoma, but not much was available. He learned that surgery was his best chance. However, surgery on a delicate organ such as the eye required new methods. Karl went regularly to Dr. Martin for the same routine of pressure checks, field tests, and vision tests. So far, there had been no major changes in the test results since his diagnosis. Norman was working vigorously on his son's glaucoma problem. He called all his contacts all over the world and got good recommendations. Well known for his herbal remedies, he gave Karl a prescription for improving his eyes. He prescribed vitamin E, B-complex vitamins, bilberry, beta-carotene, and One-a-Day multivitamins. Norman ordered these ingredients and started a regimented approach; every morning after breakfast, he made sure Karl took these herbs and vitamins.

After Karl had been on his father's formula for three months, his general health improved. He thought his eyesight, especially his peripheral vision, also seemed to be getting better.

KARL PROPOSES TO INGRID

One day, Karl invited Ingrid out to a restaurant on top of Mount Royal. After a nice meal, he ordered a nonalcoholic bottle of white wine, as he always avoided alcoholic drinks. Ingrid was looking vivacious. He told her that today was their third anniversary of friendship, and Ingrid said, "I was going to tell you, but it is so nice you remembered."

Karl smiled and put his hand into his right blazer pocket. He took out a small, blue velvet box. Ingrid knew what was happening and began to cry silently. Tears were gently rolling down her cheeks. She extended her hand to touch Karl's hand. He held her hand and finally opened the box with the ring. He took out a diamond ring blazing with color and asked her, "Ingrid Burdon, will you marry me?"

She started crying and laughing at the same time. It was good that Karl had made a reservation in a private booth. They toasted with a sip of wine. Karl said he would like to marry as soon as possible.

"You can still finish your experimental work on flowers," he said. She was smiling, so Karl asked her, "Did you hear what I asked you?"

"Oh Karl, I am sorry. What did you ask me?" They both started laughing. She told Karl, "I was wondering when you would. You know Karl, I love you so much that every time you drop me off at my dorm, I feel so lonely and I miss you. Sure, we can set the date, but let's go to your house and get your parents' blessing. From there I will call my parents in Calgary."

They left the restaurant hand-in-hand and very happy. She had the ring on her finger and looked at it admiringly every once in a while. When they arrived at Karl's home, it was nine o'clock. Karl rang the bell. Krista and Norman were wondering who it could be. Krista opened the door and was delighted to see Karl and Ingrid.

"Why did you ring the bell, Karl?" she asked. "Did you forget your key?"

"No, Ma, I have my key, but we are here to give both of you the best news of the day." Karl was smiling, and so was Ingrid.

"Come, come. Your father will be delighted to see both of you." They walked in to see Norman who got up to greet them.

"What a surprise to see you, Ingrid," he said, shaking her hand.

"We have another surprise for you," both Karl and Ingrid said together. Ingrid held Norman's hand, and Karl took his mother's and asked Ingrid to tell them the surprise.

Ingrid smiled and asked them, "Are you ready for the surprise?" She lifted her finger with the brilliant diamond ring. "Karl asked me to marry him, and I said yes."

"Wonderful!" Both Norman and Krista were happy. They all hugged. "Congratulations are in order. Let us have a drink."

Norman asked Krista to bring him the special Canada Dry ginger ale, and Ingrid told Krista all the details about how, when, and where this magic took place.

"Karl, oh look, it is about ten p.m.," Ingrid eventually said. "I have to be in my dorm by ten-thirty. Please take me home. I hate to leave this emotional high." She kissed Krista and Norman.

"What about calling your parents?" Karl asked.

"I will call them tomorrow." Ingrid was so happy that she had forgotten to call them.

"Ingrid, tomorrow is Saturday, so why don't you come here for lunch and we will all congratulate your parents?" asked Karl.

"That would be nice," she agreed. She shook hands and kissed Norman and Krista and said, "Good night, Ma and Dad. Is it all right if I call you Ma and Dad, just like Karl does?"

Krista and Norman said, "That would be sweet. We now have the daughter that we never had."

Karl went with Ingrid, and Krista and Norman were giddy with happiness. They needed these moments.

Karl dropped off Ingrid at her dorm and headed home. He wondered whether he should tell Ingrid about his eye problem and promised himself that he would tell her about his glaucoma the next time they got together.

It was late when Karl arrived home, so he took a hot shower. He let the warm water wash over his eyes, and it was soothing. He was relaxed and prepared to get into bed.

The next morning, Karl and Ingrid sat down with Krista and Norman. Karl said to Ingrid, "Go ahead and ask my parents what they think about your idea."

Ingrid said, "Okay, I will. Ma and Dad, I would like my mother and father to come back here so we can all sit down and set the date for our wedding."

Norman replied, "Ingrid that is a wonderful idea. That way we will all pick the wedding date, and no one will complain."

Karl suggested, "Can we call Ingrid's parents now, Ma?"

Krista agreed, "Go ahead and do it now. What is the time in Calgary?" Karl replied, "It is about ten in the morning."

Ingrid brought the phone to the living room table. She dialed the number. It rang six times before Ingrid's father finally picked up the receiver and said, "Hello."

When he heard Ingrid's voice, he said, "Oh, my dear Ingrid." His voice was clear. "How are you? I am sorry we did not answer at first. We were outside in the backyard. What's up, Ingrid?"

Ingrid said, "Dad, I am at Karl's house, and Mr. and Mrs. Schoulz are here. I will ask Mrs. Schoulz to pick up the other phone, and you can ask Mother to do the same, because I want to have a conference call."

So both parties were listening to each other. "Dad and Mom, as I explained to you last night, Karl asked me to marry him. I was delighted to say yes. I want to introduce you to Karl and his parents. Dad, here is Karl."

"Hello, Karl." Ingrid's father introduced himself, "My name is Jeffrey Burdon and here is Audrey Burdon."

"Hello, Karl. I am Audrey Burdon. It is our pleasure to have you in our family. Ingrid has told us about you, and she is crazy about you."

Ingrid said "Mom, here are my—well, I call them Ma and Pa. They are Mrs. Krista Schoulz and Mr. Norman Schoulz."

Both Krista and Norman voiced together their pleasure at having Ingrid in their family. Ingrid invited her parents to come as guests of the Schoulz family the following Friday, to discuss and plan the wedding date.

"Oh, darling, we don't want to disturb them; we will stay in a hotel."

Karl, Krista, and Norman said collectively, "No, you are going to be with us for Friday night and Saturday. We will let you free on Sunday."

Jeffrey and Audrey said, "It will be our pleasure."

Ingrid then suggested, "Dad and Mom, you go ahead and make plans, and Karl and I will pick you up at the airport. Call me and tell me details of your flight. Ingrid said. "Okay, Dad?"

"Okay, Ingrid. See you soon," her parents said. "Thank you, and good-bye till Friday." They hung up.

A few days later, Karl picked up Ingrid from a class at the north building. It was at least five miles away from proper botanical building, but she attended some classes there. He opened the door of his mid-sized Volkswagen, and Ingrid stepped in. They were on their way to Karl's home for dinner and to discuss further plans for the wedding with his parents. The ride to his house should have taken twenty minutes, but he turned onto another street.

Ingrid was surprised. "Where are you going, Karl? The house is nearby. Why are you taking another street?" Karl was a little nervous as he entered a small parking area. "Are you all right, my love? What is the matter?" Ingrid was puzzled.

"Ingrid, I just wanted to talk to you in private. I have a problem, and I want to tell you about it," Karl answered her.

Ingrid's eyes were now getting cloudy with little tears. Karl kissed her eyes; his lips were wet with her tears. "Ingrid, I have a problem with my right eye. My dad took me to his friend, an ophthalmologist who is in our medical building."

Ingrid was getting impatient. "So what's wrong with your eye? Is it dangerous?"

Karl said, "Well, it may be. I don't know. Are you familiar with an eye disease called glaucoma?"

Ingrid said, "Yes, I know. My mother's cousin has it, but he is seventy-two. Apparently, it is a silent disease. If you don't treat it early enough, you could lose your eye."

"That is what I want to tell you," Karl said. He then told her that the doctor told his dad that he needed another checkup every six months. In the meantime, he had some eye drops to use during the day and others to be used at night before going to bed.

"Oh, Karl, my love, that makes me a little sad, but you are young, and I will take care of you." She raised her head and kissed his eyes.

Karl continued jokingly, "You still have time to cancel the wedding."

Ingrid said, "Karl, you can't get rid of me that easily. I love you, and *que sera, sera.* We will help each other. I will not let you lose your eye."

Karl said "It was better to let you know more about me."

"That is one more reason I love you so much; you are such a gentleman and so sincere. Where could you find a better human being?" Ingrid replied. "Let's go home. And let us not talk about it unless I ask you, please. I will start to keep a diary from now and keep track of details as far as you are concerned."

They arrived home, and Karl opened the door. Krista heard the garage door open and asked, "What happened? You are a little late."

"Ma, we were sitting in the car talking about my eye."

Krista and Norman were a bit upset. "Did you have to tell her now?" Krista questioned Karl.

"Yes, Ma, she has a right to know before we get married." Krista and Norman both agreed it was the right thing to do.

"Go wash up, both of you. Dinner will be served soon." Ingrid was impressed by Karl's openness about everything. They were holding hands when they returned from the wash room. Ingrid was trying to find any defect or difference in his eyes. They were nice, sort of bluish and sparkling as they looked back at Ingrid. He squeezed her hand, and both smiled.

Mother and Father saw the sparkle in their eyes and were satisfied. Krista squeezed Norman's hand, and they both smiled. Everybody sat down, laughing. Karl poked Ingrid's side to make her giggle, and she did.

Karl took Ingrid to her dorm around ten o'clock. They could not stand being separated anymore. He told her, "I have never felt for anyone like I feel for you. I don't want to be without you, day or night. How about instead of living at your dorm, you move in with us? I have already discussed it with my parents, and they are okay with the idea, as long as you are never in my room for more than twenty minutes."

"Yes, I think I feel the same. You know, someone up there is looking after us. How wonderful that nature has arranged for us to be together and to be supervised by your parents. And next Friday, my parents will be coming to stay there, too. Oh, Karl, this is magical, just wonderful."

Karl, too, was delighted. He even suggested that she sleep at his parents' house that very evening.

"But Karl, I don't have my pajamas, clothing, toiletries, or anything. How about after school tomorrow you and I go to my dorm and load up my belongings? I can move in tomorrow. I don't have any classes any more, and you are free also, so it is decided."

Karl shook her hand saying, "Okay, okay."

The next day, the girls from Ingrid's dorm teased Karl as he loaded up his car with Ingrid's boxes. "Now you can't live without her," they teased. Finally, they said good-bye to Ingrid's roommate and classmates. The dorm was only for female students.

They arrived home, and it took a few hours for Karl and Ingrid to arrange everything in the room.

Friday soon came, and Karl gave Ingrid the telegram that had come from her parents. It read, "Flight number 239 arriving at the airport at 11:05 a.m." All four of them drove to the airport in the Schoulz's' station wagon, which seated six with enough room for luggage left over. The airport terminal was small and easy to find. They all hugged and were pleased to see each other.

After returning home and refreshing themselves, they sat together in the living room. Ingrid told her parents that in their honor, she would be staying there in the third room upstairs. "Mommy and Daddy, you will take the guest room down here."

Karl, with the help of the housekeeper, brought in the luggage and set it up in the guest room. This was a big room with large windows and an attached bathroom. Lunch was served: bread, cheese, cold cuts, and fruit. Audrey and Jeffrey were coffee drinkers, as was Karl. Krista and Norman as well as Ingrid took tea.

Friday was spent getting to know each other. Jeffrey said, "I am retired now," and Norman said, "I too am retired." But Krista told Audrey that Norman could never truly retire: his university and his sponsor, International Pharmaceutical Corporation, kept calling him for consultations.

Norman said, "Ingrid tells me that you, Jeffrey, are a chartered accountant."

"Yes, Norman, I liked the job. You have to be an accountant and lawyer and many other professions to do the work well," Jeffrey commented. He continued, "I understand you are a world traveler and you like nature and rain forests. Boy, I don't know how you did it. I would not be caught in a rain forest."

Audrey said laughingly, "That is why you have a big tummy." Everyone laughed.

The next morning after breakfast, they started to discuss the wedding date, and everyone agreed on June 21, a Saturday. Karl said, "The most important part is done. Now we have to go and discuss all the arrangements and guest list with Norman Jr."

Jeffrey said, "Karl, you better contact your cousin, Norm Jr., and ask him to design the invitations card. He is fantastic. Can you believe we have the grandson of artist Norman Rockville with us? You told me that he is doing graduate work in arts at the university."

Karl agreed to talk to Norman and to tell him they did not want to receive boxed gifts. "He will also design another modern box to hold cards and, hopefully, big money."

Krista said. "Okay, you go and look after that. We will do the rest. So Ingrid and Karl left.

Karl and Ingrid went to see Norm Jr. at his studio. He had already promised to design an art nouveau wedding invitation card; Ingrid asked him, "Could I select the color of our card?"

Norm Jr. looked at her for a while, and she said, "I am just suggesting that there are three basic colors I will love to have as our theme."

Norman Jr. interrupted her. "What are those basic colors?"

Karl knew Norm was a little upset.

"The colors are pastel pink, green, and pale yellow."

Norm extended his hand to Ingrid and said, "Excellent choice."

Karl was delighted to see Norm accepting Ingrid's choice of colors. He looked at Ingrid, and both smiled.

"Don't worry, we have lots of time," Norm Jr. said laughingly to them. "Listen, I have a lot of work. I am getting ready to open my show at Art Deco Studio at Westmount Gallery, so good-bye and good luck."

Norman, Krista, Audrey, and Jeffrey were at home when Karl and Ingrid arrived. "So did you accomplish something?" Krista asked.

"Oh yes, NRJ has promised to design invitation cards as well as an art deco collection box. What about you? Is the list ready? What about a list of work assignments? Who is doing what and when?" Audrey suggested.

"You have to hire a wedding planner if you want proper execution and a choice wedding," Norman and Jeffrey agreed. They all thought it was a super idea.

Dinner was ready, and they all went to wash their hands. Ingrid kissed Karl and said, "Is it not fantastic? Everyone is in agreement. I thought weddings always caused problems because both families can never agree completely." Karl explained, "Ingrid, that will always be the case as long as two people are not clones of each other. There is a good chance we will have a good life, and hopefully we will agree on most things. I have to admit, when you asked Norm about suggesting colors, I thought, 'Oh, why she is doing this to a master of his work?' Yes, I must admit I was nervous, but when he shook your hand and kissed you, it was worth it."

They went hand in hand to the dining table. Ingrid looked at her parents. "I am going to miss you both. You are leaving tomorrow night."

"I know honey, but we are a phone call away," they said.

The following day, Ingrid's parents left for Calgary. Karl and Ingrid took them to the airport. Time was passing by in a hurry. The wedding planners were having a meeting with Norman Schoulz, Krista, and Norm Jr. about the box and invitation cards. Finally, half a dozen cards arrived for final approval. Norman and Krista were delighted with the stunning results. Karl sent a sample card to Ingrid's parents in Calgary, and they too were delighted.

The wedding planners were handed the cards, guest list, and location. Norman's old friend Armand Mercier, owner and operator of the Hotel Ritz, had promised the best hall for the wedding. He told Norman, "I will never have another opportunity to show my admiration for you, so you will have the best food and an excellently decorated hall for your son's wedding."

Karl was happy that his father's old friend was doing his best. It was already March, which made it difficult to reserve a nice location for June. It seems everybody gets married in June. University exams were about over, and the holidays would start soon. The wedding plans were almost complete. The only thing that was worrying Ingrid was her wedding gown. Her mother knew a European seamstress, Sara Argil, who worked for a Montreal wedding gown designer and was authorized to use the mark of St. Laurent, the hot young French designer. Audrey, Ingrid's mother, made an appointment with her. Sara was delighted to design for a well-known family and invited Ingrid and Krista, to the high-class boutique. They spent two hours looking at materials and designs imported from France.

Ingrid wanted Karl's approval, but the designer, Sara, said, "It should be a surprise for the groom. However, if you want the opinion of your friend, you can bring him tomorrow. But you and Mrs. Schoulz should choose the material now. I must tell you, there is not much time left."

So reluctantly, they selected the material. Sara Argil promised Ingrid, "I will send pictures and a small piece of material to your mother in Calgary."

Ingrid asked, "If my mother does not like it, then what we do?"

Sara assured her that not too many people would reject the material she had chosen.

Ingrid was still not satisfied, and she asked Sara, "Can you at least show our artist friend, Mr. NRJ, if I bring him here?"

Sara was surprised to hear NRJ's name. "You mean the grandson of the famous artist?"

"Yes, that one," Ingrid smilingly replied.

"Now, that's one artist I sure will listen to. He should look at the design too," said Sara. Ingrid and Krista asked her if she knew NRJ had an art show coming up the next month. Sara said, "Yes, I do, I do."

Ingrid and Krista drove back to their house, where Karl and Norman were waiting. Karl jumped and threw his arms around Ingrid. "So, did you make a decision? And Ma, what did you think of the designer?"

Krista and Ingrid both told him that they liked her and the material they had chosen.

"Karl, I asked Sara to get an opinion from Norman Rockville Junior."

"Wow, Ingrid, you are a sweetheart and a genius," Karl said, kissing her.

Krista was tired and happy that another big job was done. They were late for dinner; the table was already set for only two. Krista went to her room, where Norman was already fast asleep with his mouth open.

Ingrid could not go to sleep and asked Karl to phone her mother as she wanted to tell her all that had happened at Sara Argil's shop. They dialed the Calgary number and spoke with Audrey, who was happy and said, "Honey, when Sara Argil is involved in designing a wedding gown, she becomes more famous. Don't worry: she will make you look like a princess. That is what you deserve."

They hung up, and both went to bed. Ingrid asked Karl to keep his door wide open.

The next day, NRJ went with Ingrid to Sara Argil's shop. As they entered the room, all the well-dressed young designers came out to see Norm. Sara shook his hand, but he bent and kissed her on her cheek.

"Sara," he said, "I have heard about your talent, and I am delighted to see that you are looking after Ingrid. Karl and this sweet angel are my favorite people." Norm looked at the designs Sara gave him to look at, and he picked one of them. "Sara, you have to include one little addition to the design. Here is the wedding invitation card I have designed and am authorized to give to you. You see, Sara, the three colors I have used here are an Ingrid color trademark. These three colors have to appear in some form—ribbon, a flower, or a delicate waistband. I leave it to you to choose."

"NRJ, you are remarkable. I have never had any requests or suggestions before to add the bride's theme colors. What a lovely touch to the bride's image. I think this may become a standard feature as a royal symbol in the class weddings." Sara asked some of her assistants to come and look at the unique art deco invitation card. They wanted to take pictures of the card, but Norm requested they keep it under their hat until the wedding.

"I will see that you respect my request. I am sure you will not disappoint me." Everyone clapped, and Ingrid felt very special to have Norm as her guardian angel. They disappeared in the dusk. Norm was driving his red Jaguar. He dropped her off and told her, "I wish I could stay, but I must go. I have so much work."

Ingrid entered the house, and Karl came running to see Norm, but he had already left. Ingrid fell into Karl's arms exhausted, not because she was tired but because of how she had been transformed in her mind to real royalty. She told him, "You have no idea how your friend is worshiped by artists. Sara, who is well known in design throughout the United States, France, and Canada, was so humble in front of him. He gave her our wedding invitation card, and you should have seen how their eyes open wide. Norm Jr. asked them all, the staff and Sara, not to show the card to anyone before the actual wedding. Karl, my darling, the card is art deco, you have no idea how the design is; it is absolutely unique. Norm said the cards would be delivered shortly. What a day; there is magic in the air."

Ingrid was emotionally excited, and after dinner she went to her room and fell asleep very quickly. Karl and his parents stayed up together marking a programmed chart from the wedding planner.

Krista said, "Today the phone did not stop ringing. You know who called?"

"No, Ma, who called?" Karl asked.

"Do you remember the eye surgeon in Rangoon who looked after your eyes when you were sick?" Krista replied.

"What did he say?" Norman was surprised.

"After such a long time, I thought they had forgotten us," Krista casually said. "It was really just to say hello and that they at the university still remember you, Norman. They heard that you retired and that your son became a professor and is about to marry in June."

"Well, they seem to know a lot about faraway happenings," Norman told Krista. "You see, each university has a method of keeping in touch with visiting professors and their families. Things are published in the *University Gazette* and university news reports."

By this time it was getting late, and they were tired. Karl was following his routine of using eye drops just before going to bed. His right eye had been bothering him lately. He reminded himself that next month he would go for an eye examination. With these thoughts, he went to sleep.

Next month came. The holidays had started, and tomorrow he

would be seeing his doctor. April started with showers. Karl picked up his umbrella and after breakfast told Ingrid that he was going to the eye doctor for some tests.

Ingrid said, "I will come with you; it will take me less than five minutes."

"No, darling, I have to go alone this time. On my next visit, you can come with me. By then we will be married, and you can share my bad and my good in sickness and in health. Don't worry your lovely head. Okay?"

KARL'S EYE TEST

Karl met Dr. Martin, who told him to go into the field test room. The university eye specialist, in consultation with a German glaucoma expert, had devised a five-foot-by-three-foot board that was studded with tiny little bulbs in a very special fashion and hung on the wall. Karl was asked to sit in a chair with a head support. He was told to click a button in his hand when he saw a light flash momentarily. The lights were switched off in the room, and it took him a good twenty minutes to go through the exercise. After the test was completed, Karl came out for other tests, like pressure and vision, etc. The light board was a unique design to determine peripheral vision loss. Dr. Martin told him that his right eye did not see as many lights as his left.

"You can see, you indicated seeing most lights on the board except few on either side or up and down."

"My goodness, Dr. Martin, it really shows the loss of sight on the right side more than the left." Karl was perspiring, and his hands were damp. Dr. Martin assured him that some brilliant doctor one day would come up with a solution to this dreaded silent disease.

Karl went home and promised not to disappoint anyone, including Ingrid, with a negative attitude. His father knew his son. Norman did not say anything and came forward to hug and kiss him. They did not say anything. In the meantime, Ingrid, happy as a lark, came downstairs and hugged Karl.

"So what did the doctor say?"

"It was just a routine test. My next eye exam is scheduled for July fourteenth. So we will not bother with any eye or other problems. Let us go out for lunch at Sheehan Restaurant. They have a good lunch menu."

During lunch, Karl mentioned, "I met Norm Jr. at the hospital, and he asked me to bring you to see his creation of the collection box and the original invitation card on Thursday at four. He has arranged a lunch, and he will also give us a preview of his art exhibition."

Ingrid could not hold back her excitement. Two tears rolled down her ivory pink cheeks. Karl held her hand and caught a reflected ray from the diamond on Ingrid's finger.

On Thursday, they went to visit Norm Jr. He was waiting for them. He greeted them and suggested they have lunch first and then visit the *World of Art Deco*. The catering master had prepared an art deco table with unusual candle holders; even the cutlery was in the art deco style, and the food was really special. There were other guests including Sara Argil, the wedding gown designer. Everybody sat down, and Norm made a little speech.

NORMAN ROCKVILLE CELEBRATES KARL AND INGRID'S UNION

"This is my moment of honoring our guest. Karl and I have been childhood friends. Our fathers and grandfathers have traveled the world together, so this is a tribute to our generation. I am honored to have both of you along with my friends today."

Everyone clapped and raised their glasses to honor the occasion.

"No, please, let us start. The art deco dessert is waiting." They all finished a sumptuous lunch and followed Norm Jr. to visit the masterpiece invitation card, which was beautifully set in a golden frame. The card was five times larger and was part of his art exhibition. Karl and Ingrid had agreed to let him use it. The box was presented to Karl and Ingrid. Everyone was excited to see the way it was designed. It was designed as a Pandora box but with simple lines, in Ingrid's color combination of powder pink, pastel green, and just a fine yellow thread running through the body of the box. The entry to the box for dropping envelopes was in a shape of lips. The aesthetic was not vulgar but fine, with a pastel pink touch. A bird sat on a little branch with an envelope ready to drop between the two lips. Ingrid adored it and could not keep from hugging and kissing Norm Jr.

Karl looked at them and said with a wink, "You certainly have stolen my Ingrid's mind. I may have her heart, I hope."

They all followed Norm Jr. into a larger room where the artists were still organizing the show pieces. Everyone was a masterpiece.

"Ingrid, when you have children—I hope lots of them—and if someone asks you which one of your children is …"

Ingrid put her hand over his mouth. "I know exactly what you mean. You are not only an artist; you are a romantic artist."

The tour came to an end, and everyone said good-bye and wished him good luck.

As Karl and Ingrid reached home, it was still thundering, but the rain had stopped for a while. The sun was spreading a golden glow low in the western sky. Karl had his arm around Ingrid and pointed to the golden sky. "Do you know what that means?"

"Yes, I do, Karl. My father told me when I was maybe eight. Red skies at night are a sailor's delight—something like that. Which means tomorrow will be sunny with no rain."

Karl applauded her and said, "You are so smart, Ingrid. I just love you, and every day it is just a delight to see your face." "Me too," said Ingrid as she hugged Karl and kissed him gently.

They were home early. All four sat down in the living room and Krista said, "You know, we have only twenty days remaining. We have a message from Audrey and Jeffrey asking us to have a review meeting and find out where we stand and what remaining items on the list need to be completed. Norman said we had better have a meeting with the wedding planners tomorrow or at least set one to do exactly what Karl just told you."

Karl and Ingrid reminded Norman and Krista that the invitations would be going directly to the wedding planners.

"Ingrid, your friends at school want to give you a shower," said Krista. "You had better call Sylvia Shriver. She said Saturday the eighteenth has been arranged at the dorm. They are still a few days, so you can invite your friends. The shower is at Windsor House at two-thirty p.m. There will be coffee and cake, so have your lunch at home but no dessert. So there; it is your job to finalize it."

It was approaching time for dinner, so Krista said, "Let's call your parents in Calgary and bring them up-to-date."

The following day, Ingrid went to Windsor House and Karl stayed behind. He noticed that two types of eye drops were almost empty. He noted also that the medications had apparently come from Germany and made a note to speak with Dr. Martin the following day to renew the prescription in time for the wedding as he would be away for one week. He wrote himself a note with an orange marker and placed it on the side table in his room.

At around four o'clock, he heard Ingrid's car arrive and went out to meet her.

"How was it?" Karl asked.

"Well, everybody was real nice, and the girls gave me nice little gifts. One of the girls was talking to me. I don't know her very well; she is from Calgary, and she knew where we live. She said her uncle worked at the Canadian High Commission as first secretary in India for four years and returned recently for an extended leave. It was very hot in the summer, and instead of coming home he decided to go to a summer resort in Sheila, a town in the Himalayan range, where some officers work. It is very healthy, pure air, and he and his wife stayed at the summer office, all paid for by the foreign office. She wanted to talk to me because her uncle saw your name on Dr. Martin's appointment board. It appears that her uncle is having eye trouble, and the doctor thinks he may have the beginning of glaucoma. She looked it up in a medical book and found out that it is a disease that silently creeps up on you. Apparently eye infection is common in India, where hygiene is poor, flies are plentiful, and if they land on your eye, they can cause infection and eye disease, depending on where they come from. I panicked and ran home to speak to you."

KARL HAS GLAUCOMA

Karl and his parents were surprised by how upset Ingrid was. Karl took her into his room, gave her some orange juice, and said, "Ingrid, my darling, I told you about my exam, and so far Dr. Martin assures me that no one, not a single specialist or scientist, knows anything about the disease, so please stop torturing yourself. You know when you are sad, I will be twice as sad. We have decided to live our lives for each other and our children."

Ingrid's eyes were glassy, filled with tears. Karl took out his handkerchief, wiped her eyes, and was going to put it back in his pocket when Ingrid said, "Can I have your handkerchief? It is the handkerchief you used to wipe my tears. I will treasure it, and it will give us hope and strength."

Ingrid was feeling better, so they went downstairs. Krista and Norman were worried about Ingrid. Karl explained what happened at the shower party, and they hugged her and started to talk about the discussions with Ingrid's parents.

"Everything is okay; don't worry," Karl said. He held Ingrid's hand

and told her that Dr. Martin had assured him that the eye drops were at his office.

"Karl, we will go together to Dr. Martin's office to pick up your eye drops," Ingrid said and looked at him with gleaming eyes.

The next day, Karl and Ingrid made up a to-do list and after dinner went for a walk. There was still a bit of chill in the air, so they both put on jackets. They walked hand in hand, talking, stopping, and talking more.

"Oh, I forget to tell you. There was a message from Henry, the master tailor. He wants you to go for your fitting. Your tuxedo is waiting," Ingrid said lovingly. "I can't wait to see you in a tuxedo."

After breakfast the next day, Ingrid was anxious to accompany Karl to Dr. Martin's office. They were ready to go at nine-thirty. Karl was driving. Traffic was building up, and Karl started to rub his eye, as he did once in a while. Ingrid was starting to worry whenever the subject of his eye came up. She looked at him suspiciously.

He immediately recognized the look and said, "Ingrid, it just may be dust or pollen. Don't get like that. I will have to suppress all my activity with my eyes." He winked at her twice, and she burst out laughing.

They arrived at Dr. Martin's office. The receptionist recognized Karl and said, "This must be Ingrid, your fiancée. Dr. Martin has mentioned her a few times."

Ingrid noticed a tall, handsome man was sitting nearby. "Good morning," the tall man greeted them.

Ingrid said, "Good morning. If I am not mistaken, you must be Mr. Crowsky, Stella's uncle."

"Yes, you are right. How did you guess? Oh, I know—Stella was talking to you. My name is Arthur Crowsky. I am here to see Dr. Martin."

Then Karl said to Arthur, "We do have something in common. How about having lunch one day? We are very busy these days; however, we could exchange notes and maybe we can form a support group." Karl turned to the receptionist and inquired whether he could have the eye drops that Dr. Martin promised him.

"Yes, Mr. Schoulz, they are right here, ready to go," she said and handed him the bottles. Karl shook hands with Arthur, and they headed home. They sat down in the car, and Karl could see that Ingrid was again disturbed.

"Ingrid, let me see the job list." He took it from her and scratched off a few items as completed. "The day after tomorrow, I will go to Henry, the master tailor. Will you come with me?" Karl was asking her these questions to distract her from the glaucoma concern.

She said, "I would not miss that for sure." Karl asked her how it was that she was allowed to see him in his wedding attire, but he was not allowed the same privilege. Ingrid assured him that there must be a reason behind such a tradition. She was again in good humor. She suddenly sneezed and used Karl's handkerchief to wipe her nose. *"You see, I have some use for it. I am sure if I feel sad and I am alone, I will take your kerchief out, and by looking at it and kissing the corner, I will be at ease."* Ingrid really believed it.

Karl got up and went to Ingrid's room to see if she was awake. Ingrid had gotten up earlier and was in the bathroom. He went close to her bathroom door and told her, "Ingrid, it is almost nine o'clock. We have an appointment with Henry the tailor at ten. What are you doing?"

She heard Karl at the door and came out. She had her toothbrush in her hand, and her mouth was full of toothpaste. Karl understood and told her, "I will be downstairs in the dining room for breakfast."

Ingrid got ready very quickly and came down. They had breakfast and had to get up and go. They had to drive through heavy traffic, but they arrived on time. As they entered Henry's shop, Henry brought out the complete tuxedo, ready for final fitting. They tried on the pants first and made few marks using a white, flat piece of chalk; next, the assistant tailors tried the vest and found it fitting. The final fitting was that of the jacket; this required a few corrections.

Henry came and told Karl, "Mr. Schoulz, I think everything looks okay. Come next Monday, we will deliver your suit." Henry wished him lots of luck, and they left.

Time was marching on, and only two weeks were remaining until the big event. Karl's suit was delivered; Audrey and Jeffrey, Ingrid's parents, were also in town, staying at the Ritz, where the wedding was taking place.

Audrey told Ingrid, "You have to move in with us at the Ritz one week before the wedding. By the way, Ingrid, your bridal gown is being delivered today to our suite at the Ritz. If you want to try it on, you have to come here without Karl."

Ingrid was so excited and told her mother, "Yes, Mama, we will come after lunch, and Karl can stay in the lobby while I try on the gown."

After lunch, Karl drove Ingrid to the Ritz. He stayed behind in the lobby while Ingrid took the elevator to her parents' suite. Karl was getting impatient; Ingrid was taking too long. Finally, Ingrid came out of the elevator, and they went home. She told Karl, "I wish you could see me in the gown. It is a dream. I feel and look so good. Mama said I look like a princess."

They arrived home; Karl was tired and suddenly remembered his eye drops. "Oh, Karl," said Ingrid, "I am sorry. With all the excitement, I forgot." She got the bottles and put drops in both of Karl's eyes. Then she told him to lie down on the couch and relax.

The next day, the wedding planner had an appointment with the parents of the bride and groom. As the parents waited for the wedding planner to arrive, Audrey told Krista that Ingrid would be moving to her parents' suite at Ritz one week before the wedding and would not see Karl again until the wedding rehearsal. Krista agreed with her. Audrey was happy to see that everything was going so well. She and Jeffrey thanked Krista and Norman and then headed to their hotel. Krista was getting a little tired and nervous; she decided to call her friend Morgan for help in carrying out all the assignments handed to her by the wedding planner.

The wedding planner arrived at Krista and Norman's house exactly on time, with a helper. Together, they drew up an hour-by-hour program for the day, and the wedding planner gave each set of parents a list of tasks to complete. "You must follow this program. I have brought Anita, who will help you to do whatever the program requires," the program director addressed Karl and his parents.

Karl pointed out, "By the way, you did not tell us your name."

The wedding planner said, "Oh, I am sorry. My name is Judy, Judy Larose. I am the president of Wedding Plan Inc." Judy Larose told them that she was coordinating the complete reception program with Norman Rockville Jr. and that they were developing a printed program that would be distributed to the guests. The program was to start with a welcome speech by the master of ceremonies, who also happened to be the best man of the groom, Norman Rockville. "Don't forget he is your best man as well as the master of ceremonies! Karl, you and Ingrid are fortunate to have such a talented and lovely person in your lives." Judy Larose excused herself from the meeting, saying, "We have a lot of work to do. Good luck."

Honeymoon suite in Florida

Norman came down and asked Karl and Ingrid if he could talk to them. The three of them went into the living room, and Norman handed the couple an embossed and decorated envelope, saying, "Here, take this. It is a gift from the chairman of the International Pharmaceutical Corporation. Charles Heber asked me if you would accept a honeymoon suite at La Baron Imperial in West Palm Beach as a wedding present."

Norman was hoping that they would accept. "Charles Heber had been a long-time friend and colleague. His company financed my rain forest expedition and other projects in search of herbal medicine."

Karl and Ingrid told Norman it would be a privilege to accept the gift. Ingrid did want to go to Florida, and NRJ had talked about arranging a trip a few weeks ago, but due to his busy schedule it had been forgotten. Karl and Ingrid both thanked Norman and asked him to give their best regards to Mr. Heber. They opened the envelope and looked at the picture of a royal suite situated on the ground floor with a large balcony facing the ocean. There were two first-class train tickets to and from Palm Beach, with instructions on whom to call for transport and all other details. A limousine was to pick the couple up at the station and bring them to the prestigious La Baron. Both families were in awe and told the couple that they could not have asked for anything better.

According to Judy Larose's program, a limousine would pick up the parents of the bride and groom at nine forty-five a.m. on the day of the wedding. Other friends, relatives, and associates would arrange transport to the church on their own and should be at the address mentioned on the invitation card by nine-thirty. The venue was a large Unitarian church at the corner of Sherbrook and Water Avenue. Guests would be guided by the attendant, who would also be traveling in the limo with the parents. The attendant would also be responsible for bringing the bride and groom to the office of Reverend Oskar Mayer, where documents would be signed before and after the marriage ceremony. The reverend would give a prearranged speech and say a few prayers from several different religious books, including the Bible. There would also be a box for donations to the church and charities. The ceremony would start at ten-thirty, which would give enough time for the guests to mingle with one another. Refreshments would be served after the marriage ceremony, and the mayor of the city, a guest of honor, would present the married couple with a golden key to the city and would address the guests. Judy expected that his address would probably be political in some manner, as the elections were not far away. Ingrid and Karl gave the wedding planner information about their honeymoon for her help with coordination.

The time had come for Ingrid to go to her parents' suite. Judy had arranged a transport that had already picked up her university friends so that Ingrid would not feel lonely. When the car arrived, Karl brought Ingrid out to meet it. The driver opened the back door, and Ingrid's friends burst out, "Surprise!" and started singing.

Karl and Ingrid were pleasantly surprised. Karl was glad to see Ingrid laughing and happy. He praised the wedding planner and told Ingrid, "Judy Larose and her team have done an amazing job. They are good!"

Karl asked Ingrid, "How did your first bridal gown fitting go?"

"Karl, I wish you had seen how beautiful it was! You will have to wait until next Saturday now. I will see you soon. I love you," said Ingrid. The car pulled away and drove off with Ingrid and her friends.

On Friday came the wedding rehearsal, a dry run of the marriage ceremony with both parties in casual clothing. The planner came to pick up the Schoulz family and their support groups, and another group brought Ingrid's mother and father along with their friends. Karl asked his mother if she had talked to NRJ recently. As they were starting to talk about him, Norm entered the limo from the other side and sat in the back seat. He told the driver not to reveal where he was sitting so he could surprise everyone in the limo. Karl was still hoping to see his best friend and best man before the wedding.

"I wonder where NRJ is?" he mused. "I hope he is all right."

Krista was sad and asked Karl, "Do you know if NRJ is coming?"

In the meantime, the wedding planner came into the house and told everyone there to get in the car. They helped Krista and Norman to get into the car. As Karl entered the back of the car, he saw NRJ, who shouted gleefully, "Surprise!"

"Norman, you really worried us. We were going to send a search party! Thank God you are here."

"Karl, don't thank God, thank me! I am sorry, but you and your fiancée have kept me so busy, and I can tell you, I have never been so busy in my life!"

Karl put his arm around his friend and kissed him on the forehead. "You are a real friend, and now that Ingrid has adopted you as a brother, you are my brother-in-law."

They both laughed. The limo rushed through the traffic. They passed the hotel, which was being decorated, most likely with pink and yellow lights at the request of Norman. In front of the church, Karl saw the limo that held Ingrid and her party. He was excited to see her after a week apart. Everyone got out and walked toward the church entrance. Karl and NRJ rushed to catch up with Ingrid.

Ingrid scolded NRJ, "Why did you leave me alone? You are supposed to look after me. I was worried for you, but something told me you were playing your childhood game of hide-and-seek.

Karl was laughing and said, "Just as we used to do. It was such a relief when I saw him."

"Hey, I hear you have a honeymoon suite in Palm Beach fully paid for!" said NRJ.

Ingrid laughingly said, "Norman, it is unbelievable. A train and a limousine from Montreal to Palm Beach station and back. Dad's friend thought of everything."

NRJ said, "I have to tell you a secret I have kept from both of you. Karl, you remember when I was invited to Paris to open my show? Anyway, I met the most beautiful girl there. This was a very romantic encounter. Ingrid, I cannot believe it; she has accepted my invitation to attend the wedding, and she is arriving tomorrow from Paris. I will keep you posted with my adventure. I didn't believe one could fall in love so badly. I can't sleep, and I am waiting so anxiously. You know, soon I will not be lonely anymore. I will be with my friend. Her name is Sybille Savera."

The assembly in the church was ready for rehearsal. Judy Larose and her staff were directing everything. First, she introduced Reverend Oskar Mayer as the representative of city hall and God at the same time. They went through all the steps, pretending to sign documents. Judy had a copy of every real document necessary for the marriage ceremony so there would be less risk of making a mistake. After all this was done, a breakfast was prepared by Judy and her company for the rehearsal guests. Their plan worked according to the schedule. Both parties along with all their guests left the church by eleven-thirty.

The wedding planners had organized a lunch for fifty people at the Ritz at noon on the next day. The idea for this lunch was to show the parties how elaborate the decoration and how detailed the wedding reception was to be. Judy expected that this highly publicized wedding would have a big positive impact on her business.

NRJ asked Karl and Ingrid to excuse him from the lunch. "I have to go and pick up my sweetheart at the airport—I have a lot of stuff to prepare for Sybille and for the reception later on."

Ingrid and Karl were so happy for NRJ that they did not know what to say. He hugged them both and said good-byes to everyone.

- You better be ready at six tonight!" Karl warned his best man. Everybody laughed, and the parties went back to their hotels to rest before the big event.

Karl, of course, could not sleep. He lay down and put drops in his eyes. He dozed off for a few minutes and woke up when the clock struck four. Norman and Krista came down to see Karl.

"Are you all right?" asked Norman.

"Yes, I am okay, Dad," replied Karl. "Whenever I use the eye drops, my eyes get red and my vision goes blurry momentarily."

Norman said, "Come, my son, it is a big day for all of us. Let us get dressed. Your friend NRJ called and said that he would be here shortly; he picked up Sybille at the airport and is coming over here with her. Karl, you are a lucky man. Thank God, he gave you a friend who will be there when you need him. He is more than a friend and has more unusual qualities than anyone I know. Now, let us go and get ready, son. By the way, who is this girl that he is bringing?"

Chapter 12

NORMAN ROCKVILLE'S FRIEND
SYBILLE ARRIVES FROM PARIS

Everyone got ready for the wedding. Karl was looking around for NRJ. His father was having a cold drink downstairs when he saw Norman Jr. enter the house with a ravishingly lovely young woman. "Where have you been? Karl is going crazy without you," Karl's father asked Norman Jr.

"Here, Uncle, meet my friend Sybille. I went to pick her up at the airport."

When Karl heard Norman Mr.'s voice, he came down to see him. They hugged, and Karl said, "I know who this beautiful young lady is. You are Sybille." He bent over and kissed her hand. "When Ingrid sees you, she will be so happy. Ingrid is dying to meet you."

Norman Junior asked Karl to get ready.

"I need this bow tie fixed," Karl replied. "Norman, can you do it?"

"I will do better than that. Sybille, can you please help my friend?" Sybille tied Karl's bow tie, and he was ready. During this moment, Karl expressed how much he had missed Ingrid during the past week. Norman, the father, complimented his son and looked at his wife. They were both in tears, and all three of them hugged.

"My beautiful son, remember this precious moment. It will never happen again!"

Karl sobbed and told his parents how well they had raised him and how happy he was at that moment. "To be here with you and for you to receive my wife so well is a blessing on us. Mom, forgive me if I gave you reasons to be annoyed with me. Dad, you were always with me, in my heart with Mom. God kept you well so you could see this day and, hopefully, the arrival of my first child." Karl was emotional, and these words were not easy for him to say. The limo came with the wedding coordinator. They arrived at the wedding with everyone waiting for them, as the bride had already arrived. Ingrid had missed Karl so much that she nearly broke tradition and tried to go and see him, but luckily she was pulled away by her girlfriends. One at a time, Karl and Ingrid went with their bridesmaids and groomsmen to Reverend Meyer's office. The reverend offered words to relax them and said, "There is still time to change your mind before we wrap you with the most beautiful chain of love, grace, and dignity, which is bestowed upon you by the Almighty God." The reverend's office was silent, and the church was packed with men and women looking their best.

As the bride entered the church, everyone applauded. The organ played, "Here Comes the Bride." Ingrid looked beautiful and radiant; she had her hand on her father's arm as she walked down the aisle. Karl was patiently waiting with his friend NRJ, who was dressed in an ivory suit; the handkerchief in his upper left pocket had a border of pink, yellow, and green. The cameraman continued shooting pictures. Ingrid arrived with her father, who handed her over to Karl. "Take very good care of her," said Jeffrey as he took his spot with Audrey. His eyes grew misty as she squeezed Jeffrey's hand. The big time had come, and the couple approached the area where Reverend Meyer was waiting.

"Ladies and gentlemen, it is my privilege to unite these two lovely personalities," said the reverend in a broad voice. NRJ was behind them as the reverend continued with his standard matrimonial speech. The only thing Karl remembered after the ceremony was the moment when the reverend asked for the ring. NRJ took out a beautiful box for everyone to see. The colors of the box were satin pink, green, and golden yellow. He slowly opened the box and took out the ring. One of his technicians had arranged for a beam of light to fall and hit the diamond in the ring. When NRJ took out the ring from the box to hand it over to Karl, the beam of light reflected off the diamond lighted the whole hall for a split second. Everyone murmured, "Wow."

Karl and Ingrid were surprised but had already known that NRJ was able to astonish and amuse everyone with his little tricks. The audience started clapping. Finally, everyone was quiet. It took the reverend only seconds to tell Ingrid and Karl to put the ring on each other's fingers. "With this ring I thee wed," Karl repeated after the reverend. At the reverend's command, the couple kissed gently. The couple thanked the reverend and hugged and kissed their parents. There were tears of joy in many eyes. After a few more formalities, Judy took the couple to Karl's house to rest before the reception. The housekeeper served everyone cold drinks, tea, and coffee.

Karl said, "Ingrid, I am exhausted!"

"Me too," she responded. "Let us go into your room. I can stay as long as I want, with no curfew now. What a change in a few hours!"

"Yes, Mrs. Schoulz! I agree." Karl tickled Ingrid to make her laugh. While they were lying in Karl's bed. Anita brought fresh pomegranate-and-blueberry juice for both of them. Karl suddenly remembered his eye drops, so he went to the bathroom.

"Can I come too?" asked Ingrid. Without waiting for Karl's reply, she barged in and saw Karl putting the eye drops in his eyes. She said, "I am sorry, Karl. Don't keep any secrets from me. Let me be in charge of helping you with your eye drops."

"Ingrid, I did not want you to think of my eyes today." Karl gave her a kiss, and she gave him a bigger one in return. She said "Let's go drink our juice; we do need our strength, so here's to you."

They drank the juice and finally relaxed; they were tired, emotionally and physically. They lay down only to be awakened by the telephone and Krista and Audrey banging on the door.

"Can we come in and stay with you two?" Both Karl and Ingrid felt good, and Ingrid began crying.

"Ingrid, we did not want to disturb you. We just wanted to see you after the big event," said Audrey.

Ingrid replied, "Mommy, it is the joy you bring to me that brings these stupid tears. I can't help it! Stay, please stay!"

Karl agreed and said, "We will miss you for the ten days of our honeymoon."

"Oh sure!" both mothers said sarcastically.

Dr. Norman was wondering why he had been left alone, so he came up and saw Karl's door open. He said to Karl, "I want to talk to you. Come and stay with your dad for a while."

Karl suggested that they go downstairs and have lunch; Mrs. Morgan had prepared delicious food and his favorite rice pudding. Growing hungry, Ingrid, Krista, and Audrey came down, and they all got to laughing and joking with one another. Norman said, "This gathering was actually to celebrate the end of curfew for Ingrid and Karl. Now they are free and can do what they want."

They all sat down at the table, which was decorated with flowers and new china and cutlery. Mrs. Morgan asked Karl, "What will be your pleasure? I have your favorite rice pudding and coffee. Ingrid and Krista, you have your choice of crumpets, bagels, toast, or your favorite Italian bread. Norman, I have your favorite snacks that can be lightly toasted with butter or jam."

As they finished eating, Norman Jr. called to say he was coming over. He came and sat down near Ingrid and Karl. "Finally, we meet after a pleasant storm. What a hectic day it has been for me. Listen, both of you. I did not want to tell you until now."

Ingrid and Karl were wondering what Norman Jr. had in mind. He told her the details of his meeting Sybille. They talked for a while before NRJ excused himself, saying that he still had more work to make this reception one that would be remembered for a long time. He kissed Ingrid and told her she looked like a princess in her gown. Then he gave a big hug to his best friend. "I have to go and get my sweetheart. I think she is waiting for me to pick her up. Ingrid, I hope you like her. She has agreed to sing at your reception. Ingrid, Karl has already met her." NRJ left in a hurry.

Judy Larose called. "I will be coming over shortly. I hope both families are there. I will go over the schedule and the speeches by the mayor, who will be there to present the couple with a golden key to city hall. This really does not mean much, but I assume his objective is to prepare the audience for the new election coming up in the next year."

Judy arrived at the same time as NRJ. He was holding Sybille's hand. When he entered the hall, everyone turned and looked at them. He had brought Sybille to meet Ingrid. He said, "Ingrid, meet my Sybille, who flew from Paris only few hours ago to attend the reception."

Everyone gathered around Sybille. Ingrid got up from the chair and shook hands with Sybille. She said, "What a lovely name. And you are so beautiful."

Sybille replied, "Ingrid, Norm has talked about you, about Karl, and about the wedding since I met him."

Sybille told Ingrid how NRJ had asked her to come to the reception and sing. "I have been planning and rehearsing in my mind since the plane ride. I have been very busy traveling, but when he asked me, I just could not refuse. Can you imagine that? Either I am in love or I am stupid "

"I think you are in love," Ingrid replied. "I am sure he is in love, too, because I could see that something was bothering him. Now I know. He was worried that you would not come. He did not even tell his best friends, Karl and me. So there, you see him now? He is happy. The way he looks at you, he sure is in love. Sybille, you are so sweet. I love you." Sybille kissed Ingrid and Karl.

Krista and Norman were so happy for NRJ that they all hugged both Norman Jr. and Sybille, saying, "What a pleasant surprise." Mrs. Morgan offered them lunch. Judy had already eaten, so she politely declined. NRJ was still in his suit white shirt.

Judy said, "Please follow the schedule and be ready at to be picked up at five-forty. That means all of you, including NRJ, must be dressed in your best. I will send a hairdresser and make-up party at five-ten, and I am sure everything will fall in to place." She left after these final instructions.

NRJ spoke. "I must say, Judy is good; I think I will hire her for my wedding."

"Sybille and Karl, did you hear that?" Ingrid was clapping and happy.

Norman said, "If you people want to rest for a while, the girls and Mrs. Morgan will help to bring your clothing, shoes, and anything you need to get ready." Everyone agreed, and they went upstairs to rest. Karl's room had a king-sized bed, so Ingrid invited NRJ to sit down on one side while Ingrid sat down on the other side near Karl. They joked, made fun of each other, and were all really happy.

Ingrid asked NRJ, "How did you manage to have the beam perfectly on the ring when you took it out of the box?"

"Yes, that was truly a magical feat," said Karl. "Are we going to rest or what? Ingrid, I will tell you another time."

Gradually, they all went to sleep. They woke up when the phone rang. The phone call was for Dr. Norman from Switzerland. It was Chairman Heber. Norman said, Oh, so nice of you to call. Both the kids were grateful in accepting your offer for the honeymoon suite!" Norman said.

"I am so glad, Norman. Congratulations to you and Krista! Have fun, and take care of Krista." The chairman said good-bye and hung up the phone.

By now, everybody was up. The girls started to get ready in one room and the boys in another. Karl and NRJ helped Norman first by assisting him with his socks and shoes as well as adjusting his suspenders. Norman enjoyed this, as it reminded him of his own wedding. When they were finished, Norman, NRJ, and Karl went downstairs and waited for the ladies to come. The makeup and hair teams came in for the final touches, and the ladies all looked beautiful. Ingrid did not have time to sit next to the boys; she was taken upstairs and had her hair groomed nicely to further complement her face. They touched up Krista and Audrey, and everyone was ready when the limo showed up. Just before six, the party arrived at the entrance of the hotel. All of Norman Schoulz's old friends, including the owner of the Ritz, were there to receive the guests. Karl's father got out first. He did not realize that journalists were also there with cameras flashing. It looked like a wedding of the stars. Finally the party, led by Judy Larose escorting the bride and groom, entered the hall. Everyone gave them a standing ovation while clapping. Others were escorting the couple's parents, and after them appeared a beautiful blonde young lady escorted by NRJ. She was dressed in a beautiful turquoise long dress, which was flowing and designed almost like a wedding gown except for the color, which matched her turquoise necklace. She took NRJ's arm, and they entered the hall, which was tastefully decorated with blue, pink, and yellow ribbons and the bright and beautiful chandelier. The place looked lovely and colorful. Ingrid and Karl sat in the middle of the high table with their parents sitting next to them on both sides. NRJ and his lovely escort sat at the end close to the podium. Suddenly, NRJ and Sybille began making funny noises, hitting their glasses and making clinking noises, to bring attention to the bride and groom. Norm got up and asked his escort to come up to the microphone at the podium with him.

"Good evening, ladies and gentlemen. My name is Norman Rockville Junior. As you know, Karl, the handsome man over there, is my childhood buddy, with our families going way back. The beautiful bride, Ingrid, has recently adopted me as her brother. And this is my dear friend Sybille Savera, who has just arrived only few hours ago to grace our party. We welcome you all on this happy and lovely occasion!" He introduced the guests of honor at the table. "Last but not least, I want you to meet Dr. Norman and Krista Schoulz, who are wonderful parents and friends and gracious hosts."

Sybille was so impressed with the whole arrangement that she could not resist saying to a guest sitting next to her, "This Hollywood-style arrangement could not be possible without NRJ's efforts."

Norm continued, "I will ask you to please look at the program card. And now I will request Reverend Oskar Mayer to say a prayer before we start the function. The reverend came to the microphone and said a small prayer while everyone stood up.

When the guests sat down, NRJ said, "My next guest is none other than Sybille Savera. She is admired and respected in the music world, and I am sure that when you hear her, you will agree that we are lucky to hear her poetry and listen to her magic voice when she sings. Now enjoy."

He handed Sybille the microphone. She said, "Good evening." She looked at the guest of honor table and then the audience. She thanked Norman Jr. for the invitation. "I was fortunate to be able to come here and had little time to prepare this poem."

She started to sing in a melodious voice. When Sybille finished, there was a pin drop silence before everyone started to clap.

Norm Jr. got up and announced, "That was just an introduction to her voice. Now be prepared to be entertained, she will sing from *Carmen*, a famous opera. Here is our Sybille."

She had already rehearsed that afternoon with the Ritz's band. The music started, and then came Sybille's voice. The hall seemed to vibrate with the sound of her exploding voice. It was so melodious, so gentle and yet so strong. When she finished, the audience cried for more. They were on their feet, shouting "Bravo!" So the master of diplomacy walked to the podium and requested her for one more song. This time, she sang "Fascination." Her voice and manner of singing were enchanting.

After the song, NRJ invited the mayor of Montreal to speak, saying, "Please welcome our honorable mayor Claude Raymond."

The mayor, dressed in a pinstriped suit, addressed the audience. "Good evening and bonne soirée. My name, as most of you know, is Claude Raymond. This will be my last year in politics as mayor. I want Karl and Ingrid to have this golden key to the city hall." Everyone clapped, and suddenly the clinking of glasses forced the mayor to stop and go back to his seat. The parents then came to the podium and thanked the mayor on behalf of the bride and groom. Everyone clapped. It was finally seven o'clock.

NRJ came to the microphone and said, "Before we go and take our seats at the dining table, I want to thank Judy Larose for organizing and supervising the arrangements. Please give a hand to the wedding organizer, Judy, who has done an excellent job!"

Judy stood up, and everyone clapped for her hard work in organizing such a beautiful wedding. George Maher, the proprietor of Ritz, had a message that he also wanted to share. "Good evening and bonne soirée, ladies and gentlemen. My friend Dr. Norman Schoulz has asked me to present this silver key to Mr. and Mrs. Schoulz, the newlyweds. This key is for their new house located at 581 Ivory Lane, in the prestigious Westmount section of Montreal. The present comes jointly from their parents, Norman, Krista, Audrey, and Jeffrey. This is the most pleasant task I have ever had to do. Thank you!"

Everyone gave a loud cheer and stood for a few minutes. George Maher came back to the podium and said, "I am sorry, but I forgot one important detail. The house has been decorated, furnished, and renovated by none other than Norman Rockville Junior!"

The bride and groom hugged their parents and thanked them profusely. Ingrid and Karl said to Sybille, "What a pleasure and honor to have you at our reception. We thank you and are so happy that NRJ was able to persuade you to come at such short notice."

The food was served; the clinking of glasses continued; and the newlyweds got up with their parents and were escorted by Judy Larose back to Karl's home. Audrey and Jeffrey had gone back to their hotel suite. NRJ and Sybille accompanied Karl and Ingrid. When they reached Karl's house, NRJ and Sybille stayed with them till midnight. Sybille and Ingrid talked nonstop until Krista came and told NRJ and Sybille to go and let both Karl and Ingrid go to sleep. They were so happy that everything had gone so well.

The next morning at six, a limo came to pick up Karl and Ingrid. Karl went to his dad and kissed him. Both were unable to talk because of the lumps in their throats. Ingrid and Krista were crying. Karl told Krista, "Ma, please do not cry. I love you. See you soon!" The limousine drove away; Karl began to say something to Ingrid.

"Don't worry, Karl," she interrupted. "I have your drops right here in my purse. I am in charge of your eyes, tears and all." The limousine raced to the railway station and arrived with plenty of time to spare. The first sitting for breakfast was at seven-thirty. Ingrid had the full schedule of the honeymoon trip to Florida. She even had the number of their first-class coach. The sleeping accommodation was a delight. The escort from the railroad guided them to the coach, and the porters brought their luggage. A conductor came in and introduced the compartment. The conductor asked, "Mr. and Mrs. Schoulz, would you like to have your breakfast in your room, or do you want to go to the dining car?"

Ingrid and Karl looked at each other and replied, "Here, in the room." There was still half an hour left before breakfast. They both washed up and changed into casual attire. Ingrid gave Karl chamois slippers and matching socks; she had a corresponding set. The bellboy knocked on the door and entered the room with a large tray of fruit; his helper carried a large tray holding coffee in a pink-and-blue thermos. He set the dining table with croissants, toast, miniature cereal boxes, milk, sugar, fruit, and orange juice. They settled down, and Ingrid told Karl, "These ten days are going to spoil us. But when we come back, we will have an even better house, furnished, decorated, and renovated by Norman Junior."

"What about that! It was a really big surprise for me," Karl told his wife.

Ingrid suddenly stood up and said, "I almost forgot to give you your eye drops." Karl looked up, and Ingrid gently inserted the drops while he kept his eyes open. Ingrid told him, "Now close your eyes before another fly falls in love with them." They laughed. "Karl, tell me, how long has this glaucoma been with you?" Ingrid asked.

"To be honest, Ingrid, I don't know. The only day I remember is when I went to Dr. Martin's office. My father told me then that glaucoma affects older people. So it has been almost five years. My right eye was showing signs of weakness when I was working with small letters. I tested my left eye against my right eye, and sure enough, there was something wrong."

Ingrid questioned Karl, "Of course you have been using drops since you saw Dr. Martin five years ago. Try to remember as far back as you can go. Have your eyes showed any signs of improvement?" Ingrid waited while Karl ate some grapes. "I am sorry, darling Karl. This is the first day of our honeymoon. I just wanted to be a good wife and your friend and to have a fair, informative discussion so I can know you inside out."

Karl bent over, kissed Ingrid, and said, "I am interested in finding out about your inside, and I am yours to explore." Both finished breakfast and Karl said, "I will ask for a Do Not Disturb sign for our room." In the meantime, there was a jerk and pull on the train. The wheels started to screech, and the conductor blew the whistle.

The train was picking up speed. Since it was an express train, it did not stop except at major stations. The bellhop slipped a newspaper under the door. The train was moving at full speed, the rhythm of the wheels making a special sound as the train rolled over the rail joints. After coffee and tea, Ingrid and Karl checked to see whether the door was locked. It was indeed. They picked up the newspaper and saw that a quarter of the front page was devoted to wedding ceremonies. The beautiful photo of Ingrid and Karl was so good that Ingrid wanted to cut out and keep it for posterity.

"Ingrid, Norman Junior had his own cameraman take all kinds of pictures. We will have plenty." They started to read the paper. Suddenly, Karl said, "Ingrid, let us dress up and go to bed."

Ingrid smiled and winked. "Karl, it is really the best idea you have had in your married life." So they dressed up in their new silk pajamas, a wedding gift. Ingrid opened her carrying case and pulled out a green-and-pink pajama set. The sleeves and borders were piped with gold trim.

"Karl, look, it is designed by NRJ; he remembered my color scheme."

"Yes. I must wonder, what one can do for him when he gets married?"

"Karl, don't worry. By the way, did you notice that everyone was looking at NRJ's girlfriend? Sybille was looking stunning in her smashing turquoise dress, and she in turn was looking at Norman Jr. so admiringly. I am so happy that NRJ has found a partner who is so beautiful and so talented. It appears they have been going out for some time. Remember, when he gave us lunch in his studio, he introduced her to us. I am so embarrassed I forgot her name! Did you hear the poem and songs that she performed for us? What a beautiful voice!"

Slowly they were falling into each other's arms, and the train was running through a tunnel somewhere, whistling and still running at maximum speed. Later, they fell asleep, covered with blue and pink blankets. They got up around four p.m., and an attendant knocked on the door to take away the breakfast trays and replace them with afternoon tea. The crockery decorated delicately with pastel colors. The colors resembled Ingrid's colors, but with the addition of a range of blue and purple flowers.

Tea and coffee were served by a young girl dressed in candy stripes who introduced herself as Juliet. "I am your host until we disembark at Palm Beach. I will be back. Good night."

They did like Juliet. After she left, night came quickly. At dinnertime, Juliet and her helper knocked and entered the room with water and freshly made fruit juice. She prepared the table with another young woman helping her. Juliet stood in front of Karl and Ingrid and introduced the night's menu. "Here is tonight's menu. If you do not care for the menu, let me know your favorite meal, and we will do our best to provide it for you." The dinner special was roasted shrimp served in garlic sauce. Juliet added, "I hate shrimp served with the skin on. Don't you?"

Ingrid responded, "I don't like shrimp."

"What is your pleasure, Mr. Schoulz?" asked Juliet.

"Well, I would like your best roast beef with fried potatoes and some vegetables."

Ingrid quickly agreed. " I will have the same, whatever my Prince Charming eats and drinks, I follow him!"

They all laughed as Karl poked Ingrid on her side, and she screeched a little and laughed. Juliet was taken with Karl's pleasant nature. Juliet returned with her helper carrying trays full of goodies that she thought they would like. When Juliet was ready to leave, Ingrid said, "We would like you to have dessert, tea, or coffee with us. We like you."

Juliet was overwhelmed by their gesture and decided she would come back after their main course. The day was almost at an end; Ingrid and Karl were getting bored just eating and sleeping. They were wondering if Juliet could organize a card game by bringing another staff member to join the game. Juliet thought it was an excellent idea. She cleared the table and brought back a deck of playing cards along with another staff member. They played cards for a while until Ingrid and Karl were ready to go to bed. The girls wished them a good night and good luck with everything. She left a fresh batch of juice in the thermos inside the room. Ingrid turned on the radio and tuned it to a station playing soft music. She and Karl got ready to take a shower in the large stall with sides made from quartz glass etched in a style that was similar to that of Lalique, the French artist. The glass panels were capped with wide stainless steel borders. They both went in, and Ingrid used her favorite scented body lotion. They came out smelling good, again dressed in their silk pajamas and chamois sandals; the music was still playing softly. Ingrid switched on the sleep mode, and they slipped into a fantasy-filled sleep.

Morning came, and Juliet brought Florida red grapefruits that were nicely carved for easy eating. She said good morning to Karl and Ingrid, who were dressed in tropical attire. That meant a flowery shirt and white shorts for Karl. Ingrid was wearing a sailor-style white and blue striped polo shirt with a light beige pair of tweed pants. They looked quite different and youthful. The train came to a stop near the station and then started to creep up slowly. The station was colorful, with Florida colors and beautiful flowers in plain sight. When the train stopped, Juliet helped Karl and Ingrid with their small carrying bags. The conductor and the stationmaster were waiting outside on the platform. Juliet escorted Ingrid and Karl to the platform, where the station master welcomed them to Palm Beach. Juliet stepped forward and introduced Ingrid and Karl as special guests of Chairman Heber and said, "My name is Juliet. I have the pleasant task of escorting them to their residence."

The stationmaster shook hands with Ingrid, Karl, and Juliet. He told Juliet, "My office has received messages from the chairman's office instructing us to assist you in making Mr. and Mrs. Schoulz's stay as pleasant as possible."

The stationmaster and the conductor started to tell them about the chairman. "Our chairman, as we call him, is a noble person and has benefited many of us. The economy of this location is flourishing because of his efforts. There is not a single month that goes by in which we do not take care of his special guests. He and his company are building a new complex in the area with an emphasis on art and education. He is building a museum with a lot of styling involving art deco. The architecture, unusual lighting, and American artistic approaches have made it the talk of the town. The chairman's objective is to make this complex so beautiful that it will attract many educated tourists. Your own arrival and departure have been discussed in several newspaper articles. A few years ago, the chairman was presented with an Order of the Republic on the opening ceremony held at this station. This was a showpiece of American capitalism. We hope your stay is pleasant." The stationmaster escorted them to their limousine, said good-bye, and left.

As their limousine arrived at La Barron, Ingrid and Karl were impressed with the resort's location and style. Juliet took them to their suite and stayed with them until all their belongings had arrived. She checked the refrigerator, beds, and blankets. Juliet gave them her phone number and told them that her room was also on the ground floor, so she could come in just a few minutes when they needed her.

Ingrid said, "Oh Juliet, I feel so good that you will be close by."

Karl and Ingrid settled down. They were tired and needed some rest. A maid brought various cold drinks. The weather was sunny and hot.

At three in the afternoon, Juliet called. Karl answered. "It is Juliet," he called Ingrid. She picked up the other phone. "H, Juliet. What's happening?"

Juliet asked if it was okay to come and see them. The stationmaster had brought a present for them. Ingrid told Juliet to give them about ten minutes. When Juliet arrived at the condo, Karl and Ingrid greeted them at the door. The stationmaster apologized for the intrusion and presented them with a bouquet of green and yellow roses. Ingrid and Karl thanked the stationmaster and invited both of the visitors inside. Juliet was also carrying a crate of oranges from the mayor. Juliet served refreshments to the stationmaster. He said good day and left. Juliet was very happy for Ingrid and Karl.

Karl and Ingrid were enjoying their stay in Florida; the high temperatures of ninety-five to a hundred degrees outside did not allow them to go to the beach during the afternoon. They had to get up early to go to beach and enjoy the ocean and hot sun. Karl made sure he and Ingrid always used sunscreen.

Juliet took them sightseeing, driving them to Miami to see live shows eat in fancy restaurants. Juliet arrived every day at their condo and brought them breakfast; the local staff was at her disposal.

Chairman Heber knew the environment at La Barron; he knew that in the month of June, the weather was hot and the other occupants were mostly mature businessmen. The number of guests was very much reduced compared with in winter, when there were hardly enough spaces to park all the cars. Karl and Ingrid slowly started to feel alone in paradise. Luckily, Chairman Heber had assigned an experienced public relations person to counteract such a situation. Juliet was that person.

On the third day of their honeymoon, Juliet judged their mood and asked Ingrid and Karl if they would like to play tennis. Ingrid said, "Are you kidding? I can't play in this heat?"

Juliet said, "Of course not. I have arranged and reserved two hours at Chairman Heber's club. You will play against two young, very smart players."

"Oh, Juliet, that is really good news. You know, we were starting to think that everything is so posh and neat and yet we are not having fun. Is it not so, Karl?"

Karl nodded. Juliet told them that she had read their minds and was working to solve that problem. Juliet wanted to know, "So, what do you think? Can you wake up early tomorrow? I will pick you up at seven-fifteen, and we will have breakfast at the club."

When Karl and Ingrid arrived at the club the next morning, they saw a different world. The place was humming with activity. Young men and women were dressed in the latest fashions. The atmosphere was happy, and the place was cool and bright. Three people seated at one table got up to receive Juliet and her companions.

Juliet introduced Ingrid and Karl. "Meet the head coach, Brandon. Jim and Kimberly are your playing partners. They shook hands, and Brandon asked them to sit down. Juliet asked Brandon if they had eaten breakfast already.

Kimberly said, "No, we were waiting for you. Now that you are here, let us get started."

They went all together to the dining room and started to get to know each other. Juliet asked Ingrid what she would like to eat. Ingrid said, "We have been eating all fancy foods at breakfast, lunch, and dinner. I would love to have pancakes."

Karl agreed. Everybody decided to have pancakes and delicious Florida orange juice. Jim and Kimberly remembered how they had come to La Barron two years ago on their honeymoon. It was very nice for two days, but after that they grew bored and Juliet came to their rescue, just as for Karl and Ingrid. They all laughed.

Kimberly told Ingrid and Karl, "Do not worry; now you are in good hands. You know, tomorrow we are going to have lot of fun. Juliet, tell them about tomorrow."

Ingrid was curious. "Yes, Juliet, tell us. Or do you want to keep it a secret?"

Juliet said, "No, no, I was going to tell you after your game. Okay, Kimberly, you tell them."

So Kimberly told them that the club had organized an overnight trip in the famous sailboat *Skipper*. "Karl, have you ever been on a huge sailboat that is built like the ones they have at the international boat race?"

Karl replied, "No, not on a big one, but I have been on smaller ones. One time, Ingrid I were invited onto a decent-sized sailboat. The weather was slightly rough, and boy, it was hard work."

Jim and Juliet told Karl, "This is a deluxe ride. The aim is to relax, and you don't work if you don't want to. They have fishing, music, and a band you can dance to."

The group finished breakfast and walked toward the courts. The court was booked from nine till eleven. Juliet told Ingrid and Kimberly that she would return at eleven and asked Jim and Kimberly to look after Ingrid and Karl while she was gone.

Karl told Jim and Kimberly, "We hope you can give us a little time to practice, because we have not played for a while."

Jim said, "I bet you will beat us anyway."

Kimberly told Ingrid "Is it not amazing? We got married last year and spent our honeymoon in the same condo as you are doing now. Juliet was there for us just as she is for you now."

Ingrid said, "I have an idea. What do you think? If we celebrate our first anniversary here and you celebrate your third next year, you know what? We may meet a third couple going through the same routine. Eventually we can have our ex–La Barron club."

"What a great idea. Oh, Ingrid, I love your idea. I think the four of us will enjoy being together every year."

Juliet arrived after they were finished playing. They walked to the soda bar and had nice, tall glasses of orange juice. It was about midday. They all hugged each other, and Kimberly and Jim said good-bye. Juliet asked Karl and Ingrid how they liked Kimberly and Jim. Ingrid said, "We really like them a lot. We played less than we expected, but we had more fun."

Juliet said "I knew you would. I am so glad. Now, we have to plan for tomorrow. You just have to worry about your clothing and personal stuff. Anyway, I will be there to help. I am going to be sailing with you. I will arrange for your lunch or you can go down to the dining room. It will be a change for you. Do not forget you are going back to Montreal in few days. I have to arrange your return trip, and there is so much to do."

Juliet dropped them off and went to her apartment, and Ingrid and Karl went to theirs. Karl asked Ingrid "Is it okay if we take a shower and go to bed?"

Ingrid hugged and kissed Karl. "How did you know what I was thinking? You are so good." They relaxed and later fell asleep.

Ingrid and Karl got up early and got ready to be picked up by Juliet. When Juliet showed up at the condo, both were outside their door with their carrying cases. Juliet was pleasantly surprised. They took off to go to the club, where they met other members who were part of the sailing group. Jim and Kimberly came and joined Juliet, Ingrid, and Karl.

Kimberly hugged Ingrid and said, "It is nice to see you guys. Juliet, are we going to have breakfast here at the club or on the sailboat?"

Juliet replied, "I have been given this program, and it says the embarkation is at nine-thirty. That means we have to wait for another two hours, so let us go and have breakfast."

They went to the club dining room and had their light breakfasts. Everyone was warned not to have a heavy meal in case the water was rough.

When they finished eating, Juliet directed them to the pickup point where buses would take them to the boat. When the bus came close to the embarkation area, the huge boat came into view. Everyone was impressed. They had not expected the size of the boat or the number of its tall white sails. Kimberly and Ingrid could not contain their excitement. They embarked on the boat and saw many neatly dressed young sailors in uniforms; apparently, most of them were students. A couple of these handsome sailors approached Juliet's party and took them for a boat tour.

Ingrid said to her friends, "Are we dreaming this entire scene or it is real?"

Kimberly pinched Ingrid's arm, and Karl did the same. Ingrid said, "Ouch. I think it is real."

They saw the sleeping quarters, a vast spread of nice beds and changing rooms, a large dining area, and the dancing hall.

The boat whistled few times and was towed by a large barge into the open sea. Karl and Ingrid were astonished by how the students climbed high up into the sails and manipulated ropes and wheels. It was amazing. The sailing was fairly smooth. There were at least two hundred passengers and crew members. Karl told Ingrid, "I think we are in fantasy land."

Ingrid was very excited, and Kimberly kept looking at the sailors. She was amazed at their agility and quick action in response to their group leader. Juliet came and asked the couples if they knew what time it was. They all looked at their watches and were surprised to see that it was twelve-thirty. Juliet asked if anyone was hungry. They all said, "Not really."

"The only reason I am asking is that if you do not go now, you will only be served at the two o'clock seating," Juliet responded. Now suddenly all were hungry; they could not wait till that late. Juliet led the way to the dining room, where they were given a table for five. Menus were present at every seat. Ingrid and Kimberly decided that they would order very different dishes and share half of each dish. They enjoyed the food more than usual; maybe it was the happy environment or the ocean breeze, and maybe it was the good cook. After dessert and coffee, they got up and left. The ocean breeze cooled the air, and once again they all went to the deck to see the movements of the sail as they related to the wind direction and the direction of the ship's movement.

The up-and-down motion was an indication of choppy waters. They all started to feel sleepy. Juliet said, "Listen, I don't know about you guys, but I need to go and rest for a while. I will meet you in the dining area at four p.m. How is that?"

They all agreed and headed toward the sleeping quarters. The time passed very quickly; they met in the dining area at four, and everyone commented about how deep their sleep had been.

Ingrid said, "I have not had a sleep like this for a long time." Everyone agreed.

Juliet suggested, "Let's have snacks and coffee in the dining area. And then we had better book our dinner because we want to go the dance hall at ten."

Everyone agreed, and Juliet went to the dining area and booked a table for five. They all went to the deck, where the purser of the boat recognized Juliet and came over to meet the group. When Juliet saw him, she shouted, "Oh, Walter, how nice to see you. It has been a long time." She introduced everyone in her group and told them that Walter had been with the boat for a long time. "Walter, would it be possible for you to take us to the captain's deck?"

"Sure, Juliet We can go now, because the ocean is calm. It is predicted that a depression is coming, and we may not have another chance."

They followed Walter. When they stepped onto the captain's deck, they saw a panoramic scene. The captain came forward. He saw Juliet and said, "I remember you from when you came with the chairman. Anyway, Walter will give you a tour. I am sorry, but I have to organize a team to face the oncoming storm. The weatherman does not know the magnitude of the depression, so we must get ready for the worst."

Walter took them around very fast and asked the group, "Do you like to watch storms?"

Karl said, "We have never witnessed a storm while riding in a boat, but Jim told me that he loves to watch lightning and thunder. What about the girls?"

Ingrid had already discussed the topics with Kimberly, and both had said that when they were with their men, they could bear storms and even enjoy them. After the tour, they came down to the deck and watched the water become choppy.

It was almost seven p.m., and the sun was still bright. They went to the dining room and were just about ready to finish their dessert when the sky suddenly started to turn dark and nasty. The wind picked up, and the boat started to roll. Juliet told them to hold on to the rails and slowly start to walk back to the dancing area, which happened to be in the midsection of the ship. Lots of passengers were told to move there. The band started to play happy tunes to cheer up the passengers. Many started to walk to the only pub, the Bulldog. By now the pub was packed, and some had a little too much and started to act rowdy. With each pitch and roll they fell, and when tried to get up they only fell again. The storm continued for about an hour. Then the wind calmed down, the rain stopped, and daylight peeked through the clouds. The western sky was turning reddish. The boat started to cruise normally.

The band started to play dance music, which attracted a lot of couples. The hall was filled with dancing couples. It was getting late, and Juliet's group decided it was time to go to sleeping area. When they arrived, the lights were dim. By eleven, the lights were out.

Next morning, they washed and dressed and went for breakfast. The boat was heading home to the club. When it arrived at eleven a.m., they all disembarked and headed home. Jim, Kimberly, Karl, and Ingrid hugged each other and Juliet, promising to keep in touch and meet next year, god willing. Juliet looked tired and drove Karl and Ingrid back to their condo.

She said, "Ingrid, I have a lot of work to catch up on. I will see both of you at one p.m. tomorrow, and we will have lunch together."

Juliet showed up at the La Barron dining room at about one and waited for Karl and Ingrid. When they finally arrived, they said they had been so tired that they overslept. Ingrid and Karl ordered hamburgers and French fries. After lunch, Juliet told them, "Do you realize that your train leaves tomorrow at ten-thirty a.m.?"

Ingrid said, "Yes, Karl reminded me last night, so we started to gather our things before going to bed. You could say we are almost packed."

Juliet reminded them, "Your limousine will pick you up at ten. If you want to have a small breakfast here at the dining room, that is fine.

Otherwise, you can eat on the train. I have wired Karl's parents and your friend Norman Rockville Jr. your arrival time and they have already given your new addressed as 581 Ivory Lane in Westmount. I have spoken with the Montreal limo driver, and he assured me that he knows where it is."

Karl thanked Juliet for giving them the best honeymoon. He said, "This week, my dear Juliet, will remain etched in our memory."

He kissed her, and Ingrid said, "Karl, my darling, well said. I love you. Juliet, please convey our sincere our many thanks to the chairman, and thanks to you Juliet for everything."

Ingrid, Karl, and Juliet ordered lunch, drinks, and dessert. They were more tired than hungry. All three got up. Juliet turned and went to her apartment, and Ingrid and Karl entered their condo. They changed, took a hot shower, and changed into their sleeping clothes. The radio was playing soft music. It was five p.m. when they woke up. Both stayed in bed reflecting on and thinking about the last few dream days.

"Karl, promise me to write about the past few days of adventure, the tall ship called *Skipper* and the storm. Write down every detail so that we can show our children how fortunate we were to have such a heavenly honeymoon."

Ingrid was emotional. Karl promised her that he would do it. "So, do you want to make a baby?"

She told him, "You just missed the boat. We will have lots of time, when we reach our new home."

Since they had to get up early in the morning, Karl suggested that they have dinner early and shower that evening so they would not have to rush in the morning. Ingrid agreed and got ready to go to the dining room. As they came out of their condo, they saw Jim and Kimberly coming toward them. Kimberly shouted, "Surprise!" and the two girls hugged and kissed.

Ingrid was happy to see them. Karl said to Jim and Kimberly, "What a nice thing to do. We were almost depressed, but you saved us from depression."

Jim jokingly said, "That's our job! We save friends from depression and oppression." He laughed and recalled that when they had gone home from their honeymoon; they had felt exactly the same way.

"Did you eat yet? If not, let us go eat."

Karl grabbed Jim's arm, and they entered the dining room. While still sitting, they exchanged addresses and phone numbers. Ingrid told

Kimberly, "We are going to our new house. Well, it is not really new. It is an older house at the top of the hill, with a panoramic view of the city. What I was trying to say is that we don't know our phone number."

Jim said, "Listen, both of you, we like you a lot and will keep in touch. Don't forget next year's meeting. Good luck and God bless."

Karl and Ingrid told them, "Till we meet again. And we love you guys for coming down."

Jim and Kimberly left, and Ingrid and Karl went back to their place and got ready to go to bed. The next morning, they were ready to be picked up at nine-thirty when Juliet knocked at the door. The porter took their luggage, and Juliet sat with them in the back of the limousine. When it arrived at the station, they walked toward their coach, where the stationmaster and conductor were waiting to receive them. The stationmaster gave a big bouquet of yellow roses to Ingrid. She kissed him and thanked him for the Florida railroad's hospitality. It was almost ten. The conductor and Juliet escorted Karl and Ingrid to their car.

Juliet hugged both Karl and Ingrid and said, "I am going to miss you a lot."

Ingrid told her to write to them and keep in touch. They all left, and the conductor blew the whistle twice. The train started to move slowly and gradually picked up speed.

They had ordered breakfast to be served in their car. They were hungry, and they had gone to bad late last night. Both Karl and Ingrid wanted to eat their breakfast and go to sleep. Breakfast came and Ingrid told Karl, "I am really enjoying my breakfast. I enjoyed the toasted bread with jam and cheese."

Karl agreed and told her that for some reason, the coffee had seemed unusually delicious. They finished their breakfast, placed the tray in the entrance area, and went to the bedroom. The room was fairly cool because incoming air was chilled by an ingenious cooling system. Ingrid and Karl were fast asleep very quickly.

It was four p.m. when they got up. They stayed in bed enjoying light music. For the first time, the telephone next to their bed rang.

Ingrid picked up the phone and shouted, "Karl, it is Norman Junior! What a surprise, Norm. How did you get this number?"

Norman said, "Forget about the number. Tell me, how was Florida and your honeymoon? Sybille wants to know if you had a good time."

Ingrid replied, "Norm, the last few days have been amazing, talk to

Karl, I guess he missed you. Actually, we both missed you and Sybille."
She passed the phone to Karl.

Norm Jr. asked again, "Karl, did you have a good time?"

Karl said "Norm, the last few days were the best. We went on an overnight journey in one of those giant tall ships with dozens of sails. The ship was called *Skipper*. I have to tell you, it was an experience of a lifetime. Norm, when we arrive in our new house, are you and Sybille going to be there? How is your sweetheart?"

Norm responded, "Oh yes, we and others will be here to receive Ingrid and you, so you'd better sleep a lot tonight. See you tomorrow. Good-bye."

Ingrid and Karl were happy to hear Norm's voice and glad that he and Sybille would be at the house tomorrow. "Karl, do you realize we have not seen our house yet? It was so nice of our parents to do that. I am really very anxious to see our house and more so to see the furniture and decorations."

Railway manager arranges a farewell dinner

One of the men from the conductor's office brought a card inviting Ingrid and Karl as guests of honor at the conductor's table.

"It was really nice of the railway to do that," Ingrid said. "Karl, I think you'd better wear your formal suit, and I am going to wear your favorite long dress, you know that one with green and pink flowers. What you think, Karl?"

Karl replied, "Ingrid, you know my darling, you look good in anything you wear. You look good even when you don't wear anything."

She ran to catch him and pushed him onto the bed. She then jumped on him, saying, "You are bad." They laughed and played more and were happy.

Dinnertime was approaching, and they started to get ready. When Karl saw his new bride dressed like a princess, he said, "Wow, my darling, you look delicious." He picked her up and kissed her. It was very spontaneous. Ingrid started to cry. "Ingrid, why are you spoiling your beautiful eyes? We have to go now." She apologized and wiped her tiny tears. They stepped out of their condo and found a neatly dressed boy waiting with a bouquet of red roses. Karl said, "Hello, what is your name? Are these flowers for me?"

The boy replied, "No, sir, they are for Mrs. Schoulz. My name is Justin, and I am supposed to escort you to the dining room. Please follow me."

They followed the boy, and as they entered the dining room, all the guests and dining room staff stood up and cheered them. They were pleasantly surprised; they had not expected such a reception. There were at least twenty-five guests, plus journalists, photographers, and the host himself, Bernard Landry, along with the dining room staff. Karl and Ingrid waved and thanked them. The young boy, Justin, took them to the conductor's table, and Conductor Bernard Landry shook hands with them and asked them to sit down. Photographers were working hard as they entered the room.

When everyone was quiet, Bernard got up and said, "I will like to say a few words before we start our dinner. I want to thank our guests for coming at a short notice and giving us this opportunity to say good-bye and good luck. Mr. Karl Schoulz and Mrs. Ingrid Schoulz have been model guests whom we were proud to serve. We have had a pleasure serving our Canadian guests, especially because they represented Chairman Heber. As you know, the love affair between Chairman, as we call him and Florida has been going on for some time. This spirit of neighborly respect and love has brought our nations together; I hope this relationship continues for generations to come. I apologize for not informing you in advance about the press and the photographers. If you have any objection, we can change that. Thank you."

Karl got up and thanked Bernard Landry, the stationmaster, and the railway corporation. "I must admit, I am proud of the fact that Chairman Heber happens to be my father's good friend and longtime college buddy. In our opinion, Chairman deserves to be an honorary ambassador representing both countries because he loves both countries equally. As far as the press is concerned, we have no objections as long as they let us go to our car early. I understand tomorrow is going to be very busy."

Everyone cheered, and the cameras started to click. Bernard Landry stood up and offered a toast. Everyone raised their glasses. Bernard said, "Here is to a lovely couple. May God bless them and give them love and happiness."

The guests were genuinely happy for Ingrid and Karl. There was a question and answer period. Then the press representative thanked Ingrid and Karl for their cooperation and sat down. Bernard requested all to sit down, and announced, "We will be serving dinner. Dinner was served, and everyone enjoyed the evening. Karl and Ingrid got up from the table and waited till the clapping stopped. "We would like to take this opportunity to thank Bernard Landry, the chef, and the train staff for such an excellent service." There were more cameras flashing and cheers from Bernard, the chef, and the service staff that had gathered in the room.

Ingrid and Karl went out. It was already nine-thirty, and by the time they were ready to go to sleep, it was ten-thirty. Ingrid asked Karl, "Karl, I was just trying to decide. If someone gave me a choice between staying in our new home and going to Florida in this heat on our honeymoon, what would my decision have been? Before I answer that question, you tell me your answer."

"My dear Ingrid, if you want the truth, I would say I would have stayed in our new home. Now you have to tell me your answer, even though I know yours."

Ingrid was happy that her answer was the same. "Karl I am so glad we think alike." They slowly drifted into a sound sleep.

Morning came, and the sun was bright. The train slowed down, and a service person came to the door. Karl got up and went to the door.

"Sir would you like your breakfast here?" the young girl asked.

"Yes, please." Karl was still sort of sleepy. Ingrid wanted to know who it was. Karl told her that breakfast would be here soon and they should get ready. "Ingrid, you know, we are already in the vicinity of Montreal."

Ingrid was very excited. "We will be home soon, and I can't wait." The girls brought two trays of breakfast, but Ingrid and Karl were too anxious and excited to sit down properly or have breakfast peacefully. They finished their tea and went to the window, saying to each other, "Look at that. Remember that bridge? And you see how many signs are in French? We should be very near the train station."

INGRID AND KARL ARRIVE IN MONTREAL

It did not take too long before the train entered the railway station and they felt at home. In the meantime, porters came around and started to bring their luggage out of the compartment. Ingrid and Karl picked up their things and came out; hoping that maybe NRJ and Sybille would be there on the platform. The only thing they saw was a limousine waiting at the end of the platform. Soon enough, the train came to a stop, and all the porters in their red uniforms ran around to organize their passengers' departures. The Montreal stationmaster was waiting at the first-class coach location and had been informed earlier about the arrival of Chairman Heber's guests.

The train came to a complete stop, and the conductor escorted Ingrid and Karl to the platform, where the stationmaster, Mr. Believe, was waiting. Bernard Landry introduced them to the stationmaster. After the formalities, they were taken to the waiting limousine. Their luggage was already there. It was a nice day, and warmer than usual; the limousine drove freely without encountering traffic problems. It climbed the little hills of Westmount and arrived at 581 Ivory Lane. As the vehicle arrived at the door, NRJ, Sybille, and Karl's parents came out to greet them. Krista hugged them and said, "Welcome to your new home. May you have peace and happiness in this house?"

Karl and Ingrid thanked Krista and Father Norman. When they were inside, Norman Junior and Sybille gave a bouquet of roses to Ingrid. Mrs. Morgan came and kissed both of them. Ingrid and Karl looked around the hall, admiring the decor and the color of the walls. They were delighted to see the furniture, drapes, and decorations. Norm Jr. said, "I know you are not tired, so we will give you a little tour of the place. I have to tell you, Sybille had a big hand in decorating. Ingrid, come here. You can see the city down below, especially at night. It is a sight to see. Sybille loves it. As a matter of fact, everyone loves the place."

Ingrid and Karl hugged and kissed Sybille and NRJ. Mrs. Morgan came and asked everyone to come and have little snack, so they went to the kitchen and its attached eating area. Ingrid said, "How cute! Look at the appliances and the light fixtures."

They sat down at the dining table, and Mrs. Morgan set up lunch for Karl's parents, Ingrid, Karl, NRJ, and Sybille. She sat next to Ingrid at the table. Ingrid's admiration for Sybille was much higher now than before.

Sybille told Ingrid, "Ingrid, you know, Norman Junior missed both of you. He was almost ready to go to Florida just to see his friends. I must say, I missed you too, because arranging the drapes, beds, and furniture in your house made me feel so close to you. You know, I have taken a one-year leave of absence from my singing engagements. My program director and his organization had booked me fourteen concert tours in Milan, Zurich, Berlin, and few other cities. I did not mind working when I was not attached and was free, but now how can I leave NRJ, my love? On top of that, they booked five recording sessions at different studios for me.

"I was in Paris to sing at a fund-raising concert for the university. Strangely enough, that is where I met Norman Junior. You will never believe how that happened. I will tell you later. I had a prior appointment to meet my father in Paris. He could see that there was something different. He asked me, 'Sybille, what is happening? You seem to be too anxious. Your behavior is not the same.' I told him, 'Papa, believe it or not, I think I am in love.' My papa was so happy for me. He started to ask all kinds of questions, so I explained to him about my NRJ and how we met. I told him that I had never felt so painfully strong about someone. It seems that nature or some power had programmed our destiny. This happened before I accepted his offer to come to the wedding."

Karl and NRJ were wondering what Ingrid and Sybille were talking about. They had not touched their lunch and seemed to ignore everybody else. Finally, NRJ spoke up. "Hey, what are you two talking about? It looks so serious. Sybille, you and Ingrid have ignored me and Karl."

Both Sybille and Ingrid apologized. "We were talking about each other's backgrounds. Sybille was telling me about how the two of you met."

Everyone went back to having lunch, and Ingrid started to tell the group about their Florida honeymoon. She told Karl's father, "Dad, your friend Chairman Heber is such a huge figure among the businessmen and professionals that they regard him as the savior of Florida's tourist industry. And you should see his contributions to art, education, and museums."

After lunch they moved to the living room, and Ingrid told Sybille, "The more I talk to you, the more I want to know you."

Karl said, "Sybille, the way you sang at the reception, I can see why every country in the world wants to hear you. How lucky Norman Junior is."

NRJ told everyone, "You know, she has decided to cancel all but three concerts. The program directors think that she must be sick, and you know why? It's just because she wants us to be together. She really has made my life worth living. Sybille is going to sing in Paris next month on the same dates as I will be opening my show, and she convinced her directors to sponsor my art show on the same dates as her engagement at the Paris opera house."

Sybille hugged and kissed NRJ. Karl's father said, "You know, you are one couple in the world that God has given a wonderful gift of art in every direction. Krista and I were discussing and visualizing the children of two extreme artists. We hope we will still be here to see them."

It was almost dinner time. Ingrid asked Karl, NRJ, and Sybille, "You know, we have been sitting here for so long. Can we go for a walk? The weather is perfect."

Karl's parents decided to go with the young couples. Krista asked Norman Junior if they were staying for dinner. Karl answered his mother, "Yes, Ma, they will."

They all went out. The streets were not very wide, and they wound downhill. It was easy to go down, and Karl thought about his parents. "Ma and Dad, I don't think it is a good idea to continue because when you go back to the house it will be hard to climb up. I will come back to the house with you."

His father Norman said, "Karl, we can go back. You stay with the rest, but even you should not be going down too far."

So Dr. Norman and Krista started to go back home, and they realized that Karl had been right. Krista was really tired when she arrived home. Dr. Norman was a veteran as far as walks were concerned, and in his hunts for herbs and plants, he used to walk miles in all kinds of weather. When they arrived, Krista had to sit down in a recliner and almost fell asleep. An hour passed before all four entered the house, feeling good. Sybille and Ingrid were still talking, and in the meantime, Karl and Norman Jr. were reminiscing about their good times in their school days.

Ingrid asked, "Sybille, Norman Jr. was saying that both of you would be flying to Paris, where Norman will be opening his art show and you will be starring in the opera *Nabucco*."

Sybille answered, "Ingrid, yes, that is correct. Next month, we will be in Paris for one week, and we will be back in Montreal for the International Expo, where Norman's art deco furniture will be exhibited. He, along with his firm, has been building and manufacturing 1930s art deco furniture especially for the expo." Sybille continued, "And our next trip will be to introduce my Norman Rockville Jr. to my father and family. I have only one concert to attend in Madrid. The local opera house will be playing *Madame Butterfly*, and I have the leading role. After that, we will have a week of free time, which we will spend in my father's condominium. I have an idea: you can come for few days and stay with us in our condo in Majorca. I have to tell you so much about my mother, my grandfathers, and my grandmothers."

Ingrid wanted to talk to Karl and NRJ about the idea. "Karl and Norm, can we talk to both of you, please?"

Norman replied, "Finally you have some time to talk to us."

They both came and sat very close to Norm and Karl. Sybille asked, looking at both of them, "I have suggested to Ingrid that next month that after we are finished with my singing and Norm has met my family, she and Karl come to Majorca and spend two nights with us."

Norm said, "What an excellent idea. So what do you think, Karl?"

"It is okay with me. It is up to Ingrid."

Ingrid jumped with joy and said, "Karl, let us do it."

Sybille was so excited that she kissed everyone, saying, "Thank you, thank you."

It was getting late, and Norman Junior suggested to Sybille that they go home. As they were leaving, Karl told Norm, "Tomorrow, Mom and Dad will sleep in their home, so it will be nice if both of you came to have dinner with us and sleep here. I know we are enjoying talking to each other, so what do you think?"

Everyone agreed to see each other the next day. Norm told Karl to say good-bye to his father and mother, who were now fast asleep. Karl and Ingrid were tired and went to sleep without any trouble.

The next day, Mrs. Morgan was still there helping Ingrid adjust to the new situation. "Here is the kitchen. I will show you the best way to prepare a cooking schedule for the whole week."

Mrs. Morgan showed Ingrid the tricks of the trade. She showed Ingrid the way lunch and dinner menus were prepared and how she prepared a grocery list. Today would be Ingrid's first day to go grocery shopping. Mrs. Morgan was happy to see that Ingrid was taking interest in what she was showing and doing; she let her stir-fry the veggies Chinese style.

She asked Mrs. Morgan, "I wonder how long I am going to need to get used to all this every day."

Mrs. Morgan replied, "If you have some desire and interest to learn, between you, me, and Krista Schoulz, you will be good in about one month. Luckily, you have free time between now and then."

The doorbell rang, and Karl received Sybille and Norman Junior. Ingrid came running to meet them. Sybille said, "Something smells really good."

Ingrid said, "I guess it is the Chinese stir-fry that Mrs. Morgan allowed me to do."

They sat down in the living room. Karl asked, "What would you like to drink? Can I get you a fruit juice?" Ingrid told Karl that she would be glad to bring the drinks.

Ingrid sat with Sybille. She told her, "You look so good, Sybille. I love your choice of colors in dresses. Remember how you told me about your trip to three big cities? I know the first one was Paris and the second was Madrid, where we will be your guest for few days, but which was the third city?"

Sybille replied, "That will be Moscow, the city where I was brought up, educated, and loved by four important people in my life, my grandfather, my grandma, my dad, and my mother." She started to choke. Her voice was hard to hear, and she could not help crying. Norm got up and hugged her, almost lifting her in his arms. Sybille's pink cheeks were wet with tears, but now in Norman's arms she was quiet.

He said to Ingrid and Karl, "Every time she talks about her mother, this is what happens."

Sybille was coming out of the situation, and Ingrid was afraid to ask her any more about her family.

Sybille said, "I am sorry I became too emotional. It is hard for me to talk about my mother. When I have a little time, I will complete my story about my father, Russia, and my mother's family. I will mail you the story as soon as possible, I promise."

Mrs. Morgan came into the room and asked them to have dinner, saying, "I am sure you all must be hungry." They finished their dinner and, before leaving, thanked Mrs. Morgan for a delicious meal.

Days passed. Ingrid was enjoying cooking more and more, especially when Karl was helping her in the kitchen. Karl's mother and father visited them every now and then. The day came when Sybille and Norm were ready to fly to Paris; they drove to Karl's place and decided to leave their car there. Karl and Ingrid were ready to take them to the airport. When they came back from the airport, they just wanted to relax on the sofa and talk.

Chapter 13
Rumors about Quebec separation

Ingrid said to Karl, "I don't know what to do about my studies. Should I go back and finish my master's degree or just wait and see what happens? You were saying that there are some rumors about Quebec separation and nationalism."

"Yes, I know, it is difficult to plan your life under these circumstances. You know who can advise us better?. Let's go and see my parents."

Ingrid agreed with Karl's idea. She told him that she still had a few months to decide. She asked Karl, "Now that you are a full professor, when do your classes start?"

Karl explained that sometime in August, he would meet with his department head and the retiring professor he was replacing to find out the exact date. "It appears that we will be in Spain in early August on a weekend. That looks all right. Now, don't forget, I have to prepare for my classes. I will do that when we come back from Spain. Ingrid, let us go out to eat. You don't have to cook tonight."

Ingrid came to him and kissed him. "That would be nice."

A few days later, Karl and Ingrid drove to the airport to pick up Sybille and Norman Jr. They were glad to see each other; they went back to Karl's place and stayed till dinnertime. Ingrid told Sybille that they had gone to a restaurant called Bona Petite. "It's really nice, if you like Italian food."

Norman said, "That is a good idea." It was already night, and Norman told Sybille, "Look, Sybille, you can see the city lighted up. This is what I like about this house."

Sybille agreed with Norm. Sybille addressed Ingrid, "You remember when you were asking what city we would be in after Spain? As I told you, it will be Moscow. There I will be singing for three nights in an opera called *Anna Karenina*. We will be at my grandparents' house. They are looking forward to it, and so am I."

It was getting late, so they all kissed and said good night; Ingrid and Karl came outside with Sybille and Norm. Sybille told Ingrid, "I will call you in couple of days. I have to practice my part in the opera. This is the first time I will be playing the part of Madame Butterfly, although I have played other roles in the opera before, and I am a little nervous. Norm is also going to be really busy. The Paris show was a big success for him, and he sold lot of art deco furniture that he promised to ship in two months' time."

They said good night and left. Karl showed Ingrid the big moon. The air was just right, and a smell of orange blossoms was in the air. Karl put his arms around Ingrid and kissed her behind her ears, and they walked hand in hand inside the house. They sat in the living room for a while and looked at the city lights. Ingrid said, "Karl, how wonderful it is to be near you, touching you and kissing you. How fortunate we are to have this lovely house, decorated by the best artists."

Karl agreed, "Yes, my love, you are right." They changed to go to bed and headed towards their bedroom.

The next day, Karl called his parents and told them he and Ingrid would like to come down and take them out for lunch. Krista told her son, "That will be nice. We have not seen you for more than a week. See you soon."

Ingrid and Karl arrived at his parents' house. Karl's father and mother hugged them. Norman said, "Karl, if I knew that I would not see you for more than a week, I would not have given you the house."

Karl and Ingrid laughed, and he said, "It is too late now, Dad and Mom. I am sorry. I promise to call often and visit more often." It was getting close to lunch time; both Norman and Krista were ready. Karl and Ingrid took them to their favorite restaurant. As they were waiting for the waiter to arrive, Karl turned to his father and asked, "Dad, there is something Ingrid asked me about. I could not give her an answer, so I told her that the best person to ask was my dad."

Norman was curious. He asked, "Is it something to do with old age?"

Karl lowered his voice and said, "What she wants to know is whether she should go back to finish her graduate work here. She has heard about the political situation in Quebec, and these rumors are getting louder and louder. I thought you have inside political contacts who would know better than us."

They saw their drinks and food coming. Norman raised his hand and said, "Let us eat now. We will discuss this subject at home. And if you sleep at our place, we can not only solve the problem but also make a plan without waiting too long."

They enjoyed their meal, but as Karl and Ingrid looked at Norman and then at Krista, they saw that their eyes and expressions seemed to warn of danger ahead. Before they got up to leave, Silvia, the owner, came to see his favorite client. They said good night and left.

They started to discuss the political situation in the car. Dr. Norman told Ingrid and Karl, "Karl, you are right; the talks are turning into plans of action among young men and women. I know one student of political history who is not even Canadian, but he is married to a French Canadian and has few children from her. He met me near the French university. He was talking with fire in his eyes. He has just come back from Cuba, where he was trained by Che Guevara, the famous socialist."

Everyone was silent; even Krista was astonished. Karl and Ingrid asked, "So, Dad, what are we going to do?"

Chapter 15

RUMORS OF QUEBEC SEPARATION FROM CANADA

Norman became very serious and told Karl, Ingrid, and Krista, "Let us go into the house. I will show you my plan of action. And by the way, you must follow this plan starting tomorrow. I forgot to remind you that the visit of General De Gaulle to Quebec started this separation mania, when he addressed our French citizens with the famous phrase 'libber Quebec.'"

Krista, Karl, and Ingrid all said, "Yes, we remember him saying that. It was so irresponsible of him."

Norman gave Karl the card of a real estate agent. "Tell him to put both your and our house on sale immediately and instruct him not to place any sale signs on the properties. Do not under any circumstances give him the real reason for selling. The second immediate task is to contact your professor friend in Toronto and tell him you want to join his university as a professor. Here, you can give him the reason. Fax him your application, addressed to the head of the mathematics department. Here is the dean of the faculty's name and address."

They all looked at each other. Ingrid was in tears. "Dad, I loved our house so much."

Norman, Karl, and Krista all were sad about what was happening. Karl took Ingrid in his arms and told her, "If we do not do this now, we will probably lose everything. Property values will go down, and there will not be many who would want to buy?"

Norman told Krista and Ingrid, "I promise you and Krista that we will buy a better and bigger house later. If we act now, when not many people know the situation, the market will still be good here. The market in Toronto is still reasonable, too."

Karl asked his mother, "Mom, do you understand what Dad is trying to say?"

Krista answered, "I know, my son. I know what is at stake here. Karl, what about Norman Jr.? He does not know what is going on. He has a big studio, a manufacturing facility, his clients, and his workers. Are you going to tell him to move?"

Norman asked Ingrid, "How about you, Ingrid? Do you understand?"

"Yes, Dad, I understand. I am still sad to lose the house with all the decorations and the furniture."

Karl tried to reassure her. "We will take everything when we move. We'll bring all your furniture, the drapes, and whatever you want."

Norman told Karl to call Norman Jr. and ask him to come for breakfast the next morning with Sybille. It was getting late, and Karl and Ingrid went to Karl's old room and soon went to sleep. Karl got up early the next morning and went downstairs. Krista and Karl's father were already there. Karl waited till eight while his mother made some biscuits and coffee.

When Norm Jr. and Sybille arrived, the family was sitting in the eating area, and Krista had made pancakes, favorites of both Karl and Norman Jr. They sat down. Krista and Dr. Norman said that after the meal, there were important things to discuss. When they were finished with their pancakes, Norm Jr. could not hold his curiosity anymore.

"Uncle Norm, I am nervous. Please tell us what is going on."

Norman explained the situation to both Sybille and Norm Jr., and Karl told them that as of tomorrow, their houses would be on the market and they planned to move to Toronto as soon as possible. Both Norm Jr. and Sybille were astounded the speed at which Schoulz family was moving.

Dr. Norman told Norm Jr., "You don't have to panic. Luckily, you do not own any property, right? Whatever you have is rented. Before the situation gets worse, I will formulate a plan that will take care of you and all your assets, like your art gallery, your office, and your workshop. We will be there for you. It is only a six-hour drive to Toronto."

Norman Jr. wanted to know, "Uncle, so what do I do now? What about tomorrow?"

Karl said, "Norm, Dad has a plan for you that will be executed when Ingrid and I go to Toronto. I will get a job and buy a house, a big house suitable for two families. We will look for a house for you and your family, and then you and Sybille can come down and see if you approve. Otherwise, we look for some more until you and Sybille find one you do like."

Sybille said, "Norm, I think what Uncle and Karl are planning makes sense. In the meantime, we just continue to do what our plan calls for. Am I right?"

Everyone agreed. Norm Jr. told his uncle, "So, we will leave now. We have so much to do. We must prepare for the expo show, go to Spain for a week, come back, and work again. Thank God I have very good help from Sybille for mental health and my group of artists for the workshop. I leave our fate with you, Aunty, and you, Uncle Norm. Karl and Ingrid, we do want to go where ever you go."

They hugged and kissed everyone and left. That day, Karl called the real estate agent and told him that his family wanted to sell both houses. He asked the agent to come down to his house to discuss the details of the sales. He and Ingrid were still at his father's house. When he finished talking to the agent, Norman said, "Karl, call him back and tell him to come over here. I know some information about asking prices and other details you may not know." Karl called back the agent and gave him his father's address.

Time was passing. Both houses were sold within the month, and closing was to take place the same week for both houses. Both Ingrid and Karl were in Toronto, staying with his friend Robert Gamble, who was a senior professor at the university. Robert had arranged interviews for Karl and introduced him to some senior members of the board. The dean of the mathematics faculty and others were impressed with his credentials. Karl was appointed as a senior professor, and Ingrid was accepted in the department of botany to do her graduate work. The university was offering her a grant to work on her selected field of "Nature's fragrances."

Karl's parents were delighted to hear the outcome of their effort. Karl called Norman Jr. and gave him the good news. Sybille talked to Ingrid to congratulate her and asked her, "Did you see any houses that you liked?"

Ingrid was dying to tell Sybille about a big house she had seen. "Sybille, you have to see this place; it is so great and charming. It is in a very nice neighborhood with tall trees and a superb garden. You will love it. Not only that, but we found a smaller house behind our house, a real beauty with a rose garden in the front yard. Karl's parents are coming, and they want both of you to come with them."

Sybille asked, "Did you say, 'the small house is behind our house'? Does that mean you already bought the house?"

Ingrid answered, "Sybille, no we did not, not without showing Karl's parents and both of you. Mind you, I wish we had, I like it so much. Karl said that the houses here are not too expensive yet."

NRJ came on the line. "I hear you found one for us too. I will talk to Uncle and see when they want to come. Maybe we can come this weekend. Karl, talk to your father. Hopefully we will see you soon."

Karl and NJR both talked to Dr. Norman and Krista and finalized their arrival in Toronto. Krista did not want to go by car because of the time and stress required. "Let us go by air," she said to NRJ. "Your uncle wants to know if we can leave tomorrow morning."

So they decided to leave by morning flight. NRJ called Karl and asked him to pick them up at the airport. He gave Karl their flight number and time of arrival.

Karl borrowed his friend's van, and he and Ingrid picked up their guests at the airport and took them to the real estate agent's office. The agent took them to the big house. Krista, Norm, NRJ, and Sybille all loved the location, the house, and, best of all, the garden with a manicured lawn. The agent told them, "Did you know that the average temperature in Toronto about four degrees higher than in Montreal, summer and winter?"

Dr. Norman asked about possession date. The agent told him that the owners didn't presently live in the house, having moved to Europe, "So possession date is your choice."

Karl and NRJ looked at each other and at Dr. Norman. The agent warned them that this property had just come onto the market and would not last long. Father Norman asked the agent to give them some privacy to discuss the issue. When they got together, Dr. Norman and Krista asked, "Tell us, do you like this place?" The children unanimously said, "Yes, we love it."

Krista asked Norman, "Norm, what about you?"

He said, "Me too. What about you, Krista?"

Karl said, "Me too."

The decision was made. They went to the agent's office and signed the papers, and Karl called his friend to find out the name of his lawyer. The transaction took only couple of hours. Dr. Norman was an experienced home buyer, so he wrote down all the conditions necessary to ensure a safe and sound house.

Sybille and NRJ were anxious to see their house, which was just behind Karl's. They walked over.

Sybille looked at Ingrid. "You were right; it is a doll house. Everything outside is just perfect. Norm, what are you thinking?"

"I was just thinking how am I going to take care of the garden?"

She said, "The gardener will, of course."

They stood outside admiring the heavy, embossed front door, which was painted light green. Inside, the floor was covered with white marble tiles, set tight to each other. The hall opened to a decent-sized living room adorned by a shining baby grand piano. That was the selling point for Sybille; she went to the piano and started playing. She was surprised at the sound quality. Norm Jr. said, "I guess Ingrid and Sybille both want this house. It is in a good neighborhood, and as luck would have it, it could not be any closer to your house, Karl."

Sybille was enchanted with the house and the piano. She asked Uncle Norman, "Can we include the piano, the oriental carpets, and other items that Norm Junior may want?"

"Sybille, the agent told me that Mr. Sims's wife passed away two months ago, and his son has arranged for his father to move to a senior home, so everything is on sale. Sure, we can include all the items in the offer. You will not get a better bargain like this anywhere, so get together with Norm Junior, Ingrid, and Krista."

The girls started to go from room to room, making a list of items they wanted to purchase. Karl and NRJ both went over the list and made some adjustments. Norman Schoulz gave the list to the agent and asked him to prepare the offer papers while they went to lunch. They went to a restaurant close by and returned in one hour. The papers were signed by both Sybille Savera and Norman Rockville Junior. Norman Schoulz shook hands with the agent and told him to get in touch with him if needed. They all left to join Karl's friend Robert Gamble at his house. Robert had already made reservations in a hotel for them to spend the night. Norman Schoulz gave Robert his real estate agent's card and asked him to check with him on the status of the offer. Robert invited everyone into his house for snacks and coffee. He introduced his wife and his two boys, aged four and six. They all enjoyed the evening. At almost six p.m., Robert's phone rang. It was the agent. He brought the phone to Father Norman. The agent said, "Mr. Schoulz, I have been running around to get both of these offers accepted. The good news is that both offers, with all conditions, were accepted. But there is a problem with the possession of the smaller house located at 61 Jasmine Crescent. This house will not be ready for occupancy, because Mr. Sims will not be able to get into the senior residence before December first. The big house, well, you can have the occupancy at the end of next month as per your offer."

Norman Schoulz praised the agent for his fast work. Norman told his party that he needed to know their decisions immediately because they were flying back to Montreal tomorrow. He said, "I think it worked. Congratulations to you all."

The agent said good night and hung up. Norman Schoulz asked Robert, "Can I ask you to follow up with your lawyer and let us know if everything was okay?"

Karl told his father, "Dad, you must be tired. Let us go and eat." They all agreed, thanked Robert and his family for their hospitality, and said good night. Karl had called a taxi, which had just arrived. They left Robert's place and arrived at the hotel. Karl asked the taxi driver to pick them up in the morning at seven. They were tired and checked in to the hotel. After a fairly decent meal, they all went to sleep.

The Schoulz family, Norman Junior, and Sybille arrived in Montreal, picked up their car from the parking area, and drove off to Karl's father's house. Mrs. Morgan was waiting for the family's arrival; she had prepared a good brunch for all. They all sat down at the dining table. Karl told his father, "Dad, it is funny. The agent told me that in the last few weeks, there have been hundreds of calls every day from Montreal asking for residential and industrial properties. Tell me what is going on."

Norm Schoulz told everyone, "You see what I told you? What we did yesterday was the best for all of us, and believes me, it is not finished yet."

Norman Junior and Sybille expressed their amazement at his foresight and prompt action. Norman Jr., Sybille, and Ingrid went to Father Norman and thanked him for his guidance.

Sybille said, "It is unbelievable that you are getting occupancy of your house when you need it and we are getting possession when we need it."

Krista asked Norman Jr., "Norm, can you once again tell us what is happening in your life? I know you have to go to Spain to meet Sybille's father and family. Is that next week? I don't know anymore; things are happening so fast. Sybille, I don't know if Norm told you about our relationship, but I will tell you. Norm is my sister's son, and we treat both Karl and Norm Jr. as our children."

Father Norman said, "Yes, that is a fact."

Both Ingrid and Sybille hugged Krista, and there were tears in the girls' eyes. Sybille thanked Krista for clarifying the situation. "I wanted to ask Norm but did not know how to go about it. Thanks again."

Krista continued her line of thought. "Let me ask you, and I will be blunt. Both of you are so happy together. What is your intention? You are going to Spain to meet Sybille's parents and buying a house together, and so far I have not heard anything about marriage. I don't understand, Norm. My son, tell me if I am out of line."

Chapter 15

NORMAN ROCKVILLE WANTS SYBILLE TO MARRY HIM

Norman Jr. got up and said, "Aunty, you are so smart and loving. Today you have given me my courage back. I have been ready for this for some time." He walked to Sybille's chair, took out a red velvet box, and knelt before Sybille, saying, "I would love you to be my wife. Would you marry me?"

Sybille put her arms around him, Norm got up from the floor, and Sybille started to cry and smile at the same time. So did Ingrid and Krista.

Sybille was quite surprised by the way Norm had proposed. It was the sweetest shock. Sybille said, "Norm, my love, I will, I will." They hugged, and all gathered around the newly engaged couple. Mrs. Morgan congratulated Krista for her role in this romantic affair. Father Norman asked Mrs. Morgan if she could find a champagne bottle. Mrs. Morgan gave the bottle to Karl and Krista.

Krista said to Karl, "My son, do the honors for your best friend and brother." Karl opened the bottle; the cork popped out with a bang. Father Norman presented a toast to the couple and wished those lots of luck, love, and patience. "May your beautiful children be even better artists?"

The friends teased, joked, and laughed together. Norman Jr. could not believe his luck. In twenty-four hours, he and Sybille had gotten a house and a diamond ring. Sybille said, "Norman, you gave me the ring box, but you did not put the ring on my finger."

Everyone said to Sybille, "You'd better check the box. Maybe there is no ring in the box."

Sybille picked up the box from the table and opened it. It was empty. Everyone was quiet for one moment and said, "Shame on you, Norm."

Poor Sybille was embarrassed. Norm sensed the danger and took out another box immediately. "Oh, my darling, I took out the wrong box." Norman Jr. took out a ring from the new box. There was a big diamond as bright as the North Star. He held Sybille's hand and slipped it on her finger. Sybille was emotional; she had not expected to be wearing a ring.

Norman Jr. said, "I am sorry. I forgot which pocket had the empty box and which had the ring."

Sybille got up and kissed Norman Jr. Ingrid, Krista, and Mrs. Morgan came and looked at the ring, admiring the brilliant diamond.

Ingrid told Sybille, "Sybille, you deserve this and more. I am so happy for you."

Sybille asked Father Norman, "Uncle, what is the time in Madrid?"

Norman looked at his watch and said, "It is six p.m."

"Can I call my father and tell him the good news?"

Norman gave her the phone, and she called her father. Peter Savera answered. "Hello, Sybille how is you?"

"I am here at Uncle Norman's house, and my Norman just asked me to marry him, and I said yes."

Her father called his wife, and Sybille's grandmother. They all started to sing. Peter talked to Norm Jr. and told him that he was lucky to have Sybille, who loved him so much. He wished them good luck.

Sybille sat down near NRJ; finally, she was calm and relaxed. They both went first to thank Krista for her lovely intervention. Norm told Krista, "Thank you, Aunty. You saved my life again."

Father Norman, Karl, and Ingrid hugged and kissed good night. When Sybille and Karl left, everyone waved good-bye at the main door.

When Sybille and Norm arrived at their condo, she asked Norm to figure out what time it would be in Moscow. He calculated mentally and said, "I think it is nine a.m."

Sybille went to the phone and called her grandparents. "Is that you, my Sybille? We thought you had forgotten about us."

"No, Nana, I dream of you and Grandma almost every day. I have good news, Nana. Tell Grandma that I am engaged to a wonderful, charming, and very talented man. His name is Norman."

Grandma came to the phone and said to Sybille, "Finally you fell in love. Oh, my Sybille, you deserve it. Your grandpa is so happy. When do you think you will get married?"

"Grandma, the date we are thinking of is the last Saturday of November. The place will be my papa's house in Spain. Grandma, the weather in Spain is beautiful then. You will love it. Make sure you come; my papa and our family will be so happy. They love you both."

Sybille was talking to her grandparents in Russian. Norm was curious. He asked her, "Tell me what they said! Are they coming to the wedding?"

She told Norm that they thought she had forgotten them. "I am sure they will not miss my wedding. Oh, Norm, they are so wonderful. You will like them too. They do speak English, but not very fluently."

She and Norm were mentally and physically exhausted. They went to sleep.

Time was passing fast. Dr. Norman Schoulz called and told Norm Jr. that the semi-industrial unit he had rented in Toronto for Norm's furniture manufacturing was ready to run. The machines and equipment were installed and running. "Your manager and artisans are here and happy. When are you going to Spain?"

Norm answered, "We will be in Spain in two days' time. Sybille is excited, and I am too."

Dr. Norman's family moves to Toronto

"By the way, Uncle, how did you make out on your move? No surprises?"

"Norm, your aunty wants to talk to you. Here, talk to her."

"Aunty, how do you like your new house? Is everything set?"

"Yes, Norm. It is peaceful, and the garden and everything are just nice. Your brother Karl is already missing you. As a matter of fact, we are all missing you and Sybille."

When Sybille and Norm arrived in Spain, all the family was there at the airport. Norm and Sybille were received like royalty. Sybille's papa and stepmother along with her grandfather and grandmother were there. Sybille introduced Norman Jr. to her father and other family members. The Savera limousine picked them up and took them to the Savera house. The weather was perfect, sunny with a cool breeze.

161

SYBILLE AND NORMAN JR. GO TO MADRID

Sybille and Norman were received warmly. Children and young cousins gathered around them. Grandfather and Grandma were speaking to Norman in English. Sybille had briefed her father about Norman Rockville Junior's fame as an artist. His work was very much liked in Europe.

Norman was so impressed with the Savera family's sincere love and affection that he told Sybille, "I love your family's happy reception; I have never experienced such an outpouring of love before. You are lucky to have a big family like this one."

Sybille was answering lots of questions from younger cousins. Peter Savera came to escort Sybille to the dining room. When everyone sat down, Norman counted twenty-five family members at the table. There were at least five toasts. Peter Savera welcomed Norman Rockville Jr. into Savera family. It was getting a little late when they left the table. Everyone moved to the large parlor, and there each member was introduced one by one to Norman. There was a lovely little girl who asked Sybille in Spanish if she could kiss Norman. Norman understood what she wanted; he picked her up and kissed her. Everyone noticed how spontaneously he showed his love to this little cousin.

Finally, the couple was shown their rooms, with separate beds. Sybille was instructed to leave the doors of the bedroom open during their stay at the Savera house.

Sybille and her father and stepmother took Norman sightseeing and gave him a glimpse of their city. Sybille took them to the opera house where she would be the star of the show in *Madame Butterfly*. She told her father and mother not to forget to come to the show. Sybille told Norman, "You will love the show."

The night came to go to the opera. Father Savera, his wife, and Norman were dressed in semi-formal attire. Sybille had gone to the opera house in the early morning to rehearse and practice her lines. The full orchestra was taking part in this program, and there was going to be only one show. Norm, Peter, and Andrea left in a chauffeur-driven car and arrived fifteen minutes before the curtain time. They had the best seats in the house. Sybille was the star of the show; she looked beautiful in her Japanese costume. When Sybille sang the last song, it was so powerful and moving that you could hear women crying. Sybille's stepmother was also crying at the end of the show. When it was over, no one moved; it appeared that the audience was under a trance. Even Norman and Peter Savera were quiet. After a moment, the audience was up on its feet and clapping endlessly. The air was filled with "Bravo" and "Encore," and Sybille had seven curtain calls.

When people started to leave, an attendant came to guide Norman, Peter, and Andrea backstage. When Norman saw Sybille, he could not help rushing to hug and kiss her, saying, "Sybille, I had no idea of this magical world you created with your melodious and powerful voice. Oh, Sybille, you are wonderful."

Her father and stepmother could not agree more. Her stepmother hugged her and gave her a bouquet of roses they had brought with them. Sybille told them to go home; she had to change and would see them later. She said to Norm, "Please wait for me, don't go to sleep." They went out to their car and were driven away.

When Sybille arrived home, Norm and others were waiting for her. Her grandmother asked Peter and his wife, "So how did you like it?"

Peter told his mother, "Mama, you cannot imagine how brilliant she was. She had seven curtain calls, a standing ovation, and constant clapping. Oh, Mama, you should have been there."

"Grandma, our company has produced a record of the show. I will get it for you," Sybille said.

Norman asked Sybille, "Can you do us a favor? Would it be possible for you to sing few bars of the song 'The Calm Ocean'? It was such a powerful rendition."

Sybille said, "Norm, I have never done it before without an orchestra, but I will try just for you and my grandparents." She stood up and sang. Her voice was amazing. When she finished, her grandparents and others clapped and approached her with admiration, hugged her, and kissed her. Her stepmother, her grandma, and the other women were wiping their eyes. The girls had prepared a snack. They all came to the table and everyone had their midnight snack. Then they all said good night and left to go to their rooms.

The next morning when they woke up, Norm and Sybille got ready to go to the dining table and found her grandparents, parents, and others already there. Sybille noticed that they were reading the morning papers. They got up and received Norman and Sybille at the table for breakfast. Her father and grandparents gave the front page to Norman and Sybille.

Her picture in Japanese costume was in three papers. Peter Savera said to Norm, "Look at the pictures and the write-up." Peter translated the article into English for Norm.

"You know, Norman, they call her a diva. Our main paper described the performance as unparalleled."

Norman agreed with the papers' assessment and kissed Sybille's hand. Breakfast was served, and later they moved to the drawing room.

Sybille asked Norman if he wanted more coffee. He nodded his head. Carlos Savera, addressing everyone said, "We understood that you, Norman and Sybille, have decided to get married on August 25. That is not a lot of time to prepare a big wedding, and there are some important friends and relatives who may be left behind if we do not start the list and act swiftly. Time is short. If it is all right with both of you, I will appoint a committee to organize a list and act immediately to send off invitations. If you permit, we will authorize the committee to program and plan a civil ceremony, the receptions from our side, and a reception on the side of Norman's family. I understand that Norman's aunt and uncle will be consulted in this matter. If everyone agrees, I will chair the committee. Here we will say a prayer. Please join me to pay homage to my father and the grandfather of Peter, whom my father loved very much. Please say a silent prayer for Juan Savera. Thank you."

Norman Rockville Jr. stood up and thanked Carlos Savera. "I wish my aunt and uncle were here to thank you for organizing a reception on their behalf as well. They happen to be my beloved guardians. If you permit me, I will like to call them and introduce them to your grandfather and family."

Norman asked Sybille to dial the number of Krista and Norman. Krista answered. Sybille said, "Hello, Aunty, this is Sybille. Norman and I are here in my grandfather's house. Norman wants to talk to both of you."

She gave the receiver to Norm. "Aunty, it is Norman. As we talked to you and Uncle Norman about getting married, we have been discussing dates and ceremonies, etc. Grandpa Savera has kindly offered to organize and work out the details of the marriage ceremony and reception from his side, and he offered to take care of things from our side as well. I will introduce you and Uncle Norman to Sybille's grandparents as well as Peter and Andrea Savera, Sybille's parents. Here are her grandparents."

"Good evening, Mrs. and Mr. Schoulz. I suppose it is night in Toronto.

House of Savera

You have a fine, charming boy, and we think they will make a very nice couple. I have offered to accept the responsibility of organizing the details of the happenings and will wire you details for your approval."

Karl and Ingrid also talked to Sybille and Norman Jr. It was a nice feeling for everyone. Norm told his aunty Krista that they would be home in four days' time. They all said good night and hung up.

The next day, Norm and Sybille were told that Grandma wanted to talk to them. They went to the family room, and Grandma introduced a young girl called Elizabeth. "Sybille and Norm, tomorrow you will be leaving for Majorca for two nights. I want Elizabeth as your chaperone while you are there."

Norm and Sybille enjoyed their two nights in Majorca, and they even enjoyed Elizabeth's company. The time came for both to fly to Toronto. They were driven to the airport, and everyone came down to the front gate to bid farewell to their favorite young couple. Without too much delay, they took off for Toronto.

Karl and Ingrid were waiting at the airport lounge. They were happy finally to see Norm and Sybille. They all went together to pick up Norm and Sybille's luggage, loaded it in the car, and drove off. Traffic was light, and they arrived just in time for lunch at 61 Begonia Drive. Krista, Norman, and Mrs. Morgan came to the front door while Karl parked the car. She hugged Norm and congratulated both of them. Krista and Ingrid both told Norm and Sybille that they had missed them a lot. Norman said, "Me too."

Sybille went around the house with Ingrid. "It looks like somebody has been painting, decorating, and buying new furniture. Ingrid, you and Aunty have really been busy. I must say, it looks nice."

"Oh, Sybille, we wanted to surprise you and Norm. We did not know when you and Norm would be free to help us. I forgot to congratulate you: it seems that your pictures were in every newspaper. They all called you a diva; the papers said that your rendition of *Madame Butterfly* was the best they had ever seen."

Father Norman and Krista sat down with Norman Jr., Sybille, Karl, and Ingrid. Krista wanted to know the details of how the family had reacted to Norman Jr. and Sybille's relationship.

Norman said, "Aunty, they were very nice, and they were happy for us. They did show a little disappointment that we did not give them enough time to organize in the manner that they are used to. Grandfather Carlos

Savera did say that we may not be able to invite some very important guests because of the short time frame. We are talking about ambassadors, Soviet army brass, and of course the top aviation men who were close friends of Peter Savera. Grandfather is a pragmatic man and understood our position, so there was not a problem. Sybille's father pointed out to his dad that we will do the best we can. Sybille's grandfather is wiring a total program to you, which you will probably receive tomorrow. Aunty, I have to warn you that the family is a bit old-fashioned. Grandmother did not allow us to sleep together, would not allow the door of our bedroom to be closed, and sent a chaperone with us to Majorca during our short stay."

Father Norman hesitated and said, "Norm, I really like that kind of culture. It is safe and respectable."

Norman Jr. said, "Uncle, we have been living in the same room, but never have done anything. Sybille will not allow it. That is why I cannot wait and we decided to marry early."

Krista and Ingrid said, "Bravo."

Father Norman said, "I think it is time we discuss a plan that will fulfill our obligations in Madrid regarding the wedding."

Krista answered, "Norman, wait till tomorrow when you receive Carlos's plan. Apparently he is an expert in planning things."

It was getting time for dinner, and Mrs. Morgan called everyone to the dinner table. Sybille and Norm started to tell everyone about how beautiful Majorca had been, although unfortunately, their time there was too short.

Karl asked Norman, "How is your expo project going, Norm? You have too many things going at the same time. You have the expo, both of you have to be in Moscow where Sybille is taking part in the opera *La Traviata*, then the wedding and the honeymoon, and last but not least, moving into a new house."

Father Norman agreed and said to Norm and Sybille, "I can help you in the legal process concerning the house. Karl and I can help you with expo stuff, but you have to sit down with us to explain what you would like us to help you with. I suppose you have already designed the art deco pieces."

They sat down after dinner and stayed till midnight, drawing up plans with starting and finishing dates. The time came for Sybille and Norm to go to Montreal to oversee the art for the expo. Father Norman and Karl took Sybille and Norm to the airport early in the morning. After breakfast, both father and son started on Norm's plan. They went to the factory, met with the manager and artisans, and left a copy of the plan with them.

Sybille called Ingrid and Krista. She thanked them and the men for helping Norm. She said, "Norm told me to tell you that he is very busy and will call them from Moscow. We are leaving tomorrow for Moscow. I have been busy practicing my arias from the opera *Traviata*. Uncle Norman was right when he told Norm that he has taken on too much work and too much travel in such a short time."

Sybille and Norman Jr. go to Moscow

Sybille and Norm arrived in Moscow in the afternoon of the next day. Sybille's grandparents and his friends, including the retired Ambassador Chernoff and his family, were present to receive Norman Jr. and Sybille, and they were treated like dignitaries. Norman Jr. and Sybille were impressed. After all the formalities, Dmitri and Katharina hugged both of them. Katharina could not stop hugging and kissing her granddaughter; she was crying and saying, "I missed you so much." They were driven in a large, black, shining Russian car.

When they arrived home, there were other relatives and family friends waiting for them. At this point, Norman Jr., was staying close to Sybille; he had the impression that nobody but her spoke English.

Sybille told him, "My grandfather speaks fairly good English. I will tell him to talk to you. He is going to take us to an art museum and show you some unusual pieces that are shown only to special visitors."

The telephone was ringing. Sybille picked up the phone. It was Karl.

"Hello, Sybille. I just heard that the political situation in Quebec is really getting worse."

Sybille called Norm over and gave him the phone. "Karl, what is happening?"

"Norm, my dad wants to know how quickly you can arrange to move your belongings from your condo. He is asking if you have prepared all your belongings for moving and arranged to move in a hurry when you need to."

Norm was surprised that things were really getting so bad. He answered, "Oh, sure, I arranged everything for the move. What about storing our belongings in my house's garage? There should be enough room."

"Norm, my dad has done that through the lawyer. The house's owner has agreed for us to use his garage, and as you know, the possession and closing of the house can be done in the last week of August instead of September, so when you come here around August fourteenth, all your stuff will be almost in your house. We will get the keys, and Ingrid and I will help you to decorate and set up. What do you think?"

It appeared that everything had been organized, mostly by Karl's dad. Norm sat down with Dmitri, and after making small talk, Dmitri asked Norm, "I overheard that there are political problems in French-speaking areas of Canada."

Norm said, "The problem has been going on for some time, and it appears that a large English-speaking population has started to move away from Montreal. My uncle knew about this problem early from very close contacts. As a result, he sold his and his son's houses quietly and at a good price. Those who want to sell now will not find any buyers. Sybille and I bought a lovely house near my uncle's house in Toronto."

Norm asked Dmitri, "Nana Dmitri, are we going to see Sybille sing in the opera?"

During this conversation, Sybille and Katharina came and sat down with Norm and Dmitri. Sybille said to her grandfather, "Nana, you see, I know you will love Norm even more when you see his art and sculptures. People are willing to pay a lot of rubles for his art deco pieces."

Sybille left early to go to the opera house. Katharina, Norm, and Dmitri sat down at the table for breakfast. Katharina poured coffee in Norm's and Dmitri's cup. She asked Norm if he took his with sugar and milk. He smiled and looked at Dmitri and said, "Nana, she speaks good English."

"Norman, Katharina was an English teacher and taught Russian air force pilots."

Norm got up and kissed Katharina. After breakfast, she told Norman and Dmitri to get ready. Luckily, Norm had brought his tuxedo with him. Everyone got ready.

Norm told Katharina and Dmitri, "Both of you look so nice."

Both hugged and kissed Norman. Dmitri told Katharina, "We have found a grandson who was missing."

Norman goes to see Sybille singing in an opera

The driver of the car dropped their party off very close to the opera house. They arrived just in time. As everyone settled down, the curtain went up. The music started very slowly and reached a crescendo. By the time the opera was over, it appeared that the audience was almost hypnotized.

Norm said to Dmitri, "Sybille's super voice is unbelievable. I have never heard such a melodious and powerful voice."

Katharina told Norm, "You are right. She has a quality of voice control that she worked very hard to achieve after her mother died. She was only in her teens, and she dedicated herself to mastering voice control. Norm, don't forget, on my side of family we have musical genes that provide the means to achieve the desired effect."

After the show ended, an official car from the opera house brought them home. They sat around in the living room, waiting for Sybille's arrival. Finally she arrived and was hugged, kissed, and admired for her part in the opera. They congratulated her on the success of the show. Norm was so impressed that he picked her up and started to dance with her. Sybille came to Katharina, placed her head on her shoulder, and said, "I am so happy and sad at the same time. I have achieved my goal, but my mama is not here to enjoy it."

Katharina wiped her eyes and told her, "My precious Sybille, I am sure that your mama is listening and that she is happy for you."

Dmitri said, "It's getting late. And you, my best girl in town, look tired."

They said good night and went to their rooms. The next morning, everyone got up a little late. Sybille went to help her grandma in the kitchen and set the table for breakfast. Dmitri and Norm came and sat at the table. The newspaper *Pravda* was at the table.

Dmitri asked Sybille, "How do you feel, my dear Sybille? Both of you look much better this morning today my plan is to go and show my grandson Norm all the sights and sounds of Moscow. We will take you to see my friend Yevchenco, who has invited us for a nice dinner."

Sybille looked at Norm. "Oh, Norm, you will like what Nana has planned for you. Unfortunately, we do not have enough time." She told her grandma, "Grandma, you know we are leaving for Toronto in two days. You and Grandpa will be in Madrid for our wedding, and then you will travel to Toronto and stay with us in our new house in Toronto. Norm and I will love it. Grandpa, I told Norm that we will take him to art museum, where there is an exhibition of art deco. Norm, my grandparents are good friends of Alexi Yorkin, who is the curator of the museum here in Moscow."

A BOMB EXPLODES IN MONTREAL

Sybille and Norm left the table to get ready. As they were changing, Dmitri called both and started to read a news article about a bomb blast in Montreal. Both Norm and Sybille came running. Dmitri read all the details about the explosion.

Norm reminded Sybille, "Remember what my uncle told us about a Montreal student who was trained in Havana? He told my uncle that they were ready for action."

Norm told Sybille, "I wonder if my friend moved our stuff from our condo in Montreal to our house in Toronto. Let me call Karl. He will know if it has arrived. I will talk to Uncle Norman as well."

Sybille agreed, and Dmitri brought the phone. Karl answered, "I know. Yes, it is true. The bomb blast did not do too much damage, but everyone is in a panicked situation. All your furnishings and other stuff arrived yesterday. How lucky can you get? My dad and mom want to say hello to Sybille and her grandparents."

Norm and Sybille were happy to hear that everything was working out so far.

Dmitri gave Katharina, Sybille, and Norm a grand tour of Moscow, visiting museums, the aviation academy, and the Dumas with its onion domes. Dmitri and Katharina enjoyed having their granddaughter and Norman with them. At one art museum, Dmitri introduced Norm to Alexi Yorkin, the curator. He looked at Norm and asked Dmitri, "You mean Norman Rockville Jr., the famous American artist called NRJ?"

Sybille answered, "Yes, Alexi, that is him." The curator was so impressed that he called his Soviet artists over to meet Norm. Dmitri excused himself and told them that his granddaughter would be getting married to Norm next month and they were leaving for Canada in two days, so they had to move on to other things. The curator and other artists wished the couple good luck.

Dmitri and Katharina took Norm and Sybille to the airport and said good-bye to both of them. Katharina did not cry in front of Sybille, but when Dmitri was driving her home she broke down and cried, "Dmitri, I already miss my baby. I don't know if you understand it."

Dmitri told her, "I understand. If I were a woman, I will cry too, but I am not. Men are not supposed to cry. You should stop crying because soon you will see Sybille, Norm, and your favorite son-in-law, Peter."

The next day, Sybille called and told her grandfather, "Grandpa, we arrived safely, but there is definitely political turmoil here in Montreal. It appears that a lot of English-speaking people are moving to Toronto and suburbia."

Dmitri asked Sybille, "Do I understand that all your and Norm's assets have been already moved to Toronto?"

"Yes, Nana, that is correct. Uncle Norman had advised us to settle in Toronto. Norm's uncle, Aunty Krista, her son Karl and his wife Ingrid have been living in Toronto for few months already. Norm went with them when they sold both houses in Montreal and bought a beautiful big house for them and a lovely small one for us. Karl got a job as a professor in the department of mathematics, Nana. He has a doctorate in mathematics. How is my sweet grandma?"

Dmitri told Sybille, "When you and Norm left, she started to cry, but now she is all right. And here she is. Talk to her, and give my greetings to Norm."

Sybille and Katharina started to speak in Russian, which made Katharina more comfortable. Sybille told Katharina, "Once we have received details about the wedding from my grandfather in Spain, we will write a detailed letter to you and Grandpa. Grandma, please promise me you will not cry, because that makes me sad. See you soon. I love you, Grandmamma."

Norman Jr. was busy with organizing an office in Montreal and signing a legal agreement to appoint one of his old artist friends, George Shiver, as his representative in Quebec. There was a complicated arrangement regarding profit sharing. Norm knew that Quebec was a very lucrative market, with many clients who appreciated his kind of work. He had discussed the deal with Sybille and his uncle Norman. He told Karl in Toronto, "I don't have to worry about Quebec business anymore. The contract that I signed with Shiver frees me to move to Toronto, where I will establish an art gallery. It will be easy, since the workshop and studio are already functioning there; I have my best working artists in the Toronto workshop. I hear many businessmen and entrepreneurs saying that Toronto will be an international city in the very near future. The best part is that we all will be very close. That really makes me very happy."

Norman Jr. called his uncle and told him that the business operation in Montreal was finalized. He said, "Sybille and I will be flying to Toronto at ten a.m., and we are shipping our cars to Toronto by truck. We will see Karl and Ingrid at the airport around noon. Uncle, can I talk to Karl?"

Karl told Norm, "Sure we will pick you at noon. By the way, the lawyer called and asked me to tell you and Sybille that the closing documents are ready for you to complete the deal, and you can move in any time after that. The house is vacant."

Norm said, "Can we meet him after we arrive tomorrow, or do we need an appointment?"

Karl said, "According to the lawyer, the seller has already signed off on the documents. What is needed now is a certified check. With that, you will get the key."

Norm thanked Karl and said that he had everything ready. They said good-bye till the next day.

Karl and Ingrid were excited to have Sybille and Norm back with them. Krista had told her husband how much she had missed Norm Junior.

The plane arrived, and all four of them were happy to be together. Ingrid said, "Norm and Sybille, you have not said anything about your trips to Spain or Russia."

Sybille replied, "Listen, tonight after dinner, we will go for a walk, and when we come back, we will tell our stories. And Karl, you and Ingrid will tell us about what is happening here."

SYBILLE AND NORM ARRIVE IN TORONTO

When they arrived home, Uncle Norm and Krista hugged Norm Jr. and Sybille, and Krista told them, "I don't know why, but this time I missed both of you a lot. You were so far away for so long."

"Aunty, these three months or so have been so busy that we did not know if we would be able to finalize everything. Norm had his art gallery and investments, and the trips to my father's house and my grandparents' house plus my singing engagements in both cities took a lot out of us."

Norm Junior agreed with Sybille and said, "Uncle Norm and Aunty, I feel safe and at home now."

NORMAN JR. AND SYBILLE MOVE TO TORONTO

Father Norman told Karl to take Sybille and Norm Junior to the lawyer's office. "It is already one p.m. I called the lawyer and made an appointment for one-thirty. If you wait too long, the traffic will be heavy."

So Karl, Norm, Sybille, and Ingrid left for the lawyer's office. They were back around five. They entered the house, and Ingrid and Sybille together showed the house key to Uncle Norman and Aunty Krista. Norman Junior came to Krista and asked them to come and open the house all together. He told them that it was a good omen when a whole family entered a new house together. Norman, Krista, and the happy children walked to the house. They entered, and Krista said, "Oh, Sybille, look how cute the piano is."

There were other pieces of furniture and fixtures that Sybille and Norm Jr. had opted to buy. Uncle Norman told Norm Junior and Sybille, "If you bought this house today, you would probably pay twice as much. You remember what I told you about what the young man, George, had told me? I am thankful to our programmer for giving us advance notice. And it was fortunate that we could buy two beautiful houses close to each other at the right time."

Krista told Sybille, "I have asked the cleaning lady who cleaned our house to come tomorrow and do your house, so be ready to come here with her at nine a.m. and open the house. Do you have another key?"

Norman Jr. showed Krista a whole bunch of keys he had gotten from the lawyer. Sybille locked the house; they came back to Krista's place and finally relaxed in the living room.

Sybille looked around and asked Ingrid, "Who did the decoration? I like your window treatments, and you repainted the house. Norm, do you like the colors? Look at those drapes. Whoever did your decor did a nice job. Norm, you didn't have time to do all this."

Norm said, "Sybille, before we left for Paris, I asked one of my men to come here and help Ingrid with the decoration. I must say, he did okay. If you like his work, I can call him and we can sit down together. Whatever you decide will be done, but don't forget we will be busy with our wedding. The twenty-fifth of September is not too far away. I was going to suggest that you postpone your recording engagement till the middle of December."

Mrs. Morgan came and invited everyone into the dining room. After dinner, they went for a short walk. It was getting a little chilly.

The next day, the house was cleaned and the furnishings and other belongings were brought in from the garage. In the afternoon, Mike

Bishop, the house decorator, came and discussed the colors and details of decorations. Mike asked Norm to give him the house key and said he would look after the assignment.

Norm Jr. was enjoying the company of his family. His friends Karl, Ingrid, and Sybille were always there. Krista and Uncle Norman were his closest relatives and loved parental figures for him. It was a very special time for him.

Dr. Norman eventually received a complete wedding program from Sybille's grandfather in Spain. Sybille received a letter from her father informing her that he had sent a special letter to her grandparents in Russia inviting them to stay with them at the Savera house.

"I also told them that you are coming one week before the wedding and you would like them to be here the day you arrive, which is September 18," he wrote. When he called his daughter in Toronto, he asked her to call her Nana and tell him that she would be sleeping in the same room as them before the wedding.

A week flew by. The decoration of Norm and Sybille's house was complete, and they would be moving in the next day. Their car had arrived from Montreal and was parked in their garage.

Krista and Norman called Mr. Carlos Savera and thanked him for his letter outlining the wedding program. Norman also told him that Sybille would be in Madrid on September 18 and requested that Carlos arrange hotel accommodation near the Savera house for his family.

Carlos Savera replied, "You all are our family. We could never allow you to stay in a hotel. We have lots of room here at the Savera house. I assure you, your family and you will be more comfortable here. And besides, we would like to strengthen our relationship, especially since your family will be Sybille's second family."

Norman replied, "Carlos, I can see where your Sybille gets her values. You are a nobleman. Thank you. We are looking forward to this international gathering. Good-bye."

The atmosphere at the Schoulz family home was relaxed. Everything was going smoothly. Karl addressed his father and mother, "Dad, you know my classes start on September twelfth, and Ingrid's graduate classes also start the same day. Luckily, the week of September twenty-fifth is a long weekend, but what I am trying to say is that Ingrid and I cannot stay too long. We must return on the Monday after the wedding."

Ingrid, Krista, and Norman agreed, but Norm Jr. and Sybille were disappointed. Sybille wanted to know why both could not take couple of days more. Norm Jr. explained to Sybille, "Sybille, my dear, this is Karl's first time at his job, and the boss is expecting him to be there in the classroom. But I think Ingrid could miss a couple of days. Am I right, Ingrid?"

Ingrid said, "I know my classes are not as important as Karl's situation, but look, Sybille, would you leave your husband for so many days?"

They still could not settle on what to do. Sybille pleaded with Ingrid, "Ingrid, what about me? I will be alone without you."

It was fall, and all the maple trees were turning golden. At night, it was a little chilly. Karl had been attending regular orientation courses at the university, familiarizing himself with the graduate students and general topics like the locations of campus libraries and lecture halls. He had already discussed his absence between September 23 and 27 with his department head, which was very understanding. Dr. Smith and Karl manipulated few dates to fit Karl's needs. Karl came home and gave the good news to Sybille and Ingrid that he would be able to stay longer and come back home with them. Everyone was happy.

Mrs. Morgan told Krista that it was supper time and that she had prepared a delicious soup with croutons. "Tell them the soup is getting cold, and a cold soup is boring."

They all came and had a hearty meal. While they were having their dessert, Norm Junior suggested that they go to his place. "My expert decorator Mike Bishop called and asked us to go and see the finished job. I told him that we would meet him at nine. Let us go and see."

The whole family, including Mrs. Morgan, came. Mike came out and greeted everyone. He told them, "Let us start with the garage."

He pushed a button on a little remote control, and the garage door started to lift gently. Flood lights exposed nice white shelving and hooks on the walls to hold tools. Father Norman and Krista said loudly, "How neat! We would like to have that."

When they entered the hallway to the living room, they saw the baby grand piano decorated with flowers and a lovely, colorful sign that read, "Welcome home, Sybille and Norm." They were all impressed by the arrangement. One side wall was painted with crimson flat paint, and the drapes were pastel green. Everyone was in awe. All the girls approached Mike Bishop and shook his hand. He then introduced his team of three neat-looking men. Mike said, "Norm, I could not have achieved all this in this short time without their help."

Everything they saw was a delight. The bedrooms were very inviting, with a warm and pleasant atmosphere. The master en suite and the other bathrooms were, according to Sybille and Ingrid, "heavenly."

Norman Jr. thanked Mike and his team and said, "I am not surprised at all. I know they are professionals."

Ingrid said to Sybille, "Sybille, you don't need to go anywhere far away for your honeymoon." Sybille and Norm agreed. Sybille was so impressed with the work done by Mike Bishop's team that she came up to Norm Jr. and told him that he deserved a big kiss.

NORMAN AND THE SCHOULZ FAMILY LEAVE FOR MADRID

The next morning after breakfast, Krista reminded everyone that it was time for Sybille to pack and get ready for tomorrow's flight, which would take off at seven-thirty a.m. Krista helped Sybille organize her essential papers and choose dresses, purses, and other paraphernalia. Krista also suggested that the family dine out that evening to celebrate the upcoming wedding and Sybille's trip tomorrow.

They all got up early at the next morning. The air was crisp, and Ingrid and Sybille admired the maple tree leaves turning deep orange. They drove off and arrived just in time.

Sybille called when she arrived in Madrid. She told Norman Jr., "Norm, there are so many guests here. And you know my grandma and grandpa? They are already here. They flew from Moscow yesterday. My father, my grandma, and my grandfather Savera were at the airport to receive me. My stepmother was so sweet. She gave me a small bouquet of yellow roses. The best thing was the happy, happy atmosphere, and everywhere there was laughter and fun. Norm, I miss you, but I know that you will be here in two days. Give kisses for me to Ingrid and Aunt Krista and regards to Uncle Norman and Karl. I love you. Good-bye."

Norman, Karl, Krista and Norman Jr. landed at Madrid airport the day before the wedding. Everybody, including the grandparents from both sides, was there to meet their plane; Sybille's father and stepmother were inside the reception area. The press from the Soviet Union, Spain, and Canada were present. It was an international gathering to report a union of the two world-renowned artists. After all the formalities, they arrived at the Savera house, a big mansion decorated with lights, bunting, and balloons. After everyone was settled in, the newly arrived guests were invited to the dining room for dinner. Later, as per protocol, Carlos Savera invited all parents, grandparents, and immediate relatives to the family room and introduced them all.

Norman and his family came to know most of the family members and other guests at Savera mansion.

The following morning was nice and cool, but the sun was beating down, and by ten a.m. it was fairly warm. Norm was dressed in an ivory suit, and Sybille wore a traditional white lace gown. They both got into a stretch limousine along with their parents. Many other limousines followed. They arrived at the city hall. It was an impressive building; the garden around the building was crowded with well-wishers and newspaper reporters along with photographers. The bridesmaids and Sybille's friends lined up on both sides of the path. The mayor and council members came to the main door to receive the Savera elders and special guests, such as Sybille's grandparents from Moscow and the Soviet ambassador to Spain with his wife. They were followed by the bridal group, relatives, and immediate family members. The press was busy snapping pictures and taking notes.

Sybille and Norman Jr. get married

The ceremony was over in a short time. The bridal group came out singing, dancing, and happy. All the special guests and others came out of the city hall escorted by city officials. Limousines picked them while the reporters and photographers kept themselves busy.

The festivities began inside the Savera mansion. There was music and laughter, and for parents and grandparents, it was time to renew old relations and to discuss the happenings of the last decade, the pleasures and pains of their lives, and, finally, world affairs. Dmitri and Katharina's joy that day brought back vivid memories of their daughter Anna and five-year-old Joseph, who had been brutally murdered in a suicide bombing twenty years ago...

Dmitri and Katherine felt somber at the memory, but the appearance of Norm Jr. and Sybille brought back the joy in everyone's hearts. Grandfather Dmitri extended his arms toward both of them, and Norm and Sybille responded with love and affection. Sybille saw tears in her grandparents' eyes and said, "Nana, why are you …"

He told her, "There is joy in my and grandma's tears. Thank you for bringing this joy."

The Savera mansion was bursting at its seams. Friends and business associates of the family and foreign dignitaries were coming and going, bearing gifts and messages of good wishes, all day long. It was getting close to the starting time of the reception, which would be hosted by the Savera family at their golf club. Limousines, cars, and buses were employed to carry guests and the bridal party to the club.

The club was decorated and lighted to receive the guests for a memorable dinner. The head table held close family members and honored guests. As the bride and groom entered the hall, the band started to play "Here Comes the Bride." When everyone sat down, introductions, speeches, and congratulatory notes from people from Moscow to Montreal were read. After the meal, limousines drove some guests back to the Savera mansion. All the young and young at heart stayed behind, dancing to a very versatile band that played waltz, jazz, and Frank Sinatra music. The band stopped playing at one a.m. Buses and limousines brought back all the Savera mansion guests. All and all, the wedding and dinner were a smash hit, according to the morning papers.

Dmitri and Katharina got up late the next morning and went down to the dining room for breakfast, where they saw Sybille and Norm Jr. having coffee and talking about the wedding reception. Dmitri told his granddaughter that they had met more old friends here in Spain than in Moscow. Peter Savera and Andrea showed up and sat with Sybille, Norm, and Sybille's grandparents.

Sybille came closer to her parents and said to her father, "Papa, Norm and I will be leaving tomorrow for Toronto, and we will stay in our new home for five days to relax and arrange our things. After that, I would like Nana and Grandma to come and stay with us for two weeks. We will send a return ticket for them here to you. You can see them off, and we will pick them at the airport in Toronto." She turned to Dmitri. "Would you like that?" Both grandparents agreed. "And Papa," Sybille continued, "After two weeks, we want you and mother Andrea to arrive. You will enjoy the best fall weather in October. The trees are golden, and the air is cool at night and warm during the day. Papa, you can help Norm. He is overloaded with work. And mother will help me to cook and set up the house."

Peter said, "That sounds good. Your grandpa and grandma seem to like the idea of visiting Canada."

Norman Jr. was sitting quietly, not understanding a word, because they were talking in Russian. After breakfast, Sybille's grandparents went to lie down and relax. Peter and Andrea also needed rest. Last night had been a little too much for them. Peter told them that at almost sixty-seven years old; he was officially a senior.

At five p.m., there was a call to get ready for the Norman family reception at the Hotel Alhambra. This time, there were fewer than seventy guests. Again, the buses and limousines picked up all the guests and drove them to the hotel. Norm told Sybille, "Look at the beautiful architecture. Sybille, please ask your house photographer to take pictures from all angles."

After short speeches and congratulations, dinner began. The menu mixed Arab and Spanish cuisines. The night was lovely, with an intoxicating fragrance of jasmine and orange blossoms. Karl and Ingrid along with Norm and Sybille sat outside near a fountain. The fragrance in the air and the light, cool night breeze of the Spanish fall created a surreal romantic air and forced Ingrid and Sybille to sit in the laps of their admirers. This romantic magic was enhanced by the arrival of the limousine. The passion continued in the plush environment and subdued lighting of the limousine.

They arrived at the Savera mansion, where they were met by Katharina and Krista. Both said, "We knew you would come tired, so we prepared your luggage for tomorrow's flight. Don't forget, the flight is at seven tomorrow morning, and we have to be at the airport by six-thirty. The airline will serve breakfast, so go get your sleep."

ALL NORMAN'S FAMILY RETURNS TO TORONTO

The next morning was cloudy. There was hugging, kissing, tears, and sadness at seeing the lovable young couples going away. The flight left on time. Norm and Sybille sat together; Karl and Ingrid sat behind them. The seats were comfortable, with plenty of leg room. Father Norman told Krista, "You know my dear, I enjoyed the trip, but I am happy to go home. What about you and Mrs. Morgan?" Krista was sitting between her husband and Mrs. Morgan, who was on her right next to the window. Both agreed. Mrs. Morgan told Krista and Norman to look on their left side.

"Look, they are all asleep. They look so cute and in love. You see, Dr. Norman? Were you like that, when you got married?"

Krista answered before Norman did. "Mrs. Morgan, are you joking? Norman, instead of being romantic, was telling me about the time he

went to the Amazon, where he found the most potent love-making herb."
They laughed. Breakfast came, and no one dared to wake the lovers, who
were still sleeping in each other's arms.

When they arrived home, it was three p.m. Karl, Ingrid, Sybille, and
Norm were hungry. They stayed at Krista's place while Mrs. Morgan
prepared a tray of omelets, cheese, jam, muffins, and coffee. They enjoyed
the brunch. Sybille wanted to go to her place. Krista asked Sybille, "By
the way, what is the name of your street?"

Sybille was happy that Krista had asked. She was wondering why no
one had asked her address. "I am glad you asked. I bet you don't know our
new address either, Ingrid. Aunty, it is 61 Tulip Circle."

Ingrid said, "Oh, what a nice name."

Karl told Norm Jr., "Norm, we just had our brunch. Let us rest a little
while, and then we will go together to 61 Tulip Circle."

He asked Ingrid, "Do you know where my eye drops are?"

Ingrid opened her little purse and came to put one drop in each eye.
Ingrid said, "Karl, you had two days without drops. We were so busy. I
am sorry; it is my fault."

Sybille got up and said, "Come on, let us go. I want to see my place."

Ingrid said jokingly, "You mean 61 Two Lips Circle?"

Sybille ran after Ingrid and caught her. "It is not Two Lips, it is
Tulip."

They were fooling around. Ingrid started to tease Sybille. "Two Lips,
Two Lips."

They walked to 61 Tulip Circle. It was just behind Ingrid's house at
61 Jasmine Crescent. They entered the hallway, where Sybille found more
flowers and a large bouquet with a card reading, "Congratulations, enjoy
your honeymoon!" from the members of the NRJ Corporation.

Sybille, Ingrid, and Karl were happy to see that Norman Junior's
workers had such affection for him. Sybille told Karl that she had heard
Mike Bishop, one of the designers; say that he was their Michelangelo.

Satisfied with the final results, Norm Jr. hugged Ingrid and Karl and
thanked them for helping to make this possible. He said, "Uncle Norm
gave us good guidance and advice. His timing was so right. I will never
forget that."

While they were enjoying every inch of the house, Sybille asked
Ingrid to go and get Uncle Norm and Aunty Krista; she planned to sing
and play "Va Pensiero" from the opera *Nabucco*. Ingrid looked at Sybille

and pursed her lips to tease Sybille. Then she ran away before Sybille could catch her.

Uncle Norman and Krista came and looked at the living room, which was half-filled with flowers. Krista asked Karl, "Would you go and bring Mrs. Morgan? She would love to hear Sybille."

Sybille said, "Oh, Aunty, I am sorry I forgot about her. I know how much you like your friend Mrs. Morgan."

When everyone was there, Sybille sat down at the piano and started to play. Her voice was so magical that Krista and Mrs. Morgan had tears in their eyes. Ingrid was hanging on to Karl with a sad face. After Sybille was finished, everyone just wanted to hug and kiss her. Ingrid asked Sybille if she could sing a happy and funny song, so she went back to her piano and started to sing a Dean Martin song. It was getting close to dinnertime; Mrs. Morgan had gone back to Krista's house and was busy preparing food. Because all the passengers had slept throughout the flight to Toronto and eaten their brunch at three p.m., they were really not so hungry.

The days turned into weeks and the weeks to months. Karl was busy teaching and coaching some brilliant students toward their PhD degrees on very unusual concepts from the modern approach to mathematics. Ingrid had already started her study of the birth of fragrance. She was so engrossed in her research that began coming home late. Uncle Norman and Krista were worried. Whenever her parents called the house, Karl could only say that she was at the university. So Jeffrey and Audrey decided to fly out to Toronto to see if their daughter was all right. They arrived one day around four p.m. Karl had gone out to the airport to pick them up. Jeffrey and Audrey relaxed and waited for Ingrid to come home. She entered the house happy and was surprised to see her parents. She rushed to hug them and kiss them. She hugged Karl and asked her parents if they were okay.

Ingrid said, "Mother, I am surprised you did not call. Karl and I would have picked you at the airport."

Audrey told her, "We have been trying to talk to you, but you are never there."

She replied, "Mother, I am so busy at school that I just cannot get away. By the way, Karl was here. His parents are here all the time. You could talk to them. But I am glad to see both of you." She turned to Karl and told him, "I have good news. I have made a breakthrough, and there are definite indications that I am very close to my objective. My professor thinks that I have found the source and the origin of the fragrance in flowers as well as their method of distributing smell in the air. The purpose of fragrance in the air is to attract pollinators."

Her parents realized, just as Karl had, that Ingrid was obsessed with completing her project. Karl told Ingrid, "Your parents have come to see you from far away, and they have not eaten yet. We were waiting for you. So let us go to the table and eat, and then you can tell me the rest of the good news."

Ingrid was more relaxed and was enjoying talking to her parents. The next day was a holiday, and Ingrid and her parents were talking about going downtown. Karl told Ingrid that he would drive them.

It was December, and there was a chill in the air. Karl was teaching at the university during the morning, but Ingrid arrived home early. After lunch, Karl took her and her parents downtown. They all came back before dinner and sat down in the living room. Ingrid saw Karl rubbing his eyes, and she abruptly got up and brought Karl's eye drops. Gently, she opened his eyes one by one and carefully squeezed one drop into each eye.

Jeffrey and Audrey were leaving for Calgary the next morning. Karl and Ingrid took them to the airport. As Karl and Ingrid were leaving the building, they met Norm Jr. and Sybille. The couples asked each other, "What are you doing here?"

Ingrid explained that they had been dropping off her parents. Sybille said, "We invited my grandparents to stay with us for two weeks, and we are here to pick them up. Do you want to stay for a little while? We can all go back together."

Sybille's grandparents arrived and were happy to see their granddaughter, Norman Jr., Karl, and Ingrid. Sybille took them first to see Karl's parents and then to see her place.

KATHARINA AND DMITRI VISIT TORONTO

Sybille's grandfather and grandma enjoyed their visit. Sybille took care of them, taking them sightseeing to the Toronto museums and an art gallery, where she showed them Norman Junior's masterpiece hanging in the middle of the rotunda. She took them to an authentic Russian restaurant. The owner, without knowing who her grandparents were, brought them to a large table. They met some older Russians who had heard about the famous Dmitri Yevchenco and had read about the tragedy at the Black Sea resort. They told Katharina, "Here in Toronto, we have our own little Russia; we follow everything that is happening in Russia."

An old man, Alexander, told Dmitri, "Mr. Yevchenco, we are proud of what people like you do for Russia. We read about your daughter Anna's wedding. That was an affair to remember. And we listen to your Sybille. Her singing is amazing. We read about her wedding in *Pravda*."

Sybille stood up and thanked them. When the owner saw that a crowd had gathered around the large table, he approached the table. Alexander got up and introduced Sergei Smirnoff to Dmitri. Sergei hugged and kissed Dmitri, and then he ordered free drinks for everyone. He went to his microphone and announced, "We are honored to have two world-renowned personalities with us, Comrade Yevchenco and his granddaughter Sybille, the world-famous Russian singer, along with her pianist grandmother Katharina Yevchenco."

Sergei asked Sybille if she would honor the company by singing two Russian songs. Sybille looked at her grandfather. He gave her a nod and told her to go ahead. Sybille asked her grandma to play the piano. She sang, and with her grandma at the piano, Sergei's place became an opera house. People gathered outside to listen to her powerful and vibrant voice. The second song got everyone up on their feet. All the Russians went crazy. Alexander and Sergei Smirnoff thanked the Yevchenco's for providing a pleasure they would remember for life. They gave them an ovation as the family left.

Katharina said, "Dmitri, this was the best gift ever. We will cherish and remember it."

The time came for Sybille and Norm Jr. to take her grandparents back to the airport. They thanked Sybille for the visit, especially to the Russian restaurant, and waved good-bye.

Norman's business was getting bigger and bigger; he was very busy. When the day came for Sybille to go and pick her father and mother from the airport, Norman Jr. could not go with Sybille to the airport because he had an important business meeting. They arrived and were surprised to see Sybille alone. She told them, "Papa, you arrived just in time. You see how busy Norman is. I hope you can help him with the administration of his business."

Just as they were talking about Norm, he entered the house. He came in and hugged them. "I am sorry I could not come to the airport, Papa and Mother. Welcome to our new home. I am delighted to have you."

Peter Savera thanked Norman. Sybille said to Norman, "I have discussed with Papa the fact that you need administration help. Norman, Papa is a good administrator, and I hope he will have time to help you."

They sat down in the living room. Andrea and Peter told Sybille, "You have a beautiful home. I love your decorations. And look at the lovely piano."

They settled down, and Peter Savera assured Norman that he would try his best to help the son that he never had. Sybille's father's help made a big difference in Norman's work; everything was falling into place. Norman was thankful to Peter and Andrea for getting his life back on track. He told Andrea that he recently had not talked to Sybille for a week. He had been so busy that he had left the house while she was still sleeping and arrived after she had gone to bed again. "That is not a life for us," he said to Peter Savera. "Papa, I am so glad that Sybille got you involved in our operations."

Sybille's parents visited Uncle Norman and his family before leaving for Spain. Norman Jr. could not believe his eyes when he saw snow flurries; he thought it was a little too early for snow. It was Saturday morning, and Ingrid had asked Sybille and Norm to have breakfast with them. There was quite a chill in the air when they put on their warm jackets and walked up to Uncle Norman's house. When they arrived at the house, both Ingrid and Karl came rushing to greet them. "We missed you! Come in. It is getting colder, and Mrs. Morgan is making your favorite pancakes, Norm."

They came into the living room, where Uncle Norman was watching a Quebec news program. Norman Jr. asked his uncle, "How is it going in Quebec? Are they really going to separate?"

Dr. Norman gave a short summary of the affairs in Quebec, which were not very pleasant. Sybille asked Krista how Uncle Norman was feeling. She asked, "Has Uncle lost some weight? He does look a little pale."

Aunty Krista tried to explain to Sybille. "Your uncle loved to travel to rain forests in his younger days. As a matter of fact, just one month before retired, his supposedly good friend the chairman sent him to the Brazilian rain forest. Can you believe it? Just one month before he was to retire from the university, just because his friend Chairman Heber asked him, he left. A month later, he was brought back home on a stretcher.

I almost fainted. If not for Karl, I don't know what I would have done. His so-called friend, Heber, did not even visit him. He did call, but I refused to talk to him. Sybille, in my opinion, Chairman Heber was using his friend's knowledge to bring back valuable herbs that would make millions for his company. He arranged travel services, accommodation, and graduate student assistance whenever and where ever he went. And for that your uncle thanked this cheap, selfish Heber."

Everyone was listening quietly, but Norm could not take it anymore. "Krista, Heber never pushed me. He was always nice. He sent you gifts, he did come on my birthday, and he sent Karl and Ingrid on their honeymoon for free."

She said to Karl, "I asked you and Ingrid if it was really a good honeymoon resort, and you told me it was not bad. Ingrid, you told me that maybe it was good for very old honeymooners because it was a little too quiet."

"Well, let us go," said Norm. "Mrs. Morgan is calling." They all came to the table and enjoyed freshly made pancakes with delicious coffee and tea. Sybille could not help thinking about Aunty Krista's hidden anger. She knew Krista's anger was related to Uncle Norman's health.

She asked, "You think Uncle Norm's rain forest trips may have something to do with his health issues?"

Before Krista could answer, Karl cleared his throat and said, "Sybille and Norm, I have to tell you that dad is under the care of a liver specialist. He has not been well since he returned from Brazil. I must say, I have to agree with my mother in all her analysis about his condition and Chairman Heber. Dad has been going through all kinds of evaluations. His white blood cell count is up, and he had a liver biopsy."

Karl could not talk anymore; his eyes were misty. Ingrid and Norm Jr. took him into the living room; Ingrid wiped his tears and kissed him. Now the snow was coming down. Norman Jr. told everybody, "Let us all go to see my factory. You should see what my unbelievable products my men are turning out. Then we are going to a real Chinese restaurant. You will love it. So what do you say to that?"

Sybille said to Norm Jr., "Norm, I love you. You are a medicine with no prescription needed. You bring happiness into lifeless people. You are just wonderful."

Ingrid told Sybille, "You and your father injected life in Norm Jr., too. He came back to us. He was trapped in his work before."

185

They went to see his factory; they saw artifacts, copies of old art, and furniture of the thirties. Norman showed them orders he had on hand and described how he was looking for master carpenters, carvers, and artists with original concepts. Dr. Norman was busy examining and admiring the craft and the craftsman. After the tour, Norman Jr. took the family to his favorite Chinese restaurant. When they entered the place, there was an unusual aroma that appealed to the taste buds. The owner came to greet them, and they all stayed at the restaurant for a bit too long. Krista and Norman were tired and wanted to go home. Karl told Ingrid that it was a mistake to have taken his dad to eat outside. They all went home.

After their supper at the Chinese place, Norm's digestive system was suffering. Krista gave him digestive pills, but the stomach pain was still there. Krista asked Norman, "Don't you know an herbal remedy for indigestion?"

Norman replied, "Sure, I know one, Krista. It is called slippery elm. It is a powder made out of the bark of an elm tree. It works wonders without side effects."

Krista was annoyed that her husband knew about herbal remedies for almost every disease but did not use them for his own benefit. She said to Norman, "I do not understand your logic or your thinking. You know products that will cure your indigestion, your adult life has been involved in nothing else but herbal medicine research, and you don't bother to utilize products that you helped to develop."

Karl went to an herbal medicine store and bought slippery elm powder. Krista was worried on one hand and annoyed on the other. She decided to take charge of her husband's well-being. She gave Norman slippery elm, and it appeared to help. The pain was gone, and he finally went to sleep.

A few weeks passed, and Norman Schoulz was having constant problems with his health, including lack of appetite, constipation, and restlessness. Krista and Karl realized that there was something unusually wrong with Norman's health. Krista made an appointment with Dr. Charles Forest, their family doctor. She told the doctor, "Norman is not well. I suspect that last time he went for a checkup, his white blood count was up and ..."

At this point, Dr. Forest told Krista, "I have to look at his biopsy result. I will call you back."

Chapter 16

Dr. Norm Schoulz is ill

K rista was getting anxious. When Dr. Forest called back, he said, "Mrs. Schoulz, I have looked at the report. The results are not very clear. The white blood cell numbers are still high, but they have remained at the same level. Mrs. Schoulz, it is important that we keep a constant watch." She thanked him and hung up.

Norman Jr. was busy, but he had time to go out with Sybille and get together with Karl, Ingrid, and his aunty. He was worried about Uncle Norman. He noticed that his uncle was not as active as before; he was spending most of his time in his recliner.

Sybille's singing career was booming again. She was booked for a Christmas engagement at the Boston music hall and had accepted five recording sessions starting in January.

Norman Jr. told Ingrid, "Sybille has received an offer to act and sing in a movie about Mario Carouso's life. She was not interested. The highlight of her career right now is an invitation from the Kremlin to take part in a Soviet celebration of achievements in Moscow. She will be a prime singer at the Bolshoi Theater."

Ingrid asked, "Norm, are you going with her?"

"Ingrid, I will certainly go. At that time, the Moscow artists' association has asked me to curate a show on art deco subjects, so I have to organize a show and at the same time is with Sybille and her grandparents."

Ingrid asked Karl if they could go to Moscow along with Sybille and Norm. Karl replied, "I will like to, but I am worried about Dad and Mom."

Ingrid asked Norm where Sybille was. He told her that she was practicing.

Karl asked Norman Jr., "How is your business doing? When are you going to open your show in Moscow? I bet you the timing of your show will coincide with Sybille's concert at the Kremlin. You are so smart."

Norman Jr. laughed and reminded him, "We never discussed the progress of your teaching job."

Karl said to Norm, "You remember how my dad told us to get out from Quebec? He was right. By the time a big crowd moved from Montreal, we were already settled. My dad is something, Norman. You are my closest cousin and friend, so I have to tell you that Dad is not well. I am afraid for him. I don't know what we can do for him."

Norm thought and asked Karl, "Have we done a real medical evaluation of Uncle's condition? I will tell you what: I am going to ask my brilliant Dr. Lee and see what he says."

Chapter 17

DR. NORMAN SCHOULZ IS ILL

Norman and Krista took Norman Schoulz to Dr. Lee; he greeted Norman Jr., who introduced Krista and Dr. Norman. Norman Jr. said to Dr. Lee, "I hope that when we talked on the phone, I gave you enough background information about my uncle's condition."

Dr. Lee told Norm Jr. that he had enough information to draw up a basic testing program and procedure that would give them some direction. First, he did a basic physical exam. Norm and Krista were ready to go out of the examining room, but the doctor said, "No, stay with me. You will appreciate and understand the results much better. I will show you what tests I want to carry out. There will be an X-ray of the total stomach, which will include the kidneys, appendix, and gallbladder. Since I have these facilities here in my clinic, the results will be available very quickly. I know Norm wants results almost immediately."

One team performed an X-ray test and another ultrasound. When the tests were complete, the results were handed over to Dr. Lee, who spent some time in his lab carefully examining results. He asked Norman Jr. and his aunt and uncle to wait in his office. The review took him only twenty minutes. The doctor came in and calmly sat down in his big chair. He asked Uncle Norman, "So what was your major complaint, Dr. Norman?"

Norman told him that he had constant pain around his stomach. "I thought maybe my liver has a major problem, like cancer."

Norm Jr. told the doctor, "My aunty has been giving him digestive pills."

The doctor said, "Norm, your uncle does not have any major problems anywhere except his gallbladder. He has fairly big stones in his gallbladder, and those are the source of his pain. The affected area has an infection, as indicated by an increase in his white cell count. His stones are causing irritation, injury, and pain."

They were stunned and happy. Norm Jr. screamed with pleasure, Krista hugged the doctor, and Norman Schoulz had a big smile on his face. Dr. Norman said to Dr. Lee, "I was slowly dying, not because of any disease but just from the thought of it. Doctor, I thank you."

Krista asked the doctor, "So what is the next step?"

The doctor replied, "He needs surgery. We can book an operating room now and quickly remove those stones."

Norman Schoulz said, "Just a minute. Can we come back to you tomorrow? I want to discuss this with my son first."

The doctor said, "Listen, Norm. You are my friend. If we wait too long, it may not be possible to get the OR. And honestly, Mrs. Schoulz, the white blood cell count is high enough. I warn you, you have to book now."

Krista and Norm agreed with the doctor. In spite of Dr. Norman's objections, Norm Jr. told the doctor, "Sam, go ahead and book him."

Krista said to her husband, "When all the kids are home tonight, we will surprise them with this good news."

While Norman Jr. was driving them home, Norman Schoulz told Norm and Krista, "I have an herbal formula for gallstones that is painless and works within days."

Krista said, "If your formula does not work, then what we do? Dr. Lee cannot guarantee the availability of the operating room. It is not in his control."

Norman Schoulz wanted to know how safe the surgery was and what could go wrong. "Norm, can you talk to Dr. Lee and ask him the safety factor? I know nobody can guarantee anything, and let us all talk to Karl."

Krista answered, "Sure, Norman, we will not do anything without Karl's approval. He is your son."

Norm Jr. told his aunt, "The operation is booked for three weeks from now; we still have lots of time."

Krista wanted to know, "Norman, how long would it take for your formula to work after you get your ingredients?"

Norman said, "Krista, it will just take few days."

Krista looked at Norm Jr. "Why don't we let him try? If his formula works, we cancel surgery. If it does not work, we just wait for the surgery."

Norm Jr. said, "Aunty, you are a genius."

When they arrived home, Karl, Ingrid, and Sybille were still not home. Krista, Norm Jr., and Norman walked into the kitchen and found Mrs. Morgan busy cooking. When she saw the three of them, she stopped cooking and waited for Krista to say something.

"Mrs. Morgan, good news. Norman is not seriously sick. His bladder is full of stones."

Mrs. Morgan replied, "Oh no! How it is possible? I never heard that a peepee bladder could have stones."

They all laughed. Krista said, "No, silly, his gallbladder."

At this point, Ingrid, Karl, and Sybille arrived home. They were surprised to hear laughter. It has been some time since anyone had laughed with such enthusiasm around the house. Karl looked at his mother and she rushed to hug them all at once, saying, "Oh, my children, we have good news. Your dad is not sick. He is hiding precious stones in his gallbladder."

Karl said, "You mean he has gallbladder stones causing so much trouble?"

Everybody was happy, dancing around Dr. Norman. Krista told Mrs. Morgan, "Stop cooking. We all are celebrating at Dolce Vita."

They all went to the restaurant. At this point Krista told everyone, "We all have been miserable not knowing what was wrong with Norman. And children, I found out what was eating my Norman. He told the doctor he thought he had liver cancer."

Norman Jr. lifted his glass and said, "Here's to Uncle and Aunty to their health and happiness.""

Karl got up and said, "Here is to my brother Norm Jr., who brought happiness to all of us. He is the one who promised to take Dad to his friend Dr. Lee. Thanks, Norm, for doing this." Everyone cheered. They went home and relaxed there, enjoying coffee and tea with Mrs. Morgan's apple pie. Karl said, "Ma, I have had apple pie many times, but no one can beat Mrs. Morgan's apple pie."

Karl was sitting near his father. Norman Schoulz asked Karl, "Do you think gallbladder surgery to remove the stones is safe?"

Karl told his dad, "If there is no alternative, you have to have surgery. There is no other method."

Dr. Norman explained that there was an alternative, a herbal method formulated to remove gallstones. "Your mother and Norm Jr. have given me one week to try the herbal formula. If I don't succeed, then I will accept surgery. I think it is fair. I have accepted the challenge; I need your help to get these ingredients today."

He wrote a list of ingredients and gave it to Karl. They went together to the herbal medicine store, and Norman gave the list to the storekeeper. The man behind the counter immediately recognized the formula. He asked Norman, "Who is going to use this formula?"

Norman told him it was for him.

"Be careful. You must follow the procedure as prescribed. Do you have the procedure? If you do not, I have the package right here with the procedure."

He went to his recipe section and handed Dr. Norman a medium-sized envelope containing the ingredients as well as the instructions. "The only other things you have to buy are olive oil, artichokes, and lemons."

Karl was very much impressed with the herbalist even though his own father was an expert. As they were leaving, the storekeeper asked Dr. Norman if he was an herbal researcher. "I have seen your picture in many articles. I have been working in herbal science for thirty years." Dr. Norman introduced himself. The man said his name was Arthur Miller. He shook Norman's hand with both hands and said good-bye.

The next day was Saturday. Krista prepared Senna leaf tea, artichoke water, and the juice from two lemons. She made Zein tea as per instructions that accompanied the herbal package. Norman started the treatment early Sunday morning and continued taking the oil, lemon juice, and other items every hour. After each item, he had to lie down. The last item on the list was another cup of Zein tea at six p.m. At this point, the treatment ended, and now at eight p.m. he was allowed to eat if he was hungry. Norman kept lying down. It was after ten p.m. when Norman had to rush to the bathroom, where he felt a few things popping out. He noticed that the pain was gone. Tired, he went back to bed and had no problem falling asleep.

At nine the next morning, Krista started to worry. She said to Mrs. Morgan, "Norman has never slept this long. Should I wake him up?"

Mrs. Morgan went with Krista to wake him up. Krista checked his forehead and found his temperature normal. She grabbed his shoulder and shook him. "Norman, wake up. It is nine-thirty."

Norman woke up and said, "Oh, Krista, I was sleeping so well. I don't have any pain." He propelled himself out of bed. Krista and Mrs. Morgan were so happy.

Krista said, "It looks like your formula works."

Norman said to Mrs. Morgan, "I am hungry. Let's go and eat."

Krista called Norm Jr. Sybille answered the phone. "Oh, Sybille, tell Norman that Norman's formula worked. He has no more pain. Maybe Norm can cancel the surgery appointment."

Sybille said, "Aunty, maybe it is too early to do that. Let us wait for a few more days. Norman has gone to a meeting and will be back soon."

Krista agreed with Sybille, and they hung up.

Two days passed, and Norman was as active as before. One morning, the phone rang, and he answered. "Herby, it is nice of you to call. Are you all right?"

It was his friend Chairman Heber. He told Norman, "Norm, I have not been well for some time. No doctor has been able to pinpoint the exact reason for my ailment. But listen, Norm. You will be receiving an invitation to attend a reception honoring you for your contribution to herbal science and for helping our company to develop very important medications that made good profits for us and our shareholders. Norm, I have been trying to convince the board of directors to prepare a package for you that will hopefully please Krista and your son. It has been long time coming. Wait for the envelope and give me a call at my residence. See you soon."

Norman Schoulz did not tell anyone the news until everyone came home that evening, even though he was dying to tell Krista. They all arrived one by one except Ingrid. They were at the dining table. Norman stood up and told everyone, "This is the week of good news. I have two items of good news to share with you. I was just waiting for Ingrid."

As he was ready to finish his sentence, Ingrid walked in. Everyone cheered. She was happy. "Listen, everyone, I have good news. My thesis was accepted, and I will have my master's degree next month."

Karl rushed and kissed her. She came around the table kissing and shaking hands with all. Norman got up again and said, "I have two pieces of good news to share. Number one, I have no more pain. I lost my marbles three nights ago, and I am back to Norm the normal. The second piece of news is very important. Krista, you pay attention. Chairman Heber called and said that tomorrow; a courier will bring an invitation to attend a ceremony to honor me for my contribution to science. He said that the board of directors of his company has awarded me a condominium in Florida and two hundred thousand US dollars. He has written a long letter explaining the details of the events that led to this happy outcome."

There was silence for only few seconds, and then came the laughter. What a day it was! Krista came over and apologized for not trusting Heber. Karl and Norm Junior were so excited that they were dancing with everyone, including Mrs. Morgan. They all congratulated Dr. Norman.

The next morning, a courier brought a manila envelope addressed to Dr. Norman Schoulz. He called Krista and both sat down and started to read the letter. It talked about Heber's health problems and his personal problems running the company. He wrote that some of the new members of the board did not want to give Norman and Chairman Heber the recognition that both deserved. At an urgent meeting called by him, he had told the board that the majority of patents that the company was using to produce lucrative products were still in Heber's and Schoulz's names. They still held ownership of the patents.

"Norm," the letter concluded, "before I took over the company, I made sure our interests were protected, and, thank God, finally it paid off. The board agreed to my terms. Krista always asked me privately, without your knowledge, why you have seen no benefit from the work you did for so many years. I must say she was absolutely right in protecting your interest. In the end, Norm, they agreed to honor both of us because you and I both went to faraway places in the search of herbs and developed these safe and sound medicinal products. Now is the time we need recognition and compensation. Norman, I and my wife Sara are looking forward to seeing you and renewing our friendship."

Krista told Norm, "I am sorry to have doubted Heber's sincerity. But it is possible that if I had not pushed him, nothing would have happened. He certainly had a nice job, an excellent salary, and a big, fat expense account, whiles you, Norman, did not ask anything. You never got anything, and you took it easy."

The atmosphere was so nice and pleasant that Sybille and Norm Jr. stayed for the evening. After dinner, they all sat down, and Norman Schoulz was again in the driver's seat. He asked everyone to pay close attention to the forthcoming events in each other's lives during the coming months. "My award ceremony is on January 20. Next is Ingrid's graduation on the twenty-third, and last but not least is an important celebration in Moscow on the twenty-fifth. We must all remember that we all have to attend everyone's functions together. It may not be possible for all of us to see all of Sybille's concerts and every day of Norm's art exposition, but we must all travel together and attend as much as we can. Children, I am warning you, when I am gone, remember that togetherness is a big remedy for all ills. Let us join hands and promise to enjoy each other's company."

Dr. Norman called Chairman Heber, and they talked for at least an hour. Norman told Heber about his health problems. He told his friend about how he himself sidetracked every physician who examined him. He was always harping on his liver, so they did not think that it could be something else that was giving him pain. He asked his friend Heber "Is it possible that your pain was due to gallbladder stones?"

Heber said, "In the end that is what this new young doctor discovered. Norman, he was the fifth doctor I visited. He ordered immediate surgery. After that, I went through a lot of pain, and it took me more than a month to return to normal life."

Norman started to laugh. He told Heber, "How strange and ironic. Herby that is exactly what happened to me. I had the same symptoms as you and came to the same conclusions. Finally, a young doctor friend of Norman Junior came up with the correct diagnosis in only one hour. The laughing matter is the surgery. Krista wanted me to have surgery immediately, but I told them, 'Let me try my herbal formula first. If it does not work, then I will accept surgery.' And Heber, my formula worked. In two days, my pain was gone and the stones were gone. I am scheduled to go for X-ray and ultrasound tests to confirm the disappearance of the stones."

Heber could not believe that both of them had suffered from the same ailment. Heber asked Norm to call him when he had the results of the X-ray.

The next day, Krista and Norm Jr. accompanied Norman Schoulz to visit Dr. Lee. Norm had already briefed the doctor about the effects of his herbal treatment.

Dr. Lee greeted Norman. "Hello, Dr. Norman. Before we do any tests, I have to congratulate you on your award ceremony this month. Before coming to my office, I glanced at the *Globe* newspaper and saw your and Dr. Heber's photo along with a description of the award ceremony."

Dr. Lee addressed Norm Jr. "Norm, my friend, after that article I believe Dr. Norman's story about the herbal remedy." He asked Norman to come to the X-ray room with him. Both came out of the room smiling. Dr. Lee announced that Dr. Norman was free of his stones. Krista and Norm Jr. we're delighted with the outcome.

Dr. Norman Schoulz called his friend Dr. Heber and gave him the good news. He was amazed by the results. Dr. Heber asked Norman, "Why is it that both of us had the same medical problem almost in the same time period, with similar false diagnoses?"

Dr. Norman told him, "Herby, look at our history. Both of us spent time traveling to many rain forests, eating the same food, drinking the same water, and being bitten by same insects for almost same number of years before completing our graduate work. As a result, we suffered the same medical condition."

They promised to see each other on January 20 and hung up.

Three days before Christmas, Mrs. Morgan and Krista went to a local nursery and bought two Christmas trees to be delivered, one to 61 Tulip Lane and the other to 61 Jasmine Crescent. The trees were delivered in the afternoon. Sybille was surprised to receive a seven-foot tree. She had never had a tree in her house in Moscow, although she had seen them around Christmas time. As she was thinking about decorating the tree, NRJ walked in and saw the tree. He was delighted. "Oh, I am glad you bought a tree, Sybille. It will be fun to decorate it. And you should see what the boys did at the workshop."

"I did not buy the tree," Sybille replied. "Krista and Mrs. Morgan ordered one for us and one for them."

"We all will get together at Aunty Krista's house and decorate their tree, and then all of us will gather here and decorate ours, Sybille. I promise you, it is fun."

Two days passed, and Christmas Eve arrived. The trees were decorated, and NRJ was right: it was fun. Sybille and Ingrid loved decorating the trees. It was a dark night. The church singers were going from house to house, singing Christmas carols accompanied by flute and violin players.

Morning brought light snowflakes, covering shrubs and trees; it created a winter wonderland. Sybille and Norm Junior dressed warmly and walked to Uncle Norman and Aunty Krista's house. Krista and Mrs. Morgan were in the kitchen preparing a late breakfast. Ingrid and Karl were still in their pajamas. Uncle Norman was coming out of his room rubbing his eyes. Norm Jr. and Sybille had prepared a Christmas song to sing when they arrived. Ingrid came running down the hall. Norm Jr. signaled Sybille to sing. She started to sing a gentle, sweet melody that attracted all of them to the hall. Mrs. Morgan joined Sybille. They had never heard her sing before, and her voice was a pleasant surprise. Mrs. Morgan held Sybille's hand and took her to her kitchen.

Krista told Sybille, "It was a lovely thought for you to wake us up with your lovely song. And you, Mrs. Morgan, surprised us with your lovely voice."

They enjoyed each other's company all day. Uncle Norman after dinner raised his grape juice glass and said, "How nice is to be happy together. I hope to have more such occasions."

Dr. Norman Schoulz is honored for his contribution to herbal science

Everyone hugged and kissed each other.

Christmas passed, and the time came for Dr. Norman's family to go to the Royal York hotel for his award ceremony. They were all dressed elegantly; Krista was dressed in long white chiffon dress, with a gold necklace around her slender neck. Sybille was dressed in a long, flowing turquoise dress with an exquisite emerald necklace. Ingrid had selected a dress with tiny green and pink flowers and a touch of purple in the back ground. The men wore their tuxedos. Dr. Norman's family was guided to seats close to the podium. As they sat down, Chairman Heber and his wife arrived. They all got up and were introduced to each other. Norman sat next to his friend Dr. Heber, and his wife, Isabel, sat next to Krista.

The master of ceremonies was one of the directors of the pharmaceutical corporation. He discussed the history of herbs and the development of safe drugs using the careful processing and preparing methods suggested by these brave young men, these two dedicated postgraduate students of the famous university in Montreal.

Dr. Albert Houser told the audience, "Dr. Heber and Dr. Schoulz searched the ancient literatures of Peruvian Indians and the ancient Ayurvedic literature of India and southeast Asia. Their search took them to the four corners of the world. They combed the Sahara and Gobi deserts. They talked to Bedouin chiefs, Buddhist lamas, and Indian local doctors practicing herbal medicine in their regions. Their dedication did not waver when they were bitten by mosquitoes, snakes, and lizards.

Thank heavens, their love for research paid off. The contribution these fearless green warriors have made to the industry in terms of monetary benefit is great, but the biggest benefit to mankind is not measurable in dollars. So without delay, I and our board present you, Dr. Heber, the chairman of our corporation, and your colleague, Dr. Norman Schoulz, with deeds to Florida condos."

The condos were located in a very desirable part of Boca Raton, right on the ocean. The cash award was in the form of company shares. At the time of presentation, the shares were worth two hundred thousand US dollars. The hall was filled with invited guests, and many representatives from the medical field were present. There was staff from the corporation's herbal research institute, graduate students from the university in Rangoon, and Dr. Cruz, the chief from Peru who guided Dr. Schoulz on his search for rare herbs that were hard to locate.

It was time for Heber and Norman to go to the podium. Both thanked the company directors, and Dr. Norman thanked his friend, under whose guidance the corporation had flourished and became the flag bearer of nature's gift to all living creatures. Dr. Norman Schoulz asked the audience to stand up and recognize Chairman Heber's contribution and achievements. They cheered both the award winners. After the ceremony was over, people kept coming to shake hands and chat a while with Dr. Norman. When Krista and the family left, it was after midnight.

The next afternoon, Karl and the family were getting ready to go to the university to attend Ingrid's graduation ceremony. The weather was a little cold but sunny. She received her master's degree in the study of fragrance. She was happy, especially when she saw her parents from Calgary in the audience. Karl was so happy that he picked her up and danced around few times. They all congratulated her and went home. Mrs. Morgan was waiting for the family. When they entered the house, Mrs. Morgan came to hug Ingrid and told her, "I have made a special dish to celebrate your graduation."

They went into the living room, where Karl gave his wife a bouquet of roses with a strong fragrance she loved. Her mother gave her a gold tennis bracelet. She was overwhelmed and exhausted by feeling so much happiness. They enjoyed Mrs. Morgan's delicious meal.

The snow was getting heavier and staying on the ground. You could hear the snowplows very early in the morning clearing the roads. Nights were spent indoors, and television shows helped to pass the evenings.

Fireplaces made the atmosphere warm and cozy. Norm Junior and Sybille were very busy getting ready for their Moscow celebrations. Sybille was rehearsing her singing. Krista had promised Sybille that she would be her piano player. Norm Jr. was extremely busy with his artwork and with designing art deco pieces for his show in Moscow.

Chapter 18

NORM JR., SYBILLE, KRISTA, AND
FAMILY ARE OFF TO MOSCOW TO
ATTEND SYBILLE'S CONCERT

Time came for Sybille and Norm to take off for Moscow. The rest of family would follow them five days later. Krista received a phone call from Norm Jr. saying that they had arrived safely and were staying at Dmitri's house. He told his aunt that it was colder in Moscow than Toronto and asked her to bring heavy coats. He also told her that he and Sybille would pick them up at the airport and that Dmitri had arranged accommodation for all of them.

Krista, Norman, Ingrid, and Karl arrived on a Friday afternoon. It was cold but sunny. Krista had her Canadian heavy coat with a fur collar, and Ingrid was wearing a new fur coat that Karl had bought for her as a graduation gift. It was made of black mink and had a large collar covering her ears. A limousine and driver were provided by the politburo at Dmitri's request. The government had given this privilege to retired politburo officers. They arrived in style at Dmitri's house; Sybille and Katharina were delighted to have Norman and Krista's family. Dmitri's big house could accommodate the whole family, and the house was warm even when it was freezing outside. Dmitri, Katharina, and Sybille took their guests around to see the important sights of Moscow. The nights were getting longer, and the cold days were getting shorter. Dmitri took them to the famous Bolshoi ballet theater, to museums, and to the Kremlin.

The time came to go to the famous opera house to attend the concert where Sybille was a star performer. The hall was packed, and Dmitri had front-row seats for Dr. Norman and his family. Ingrid and Karl had never seen an opera singer so admired; people said that when Sybille Yevchenco sang, they felt chills down their spines. When the show was over, the audience wanted more and more of Sybille's singing. She had so many curtain calls that she was exhausted. Norm Jr. and Dmitri were aware of the stress she went through every time she sang in public. Dmitri told the family that she tried too hard. "She is a perfectionist. She puts her heart and soul in her work, and that tires her out." Sybille arrived home soon after the rest of the family. Dmitri hugged and kissed her and made her rest on a recliner, Norm Junior held her hand, and everyone praised her for a beautiful and courageous performance. She had three more performances to attend in the coming week.

The next day, Sybille started to practice for her upcoming performances. Norman Rockville Junior was busy getting ready for his art show. Karl and Ingrid were helping NRJ's man, Mike Bishop, who helped NRJ whenever they went out of the country to exhibit their art and artifacts. Stories about Norman Rockville Junior and Sybille were in every newspaper; they had a large following among opera lovers and the art world.

The official Soviet celebration would be inaugurated on Saturday morning by Marshal Karmasoff. Dmitri and his family would be seated up front at the podium along with retired ace Soviet air force pilots and the chief of the Mikoyan design group. There would be a spectacular military parade, and the Soviet air force's new jet fighters would display their skill and killing aerobatics. On the same day, Norman Junior's art gallery would be officially opened by the minster of art and culture.

There were big crowds in all directions; traffic was jammed around the parade grounds. Dmitri and Katharina and their guests were driven in a government transport to the central square of the Kremlin. They arrived with big fanfare, and a large military band was playing. Other dignitaries, diplomats, and military attachés of friendly countries were filling the podium. Many high-ranking Soviet officers had a tremendous respect for Dmitri Yevchenco and his darling granddaughter Sybille; many remembered the tragedy the Yevchenco family had gone through.

This morning was the day dedicated to the armed forces. The parade was honored and blessed by the president, three service commanders, and the defense minister. The march past the parade ground was very impressive; soldiers, sailors, and air force personnel were represented. While the parade went on, air force fighter jets thundered above. A formation of the newest fighter jets suddenly appeared, swooping down low enough to shake the ground. Everyone, grownups and children, were up on their feet in awe. Just before the last jet disappeared in the winter air, another squadron of the latest Mig fighter jets appeared, swooping down as if saluting the president and the chiefs. It was thrilling to watch. The guests had never seen a show where screaming jet fighter flew so low and as loud as they passed by, shaking the whole place. They said that this air show was the best.

Dmitri, Norman, Karl and Ingrid left the podium and went home. There, they found Krista and Katharina helping Sybille practice and prepare for the next day's royal concert. The academy called it a royal concert because it would be attended by the president, members of the communist council, and chiefs of services along with the cabinet members. This was a special treat for governing council and politburo members. After the show, the organizers had planned a dinner to celebrate the achievements of the Soviet communist party in social and scientific fields. Speeches by the president and politburo members would be short and to the point. Dinner would follow at the end of speeches; the orchestra would be playing Russian national music and folk songs. A limited number of guests would be invited.

The dinner and dance was attended by Dmitri and Katharina. Sybille was going as a special guest, and NRJ was going as her escort. They left to attend the celebration at the central committee hall. Norman Junior was amazed at the decoration and setup, which must have cost millions of rubles. The gilded walls, the exotic and beautiful chandelier, the gold-framed full-length mirrors, and the shining marble floors were astounding. The hall resembled Catherine the Great's Hermitage. Norman made some mental notes for his future designs. Dinner was remarkably delicious and light; wine and vodka were abundant, yet no one was out of control. Most members were senior in age and were not in their best form. The master of ceremonies came to the podium and announced, "Sybille Yevchenco will sing our national anthem and later will sing few Russian tunes to lift our spirits without vodka."

The younger audience members stood up and cheered. Sybille was looking like a princess. Dmitri, Katharina, and NRJ were filled with pride and love. Norm Junior could not believe the high esteem and high regard the Soviet people had for their world-famous sweet little Yevchenco, as they called her. After she finished her songs, she was presented with a bouquet of roses from the politburo central committee.

She was still standing at the microphone while the audience members were bringing long-stemmed roses and placing them on the stage near her feet. She looked tired and signaled her grandpa to take her home. By the time she came out through the back door and walked to the waiting limousine, it was eight-thirty p.m. She entered the car and sat near NRJ. He took her in his arms, and she placed her head on his shoulder. They arrived home, and Dmitri made her comfortable on the big recliner. Norman Junior went to his aunt and asked her whether it was normal for a singer to be so exhausted. Krista thought for a while and said, "Norm, my son, I have seen quite a few operas, but I have never seen a diva so tired."

Norm Junior thought for a while and asked Ingrid, "Is it possible that after her exhausting performance, her blood sugar drops and she is ready to collapse?"

Krista jumped and kissed Norm, saying, "My God, Norm, you just hit the nail on its head. You are ingenious. Krista went to see Katharina and Dmitri, who were sitting near their loving granddaughter. She asked them to come to the living room. Krista addressed both of them and started to discuss Sybille's exhaustion after every performance.

Katharina said, "I know. I have seen lots and lots of singers who can talk to people or the press after their performances. They are never exhausted like our baby. I thought it was because she put too much energy and effort into pleasing the audience."

Norm Junior remarked, "Nana, every diva becomes a diva because she tries her best."

Dmitri asked, "Then why does our little girl have this problem?"

Krista put her hand on Dmitri's shoulder and said, "Norm Junior has come up with a possible cause. Norm, tell them."

"It is just a thought. After such an exhausting work, I think Sybille's blood sugar level drops, causing her to become very, very tired. To cure this problem, she just needs to raise her sugar level."

Both said, "Norman, you may just be right."

Katharina asked Norm, "So what should we do?"

Dmitri told Katharina, "We'll just ask the doctor to monitor her blood sugar during the day, checking it every two hours. I am sure Norm is right. Then we can give her sweet drinks during her performance when she has time for a break."

They thanked Norm Junior for his excellent diagnosis. Katharina told

Krista, "Every time she attends a major performance like tonight, just thinking about her condition after the show kills me."

In the meantime, Sybille had gotten up and was looking for Norm and her grandfather. She called, "Nana, Norm, where are you?"

They came down to see her immediately. She asked her grandpa, "What happened? You left me alone." She asked Norm, "Why do I get so exhausted, Norm?"

Dmitri told her to sit down and listen. "We went into the other room to discuss your problem, and you know, I think your husband has the answer."

She could not keep back her joy. She said, "Really? Oh, Norm, you are so smart."

Dmitri asked Norm to explain his theory to Sybille. He told her, "It is possible that your blood sugar level drops when you appear on stage, if you are anxious and don't eat enough protein and sugar prior to your performance."

She said, "Norm, I think you are right. I notice that when I am singing folk songs or other songs for even more than an hour, I don't get so tired."

Dmitri explained to her their plan. "At your next operatic performance, your grandma will be there with an orange juice bottle and you will take a sip during your break. If the orange juice trick works, then you know Norm's diagnosis is correct."

Katharina, Ingrid, and Krista were pleased and waited eagerly for Sybille's next big performance in the Bolshoi Theater. They were all so delighted at the thought that Sybille might be free from her sugar deficiency. Katharina was praying silently for the remedy to work so she would not have to worry about Sybille before every performance.

Dr. Norman, Krista, Ingrid, and Karl were flying home the day before Sybille's performance. Norm Junior told Sybille to stay home while he took them to the airport. "Let the doctor do his testing. And you have to practice for tomorrow's performance. *La Traviata* requires a strong performer, and if you survive this show without collapsing, we will know we have found a solution to your problem. So, my darling Sybille, I am waiting for tomorrow. I have never waited for any tomorrow with so much anxiety. Go and practice hard with confidence. I am taking our family to the airport. I will be back soon." He embraced her and told her, "Just think of how much I love you."

She got up to say good-bye to everyone and went back to follow her training program.

As Sybille sat in the limousine between her grandfather and Norm on the way to the Bolshoi Theater for her very important performance, she felt confident. The limo dropped her off at the rear private door of the theater. She kissed Norm and her grandpa inside the car. The driver opened the door, and Norm got out and helped her down. She hugged Norm and kissed him. "Norm, I feel good. I think it will work." And she left.

The Bolshoi Theater was a beautiful place. Sybille entered the backstage area and made arrangements for her grandma to sit just behind the curtain so that she could give Sybille orange juice during breaks. The orchestra started playing very softly. One of the best conductors was leading the hundred-piece ensemble. When the drums began rolling, the curtain lifted, and soon Sybille appeared among thundering applause. She sang with her full energy. Every time she had a moment, her grandma was there with her juice bottle. Every time Sybille came backstage, she took a big sip. Sybille sang so well that she could not believe herself. When it was over, she had many curtain calls, and she was still on her feet, feeling comfortable and relaxed. Dignitaries and reporters were waiting to speak with her. She sat on an armchair and conversed confidently and gracefully. Katharina sat near her, filled with pride and happiness. Dmitri and Norm Jr. came in to escort Sybille and Katharina to the waiting limousine. As they settled down inside limousine, Sybille expressed her gratitude to her grandma for providing her with the nectar that gave her life.

Katharina kissed her and said, "Sybille, you have no idea how I prayed for this orange juice to give you what your husband said it would give. Look what happened. You were solid like a rock."

Dmitri put his arm around Norman's neck and kissed him. "My son, you saved our little girl's life, her musical honor, and her dignity. Thank you."

They arrived home. As they entered the house, Sybille jumped into Norman's arms and showered him with love and affection. Dmitri announced that they would go to a restaurant where the food was heavenly to celebrate Sybille's freedom from exhaustion. This had been Sybille's last performance in Moscow, and Norm Junior's show had also ended. They were scheduled to leave in two days for Toronto.

The next morning, the media were also celebrating Sybille's meeting with the press. She was looking healthy. The city newspapers were speculating about her well-being. The press had mentioned her exhausted condition after previous performances.

Norman Junior called Krista and told her that their diagnosis had proved to be true, and Dmitri's solution had cured the problem. As a result, after her last performance she was fit to handle the press and give interviews without any problems.

Sybille and Norm Junior were driven by Dmitri and Katharina to the airport. It was hard for the grandparents to say good-bye. Katharina was in tears. She told Sybille, "My darling, we are getting old, and I don't know when we are going to see both of you again. We love you, Norm. You are our grandson."

You could see Dmitri wiping his eyes as he hugged Norm and Sybille. Katharina joined in. It was an emotional moment. Sybille promised her grandparents that when she was in Europe on her concert tours, she would make sure to book a flight to Moscow to be with them for a few days.

When Sybille and Norm Jr. arrived in Toronto, Karl and Ingrid came to pick them up. They were happy to see each other. Sybille told them about how Norm had diagnosed the reason of her exhaustion after every major concert. "It was getting so bad that the reporters of major newspapers had started to talk about my health. Norm Junior and my grandparents came up with a solution. My grandma brought a bottle of orange juice and stood just behind a prop on the stage. Every time I had a free moment, I came back for a big sip of juice. I felt so much better and stronger. Before, I was always afraid of collapsing on stage at the finish."

Ingrid said to Norm, "You helped Norman by taking him to your doctor who cured his stomach pain, and now you help Sybille by saving her from exhaustion. That is our brother and your husband, Sybille."

It was getting colder. Snow was piling up on the ground, but the roads were clean for safer driving. Sybille said, "Norman, remember how cold it was in Moscow?"

Sybille called her father in Spain and gave him the good news. She also called Dmitri and Grandma in Moscow. They told her, "Talking to you gives us so much pleasure that we look forward to every Sunday."

March was not too far away. One day, there was a snowstorm. The roads were blocked, schools were closed, and very few made it to work. Ingrid did not sleep all night, and Karl slept very little. Karl went with

Ingrid down to the kitchen at six in the morning, when Krista and Norman were still sleeping. Karl made mint tea for Ingrid, who had complained, "I think I have an upset stomach. I have gas and feel nauseated."

Karl told her that mint tea would be good for her. She started to drink the tea, but it was too hot. They made enough noise to wake Krista and Norm up. Krista came running to the kitchen and saw Karl and Ingrid sitting at the dining table and Karl holding Ingrid's hand. Krista asked them, "What happened? What is wrong?"

Ingrid told her, "Ma, I don't feel good. I have an upset stomach and I feel terrible. I was nauseated and could not sleep all night."

Norman entered the kitchen a little later and heard only part of Ingrid's complaint. Krista started to laugh and was joined by Norman. Karl and Ingrid could not understand. "Ma, why are you laughing? Ingrid is really sick."

Krista and Norm hugged Ingrid and Karl saying, "Congratulations! We are going to be grandparents, and you will be playing with a baby in nine months."

Ingrid was laughing and crying at the same time. Karl was dancing around Ingrid and kissed her. Ingrid could not believe that she felt sick when she was going to have a baby.

Karl took Ingrid to the living room and made her sit in a recliner. They all sat near her, and Karl started a fire to warm the room and covered Ingrid with a blanket. Ingrid asked Karl to call Norm and Sybille and give them the news. Both Norm and Sybille came over and were overjoyed. They stayed for breakfast. Mrs. Morgan woke up and wanted to know what was going on. When she saw Ingrid on the lounge chair and everyone sitting around her, she knew what the situation was. She kissed Ingrid and congratulated Krista and Norman. Ingrid's sickness was only temporary; after few weeks, she sometimes forgot that she was pregnant. Gradually, she put on weight.

Karl and Krista made an appointment for Ingrid with a female gynecologist. Krista and Ingrid both wanted a lady doctor to examine Ingrid; she felt more comfortable that way. Krista always complained about male gynecologists and believed that men should not be encouraged to become doctors for women. Dr. Sara Azari was a middle-aged, experienced gynecologist who had practiced in Montreal at Victoria Hospital and was known to Krista and Norman.

Dr. Azari examined Ingrid and declared her in excellent shape.

She asked Krista to bring her back in three months unless a problem developed.

Dr. Norman Schoulz and Krista were happy with the way their lives and those of their loved ones were going. Sybille was booked for the next six months at recording studios and performances in Ukraine, Budapest, and Berlin. She told Ingrid that when she was in Ukraine, she would visit her grandparents in Moscow. Norm Jr. had arranged another art show in Moscow around the time Sybille would be visiting her grandparents there.

Ingrid was seeing Dr. Azari as scheduled and was feeling good. Her due date was approaching. Krista had advised Ingrid and Karl to sleep on the ground floor for the two weeks before the baby was due. Krista told Ingrid, "It will be a lot easier when you need to go to the hospital."

After that, Karl and Ingrid began sleeping in the guest room on the ground floor. It was a beautiful day on October 10 when Ingrid woke up early in the morning crying and complaining of pain. Karl woke up and went to wake his mother. Krista quickly dressed herself to go to the hospital. She asked Karl to call and leave a message with Dr. Azari. Karl brought the car around and drove to the hospital. When they entered the emergency room, the staff members took Ingrid inside, while all the paperwork was being handled by Karl. Krista was with Ingrid. It was eleven a.m. when Krista came out to get Karl. Krista was happy, "Come, my son. Ingrid has given you a beautiful baby boy."

Karl went in the room and kissed Ingrid. She was smiling and said to Karl, "Hold your son. Is he not beautiful?"

Karl took his son from Ingrid. Krista said, "Look how healthy he looks, Karl. He is looking at you and smiling."

Krista told them that she had to go and give Norman and Norm Junior the good news, and she left the room. Karl was just enchanted with his little boy. He handed him back to Ingrid and asked her, "Did we decide about his name?"

Ingrid told him, "Karl, you and your father decided that his name would be Paul Schoulz, and I think my parents also agreed."

Karl asked Ingrid, "So can I hold my Paul again now?"

Ingrid said, "Karl, don't you see he is having his lunch?"

Karl said to her, "I am hungry, too. Can I have my lunch too?"

She told him, "Sure, touch my breast. It is full. There is enough for you after Paul has had his. Karl, I love you a lot, but from now on, Paul comes first as far as his food is concerned."

Paul fell asleep, and Karl touched Ingrid's breast. It was full, and a little squeeze squirted out a little milk. Krista entered the room and saw him playing with Ingrid's breast. She scolded Karl, "What are you doing? Just wait. She will be home very soon."

"We were just kidding," Karl and Ingrid both said, laughing.

Baby and Ingrid were doing well, so Dr. Azari signed the papers allowing them to go home after three days. The day before, Norm Jr. brought Sybille and Norman to see Ingrid and the baby. Sybille loved the baby so much that she took him into her arms. The baby smiled at her, and she asked Norm Junior to take him. The baby was looking at Norm and making sounds as if he were talking. Ingrid was surprised because she never heard the baby making those kinds of noises before.

Grandpa Norm said, "Hey, Norm, let him say something to his grandpa."

Norm gave the baby to Norman. Baby Paul continued to talk to his grandpa. Sybille and Ingrid were both fascinated. Sybille asked Ingrid, "What are you going to call him?"

Grandpa Norm said, "Paul."

Norm Junior asked, "And when is Paul coming home?"

Ingrid told them that they would be coming home the next day and hoped everyone would come by.

When Ingrid and Paul came home, all the family was there. Karl told Ingrid that he had to go to the airport to pick up her parents. She thanked Karl. Audrey and Jeffrey arrived and were overjoyed to see their grandson. Ingrid looked as good as if nothing had changed except that she had gained a little weight. Uncle Norman and Aunty Krista were happy. The whole house's atmosphere was pleasant and full of happiness. Mrs. Morgan ran to see the baby as soon as he started to cry and brought him to Ingrid to be fed.

Sybille looked at Norm Junior and asked him, "Can we have a baby too?"

Norman told her, "Sure, but you will have to interrupt your singing career for maybe two years. We can it discuss later. Let us enjoy Paul before he grows up. You know that babies grow up very fast."

The baby became the center of attention. Karl and Ingrid had the best toy they had ever seen, and Paul's grandpa and grandma had took turns picking him up.

Mrs. Morgan said to Norm Junior, "I would love to see your baby. I bet your baby will be the best artist and the best singer."

He told Mrs. Morgan, "I am pretty sure you are right. You see, everything has its time, and hopefully it will be soon. We are working on it." Paul grew big and began running around the house. His grandparents tried to catch him, and Ingrid ran after him. Paul loved the attention, as if saying to him, *Catch me if you can.* Ingrid loved breastfeeding and cuddling him. When Karl came home, Paul always quieted down and wanted Karl to pick him up.

Norm Junior and Sybille were invited over for Paul's third birthday party. Mrs. Morgan had prepared pepper steak, stir-fried fresh vegetables, rice with saffron and peas, fruit juices, and Black Forest cake. Everyone was enjoying the food, and Paul ran around the table from relative to relative. Suddenly, Sybille ran to the washroom, and Krista and Norm Junior went after her. Krista knocked on the washroom door. She could hear Sybille moaning inside, and it sounded as if she were trying to vomit.

She opened the washroom door and came out, looking exhausted. "Oh, Aunty, I feel so bad. I think the food was too rich."

Krista told her, "Sybille, look at me." Sybille raised her head, and Krista shouted, "We are going to have a baby!"

Sybille started to cry. Norman was there next to her. Everyone left the table and came running to hug Sybille. She could not believe it. Norm took her back to the table and gave her fruit juice. She wiped her eyes and said, "I am so happy. Thank you, Aunty Krista and Uncle Norm, Karl and my lovely Ingrid. It is the happiest day of my life."

The next morning, she called her grandparents in Moscow and gave them the good news. They were very happy and excited.

Norm Junior called his doctor friend and gave him the good news. He asked him, "Dr. Lee, when could you examine Sybille?" The doctor came to the house, examined Sybille, and told Norm that everything was okay. They discussed the fact that Sybille was scheduled to appear in two shows the next month. The doctor said, "The way she is now, she can go anywhere in the world. I will check on her every month and we will decide her schedule, depending on her condition."

Sʏʙɪʟʟᴇ ɪs ɢᴏɪɴɢ ᴛᴏ ʜᴀᴠᴇ ʙᴀʙʏ

Summer came. Sybille was in perfect health. One day, Norm called Krista to take Sybille to the hospital, and her baby, Sara, was born at nine a.m. It was a moment of great joy to have a beautiful girl in the house. Sybille and the baby were in such good health that they were allowed to go home on the third day. The baby's room was decorated for a princess; everything was decorated in pastel pink and green. Ingrid and Krista loved the nursery.

Many seasons passed. Karl was going gray around his temples, Paul was twelve, and Sara Rockville was tall and beautiful at age eight. Grandpa could not bear to stay in his place during the wintertime. The cold was starting to bother both him and Krista, so he decided to go to his condo in Florida for the winter. In the beginning, Krista and Norman did not feel like leaving their grandson Paul and great-niece Sara for three months, but the comfort of Florida, the warm sun, and the prospect of meeting new people of their age finally won them over. Every time there was a long holiday, Krista and Norman wanted Karl and his family to visit. They also wanted Norm Junior, Sybille, and Sara to join them at the same time. When they were there, they all had fun. The condo was big enough to hold the whole family. Paul and Sara had been spending summers at Norm's art studio learning and practicing their skills. Sara had inherited her father's talent in art and her mother's musical capability. When she was old enough, she was admitted to a music conservatory. She was always on top of her school's talent list. Many recording companies and talent scouts had approached Sybille offering to market Sara's talent, but Sybille always refused.

The summer after Paul graduated from high school, he was tall, lean, and handsome. He and Sara were both working with Norm Junior and loved to sit in on meetings with designers, learning about manufacturing techniques.

Dr. Norman was in his mid-eighties and had been suffering from liver problems; he spent many hours in hospitals, going through all kinds of tests. Karl, Norm Jr., and Sybille often got together and tried to find the cause of his constipation, nausea, and lack of appetite.

They took Uncle Norman to Dr. Lee; he carried out few basic tests and was sure Dr. Norman's sickness had something to do with his liver. Dr. Lee made an appointment with Dr. Medlock, who specialized in liver disease.

A month after Dr. Norman saw the specialist; Dr. Lee called Norm Junior and told him, "I would like to have an immediate meeting with

Mrs. Schoulz and Karl, if you can bring them into my office around five p.m. It is, of course, about Dr. Norman Schoulz."

Norm came running to see Krista and Karl and said, "Aunty Krista, Dr. Lee called me at my house. He wants us to be at his office at five. He wants to discuss Uncle Norman's condition."

They all went to see Dr. Lee. He asked them to sit down and said, "I don't know how to say this. Dr. Norman's condition is complicated. According to Dr. Medlock, Dr. Schoulz's past bout with malaria has complicated the issue. He is in his late eighties, he has no appetite, and he is losing weight. Dr. Medlock told me he was worried about Dr. Norman's blood pressure and recommended that he be admitted to the hospital, where we can monitor his vital signs. There in the hospital, we will have access to a team of experts in related fields. We must try to raise blood pressure. Otherwise, we are going to lose him very soon. We are approaching a critical phase." Dr. Lee continued, "Dr. Medlock has booked a private room at the Toronto West Hospital, fairly close to you. He must be admitted tomorrow morning. It is hard to say how long he will be there. Be prepared for any eventuality."

Krista started to cry and left the office. Karl followed her and tried to console his mother. She told Norm and Karl, "I feel sorry for him, lying helpless. He does not talk, he has no strength even to stand up, and I can assure you, he will not like to be in the hospital."

It was Friday morning; there was not a single cloud in the sky. Norm Jr. called 911 and asked for an ambulance. The paramedics arrived. They took Dr. Norman's vital signs and transferred him to a stretcher for the ride to the hospital. Karl, Krista, and Norm Junior followed the ambulance to the hospital. After the paperwork was completed, they went to his room. Krista sat near him, sad and confused, with all kinds of opinions, thoughts, and questions. Her mind was roving. It was almost an hour before Dr. Lee and Dr. Medlock came around. They brought a special private nurse with them. She had a document with instructions for monitoring Dr. Norman's condition; the room was fitted with all kinds of devices. Dr. Lee told Krista that her husband was in a semi-coma tic condition and was not able to communicate. "We suggest it is better for you all to go home. We have to carry out a few tests to determine the line of action we will adopt. Any drastic move, chemical or physical, could jeopardize the situation. His low blood pressure and a serious liver infection are a cause for concern, so please go home. I will keep in touch."

Dr. Norman Schoulz passes away

Krista, Karl, and Norm Junior, all heartbroken and helpless, went home. Sybille, Sara, Ingrid, and Paul were together, waiting and hoping for some good news.

Norm Junior brought Karl and Krista home. They entered the front door with sad looks. Sybille and Ingrid rushed to embrace them. Krista could not hold her tears back. Ingrid asked them, "So what are the prognoses?"

Krista was still crying quietly. Norm answered, "He is really in bad shape. Dr. Lee said to be prepared for any eventuality."

They was all sad, and both Karl and Norm were wiping their tears. It was getting late, but all the family was still waiting by the phone. It rang, and it was Dr. Medlock. "I am sorry, Norm. Dr. Norman Schoulz passed away at seven-thirty."

Krista and the boys went to the hospital. They were sad. Karl could not talk about it. Norm broke the ice and told Krista and Karl, "Aunty, you know what is amazing? Uncle was always worried about his liver. He knew his trips to rain forests and tropical countries would cost him his life."

Krista finally spoke, "Karl, you remember when they brought him home burning with fever? I was so shocked, and you were crying with me. I told you that I did not want him to go on those expeditions anymore. You told me, 'you can't stop him because of his love for that kind of work.'"

Karl broke his silence. "Ma, if you had stopped him from going to Brazil, it would have made things worse. It is not the last trip that did the damage. The damage was done way before, and he always said it was programmed. You may call it destiny."

They reached the hospital, and Norm noticed that talking about Dr. Norman helped to distract him and took away some of his pain. They were shown Dr. Schoulz's body. Krista was really sad when she saw his face, which had become pale and reduced to bones in the last few weeks. Norm Jr. kissed his uncle and thanked him for giving him a good life. Karl kissed him and said, "I am going to miss you, Dad. I love you."

Krista kissed him and held his hand as tears rolled down her cheeks. "Norm, you did not have to leave so soon. We were getting better; we had more time left. But now you have time for eternity. Sleep well, my darling."

They were taken to another room, where they could cry and mourn their beloved Norman. When they came home, they were met by an anxious Ingrid, Sybille, and Mrs. Morgan and both children. Ingrid, Sybille, Mrs. Morgan, and the children met Krista, Norm, and Karl. All started to cry. Mrs. Morgan had her arms around Krista and cried a lot. The children hugged their fathers.

Time is a good healer; Krista and Mrs. Morgan grew much closer. Paul Schoulz moved on to do post-graduate work on optic nerves. His research interests were tremendously influenced by his father's suffering from that silent disease. By the time Karl was in his fifties, he had lost a fair amount of vision in his right eye.

Dr. Paul Schoulz worked on projects related to solving vision problems. His team's efforts, if successful, would benefit millions who suffered from glaucoma, cataracts, and macular degeneration.

Another team of university researchers, headed by Mark Simpson, was busy trying to achieve two-way communication between human beings and an African Gray parrot. This African Gray parrot was GG, Sybille Rockville's pet for over thirty years, whom Sybille and Norman donated to the University for Research after she retired from singing.

Before beginning his experiments, Mark Simpson did some background research on African Gray parrots. He found out that African Gray parrots are categorized into two subspecies, the Congo African Gray and Timneh African Gray. Almost all African Grays possessed high intelligence and the ability to imitate and mimic animal and human voices. They could bark like dogs, whistle, and talk with accents that sounded very close to humans. To improve and increase these skills, the African Grays needed a mother figure and a loving relationship; they loved having a great deal of attention and activity. Otherwise, they became depressed and lethargic. They liked to have a dedicated companion and a master. They learned quickly and retained information for some time. The parrot liked to have one master. If the owner became the master, the parrot listened and obeyed commands. Eventually, the relationship reached a point where two-way communication developed. Not every African Gray necessarily had the capability of becoming a real, talking friend. This depended on the bird, probably on luck, and on having a loving relationship with one person, preferably a female, with whom the African Gray became a close companion and maintained regular conversations.

This capability, if achieved, could open many doors in the learning and understanding of the relationship between birds and humans. This talent of an African parrot could be utilized to find out what other birds or other animals were saying. If there was a pet dog in the house, someone could ask, "GG, what did the dog tell you after I left the house?" One could find out whether there was a lingua franca among dogs, cats, and other animals. One might discover that the GG was an animal translator. One might find out that there were different modes of communication, some very sophisticated and some not. An educated parrot like GG might not have any idea about what mode of communication aquatic animals used. One might discover that "mute" creatures like fish might use some kind of an electronic signals or subsonic language.

Dr. Mark Simpson, addressing Sybille and Norman, said, "I know how important this investigation is. In light of this information, it becomes even more important to have a parrot like GG in order to carry out this relationship research and unfold an entire new world to explore. It is difficult to acquire a parrot like GG. In my opinion, we are lucky that you have approached us and brought us a smart specimen that wills kick-start our extremely important work. The results of this work can provide us clues too many hidden secrets of life. I am delighted to have met you and GG."

Norman, Sybille, and Sara were quite impressed with Dr. Simpson's statements. Sybille promised to make a decision and come back to him shortly. "We will bring GG next Friday at the same time, but first we want to be sure that everyone understands the situation and consequences. I must point out; it has nothing to do with money." They said good-bye to Mark and left.

When they arrived home, GG constantly talked about Pita, her new sister. Sara asked GG, "Would you like to spend more time with Pita? If you do, we will leave you with Pita, and we will visit you often, maybe on weekends. What you think, GG?"

She did not answer Sara but looked sheepishly at her mama. Sybille knew GG was looking for her support and told her, "I think it is okay, GG. Yes, we will come and see you. When you want to come home, just tell Papa Mark." She took GG on her finger, stroked her head, and tickled her belly.

SYBILLE RETIRES GG

Sybille and Norman discussed the situation. Norm told Sybille, "I would love to give GG to Dr. Mark Simpson, who represents the university, but there may be a legal problem. You know, GG is earning royalties. If she legally becomes the property of the university, they become the owners of her earnings. I really don't know all the details. Why don't you call Grandpa Savera in Spain?"

Sara agreed with Norman. She was surprised by her father's legal mind. She told her father, "I love you, Dad. In the music business, or any transaction where money is involved, you need good legal advice. Papa and Ma, I have decided to attend law school when I graduate from my music academy."

Both Norm and Sybille were surprised with Sara's impromptu decision, but they loved it. They hugged her and kissed her. Norm asked her, "Sara is you sure you want to do that? You already have so much on your plate, and you have this recording contract to prepare for."

She told him, "Lately I have been bored. Believe me, if GG were not here, I would not know what to with my time besides practicing."

Sybille called her grandpa. "Grandpa, we have a legal question. We have been looking for a good retirement home for GG, and we have found one at the university here in Toronto. They would like to use GG in their new research. She will live with other African Gray parrots. They need a parrot that can have two-way communication with a person, and GG passed all of their tests. The question is, if they own GG, what happens to her royalties?"

Grandpa replied, "Let me look into it. I will call you tomorrow." Grandpa faxed a contract to Sybille and a letter instructing her to follow his instructions. Basically, GG should not be sold or gifted to the university but rather leased to it.

Norman read the contract and instructions. He told Sybille, "Fax this to Dr. Mark Simpson before we go and see him. That will give him enough time to show it to the university lawyers." Norm was satisfied with the arrangement.

On the next Saturday, they all went to see Dr. Simpson at the university. Mark introduced Sybille, Norman, and Sara to the lawyers. They all signed the contract, Sybille handed over GG, and Sybille and Sara went with Mark to see the reaction of GG when he placed her with her so-called sister, Pita. As soon as Dr. Simpson placed GG in Pita's cage, she went to Pita and placed her wings on her sister's shoulder. GG was really happy, fluttering her wings and kissing her friend with her beak. Sybille and Sara were satisfied with GG's situation.

When they left the university, Sara was full of tears. They were all sad. Norman told Sara, "It was the best we could do for us and for GG."

He hugged both of them and told them, "You can't leave GG alone and go to your singing practice at the music conservatory or go to Paris for recording sessions; she would be depressed and sick. Look what happened when you left her at your Grandma Katharina's place. Dmitri could not cheer her up; she finally got sick and depressed."

They reached home and settled down. The phone rang, and Sybille answered. "Oh, Grandpa, are you all right? Is the new condo in the Black Sea area good?"

Dmitri said, "Sybille, it is wonderful. It is never very cold. There is no snow and no cold arctic winds, Thank you for moving us into this heaven before our death. Thank you. We will love for you to come and visit us."

Sybille promised to go and visit them; they said good night and hung up. Sybille and Norman knew that both Katharina and Dmitri were happy living in the Yalta area. They found out that some of their colleagues from the Ministry of Defense and air force academy had been living there since their retirement. They always thought that when one retires, children and grandchildren are fine, but the best companions are your childhood friends and retired colleagues from your working days. If your friends are from similar financial, social, and ethnic backgrounds, you have a better chance of enjoying their company and socializing. When they know you and your family, they are friendlier; they like to sit and talk about politics and common diseases. They love to listen to someone who knows slightly more about these things than they do.

Sybille and Norman were really happy for her grandparents in the Black Sea area; they did not have to worry about them. Norman had recently been too busy with Sara and Sybille to have time for his workshop or art. One morning, he got up early and sat in his recliner. His mind was running backward, taking him to the day he met Sybille. He realized how long ago that was. He wondered at how much he and his environment had changed. He wanted his mind to play the scene when he went to a red door with two pieces of luggage exactly like his. He knocked, a beautiful young woman came out, and the last thing he knew he was having dinner with her. He looked up, and even though he did not see any one, he felt and almost could visualize someone smiling.

Sara woke up and saw the light in the living room. She went in and saw her dad in an attitude that she had never seen. His eyes were shiny.

She could feel that her father was emotional. "What is the matter, Dad? You look as if you were far away."

He pulled her toward him and made her sit in his lap. He rubbed his eyes and told her, "Sara, it is very strange. I was watching a rerun of my life. I was at your mother's hotel door with two pieces of luggage, seeing her for the first time. It was so clear."

She said, "Papa, I know how much you love us. Come, I will make some coffee for you."

They went into the kitchen. While Norm was drinking his coffee, Sybille woke up and rushed down to the kitchen. She asked, "Norm, are you all right?"

She saw he was in his daughter's company, but he seemed subdued and sort of lost. He told her that his brain had taken him back to the day when they met. She went behind him, wrapped her arms around his neck, and kissed him. He told Sybille and Sara that he had been talking to Paul Schoulz. "He told me that he and his team have been experimenting with brain memory, especially the audiovisual part. When I sat down on that recliner, I could daydream so accurately and clearly that it was as if as I was actually there. If Sara had not come into the room at that time, I would have gone through all the episodes of our encounter." Norman told Sybille, "You know, I have not been taking part in the activities of my workshop, and I have not made a single decent painting or art deco article in few years. My manager and partner are not happy with me. Sybille and Sara, tell me. Is it because I am getting older or is it that I was too busy with my family and GG? I am confused, and I am sure of one thing: I do not want to go back to that life anymore."

Sybille and Sara both agreed with Norm. Sybille said, "Norm, it seems you are losing interest in everything. You have lost interest in us. We never seem to do anything; we do not go to movies or the theater, and we don't invite your family over. Karl is your childhood friend, and Paul has become a famous figure in the scientific world. Everyone is talking about his discoveries, but you never talk about him. I am going to call Krista and invite the whole family over. I understand Paul is engaged to a computer scientist and is going to marry in June."

Norman felt ashamed for not taking part in his cousin and best friend's life. He knew Karl was going blind in his right eye. He was ashamed to be so involved in his own life that he had forgotten his aunt Krista, who had brought him up like her own son ever since his parents had died when he was ten years old. He leaned back on his chair, covered his face, and started to cry like a baby. Sara jumped to her feet and ran to hug her sweet and loving father. Sybille came behind him, kissed him, and told Sara, "Maybe it is our fault. We did not take part in your life activities, and maybe we kept you busy with our activities. Sara, let us go to the living room. He wants all three of us to lay down our needs and desires and finalize what each one of us wants in life and what things we can do together for our happiness."

Norman wrote down his desires. He wanted to rent a hall to exhibit and sell his art objects, his paintings, and his art deco furniture, and then he wanted to sell his workshop and the remaining objects that had he produced. He wanted to present his best pieces of art to his immediate family and extended family members.

His next desire was to buy a bigger house, where he would like to make a studio to create art glass objects. He said, "I have been so in love with Tiffany art ever since we went to Corning Glass studios. Sybille, do you remember that? Sara was too small."

Sara replied, "No, Papa, I still remember those door panels."

Sybille said, "That is good. We will try to achieve those objectives. What about joint adventures for the family?"

Norman answered, "Sybille, let us see your and Sara's desire lists."

Sara said, "My list is very simple. After I get my music degree, I want to study law, specializing in litigation and contracts in the field of music. The second thing I would like is to take part in the international Queen Elizabeth music contest in Brussels, Belgium. The third thing is to buy an exquisite ocean condominium for the family."

Norman and Sybille both agreed. Sara said, "What about you, Mama? Let us see your desire list."

Sybille said, "My number one priority is to do go out and do some fun things. Let us go dancing once a week in a nice, reputable club. I want to go with family and friends so that we can laugh, without alcohol. I would like all of us to go and see my grandparents in Yalta in March. I would like to go to a nice dinner every two weeks with Karl, Ingrid, and Paul; I want Mrs. Morgan to come with us, too, though not necessarily every time. Mrs. Morgan helped me a lot when I came to Canada to be with Norman. Sara, a condo in Florida will make our lives more pleasant, especially when it is cold here. Finally, I would like all of us to become members of tennis and squash club and play three times a week. My hidden desire is for my beautiful baby Sara to meet a handsome tennis player scientist like Paul. With all this going on, I want to establish a charity for widows and their small children. We are not short of money, so we can do all this. To start off our happy program, I want to take one week off to go to Las Vegas. That will kick-start our desire program."

Both Norman and Sara clapped and congratulated Sybille for her balanced desire list. Norman called Karl and asked him, "What are you doing this week? I have been so busy and just so lazy and selfish that I have not talked to you for almost a month. Karl, you are my childhood friend, and Aunty is like my mother. I have decided to spend more time with you. If you are not doing anything, we would like to come down and see you."

Karl said, "It is funny you say that. My mother was saying the same thing and was wondering if you or someone in your family was sick. Anyway, come on over. My mom will be happy to see you. Paul will be here shortly, and Ingrid has missed you too, so come on. Bring Sara and Sybille, too."

Norman and family walked over to Krista's house and rang the bell. Ingrid came running to open the door. They all hugged each other. Sybille and Ingrid were crying. Norman hugged Karl and his aunt Krista. He apologized to his aunt for being so near and yet so far away. They exchange the latest news, and Norman asked Karl about his right eye. He told Krista that she was looking much better compared to last year. Sybille asked Ingrid about her studies.

Ingrid replied, "Sybille, I don't seem to be interested in my studies anymore. I am more interested in Karl, who has almost lost the sight in his right eye. He has been using those drops for years, but I don't even know if they work. It appears that his left eye seems to be developing higher pressure. Sometimes I worry that it is going to go the way his right eye went. What worries me is that sometimes I see him sitting down alone, worrying that he may become really blind. It makes him depressed, but I assure him that I just love to take care of him. You know, he gets tears in his eyes, and after I kiss him, he feels better."

Sybille said, "We are here to invite you to a party next week to celebrate our friendship renewal and extend a promise to become a closer and happier family. By the way, it includes Mrs. Morgan. Ingrid, can you please ask her to come here? This program that we are following came about after Norman, Sara, and I found ourselves drifting apart. We sat down and wrote down what would make our lives loving, cheerful, and cohesive. We found that we have lost touch with our friends and relatives, we do not have fun, and we are becoming lethargic. We are here because this is our first step to reverse the process, and we hope it brings us more joy and happiness."

Mrs. Morgan came and hugged Sybille. They were happy to see each other. Sybille said the party would be on next Saturday and would last for four days. "You are all invited. Will you all come?"

Ingrid asked, "Where are you going to have this party? Do you need help?"

Norman said, "We are taking you all to Las Vegas for five days for fun and getting to know each other again, just like before we all got married."

They all were overworked, it appears; their lives were going in the same direction, and they all felt lackluster and lethargic. Mrs. Morgan told them to make themselves comfortable; she and Sara would make some refreshments, just like old times. She and Sara set out crumpets, toast, different cheeses, coffee, and tea, and everyone sat down. Ingrid came and thanked Norman, Norman thanked Karl, and you could see that the program had started to work.

It was getting late. Paul Schoulz entered the house, and everyone shouted, "Surprise!"

He was thrilled to see everyone, especially Sara, who told him that she and her parents were so proud of his work and everyone was tired of seeing him working so hard, so he was coming to Las Vegas with everyone. They came home late.

The next morning, Sybille arranged the details of the trip with her travel agent. He booked an early flight and asked Sybille if he should arrange for a limousine to pick all the passengers at seven a.m. Sybille was delighted with the idea of a limousine.

Saturday came. Norman, Sybille, and Sara walked over to Krista's house. When the limousine showed up at Krista's, you could feel the happy vibrations all around. At Ingrid's request, Sybille and Sara started to sing, and everyone joined in. Krista was happy. She told Mrs. Morgan, "I feel like a schoolgirl. Why can't we do this more often? We all have money."

Mrs. Morgan replied, "Money alone does not buy this. It is friends and people like these who make it happen. Your family has the potential, but someone has to take the ugly bull by the horn and move it to let the sun shine."

Krista said, "Mrs. Morgan, Norman and Sybille are gentle souls, and I must say, my Ingrid and Karl are nice. So let us support our extended family."

Mrs. Morgan told her that she was the most gentle of them all. The limousine came to a halt, and the travel agent was there to receive them. He looked after the luggage. He checked in at the first-class counter and escorted them to the plane.

All the family returned from Las Vegas rejuvenated and recharged for love and life. Norman and Sybille were so excited with the success of the kick-off project that they looked back at the program all three had established to see what could be done next. The program was written on a large piece of paper in red, green, and yellow ink, a little like the Magna Carta. It had been designed by Sara and Norman and framed by Sybille, and it hung in the living room.

The next item on the list was to make an appointment with the manager of the Forest Green tennis club. Sybille invited Ingrid and Karl to come with them. She asked Krista to come along just for fun. Sara tried to get hold of Paul. He was hard to reach. Finally, she got hold of Paul and told him that they were all going to the tennis club, Paul told her, "My fiancée, Jolene, is already a member of the club. She asked me to come to the club and introduce her to my aunty." She said, "Paul I have not seen them yet." He promised to meet her at the club. He told Sara, "I will be there shortly. Good-bye. They all went to the club and completed the formalities to become members.

In the meantime, Paul and Jolene arrived. Paul introduced Jolene to Sara, Sybille, and Norman. Sara asked Jolene, "I understand that you are a member here. How do you like it?"

Jolene answered, "I really enjoy it here. You meet nice people, they arrange partners to play with you, and there are dances, functions, and lot of activity."

The coach came around and booked dates and times for Sybille, Sara, and Norman to play. The coach suggested that they buy their playing outfits at the pro shop. So they went to the pro shop and bought their outfits. Jolene made an arrangement with Sara to play over the weekend. She said, "Paul is so busy in his projects that he has no time to play tennis, yet he needs some exercise."

Norman was organizing his art exhibition at the international center. His partner had agreed to take over the Rockville shop and the remaining artifacts after Norman had sold or given away some of his prized possessions. The winding up of Norman's art business was covered by a legal contract.

SYBILLE RETIRES GG

It was almost a year since GG had been working with Dr. Simpson. During this period, Sara and Sybille visited GG regularly, and she appeared to be happy and was enjoying working with Dr. Mark Simpson.

Sara asked GG, "What do you do with Mark? Is he teaching you something?"

GG told Sara, "Papa Mark, he wants me to talk to dogs, cats, ducks, and chicken. After, he asked me what they said, so I tell him. One day he wanted me to talk to a boy cat. The boy cat was mad and he wanted to eat me. Papa Mark saved me and put the cat in a cage. My sister and other parrots laughed."

Sara asked if she talked to fish. GG replied, "Fish don't talk like us. They blink their eyes and do funny things. Parrots don't understand that. Sara, nobody sings here. I miss singing. Can you sing, Sara?" Sara started to sing "Spanish Eyes."

GG started to whistle and sing along with Sara. *It is amazing*, Sara thought. *Once GG listens to the words of a new song, she picks it up.* GG saw Sybille coming over to her big cage. She said "Good morning, Mama," even though it was afternoon.

Sybille and Sara found that GG was not learning any new sentences or words. Sybille asked GG, "What new word you know, GG?"

She replied, "Conversation, Mama. It is long word."

Dr. Simpson told Sara and Sybille, "The University is giving a press conference on Wednesday at eleven about the progress on human and animal relations. We would like you and your friends and family to attend."

On the day of the conference, the university was humming with the press, cameras, and lots of scientific representatives from many disciplines and countries. The big hall was filled to capacity. Outside the building were banners announcing, "International Conference on Human and Animal Relations."

Other banners announced, "GG the African Gray Parrot Breaks

down Language Barriers." A few days before, the scientific section of the *Globe* had announced that GG would take part in the press conference after the research findings were presented. The program brochure had said that there would be a two-way conversation demonstration between GG and her owner. There were rumours that Hollywood companies like MGM were represented in the hall. International Geographic top executives had already approached the university team when they were at a planning stage. Sybille and Sara had been helping Dr. Mark Simpson to arrange the conversation between GG and Sybille. They knew that GG was not intimidated by large gatherings. Another local paper had published a story about GG's past singing career. A radio station was playing GG and Sybille's solo songs. There was a big interest in GG and her human family. The stage was set; they played the national anthem before starting the proceedings. Everyone was quiet, and suddenly there was a clear voice on the speaker. "This is GG. Welcome to Toronto and the university. Papa Mark wants to talk."

There was pin-drop silence and then a big round of applause. The audience was stunned to hear a university-educated parrot talking like a real person.

The stage was cleared. Dr. Mark Simpson went to the microphone. He explained to the audience the circumstances under which the research program had been born. He said, "One day, our president was describing the behavior of his wife's poodle. He told me that this dog, whose name is Nemo, was able to communicate with us by his actions rather than words. He said that Nemo was able to bark in a sort of coded language, along with communicating by moving his eyes and feet. Dr. Berman was wondering if that was true. We needed another animal that was able to talk and decode a dog or cat's language. I told President Berman that I had bought a record on which a parrot called GG sang all kinds of children's and popular songs in a clear voice and in perfect tune with the orchestra. I told him that the record had sold more than a million copies throughout the world. He could not believe it, so we drove to my house and played the record. He could not believe that it was the voice of an African Gray parrot. Dr. Berman had read that African Gray parrots were known to understand and actually use human language. After this encounter, the hunt for GG was on. As luck would have it, the owner of the aging GG, Mrs. Sybille Rockville, called me to inquire about whether the university had any programs to house talented senior birds. It turned out to be a senior GG she was asking about. This golden opportunity convinced our president to launch our project. When we published our program with a funding request, there were all kinds of animal lovers and commercial organizations that responded generously. The offers are still pouring in. We are very much obligated to all donors, especially the owner of GG, who leased her to our university for the very unusual and important study." Mark Simpson continued, "I have the privilege of introducing Dr. David Herman, our president, a champion of human and animal relations."

Everyone stood up and applauded. He said, "I know we have taken a bold step that may open a window to observing, understanding, and hopefully communicating with animals through an intermediate like GG. She can help to decipher the languages of animals that are able to convey some sense through their barks, meows, and chirping. GG calls them vocal animals. She was asked about fish, snakes, and others who are not vocal. She told us that these creatures do not speak a language; instead, they have some kind of light signals. She ended up saying, 'I don't know.'"

Chapter 19
GG BECOMES PART OF RESEARCH TEAM

Simpson said, "The time has come to present to you a two-way conversation between an animal and a human. In this case, it is the owner of GG. We call her Sybille, but GG calls her Mama. So, I present to you GG and Sybille. Before I bring them out, I want to point out that if you are a music lover, you will surely know Sybille as the famous opera diva well known in Europe. So please meet Sybille and GG."

As they came onto the stage, the crowd gave them a standing ovation. The microphone was on, and the audience heard GG say, "Mama, every time we come, why people stand up?"

Sybille told her, "GG that means they like us."

GG said, "Mama, I like them."

Sybille had written down questions for the demonstration. "GG, what is your name?" The parrot gave her name. Sybille asked GG, "Where is Sara? Can you call her?"

Little GG shouted, "Sara!" and then whistled at her.

Sara came on stage. GG said, "Good morning, Sara," and then barked like a dog, knowing that Sara liked her barking. Sara thanked her. The audience went wild; everyone was clapping and laughing.

Sara told GG someone wanted to ask her a question. A lady from the audience said, "My name is Didi. GG, I want to know what kind of food you like best."

GG said, "Candy." Everyone laughed and clapped. GG asked Sybille, "Mama, how people make sound with their hands?"

Sybille and Sara both clapped to show GG how it was done. When GG tried to clap, she fell on her bottom.

The audience was convinced she could carry on a normal conversation.

The question-and-answer period continued with the press in front of the cameras.

At the end of the conference, Dr. Simpson thanked the audience members for their interest and said he hoped see them at the next conference, which was to be held in Florida at a time and place to be announced later. He invited some of the scientists who were already involved directly or indirectly in the project.

On the next day of the conference, a committee was formed to search for more talking birds, like Mynah birds, parrots of different species, and cockatoos. Dr. Simpson pointed out that it might be difficult to find another African Gray parrot with GG's qualifications; however, a younger parrot with some experience could be trained further using tested and improved methods. "We are planning to start a school for African Gray parrots to converse in just like GG," he explained. "We have to point out that our GG is almost forty years old and will be able to teach young parrots, especially female ones."

Dr. Simpson told the committee that the school would start in the late spring. He presented the committee with results of interviews in which GG talked to a dog and translated its responses. The same thing was done with GG asking a cat many questions in the presence of Sara and Sybille. All these experiments had been taped and were still being analyzed. The only problem was the reliability of GG's interpretation. Thus, it was very important to cross-check the results with the responses of another talking bird.

Dr. Simpson continued, "We have all the questions recorded, and if we had another educated parrot, we could see the results confirming GG as a true medium. Therefore, we would be able to continue and even expand the project."

He thanked all the delegates and guests and expressed his appreciation to the Rockville family for their generosity and help in advancing the cause. The conference was a success in bringing awareness in the field of human and animal relationship with regard to communication.

Sybille, Sara, and Norman went to say good-bye to GG. Dr. Mark Simpson took them to GG's house. It was getting late, and GG, her sister, and the other parrots were having their evening meal.

GG said, "This food is good, and we all feel great. Mama, I can sing and dance better. Look at my eyes and my beak. Ask my sister. You want me to sing? What shall we sing? The boys and my sister know the song 'How Much Is that Doggy in the Window.'"

All the parrots sang together. Dr. Martin was amazed; at this point, he recognized that GG was doing a good job of teaching the other parrots. He had to call one of the bird trainers to organize a professional school to teach human language to gray parrots, but GG was already a good teacher and had half-trained three African Grays.

Sybille and Sara were happy that GG was being part of a program that would be very value able to human and animal relations. Sara said to her mother, "Mama, can you imagine? We and GG can be part of a real scientific discovery."

They reached home just about dinnertime. The dinner was at Karl's and Ingrid's place. After refreshing themselves, they went to Karl's place. Norman was already there enjoying his friends Karl and Ingrid, just like old times. It was nice to see Norman laughing again. Everyone welcomed them. Paul and Jolene asked about the happenings at the university. Sybille told them about the school Dr. Simpson wanted to start. Sybille asked Ingrid to go with them next Wednesday to see how they were planning to teach the parrots to have conversations like GG.

Time does not stay still. As children grow, grownups are growing older; they forget that age must keep rhythm with time.

Sara graduated from her music school and finished law school, specializing in litigations in the music industry. After graduating, she joined one of the finest law firms in the field of music litigation.

Sara remained active in her singing career. One day, when she was on her way to Paris for a recording session, next to her was sitting a handsome young man reading a music magazine called *Rolling Stone*. The page he was reading had Sara's picture and an article about her going to the Queen Elizabeth international contest in Brussels. He looked at her and said, "I am sure you are Sara."

Sara hesitated and replied, "Yes, indeed I am. How do you know?"

He opened the magazine and showed her the picture. She laughed, he laughed, and he told her that he knew where she was heading. She looked at him, surprised, and asked, "How do you know? And tell me where I am going."

He smiled and said, "Same place I am."

Sara was getting a little bit annoyed, but at the same time she liked him, so she did not want to show her frustration.

He said, "I am sorry. I can see that this conversation is bothering you, so let me introduce myself. My name is Murad Noury. I am David Jordan's lawyer."

She looked at him and smiled. She told him, "Yes, you are right. I have a recording session at his studio." She extended her hand, and they shook hands.

He said, "I must congratulate you on both of your accomplishments, the music and a law degree, Sara. May I call you Sara? This calls for a drink. What would you like to drink?"

She said, "Pomegranate juice would be nice."

He ordered two pomegranate drinks. She told him that he could order an alcoholic drink, if he wanted to; he told her that he did not drink alcohol.

She thought, *He is a lawyer in the field of music, and he does not drink alcohol.* As she was thinking, the two drinks arrived. They clinked glasses and, relaxed, looked at each other with admiration and, it would appear, perhaps the beginning of love. She had the urge to call her mother, as her mother was in Paris when she met her father. She thought about her father's words, "It is the programmer."

The plane landed, and Murad helped Sara to get her luggage. He was nice; he took her hand and helped her to get up into the limousine that had been arranged for her.

David Jardin was surprised to see Sara and Murad together. It was already past noon, so David suggested having lunch before getting down to business. He took them both to a fancy restaurant, and they came back just before two. During their lunch, the conversation between David and his newly appointed lawyer revealed that Murad Noury litigation lawyer was there to discuss matters related to the Savera family. Sara was surprised to learn that. She had never heard of any conflict between the two parties.

Sara excused herself and went to call Grandpa Carlos Savera. She told him, "I am here at the Paris recording company for an audition. At lunchtime, I heard David Jardin say that there is some kind of problem between us and them. I have no idea what are they talking about. Please, Grandpa, can you fill me in? I have passed my bar exam and am registered as litigation lawyer."

Carlos said, "I know, and I also know you are working for a reputable law firm. Now listen, the problem is that they have put a stop on payment related to GG's solo LPs and VCR recordings. The excuse is that GG is working for the university in Toronto and is no longer Savera property. I naturally sent them a notice and threatened them with legal action. I have also threatened to withdraw all business relations with them if they do not transmit funds within three days, so if you are there to work with them, I advise you to postpone it."

Sara asked, "Grandpa, do you want me to discuss the problem and try to solve it while I am here? Most certainly, I will tell David that until this problem is solved, I am not comfortable working with him, and I will him know that you have told me all the facts and have advised me to cancel or postpone the recording session."

Grandpa Savera said, "Sure. You can tell them the facts about GG's lease agreement with the university."

She asked her grandpa to fax the lease document. "When I have that document, I am sure we will be able to close the case. It is ridiculous to stop a large sum without looking at the facts. Grandpa, give me a chance to deal with my first case. I will not disappoint you."

After this fact-finding mission, Sara was confident about discussing the matter.

In the meantime, David Jardin was looking for Sara. She was in the administration area waiting for the fax that Grandpa Carlos had promised to send. When she had the fax in her hand, she went to David's office and found him sitting with Murad. She said, "I am glad both of you are here. My grandpapa has authorized me to settle the case. I have a faxed copy of the lease that exists between my mother and the university."

She gave a copy of the lease to David. She told Murad, "Please look at the document. When you are finished reading and digesting it, I will be in the cafeteria waiting for you."

She went to have a cup of coffee. She had not yet finished her coffee when Murad and David came and asked her to discuss the situation. They returned to David's office, and he said to Sara, "Murad tells me that the lease explains and clears up the situation. I was given a totally different picture. Our company's other lawyer had convinced our board members that GG had become the property of the university. I am sorry for this misunderstanding."

Sara was upset. "You know, David, this was such a blunder. What were you thinking? I do not know anyone who would take such an action to block legitimate funds without checking the facts. This unilateral action would have killed your golden goose. You jeopardized your reputation and a multi-million-dollar business and now, as a result of this immature action, your reputation is tarnished. I am sure I can convince my grandfather Savera to ignore the mistake made by your ex-lawyer. I will be faxing him a note that the funds are being released immediately followed by a letter of apology."

Sara's lecture shook up Murad and David. Murad thanked Sara for her discourse and said, "I don't think your lecture will be forgotten for a long time. I accept and agree with your assessment of the situation. At this point, my suggestion to Mr. David Jardin is to transfer the funds in question immediately without any conditions."

David called his accountant and in front of Sara and Murad dictated a memo to release the funds immediately. Sara and Murad went out together into another office. Sara placed a call to her grandpa and gave him the good news. Carlos told her that he would believe it when he checked with the bank. Before hanging up, Carlos praised her action in avoiding an unnecessary legal battle.

Murad told Sara to stay put. He said, "Sara, I will try to get the confirmation from the accountant about the transfer of funds, and then I want to talk to you."

Murad was back within ten minutes with the confirmation papers. David Jardin came to see Sara and Murad. He showed the letter that he had faxed to Carlos. He apologized to Sara for not paying more attention to the legal and contractual agreements. He said, "To be honest, your mother and GG have kept me so preoccupied that I almost lost my grip on the situation. It was overwhelming. At that point, I put in an emergency call to Murad. He was recommended by an acquaintance of your grandpa. I needed people like you and Murad who can guide me before my company gets into unnecessary problems."

Sara told David, "It is getting late now, I have wasted enough time, and I will not be able to audition this week, so if you can book my seat back to Toronto tomorrow morning around ten a.m., I will appreciate it."

David agreed and asked his assistant to make the flight arrangements for Sara. She talked to Sara for more information. The assistant brought the flight information to Sara. She got busy confirming her flight. Murad came by and waited for her. He asked her if she was taking a morning flight to Toronto. She said yes.

"You see, Murad, I am too upset by what happened. I just want to go home and spend some time with my mother and father."

Murad replied, "As far as I am concerned, there is nothing more I can do here. David has offered me an advisor's job; he has agreed to pay my expenses, including airfare and hotel accommodations. My mission is complete, thanks to you. I have started to work with a fairly well-known company called William and William. Since I joined them, the firm is now called William, William, and Noury. They are located in the Dominion building in Toronto. I will be taking the same fight as you."

Sara was pleased, but she did not tell him that. She asked him, "So that means you live in Toronto?"

He told her that at present he was living immortal with his parents. He said, "Now that I have accepted this new position as a junior partner, I am looking for a condominium downtown, close to work. Pardon me for changing the subject—my task is complete here. I am going to my hotel. I understand you are booked in the same hotel. Would you like to share a cab?" Sara agreed. Murad said, "Let us go and say good night to David." His assistant told them that David had already left.

Sara and Murad took a taxi to the hotel. They went to their own rooms and promised to meet in an hour's time. Sara was tired, not physically but emotionally; this was her first legal match, and she had won. The best part was that Murad was on her side. She was a little embarrassed about giving grown-up men a tough lecture, and she worried that Murad would think she was pushy.

SARA LIKES MURAD

She promised herself that she would be more diplomatic. She called her mother and told her what had happened.

Sybille said, "Grandpa called me. He told us that you solved the payment problem within one hour. That's my girl. Oh, Sara, your father and I are very proud of you. Grandpa said that David Jardin told him that this was the first time a little girl lawyer had scolded him."

Norman came on the line and praised her. He told her, "Remember how you wanted your mama to go with you, but I told you that it was about time you went on your own? If Sybille had gone with you, maybe the end result would not be the same."

Sara thanked both of them. She asked Norman if she could talk to her mother again.

Sybille said, "Sara is something wrong?"

Sara said, "No, Mama. Nothing is wrong. How can I explain? I think the programmer is up to something, you know. David has hired a young, handsome layer. His name is Murad. We met each other on the plane while on our way to see David. I had no idea I would fall for him in just a few minutes thanks to his mannerisms and his gentle behavior. Anyway, he is a junior partner in a law firm in Toronto, and I think we will be taking the same flight home. Ma, there is something about him that seems strange. He seems to know everything about us, and he supported me to convince David to transmit GG's funds immediately. We are staying at the Hotel Savoy, in different rooms, but I am supposed to have dinner with him in an hour's time. I have to go now, ma. I will call you later and tell you more. By the way, you and Papa can pick me up tomorrow at four-thirty. Good night, Ma. You might meet him. I love you."

Murad was waiting patiently in the hotel lounge. It was dinnertime. He looked at the elevator and saw a beautiful woman, dressed in a lovely lapis lazuli blue dress, which gave her a special glow. He knew at that moment that he was enchanted with her. Murad himself was dressed in a blue double-breasted blazer with eight shining brass buttons and smaller buttons on his sleeve. His tie had blue and yellow stripes, and his khaki pants looked as if they had been freshly pressed.

Murad stepped up to receive Sara as she got out of the elevator. The two minds were judging and admiring each other. He said to her, "Oh, Sara, you look wonderful."

She told him, "It is nice to be with a handsome man dressed elegantly."

She wanted to look at him, and he kept on looking at her. He noted the difference between this Sara and the lawyer Sara from last evening. He said to her, "Are you sure you are the same person who scolded David?"

She told him, "Look at you. What a difference a few hours make. I suppose we have something in common. Your personality changes with the circumstances and situation, too. I have to tell you something. I loved the way you took care of the situation. It shows your level of confidence and maturity. I would like to be with you in Toronto. That is the main reason that I wanted to spend six hours flying with you and maybe meet your parents at the airport." Sara was curious. "Murad, I am amazed by how you assume things. I noticed that so far, all your assumptions have been correct."

Murad smiled and kissed her hand. He told her, "Let us go to the restaurant. We don't have to drive; let us eat here. The hotel restaurant is very good. It is a little pricey but the chef is superb and his menu complements both worlds."

They walked in, and the waitress guided them to a seat next to the window. The receptionist knew that Murad was a friend of Michel Sarazin. As Sara and Murad settled in, the waitress brought them menus. In the meantime, Michel came out of the kitchen and went straight to their table.

Murad said, "How did you know I was here, Michel? It is nice of you to come and see me." Michel asked, "So you finally got married? Your father told me, 'Forget Murad; he is not the marrying kind.' Congratulations."

Murad said, "Michel, wait a minute. This is my best friendly lawyer, Sara Rockville. My father thinks it is not a problem to find a girl and get married. Michel, I promise you, when I get married, you will be on my list."

Michel told the waitress to take away the menu and asked Sara if she liked filet mignon. "Sara, I have the best filet for both of you, with petite fried potatoes and delicious green beans. I must go now, and do not order anything from the menu."

The main course of filet mignon was superb, and Michel sent out a delicious soufflé for dessert. They enjoyed the dinner and asked for Michel. They said good night to Michel, who kissed Murad and shook hands with Sara. Michel told Murad, "When both of you are in town again, call me. I will make your honeymoon dinner."

Murad laughed, and he and Sara left the restaurant. They came back to the hotel lounge and sat chatting for a while. Murad told Sara, "I see you are not comfortable sitting here, especially when we are formally dressed. I feel as if everyone is watching and staring at us. I suggest, since it is only eight p.m., that we go change into casual clothing."

Sara agreed, and they went back to their separate rooms. When Murad arrived at Sara's place, she was already in fine, pale green nightgown. She asked him about his parents. "I am curious. I hope you don't mind. What is the origin of your name, and does it mean anything?"

Murad replied, "You are the first person who has not hesitated to ask a logical question. Yes, it means 'wish' in Persian. You see, during the upheaval in Russia, our family had to flee. I was not born yet, and my parents and grandparents were in refugee camps organized and financed by the American administration. They moved us from one camp to another. We ended up in Japan, from where we finally found our way to Turkey. My father's cousin was married to an Australian; she arranged our immigration to Canada." Murad got up from his lounge chair and took Sara's hand. He said, "Sara, we have so little time, and I want to know so much more about you. First, I want to meet your parents. Both of them have achieved international fame and are so talented. I admire those kinds of people, the achievers. I admire you. Look at you. You are an established singer, and I just saw what kind of lawyer you are going to be. You know, my grandfather once told me that your children are the reflection of you and your partner. He said, it is nice to be good-looking and it is nice to be smart and talented, but all these qualities lose their luster and charm without manners and decency."

Sara clapped and came up to kiss him on his cheek. She said, "You must be thirsty," and she brought him a glass of fruit punch. He admitted that he had talked too much. She told him, "When we land in Toronto, my parents may insist you come to our place. I am sure we all will enjoy each other's company. We will go to see GG; you can talk to her, and after that you can go and tend to your affairs. When is your flight from Montreal?"

Sara approached the hi-fi radio, which was playing "Fascination." Murad took her hand, and they started to dance, closer and closer. It was getting late; he said, "I think I should go."

She said, "I meant to ask you about Michel, the chef. How you know him? He has a very high regard for you."

Murad told her, "Michel was with us during our stay in Russia and was with us during our refugee period. He has served me and our family well, and we consider him family. My grandfather knew that Michal, as we called him, was very good at preparing delicious dishes. When we arrived in New York, we were already acquainted with a few successful restaurants and their central Asian owners. With my grandfather's resources, Michel started to work hard. His programmer, as you would say, made a name for him. He won the coveted New York culinary trophy, and you can imagine how his career blossomed after that." Murad Noury looked at his watch and said, "Oh, my dear Sara, I hate to leave, but don't forget we have to take an early flight."

She took his hand and made him sit in the recliner. She went into the kitchenette and brought out a cup of hot chocolate for him. Murad placed the hot drink on the table next to his seat. He took her by her hand and waist and gently seated her in his lap. They kissed and hugged. As she put her head on his shoulder, he could feel her heart beating faster. Her warm body, wrapped with a gentle fragrance, gave him a heavenly calm and inner joy. He had never known that he could achieve such joy so soon. He looked at the stars outside and found one star that seemed to be looking at him. He wondered if his programmer lived in that star. He looked at Sara's beautiful face and her cute nose.

Sara opened her eyes, and he bent down, kissing her eyes and lips. She admired him for his integrity and decency for not taking advantage of the situation. She thought, *Even if he did, I would only love him more.* She got up and kissed Murad and said, "Oh, my love, I feel I am lying in the lap of an angel, so warm and peaceful. Let us go to sleep."

He started to go to the door; she took his arm and led him to her room. After a while, they fell asleep. The front desk called to wake them up. Murad rushed to his room, got dressed, and came running to Sara's room. She got ready and went to the breakfast bar. They looked very happy and in love. The taxi came just in time and took them to the airport. Murad looked after Sara's luggage and helped her to the seat next to the window. Their first-class seats were so comfortable and warm that after a while they fell asleep. Their arms were locked; their faces were glowing and warm. The voice of the pilot over the intercom woke them up. The stewardess came around telling them to fasten their seat belts for landing.

The plane made a fine landing. Everyone disembarked, and Sara and Murad picked up their luggage and came out to the arrivals area. Sara and her parents waved frantically at each other; Sybille and Norm were pleasantly surprised to see their daughter holding the hand of a tall and handsome man.

Sybille said to Norman, "Isn't he handsome?"

Norm squeezed her hand, and they came running to meet Sara and her friend. Sara introduced Murad to her mother and father. Murad shook Norman's hand, and Sybille kissed Murad. Sara asked about her grandparents in Russia, her grandpa in Spain, and Karl, Paul, and Ingrid. Murad noticed how close she was to her family. They arrived home and settled down in the living room. It was almost dinnertime, and the table was ready. Murad was fascinated with paintings, art deco glass, and furniture; he asked Sara if the works around were her father's creations.

Sybille said, "Murad, you must be hungry. Come."

They all enjoyed Mrs. Morgan's food. Coffee and tea were served.

Murad said, "We both have been drinking coffee all the time. Sara, can I have tea?" She knew Murad took sugar and milk in his tea.

Sara said to her mother, "Ma, Murad knows all about GG, you, and Papa. He is very much interested in visiting GG."

Sybille said, "Sara, we are supposed to go and see Dr. Simpson. You know why? Well, it so happens that they want us to train GG's sister Pita to talk and sing just likes GG."

Sara said, "But Ma, we are so busy. How can we do it? Murad, I forgot to tell you. In the last week of April, I have to go to Brussels, where I have been accepted to take part in the Queen Elizabeth music contest. I will be competing in piano and singing. You see, Ma, I have to start practicing."

Murad was surprised; he knew that the international contest was open only to the top artists. He said to Sara, "I did not know the depth of your talent. Congratulations, Sara. So when do you leave for Brussels? The reason I am asking is that I have been appointed to speak at a conference in Padova, Italy, in the first week of May."

Sara was delighted. "Oh, Murad, look at our heavenly program. I was wondering how I could ask you to come to Brussels with me, because I would hate to spend more than a week without you. So when are you planning to go to Padova?"

In the meantime, Norman and Sybille were looking at each other and wondering how the pair's love had intensified in just a few days. Murad was able to read Sara's parents' latent thoughts, he interjected. "I have to explain. We think we have control of our senses and emotions, like love and sadness, but these attributes are not mechanical. It is like an allergy: you have no control over them. They are human; if you don't have those traits, you are not a balanced individual."

Sara and Sybille clapped and kissed Murad. Norman and Sybille both agreed with Murad's analysis. Sybille said, "That is what happened to us. Over just one day and night, we were struck."

Sara jumped up and said, "Murad, Mama told me one day that it was impossible for them to be away from each other."

Norman said, "I must agree with Murad; it is like an allergy. When I left Sybille to go to Montreal alone, I realized I could not live. I had to have my Sybille to achieve a balance."

Norman asked Murad, "So you are going to lecture or present a paper at the conference, and what will be your subject?

Everyone was looking for an answer. Murad spoke. "I hope I will not bore you. The title is 'The role of extrasensory perception (ESP) in achieving the maximum out of life.' This subject has not been studied and practiced by many professionals. The use of ESP could mean a big difference between failure and success. The trait of ESP is acquired genetically, like music and other extraordinary skills. It can take you to new heights in your life if practiced intelligently. You can perceive and foresee in advance physical and emotional effects, thereby directing you to act accordingly. Today, ESP is not taken seriously. People practice ESP to predict the outcome of a lottery or prepare horoscopes. These practices have diminished the importance of real applications of ESP. Forgive me, but I will have to stop my discourse now. My common-sense perception tells me that it is getting late and Sara needs rest. It has been a long day."

Norman told Murad, "It is amazing. I don't think anyone has any idea about the powers that lie within us."

Murad told Norman, "Here, I will demonstrate a little sample of ESP. Sara has been anxious to ask me when I am going to meet her in Brussels. Am I right, my dear Sara?" She said, "Yes, I did not hear one word regarding your lecture. My mind was already thinking about meeting you in Brussels. You are right; I was anxious."

Murad told Sara that he would be in Brussels on a Friday and they will travel to Padova that night. He told her that he had hotel reservations near the University of Padova. She was delighted to know that.

Murad said, "I am aware of the thoughts going through Papa Norman and Ma Sybille's minds at this point. The only thing I can say is, yes, I am in love, and my parents don't have any clue. I do not want to tell them on the phone. I will be home tomorrow, and then they will know everything, including the present and my future plans. When Sara and I come back, we will set the date."

Sara and Sybille were thrilled. Sara jumped, and Murad picked her up. She kissed him. He asked, "Does that mean you agree?"

Sybille approached him while Sara was still in his arms; she kissed him and told him, "You are the first person who has added new dimensions to our lives."

Norman shook hands with Murad and thanked him for updating them on various subjects during his short stay. As they were talking,

Karl, Ingrid, and Krista rang the bell, and Mrs. Morgan led them to the living room. They all got up, and Norman introduced Murad. Sybille had telephoned Krista and asked the family to come and meet a possible fiancé of Sara. Norman and Sara had no idea.

Norman told Murad, "These are the dearest members of my family. Aunty Krista was responsible for bringing me up along with her son Karl, my childhood buddy. Ingrid is his loving wife and Sybille's best friend. Paul is Karl's son, and I think his work on regenerating dead optic nerves stands a chance of being nominated for a Nobel Prize in biophysics."

Murad looked at the family and said, "I am delighted to be among this family of great minds. I have read few papers by Dr. Paul Schoulz, who is discovering new ways of regenerating nerve cells and probing into brain functions. I also read about your glaucoma. Someone told me that Paul has devoted two years to finding a solution to his father's glaucoma problem. That shows high regard and esteem by a son toward his father." Krista, Sybille, and Ingrid were crying. Sybille and Sara hugged Murad and said, "Murad, we have never heard anyone describe a son's devotion in such a fashion. Thank you."

Krista told everyone to come to the table because Mrs. Morgan had prepared something special to celebrate this joyous occasion. It was getting late. Norman thanked Krista, Ingrid, Karl, and Mrs. Morgan for being part of this occasion. He thanked Sara for bringing Murad into their life, and he told Murad, "There are two other families on two different continents that are also dear to all of us. We hope you will meet soon. They are the parents of Sybille's mother in Russia and Sybille's father and grandfather in Spain. We are looking forward to meeting your parents and grandparents."

They enjoyed Mrs. Morgan's cakes and pastries. Krista hugged Norman and everyone said good night. Norman and Sybille said good night to Murad and Sara and told them not to stay up too late. Sybille asked Murad, "What is your agenda for tomorrow? Do you still want to see GG?"

Sara answered, "Ma, Murad has to go to his office and attend a meeting."

She saw that Murad wanted to say something to Sybille. "You see, since my family does not know anything about Sara and me, I want to sit down with them and discuss the issue. Everything is happening too fast. Personally, I want a simple wedding. Knowing my mommy and sisters, they will want an engagement party, where I will have a chance to get my lovely Sara a very nice ring. My parents are old-fashioned, but I really don't know too much about the rituals. I am sure they will want to meet Sara and the family. Maybe next week I can bring them."

Sybille saw that Murad really did not want to say too much without his family's knowledge. Everyone went to sleep. The next morning, Sybille and Norman were already waiting for Sara and Murad when they came down to the eating area to have breakfast. Sybille asked them if they had slept well. Sara answered, "Mama, we talked a lot, and finally we fell asleep around two. Murad woke me up this morning. I am going to drive him to his office and come back. He is going to attend a meeting and collect his condo key, and then the office's driver will take him to the airport for him to catch his flight to Montreal at twelve-thirty."

Sara and Murad sat down and finished their breakfast. Murad thanked both Sybille and Norman for their affection and hospitality. He thanked Mrs. Morgan for a nice breakfast, and he and Sara left.

Later that day, Sara and Sybille waited impatiently for a call from Montreal. Sara was pacing back and forth, and Sybille was watching her in agony. Finally, the phone rang. Sara rushed to pick it up. Murad said, "Oh Sara, I missed you all day. My mother, my sister, and all my family are so happy. I am sorry I did not call you earlier. Everyone wanted to know everything about you and your parents and so on. My mother said to wait for my father, who was visiting some of his friends. He walked in few minutes ago. He was so happy that I am going to be married, and of course I had to repeat everything all over again. My mother wants first to speak with your mother to observe the protocol, and then she will hug you and kiss you. Don't be too long; everyone is lined up to talk to you. Next my father will talk to your father and mother and finally you. So, dutiful Sara, I will get my mother, and you get your mother. Switch the phone to speaker setting so that everyone can hear what they are saying."

Sybille started first. "Mrs. Noury, my name is Sybille, and I am Sara's mother."

Mrs. Noury said, "Sybille, good afternoon. My name is Samira, and I am Murad's mother. We are so happy that my son has fallen in love with your daughter, Sara. How fortunate he is, and how lucky we are to have such a talented young lady as our daughter-in-law and for Murad to have such a loving second pair of parents. Thank you, Sybille. Our congratulations are in order. I must go now; there is a long lineup of people. Before I go, I just want to hear the sweet voice of Sara."

Sara came to the phone and said, "Thank you, Mother Samira, for such nice words."

The phone was passed on from mother to sister and other female cousins. Father Selman Noury talked to Norman and Sybille. He thought that Murad's choice was perfect and told them that the engagement was a heavenly blessing on all of them. After everyone had a chance at listening and talking, Murad took over the telephone and told Sara that the plan was to fly his immediate family to Toronto on the coming Friday, arriving at ten past four. They planned to go to the Princess Hotel and come to Sara's parents' home the next morning for an engagement ceremony.

Sara said, "No, Murad. My parents and I will be there to pick up the family and take them to our place. We will go for dinner at a Malaysian restaurant, and then we will drop you at the hotel. The next morning, our limousine will pick up the family at ten and bring you here at our house for the ceremony. Oh, Murad, how I love you. As your father said, our love is made in heaven. Well, for me heaven is here, and I am in it with you. So how does our plan sound?"

Murad told Sara that her plan might as well be made in heaven. "I love it, and my family will too. Sleep well, and I will see you at the airport."

Preparations were going on at the Norman house; Karl, Ingrid, and Krista were helping Sybille in organizing the program for the wedding. Norman's studio had been completed; it was spread right across the back of the house. Norman had designed a glass dome as the roof of the studio, and Sara liked the idea of having the engagement party in the studio. When Murad called, she told him that they had decided to use the studio for the party. "You will love the studio," she assured him.

Workers from Norman's shop worked at decorating and setting up cameras, music, and microphones. Krista suggested the family go to her place for a break. She told them that Mrs. Morgan had made a special lunch and desserts. She told Norman, "Norm, don't forget what you did at Karl and Ingrid's wedding. It was wonderful, but you were young then. We were all younger. We don't expect you to work hard alone. We can combine forces under your guidance, and the work will be done. Friday is still five days away."

They sat down and enjoyed a good lunch. Karl said to Norman, "You were wise to build your studio as part of your house. Your architectural design is lovely. Your glass dome has a Tiffany style that is so delicate. The colors are pastel pink and green, representing a vine. That gives the glass a three-dimensional effect."

Norman was satisfied with the arrangements. Everything appeared to be ready and waiting for the guests arriving from Montreal. A limousine arrived to take Sara and her parents to the airport, and the stretch vehicle was big enough to accommodate all. Sara, Sybille, and Norman were waiting in the arrivals area. Sara saw Murad with all his family. She rushed to hug him, and finally they all met and were directed to the waiting limo. Norman's men had taken care of the luggage. Everyone appeared happy and gay, the limousine was able to accommodate all the guests comfortably, and the happy couple was enjoying the love and affection of their families.

When they arrived at the Rockville house, it was two p.m. The sun was still bright. The driver opened all the doors of the limo. In the meantime, other members of Krista's family and friends of the Rockville's came out of the house to greet the guests from Montreal. As the Noury family entered the house, they received bouquets of pink and yellow roses. Father Selman was introduced first, followed by Samira Murad. They were all directed to Norman's studio. The guests were enchanted with Norman's artwork and the lit glass dome. Many family members had not yet seen his studio. Ingrid and Karl came to hug Norman and congratulate him on his masterpiece.

Ingrid said, "Norm, it all reminds me of when Karl and I got married, and you did so many things for us. It was the best time. The invitation cards you designed are still a collector's item. I will love to see your design for Sara's invitations."

Karl told Norm, "You are still full of surprises." Norm became the center of attention. Murad brought his whole family to thank Norman for giving them a chance to look at his masterpieces. The sun was still bright, and according to Norm, the dinner reservation was at seven p.m., not six. Yes, it was a small, informal gathering. Dinner after a religious ceremony was over.

The engagement ceremony started with a special song sung by Sybille. It was written by Sybille's music director, and Sara was at the piano. It was in praise of life and of the dream that begins with great joy and love. The song had an undertone of sadness. Everyone loved it. Norman got up and thanked Sybille for her beautiful song, and then he continued, "I will like to suggest that we begin the engagement ceremony."

It began with little Norose, the sister of Murad, and her cousin singing a traditional Turkish song. The girls sang a nice, catchy tune, everyone clapped, and Sara and Murad kissed them. Murad's mother asked Murad and Sara to stand and face each other. She asked Murad to hold a red box in his hand. Mrs. Noury announced that her husband would say a small prayer in Arabic, blessing the ring before he placed it on Sara's finger.

Mr. Noury stood up and recited the prayer. Everyone said "Amen." Murad took out the ring and placed it on Sara's finger. Sara lifted her finger to show the ring; the diamond was brilliant. Sara kissed Murad's mother and then went to Murad's father, and he put out his hand and blessed the couple. Sara then kissed Murad. All came to the engaged couples and congratulated them.

It was getting late, so Norman said that the limousine would take them all to a Malaysian restaurant for dinner. Murad's family liked the Malaysian food and hospitality; during dinner, there were many toasts wishing the couple happiness and joy. After dinner, the guests were driven to their hotel. Sara said good-bye to Murad. Norm and Sybille thanked their guests for coming to their house and bringing good luck and joy to their family. Mr. and Mrs. Noury thanked their hosts and hugged them; they said good-bye. Sara and her family returned home.

All the family elders had decided that it would be appropriate for Sara and Murad to get married in Toronto city hall before going to Europe. Sybille and Norman agreed with the plan. Norman told Selman on the phone, "After the children return from Europe, we will give them a big reception at the university hall on the first Saturday of June." Mr. and Mrs. Noury thought the idea was good.

After Murad and his party left, Sybille made sure that Sara practiced her piano and singing at least four hours a day. Sybille said, "Sara, there are only four weeks before your trip to Brussels."

Sybille knew her daughter's capability. She knew that Sara's musical talent was a gift from nature, and she found that her daughter's memory was more amazing. Once Sara heard a melody or tune, she never forgot the music or related words. Sybille found that Sara's voice had a special clarity and tone that allowed her to move from a very low to very high note. She told Norman, "Sara probably will do better in her singing than in piano. Norman, do you know that she has picked the toughest aria from the famous opera *Thais* by Jules Massenet? It is said that only the most experienced and top-class artists can sing it successfully. I don't know why she has to select it."

244

Norman responded, "Yes, you are right. I looked at one of your opera books, and I found out something very unusual. Did you know that aria was written by Massenet for an American soprano, Sybil Sanderson? Maybe she chose it because it was first sung by her mother's namesake."

Sybille jumped and said, "Oh Norm, you are right; it was written for Sybil. What a strange coincidence. I think Sara's mind is working on the premise that if she can pull off this very difficult musical number, no other competitor can touch her. That is really good thinking. What a smart Rockville. Now I understand why she is working so hard. Did you see she left the house at six in the morning? Before you got up, she was gone. She is working with her director, Boris Conrad, at the conservatory."

Norman told Sybille that her musical career and her genes were playing a big part in Sara's success. "Let us hope she gets the top honors at the Brussels international competition. Oh, I just had a thought. If she gets to the top of the list, you know, Sybille, she will be so much in demand that the top agents in the music industry will be at her door to convince her to sign up with them. I don't want my baby to be away and traveling all the time. I would feel sorry for Murad. No one felt sorry for me when I was always waiting for you."

Sybille came to sit on his lap and told him, "Norman, I am sorry I made you wait so many times. You know, I admired you and had lot of respect for you, just because you never complained. I promise you, we both will guide Sara to conduct herself in such a manner that Murad does not have a reason to complain. You and I did not have any backup to support or worry for us. You were without parents at an early age and I had no mother at an early age as well. After my mother was killed, my father was heartbroken and very depressed. So you see, our Sara has us, and she will have our full support and lots of love for her and her husband."

Norman kissed and embraced her. They felt a new, special bond beyond intimacy between them. Sara and now Murad were playing an important role in cementing the love and respect between them.

The appointment day at city hall came soon. Sara and Murad were dressed in business clothes, and Norman and Sybille were looking young and pleasant, not overdressed. Norman had told Murad's father and mother not to go through the trouble of coming to Toronto for just one day. He told them that it was going to be just a short matter of registration. He told them, "We have booked the university hall on the twenty-eighth of next month to celebrate the real wedding, and you will stay with us and my aunt Krista."

Mr. and Mrs. Noury were agreeable and thanked Sybille and Norman for looking after their beloved son. Sybille told them, "We have gained a son and you have gained a daughter."

The ceremony at the city hall went smoothly. The groom kissed the bride. Sara told Murad, "Do you know that we are married legally? I wonder why our parents wanted us to go through this civil marriage."

Murad said, "I heard our parents saying that since we will be traveling together and staying in the same room, the urge of passion will be strong. They argued that as a result, we could have a baby. A baby out of wedlock is a no-no in good families."

Sara laughed and said, "Oh, I see. As a matter of fact, they are right. I would not like for my baby to be born with any stigma. We are smart, though, and we do not want a baby now. My doctor has given me all the information and medication necessary to avoid that. I am sure your doctor must have talked to you, too."

Before she finished her sentence, Murad told her, "You know, my friends have given me more information than the doctor. They have even given me things. We have knowledge, and we will act responsibly. I am not concerned. Don't worry; we will have a baby when we want."

They arrived home. The day's ceremony did make them feel a lot closer, and they were able to hug, kiss, and flirt without hesitation or shame. Karl, Ingrid, and Paul along with his wife came over to get the story about Murad and Sara's civil marriage. They were all happy and congratulated Sara, Murad, and their parents. Karl told Norman that his mother wanted the family to come over; Mrs. Morgan had prepared a special Black Forest wedding cake for the kids to cut. Sybille hugged Karl and Ingrid and said, "You are the best. Your mama is such a caring person, and look at Mrs. Morgan; she does so much every time she gets a chance. I think your mother will be eighty years old next month, Karl, and if I am not mistaken, Mrs. Morgan is also about her age. I am going to give them a birthday party on the first Saturday of next month. They deserve it. Karl, can you arrange to make a list of some of their friends? Ingrid and I will call them and invite them. We can arrange to pick up anyone who needs a ride."

Karl and Ingrid were delighted with Sybille's idea. Norman approached her, picked her up, and swung her. "Sybille, you are a sweetheart; you should be awarded a medal for being so good. I like your ideas."

Sara had been practicing her singing every day. When she came home from the conservatory at three p.m., she would have a snack and then go to the piano. With her mother's help, she played "Meditation" by Jules Massenet. After two hours, she would become tired and go to sleep in the recliner. She woke up when Murad came home, and then she came back to life. A few days before their scheduled departure, she went to ask her parents, "Do you think it will be okay if Murad and I took a trip to Madrid and introduce Murad to Grandpa and the family? We will be in Padova, and Spain would not be that far."

Both Sybille and Norman jumped at this idea. Sybille said, "Your trip to visit the House of Savera will give them great pleasure. And don't forget to call and invite your cousin Oskar. Maybe your Papa will not like this idea, but you ask Grandpa to let you spend two nights in Majorca."

Sara said, "Mama, actually that is where I wanted to go, to follow my loving parents' path."

Norman warned them, "Don't think you are on your honeymoon. You can go there after your reception for a real honeymoon, I promise." Sara reluctantly agreed with her father and told him that she would just visit her family for one night.

Sybille received a call from Dr. Simpson with a request for help with an experiment involving GG. Dr. Simpson had not been convinced that GG was telling the truth when she told him about her conversations with an old beagle, One day in the presence of the dog, Dr. Mark Simpson asked GG, "Go ahead, ask Mr. Beagle what he had for lunch today."

GG told him that Mr. Beagle had said, "Bones."

Dr. Simpson was quite puzzled; he did not know whether GG had really talked to Mr. Beagle. The only way to be sure would be to go through the same routine with another parrot.

Dr. Simpson asked Sybille to train GG's sister, Pita. She agreed, and Dr. Mark and another man came over to her house holding a bird house. She invited them in. The other man placed the bird house on the table. Sybille uncovered the house, and there was GG with Pita. Without any hesitation, GG shouted, "Hi, Mama!"

Sybille answered her, "Hi, GG. How are you?" That was the day Sybille and Norman started training GG and Pita. Sybille kept the birds busy talking and singing. Norman was helping out and enjoying the company of both birds. Norman said to Sybille that GG's presence made it easier to train Pita. As a matter of fact, every time Pita made a mistake, GG really scolded her.

The time was approaching for Sara to fly to Brussels. Murad would take Sara to the airport at six the next morning. Murad had spent all day at the court and Sara at the conservatory of music. They entered the house at about the same time. They were surprised to see GG and another bird called Pita. Sara and Murad went into the living room. He was surprised to hear GG saying, "Good evening, Sara." (Note: Murad was not sleeping at Sara's place.)

Sara replied, "Good evening, GG. Who is with you?"

GG replied, "This is my sister, Pita. Say hello to Sara, Pita."

Pita said, "Hello, Sara."

Murad was laughing away; he could not believe his ears. He told Sara afterward, "The voices sound so much like a human. It is amazing that GG understood what you said and answered quite correctly. Sara, I hope at our wedding reception, we can have a talking bird show. I bet you everyone would love to ask GG and Pita questions, and the birds will take part in the dialogue."

Sara said, "Let us go and see what Mama thinks. I like the idea. To be frank, receptions are boring, and this bird show will make everyone laugh. I am sure your family will have so much fun; they will remember our reception forever. I just love your idea."

They went to the living room and spoke to both parents. "Ma and Papa, Murad has a wonderful idea. He thinks we should do a GG show at our reception after the dinner and speeches. Papa, can you include that event in the invitation card? The kids will love it, and Murad is already enchanted with the birds' voices. Can we, Mama?"

Norman and Sybille agreed. Murad and Sara kissed them and thanked them. Sara said, "Papa, you can mention that there will be a talking bird show after dinner especially organized for small and grown-up children."

Murad helped Sara to pack for the trip. He checked her passport, her health insurance, her files, and her musical material. Sara told him, "Take my checklist and go through the luggage and my carrying case."

Sybille came in the living room and asked Sara and Murad, "Did both of you eat? Do you need anything?"

Sara told her that both had eaten their meals outside. Sybille helped them to set an alarm for the morning and went downstairs. After checking everything, Sara and Murad went downstairs and said good-bye to her parents. Sybille and Norman hugged and kissed them and wished Sara the top honors. She thanked Sybille and Norm and went upstairs to sleep.

Murad was up at the sound of the alarm the next morning and woke up Sara; they got ready and left for the airport. Murad wished her lots of luck and told her not to worry. "Sara, my sweetheart, I will see you in three days. I am going to miss you."

Murad took off for Brussels to join Sara after she was through with the contest. Murad arrived at the Brussels airport, where she was waiting anxiously. She saw him coming and ran to meet him. She seemed very happy. She showed him the morning paper, where her name appeared as one of the top contestants in the Queen Elizabeth competition. They called her "the woman with the golden voice."

Right in the middle of the receiving area, Murad picked her up and kissed her. There were few reporters in the area that recognized Sara and started to take pictures of both when they found out that Murad was her husband. The *Brussels Standard* ran another story about her and her husband, and her interview was broadcast on television.

The next day, Sara and Murad had dinner in their hotel dining room, waiting anxiously for a call from the music competition committee. Sara was anxious and lost her appetite. Murad heard the bellboy going around from table to table calling, "Call for Miss Rockville."

Murad stood up and called the bellboy. Sara took the phone and said, "Hello. Yes, this is Miss Rockville."

The voice said, "Miss Rockville, this is the chairman of the Queen Elizabeth international competition music committee. My name is Fredrick Gerber. Our team is pleased to announce that you are the first laureate of the singing competition. The committee will be sending an official award certificate and other details."

The manager of the hotel came over and congratulated Sara on winning the coveted award. The manager sent a bouquet of roses and announced that the hotel was proud to host the queen of classical singing. All the guests in the dining room got up and presented a toast to Sara. It was quite emotional for Murad and Sara. They went together to their room and called her parents. It was after four p.m. in Toronto. Sybille got up and rushed to the phone, knowing that her daughter had won. Sybille said, "Sara, congratulations! I knew you would do it."

Norman told her that he was very proud of her. Norman was so thrilled and proud of Sara that the first thing he did, early in the morning, was to call his aunt Krista and Karl. They came over to Norman's house and celebrated. Later that morning, music industry reporters called Sybille to offer their services for obtaining lucrative contracts for Sara. Sybille called her father in Madrid and gave him the good news. She called Isabel and told her about Sara's success in Brussels, too.

Sara and Murad left Brussels and flew to Padova, where Murad was to speak on extrasensory perception. They had the weekend to celebrate Sara's success. The weather was perfect. They took a city tour and visited the host who had organized the seminar on human behavior and ESP.

When Sara and Murad arrived at the front desk of their hotel, an envelope was handed to Murad from the director of the hotel. It was addressed to Sara, welcoming them and requesting that she meet him in his office. The letter was polite and said that the hotel was proud to host a celebrity. The clerk informed the director of their presence. He came out and welcomed them, then escorted them into his office. As they entered the office, he introduced them to the musical director of the hotel, Mr. Taboori. They sat down.

The director, Mr. Santorin, asked Sara, "We, the music lovers, are so anxious to hear your golden voice, as the newspapers are calling it. Would it be possible for you to give us an opportunity to listen to your voice?" While she was talking to the director, the phone rang. It was her father, Norman Rockville. The director gave Sara the phone and went out of the office to give her privacy. She said, "Hello, Papa."

Her father told Sara to fly home. He said, "Your mother does not want you to go to Madrid. You will put Murad in an awkward position, and she wants you to visit them on your way to Majorca on your honeymoon. Murad will meet all the Savera family at your reception."

Sara said, "Mama is right. Murad agrees with your assessment. Papa, we are coming home. Good night." Santorin came back and continued the conversation. He said, "You are a star. We do not want you to sing your new work. Please, we just want you to sing an old aria that you have sung many times."

Sara looked at Murad, and he seemed to say yes. It was agreed that Sara would sing the next day and that a short practice run would take place at ten a.m.

Armand Taboori asked them, "What time will you be dining tonight? It is already five-thirty. If it is all right with you, I will arrange your dinner at seven."

They agreed and went to their room. When Sara and Murad came down for dinner, Armand Taboori was waiting for them. A waiter directed them to their table, which was decorated with more flowers. They noticed in that two hours the hotel had managed to put up nice, colorful poster announcing "Sara's golden voice," to be heard in the music hall at ten p.m. Sara and Murad had never known such fuss about a recently dubbed "golden voice."

Sara awoke early and went over her music sheets. She was fairly confident that one rehearsal of main aria of *Madame Butterfly* would get her into the proper mood and condition. By eight, Murad was up, dressed, and ready to go downstairs for breakfast. They came into the restaurant, where the music director of the orchestra and his piano player were waiting to eat together. Their idea was to mingle and exchange ideas with Sara about immediate plans. Mr. Taboori discussed with Sara the details about her preferences for instruments. The director had read about Sara's being an accomplished pianist.

She looked at her watch and got up. Murad held her hand and took her to their room to get ready for the rehearsal. When Sara came down with Murad, she looked lovely in her simple but elegant dress. As she entered the music hall, all thirty members of the orchestra stood up. There was silence in the hall. The music director introduced Sara to the members of the orchestra, and they all applauded. They were told about Sara's aria. It was time for Arman Taboori to take his place at the podium. The music started, and Sara's golden voice came out strong. The rendition was so powerful that women in the audience were really crying. At the crescendo, a shiver went through the hall. Murad could not believe his ears. He had never been interested in operatic singing, but this was so penetrating that he had goose bumps. The invited guests and the spectators were amazed at Sara's presentation. Director Taboori thanked her for giving him and his orchestra members a rare opportunity to be the first to hear and play for the rising star. After Sara was free, she came to Murad and hugged him. He told her that he never imagined that his sweetheart had such a powerful voice. He said, "When your voice went so high, I had goose bumps all over my body. Is that normal? I have never experienced that before."

Sara laughed at the way he spoke. The hotel management thanked Sara for giving their people a chance to hear her golden voice. Sara and Murad headed to their room and relaxed before going to bed.

On the next day, Murad spoke for a gathering of legal experts from all over the continent on the subject of ESP, which was becoming more popular as a tool for prejudging people. If used correctly, it could be very useful in predicting behavior. The Soviet Union had employed experts in this field to solve crimes and to select the right candidates for Foreign Service, especially by testing the loyalty of diplomatic appointees and secret service personnel. It is said that some families have a special gene that makes them more psychic than others. The science of ESP is based on possessing an extraordinarily acute sense of perception. This was the basis of Murad's lecture; he suggested that ESP could be learned from a natural master.

The audience was impressed with the concept of learning and improving the suppressed ESP gene, thereby getting the full benefit of highly developed perception. When the lecture was over, Sara and Murad were driven to their hotel. They were tired and had to get up early in the morning to catch their flight to Toronto. Murad called the front desk to schedule a wake-up call and a taxi to take them to the airport. Both took showers and ate a room service dinner.

The next morning, they woke up, had a small breakfast, and left for the airport. The plane took off on time; they slept for most of the flight.

Norman and Sybille were waiting for them in Toronto; Sara was delighted to see her parents, and they were overjoyed to see Sara and Murad. Later, Karl, Paul, and Krista came over and joined them to celebrate Sara's victory at the Brussels competition. Sybille and Norman reminded both Sara and Murad about the wedding reception to be held in three weeks. The invitations had already gone out, and Karl had the hall at the university booked. Sara asked her father to show her the invitation. She told Murad, "Papa's invitation design for Uncle Karl's wedding, I hear, was a masterpiece."

Norman brought out a sample card and gave it to Sara. She looked at it and said, "Oh, Papa, this is so beautiful. Look, Murad. Look at the colors. Papa, the peacocks look so lifelike."

Murad looked at the two peacocks. "The one with the beautiful tail is the male. See the expression in his eyes? It seems to almost tell you that he loves her. And look at Sara, so elegant and shy. She is looking down; it appears that she is looking at Murad through the corners of her eyes."

Sybille agreed with Sara and Murad that it was a real work of art. "My husband has done it again. Oh, Murad, you should take a look at the enlarged picture of this work, framed beautifully, hanging in his studio. The peacock colors seem to jump out."

Sara and Murad rushed to the studio and saw the framed card. They were amazed by the way Norman had hand painted it using acrylic paint that enhanced the three-dimensional effect. It was almost dinnertime, so they moved to the dinner table.

Karl got up and proposed a toast congratulating Sara on her very important musical achievement. He proposed another toast congratulating Murad for adding a new dimension to the application of ESP. Sybille and Norman were so happy to see the family together. Sara was wondering, "Uncle Karl, where are Paul and his family? I miss them. They must be out of town."

Karl said, "As a matter of fact, Paul and his wife are in Sweden, being interviewed for the upcoming Nobel Prize. The rumor is that he is being considered for nomination for his work on optical nerve regeneration to cure glaucoma."

Sybille said, "Have you ever seen a son so disturbed by his father's losing his eyesight? What a son you have, Ingrid and Karl."

Sara said, "Paul and I almost grew up together, and he often talked about that. He is a brilliant man. So here is a toast to Paul, and good luck to him."

They were all hoping Paul Schoulz would be nominated for a Nobel Prize. It was getting late. Krista and her family wished Sara success in her music career and left.

Sybille asked Norman, Sara, and Murad to come into the living room. They all sat down. Sybille said to Sara, "You know, since the results of the competition were officially announced in the media, our phone has been ringing all day. Song writers, composers, and, most importantly, the top agents in Europe and North America have been calling to talk to you. I happen to know a few of them. This top agent, David Roster, represents only the best singers and composers. He knows me. When I was at the top of the charts, he was not too big, but recently he has acquired recording studios, and he has a network that covers Asia, Japan, and Western Europe. He told me that you are at your prime; Brussels pushed you way up on the charts. He told me he had spoken with songwriters and composers who had prepared a long album of classical and semi-classical pieces for you. He said we have to take advantage of your name and the fame spread by the Brussels announcement. It really makes sense; we should take advantage of this situation. I told him I would talk to you, Norman, and Murad about recommending him as your sole agent and advisor, and I asked him to come next week to discuss the deal."

Norman said, "Sara, I think this a good opportunity for you become an international star. David seems to be the right choice. Your mother is correct: your life, and especially your husband's life, will be more tranquil if you have an agent. Your mother never had time for me; she was torn between her career and her husband."

Sara replied, "Papa, I agree. I do not want to make him wait for me; I want him to be with me. What is the value of money if it robs us of our love and happiness? Mama, ask David to come."

She looked at Murad for confirmation. He nodded his agreement. Sybille cautioned Sara not to neglect her piano and singing practice. "Remember, singing helps piano and piano helps singing. They are a pair."

David arrived the next week to discuss working with Sara. Sybille, Norman, and Sara welcomed him. David told Sybille, "It is too bad you don't sing anymore. Last time I heard you, you still had a powerful voice."

Then he turned to Sara. "You are absolutely beautiful. It is too bad you do not want to be in the movies. Maybe you will change your mind later. I am glad I came. You know, not everyone who has an internationally renowned voice is as beautiful as you are."

In the meantime, Murad returned from his office and entered the room. Sara introduced him to David Roster. "David, meet my husband, Murad Noury."

David shook hands with Murad and said, "Yes, I know Murad through the media. I know he is with a large legal firm."

Murad listened to David, who talked a lot about making sure Sara recorded and marketed her songs as soon as possible. Murad got up and addressed David. "David, I have listened to you talking about releasing Sara's recording in the market, but I have not heard you talk about any program or plan to produce a recording. The important thing in recording management is to organize a meeting of essential players in the production, such as song writers, music composers, and a director. We do not want to produce an album in a hurry. Sara's reputation is at stake. Her mother Sybille has recorded many times in her career, and this family knows what it takes to make fine recording. Now what you need to do is to go back to New York and organize a meeting with those essential experts and appoint a capable manager to establish a program after talking to the experts. We also need to establish the ownership of the many recording studios you claim to have, the names of officers running those studios, and, don't forget, the production rate of the studios. If you want us to sign a contract with you, our accountants will go through your official books."

David was very quiet. He told Murad that he would try his best and left. After his departure, the whole family cheered Murad and Sara. Sybille came to congratulate Murad. Norman came to shake his hand and said, "Murad, you saved us from disaster. This man was nothing but a con artist."

"Papa, you are absolutely right. According to my reading, this guy, David, wanted to sell Sara's contract to another studio. I must say, I shook him up a bit. Let me call my office and find more about him. I will tell you what I find out."

Norman told everyone to sit down and told them, "I know you all have been busy with your affairs, but Sybille and I have been breaking our backs to organize the wedding reception to be held three weeks from today. The important thing is that both of you must not make any plans during that period. I know you have to organize your recording affairs and rehearsals, but you also have to think about your honeymoon. It is a very critical time, and I worry because you seem to be overbooking yourselves with new things. I want both of you to go through the list and see if we have missed anyone whom you would like to invite."

Murad said, "I forgot to give you the names of my bosses at the law firm."

Norman continued, "You all have the printed program. Look at it carefully. If we have missed anything, please tell me. I know that both of you wanted the African parrot show, and we have included that. Give me your opinion."

Murad and Sara looked at each other and said, "Everything looks all right. We like that there are not too many speeches, and we are glad that you gave center stage to Grandpa Peter Savera."

Guests started to arrive the week before the reception. The first ones to arrive were Dmitri and Katharine, Sybille's grandparents. They were in their seventies and getting older. Sybille had bought them a condo in a Black Sea resort where winters were not as harsh as in Moscow and summers were nice. They loved to spend time with Sybille, Norman, and Sara and were happy to be attending Sara's wedding.

Sybille said to Dmitri, "Grandpa, if you like to stay here, why are you leaving in two weeks? You are free to stay as long as you want."

Katharina answered, "Sybille, your grandpa has a big reunion of aviation experts and decorated pilots. Your grandpa is a guest of honor. The meeting will be held at the Red Memorial Hall, a few hundred miles from where we live. The hall is in a mountain area. It is so beautiful, lush and green with lots of lakes. The central committee has made sure that the aviation pioneers will receive only the best treatment and enjoy themselves. They have organized excursions and shows."

Sybille told them, "I don't think you should miss that. But you know, Grandma, when Sara has her first baby, you will be the first ones to be invited. After all, you will be the first great-grand parents for that baby."

They kissed and hugged. Peter came along with Andrea and chatted with them for a while. Sybille's house was full, but Karl and Krista were happy to share their house with other guests from the immediate family.

SARA AND MURAD'S RECEPTION

The reception day arrived, and everyone was there. Murad's parents, his sister, and his nephews and nieces were there in their bright and beautiful dresses. The head table was full of flowers, roses of different colors and fragrances filled the auditorium, and there was a good-sized band. When the band started to play, everyone was quiet.

Norman at the microphone announced, "Please welcome our most loved and admired couple, Sara and Murad."

Everyone got up and cheered them. They all sat down. On one side of the couple was Murad's family, and on the other side was Sara's family. The first speaker was Peter Savera. He thanked the guests for taking the time to attend this happy and memorable occasion. "There are some important people missing who would have loved to be here. Sara's Grandmother Anna, and my wonderful grandfather, Juan Savera Would love and enjoy being here. But we must cherish what we have. Congratulations from Andrea. My father has sent a special message of congratulations and an invitation to both of them to visit him. He has organized a two-day stay at the Savera house in Madrid and three days at the Savera honeymoon sanctuary in lovely Majorca. You see, he did not want to miss his great-granddaughter's wedding reception, but because of his health he was unable to make this journey."

Peter was almost choking. He stopped for a few seconds and then continued, "Both Sara and Murad are going to see him and are going to fulfill his wish. Good luck, my children."

Next was Mr. Noury, Murad's father. He was very emotional. "We love you, Murad, and we welcome Sara, our new daughter, with open and loving arms."

Other speakers came and wished the new couple lots of love and prosperity. Dinner was served, and Norman came to the microphone. "I have a special announcement to make. We will present a South African parrot show after you have enjoyed your dinner and wedding cake."

When the dinner was over, guests settled down for the show. Mark Simpson brought both birdhouses on stage.

Mark introduced himself to the audience. "I am Dr. Mark Simpson, and I have initiated a research program to establish a relationship between humans and the animal kingdom and to study the communication among species. Mrs. Sybille Rockville and her family have been kind enough to lend GG to the university for this purpose."

Suddenly, GG screamed from her cage, "Mark, let me out. I am hot."

Mark took the cover off her house, and GG came out. Everyone cheered. The parrot whistled very loudly and said, "Thank you."

The audience did not believe that it was the bird talking. From the other house, Pita was screaming, "Hey Mark, what about me?"

Mark had to get Pita out, too, and everyone cheered.

GG looked around and said, "Where is my mama?" Sybille came running onto stage, saying, "I am here. How are you, GG?"

She replied, "Mama, I am not good."

Sybille asked her, "What happened?"

GG sounded as if she were really sick. "I have a stomach ache, Mama. I have gas and a little diarrhea."

Sybille picked up GG and kissed her. The audience was going wild, laughing and clapping.

Dr. Simpson said to the audience, "GG is willing to answer questions from ten people. She will select the person."

The audience members wondered how she was going to select the individual. Sybille asked GG to go ahead and select someone. She said, "The little girl in the center of the first line."

The girl stood up and asked GG, "Where is your papa?"

She replied quickly, "He flew away." She selected another boy from the third line.

He asked, "Who gave you your name?"

GG replied, "Mama Isabel."

Sybille explained to the boy, "Her first owner was my cousin Isabel." She asked Isabel to come out. Isabel came on stage, and GG was excited to see her.

"Mama Isabel, I missed you. "

Everyone was sorry for GG. Isabel asked GG and Pita if they would like to sing a song. The band started to play "La Cucaracha." Both birds started to dance and sing. People were singing and started to dance. The show continued and ended with the playing of a solo recording of GG. It was hard to believe that a bird could sing in harmony with the band just like a person.

The next day, Peter Savera and his wife were at the breakfast table having a conversation when the phone rang.

Norman picked it up. "Good morning, Grandpa Carlos. Yes, everything went well. Oh yes, both are looking forward to seeing you, Grandpa. They will be leaving for Madrid with Peter early tomorrow morning and will be at the Savera house at about eight p.m. Yes, Grandpa, they regret that they won't be able to stay more than five days."

Grandpa Carlos said, "Norman, I am so happy that they did decide to come and take advantage of my offer. The girls will be happy to know that. Give our love to Sybille. Everyone here sends their congratulations and best wishes to you and Krista and her family. Tell Peter I am anxiously waiting for his arrival."

Sybille and Katharina were talking about Katharina and Dmitri's departure to Moscow. Sybille told her grandmother that she was going to miss them. "Grandpa, Sara and Murad are going to the airport tomorrow to catch their flight to Madrid around five-thirty in the morning. What time is your flight? Oh, now I remember. Yesterday you told me that your flight was at eight. So what we do? Let's leave all together at five-thirty so we do not have to make two trips."

They all left in the morning for the airport. When Sybille came back from the airport, it felt quiet and lonely in the house. Norman told Sybille, "Let us go to bed. I am very tired."

Sara and Murad arrived back from Madrid in less than a week. Norman and Sybille were happy to see them. She complained that the house felt lonely and boring without them. "I hope you don't go away too often," she said.

Sara and Murad did not want her parents to become so attached to them. "Ma, you do not want us to become your babysitters. I know Papa has hobbies; he can start painting. You have to have your own projects."

Murad said, "Just a minute, Sara. I have a few ideas. Ma, you won't be alone if you think positively. Sara will become very busy very soon. You have finally found a well-established agent for her, and he is drawing up a plan. Sara will be rehearsing for a couple of weeks per month. Both of you will be there with her in legal or music-related meetings. I know Sara is capable of handling herself, but believe me—she will appreciate the company of those who love her. No one could be better companions than parents who are skilled in music and art. Sara will feel comfortable when you are there, especially when she is surrounded by corporate wolves. Ma, I have to tell you another disturbing thing. One day not too far in future, with your and Papa's blessing, we will have our own house."

Norman agreed and said, "This is what happens to almost everyone. It does not matter how much money you have, Sybille. Children become adults and have their own children. Murad is right."

Murad told Sybille, "I have other ideas, and I am working on them. Sara and I will talk to you later. You will love the end results, but now we are hungry and tired."

They all went to the eating area in the kitchen. It had been about a week since Dmitri and Katharine had left for Moscow. Sybille asked Norm if he could call Grandpa Dmitri and find out if he had gone to the Soviet aviation anniversary ceremony."

Norman replied, "Sybille, I am sure the convention is starting today. They have to be there."

As they were discussing and worrying about Sybille's grandparents, the phone rang. Norman told Sybille to pick it up. "I am sure it is your grandpa, Sybille."

The voice on the phone said, "I am General Ustinoff. I would like to talk to Miss Sybille Rockville."

"Yes, General, I am Sybille Rockville."

"I am sorry, but I have some bad news. The transport plane that was carrying thirteen of our retired senior members of aviation academy crashed into the side of a mountain. Unfortunately, your grandfather and grandmother were among the passengers."

Sybille was hysterical, crying out of control. Norman jumped up and grabbed the phone while Murad and Sara looked after Sybille. Norman thanked the general and hung up. Norman had never seen his wife in such distress. He called his doctor friend, who arrived within minutes and immediately administered medication to calm her down.

Sara and Murad had never seen Sybille scream and cry so much. They sat quietly near Norman, who was sitting and talking to the doctor. Sybille was asleep, but her pulse was still racing. The doctor monitored her blood pressure and pulse. It took about twenty minutes before Sybille relaxed. Dr. Steven Chan told Norman that he thought she would wake up in the morning and, after a light breakfast, still be sad but calm and more realistic. Dr. Chan said good night and told Norman to call him if he needed to.

General Spinoff called back the next day around eleven a.m. When Norman picked up the phone, the general asked about Sybille. He told Norman, "Dmitri was a good friend of my family. I know how Sybille must feel. When Anna was unfortunately killed, I was the one who took care of the family, and now imagine, at my age I have to bring this bad news again. Norman, tell Sybille we are here to help. If she wants transportation from the airport and help with arranging accommodation, etc., tell her to call me. I know many things must be going through her and your minds. Take this number down and call me. If Sybille and the family want to come for the official funeral to be held in three weeks' time, I will have more information later. My wife remembers Sybille; she sends her condolence and love."

Sybille was listening to the conversation. She said to Norman, "I remember the day of the explosion. The general was very nice. He took us to his house until Grandma was calm. I never saw Grandpa cry, but I am sure he was crying inside quietly."

Norman held her in his arms and said, "Sybille. Promise me you will not do this again. I almost had a heart attack. Both Sara and Murad were worried and stunned. Promise me. We are here for you."

Sara and Murad brought Sybille to the table and served her favorite porridge. She started to eat. Norman gave her a small glass of orange juice. She finished her breakfast. Norman asked her if she had heard the general. He said, "If you want to go to the official funeral, he will arrange to pick us up from the airport. He will arrange hotels and so on. He was very nice."

Sybille said, "I think I would like to go. This way, I will not be too sad. Many of his friends died. He was not alone."

Sybille healed slowly. She started to divert her energy into Sara's career, working with new agents and traveling to New York and California. Sara, Sybille, and Norm traveled together; Sara's parents were enjoying being in the limelight of the music world. When the time came to endorse agreements and contracts, Murad was always with them.

General Ustinoff called one morning and gave details of the central socialist party's plan for the mass funeral. Norman gave him their scheduled arrival time.

Dmitri and Katharina Yevchenco
are given a state funeral

When Sybille and Norman arrived at the Moscow airport, General Ustinoff, along with other committee members were there to receive them. The general kissed Sybille and embraced her, and he shook hands with Norman. The committee members shook hands with Sybille and Norman. Sybille noticed that all the Soviet flags were at half-mast; the nation was in mourning. They were driven to the living quarters. The general gave them the program regarding the next day's funeral arrangements. Before the general left, Norman told him that after the funeral they would be taking a seven-thirty flight back to Toronto.

"Do not worry," the general replied. "I will arrange your transport to the airport. The driver should pick you up at five-thirty." He said good night and left.

The next day, there was funeral procession with the Soviet national band. A symbolic coffin was drawn by thirteen black horses. Each horseman carried a flag bearing the name of a crash victim. Both sides of the road were lined with people looking sad. It was a very somber sight; there were many men and women wiping their eyes. Suddenly, the latest Soviet fighter planes came screeching down to give their beloved aviation experts a salute fit for a king.

The central committee chairman rightly said, "Never have we lost so many who gave birth to our guardians in the sky in such a short time."

When the funeral was over, many high officials of the air force and communist party visited close relatives of the crash victims to express their condolences. Professor Dmitri had been a well-liked and much-admired man. Sybille was surrounded by his friends and her grandmother's friends, who kept hugging her and kissing her. Sybille was the closest surviving relative of Dmitri Yevchenco.

Sybille and Norman left Moscow that evening and arrived in their house in Toronto the next morning. Sara was waiting for them; Murad was away on a business trip and was expected that night. They were happy to see each other. Sara rushed to the door when she heard her parents enter. "Oh, it is so nice to see you, Ma. Now I know how you feel when no one is in the house. I was bored alone, so I went to Aunty Krista. I found Paul and his wife visiting them. I love their son. He does look a bit like Paul and Uncle Karl. I played with Junior and talked to Paul's wife—I forget her name. They were nice. Aunty asked about both of you and I told them about how Grandpa and Grandma had died in a plane crash. They all hugged me, and I started to cry. Tell me, how was the funeral?"

Norman said, "Let us go upstairs and change. Then we will eat, and my dear Sara, you will sit near the fireplace and we will tell you all about it."

They had their meal and came down to the living room. In the meantime, Murad entered the house. Sara got up and came running to meet him. She told him that her parents had been at home for some time. He kissed Sybille and Norman and asked them to sit down. "I have, I think, great news. An agent from Colombia Pictures called and wants Sara to audition for a background role singing in a musical production that will start filming next month."

Sara said, "Papa, do you think it is a good idea to work in the movies?"

Murad said, "You will not be working in the movies. No one will see you; they will just hear your singing. If you are accepted, you will be making very good money, and I know their musicals have top-notch writers and music directors."

Norman told Sara, "What Murad is saying is that to record five or six songs will not be a big problem. The only thing that bothers me is that you have to go to Hollywood, and that is far from home."

Murad told him, "No, Papa, their recording studio is in New York. I asked them whether Sara would be going back and forth to LA. They said maybe to sign a contract or to meet the directors, but not to work."

Sybille agreed with Murad. "If that is the case, then Norm and I will be glad to go with Sara to New York. Remember, Norm, when GG and I were going to recording studio in Paris, you came with us a few times."

Murad looked at Sara. "How come you are not saying anything?"

Sara replied, "If Murad does not come with us, I do not want to leave him alone. Are you coming with us, Murad?"

Murad answered, "Sure, I will come. You know it is hard for me to be without you." He came forward and lifted her up in his arms. He told Norman, "Papa, she is like you. I can see the Norman genes in her makeup."

Sara was happy, and they all agreed she should go to the New York studio for an audition.

Murad told them, "I can call the agent, Joseph Jordon. He will organize everything and send me a written invitation. By the way, it is an all-expense-paid trip for Sara and me, but you, Mama and Papa, will have to make your own travel and flight arrangements."

The next day, the invitation for an audition arrived by fax. They were scheduled to leave for New York in two weeks' time. When the time came, there was a limousine waiting at the airport to pick up the family. They arrived at the studio and were met by the studio director and manager. After a few formalities, they went for lunch, where they met the music director and composer. The music director knew Sybille and had heard about Sara's success at Brussels. They came back to the studio. They were given the next day's schedule. Their first meeting was to start at nine in the morning. Sara was given a choice: she could sing classical, popular, or opera songs.

They came back the next morning for Sara's first meeting. In another board room, Murad was meeting with the resident lawyer, discussing contracts and agreements for compensation in case Sara was approved. After all the formalities were over, the music director asked Sara, "I have heard recordings of your performances in Brussels and Italy. This is nothing to do with the audition, but I am very much interested in hearing your voice, if you will oblige."

Sybille told Charles Burman, "I am sure she will be delighted. Sara, this will be without music."

Sara got up and sang her favorite aria from *Madame Butterfly*. The place was vibrating with her voice. Studio personnel came running when they heard her sing. It looked so easy for her. Everyone clapped and cheered. The directors and all who had gathered to hear her came to shake her hand. Murad came and kissed her. He knew she would succeed and would get her asking price.

The music director, Charles Burman, came to Sara and thanked her for presenting a powerfully delivered aria. He said, "Sara, you are brave, confident, and certainly able to deliver without any musical accompaniment. I know for sure that many would not dare to sing on the spur of the moment, like you did. In my opinion, you can deliver whatever is presented to you."

Sara thanked him for his generous comments. Sybille told Charles, "Don't you think her voice and presentation are much better than what I was able to deliver?"

Charles turned to Sara and said, "Sara, before you leave this place I will let you see and practice some of the scores that we have proposed for this motion picture. We have prepared for you short excerpts from five songs, and after lunch I and some of the best men from my orchestra will accompany you. But before that happens, your mother will be at piano and you will practice with her in private, right here in the studio. I have not done this with any other contestant, but in my estimation it is you whom we want. I am sure those songs and arrangements should be a piece of cake for you."

It was noon; they all went to the dining room in the studio. Charles introduced his well-known pianist, an Oscar-winning violinist, and a philharmonic cello player. These gentlemen were very much impressed with her voice, which was, as they put it, so mellow and yet so powerful. After lunch, they went back to the studio, Sara, Sybille, Murad, and Norman went into the private studio, and Sybille started to play some tunes. Sara had the words and song sheet in her hand. After a while, Sybille and Sara started to harmonize. Sara told her mother, "Look, Mama, this score seems to be adopted from *Madame Butterfly*. Oh, Ma, I can really give Charles the best he has ever heard. This tune has pathos and drama in it."

Sybille was excited and agreed with her daughter, "Sara, many composers and arrangers are influenced by previous well-known compositions, quite often with great success."

Sybille and Sara continued practicing all day. Charles Burman came around just after four-thirty. He asked Sara, "Are you ready for a final audition tomorrow? We will have a fairly decent orchestra. Although it will not be the grand ensemble, I am sure you will like it. The audition will be held in the auditorium, so don't forget to be there at ten a.m. sharp. Good luck."

Charles left, and Sara and family left for their hotel.

The next day was a big day; Sybille had told Sara that Charles had invited other junior and senior managers and directors from the main film studio in Hollywood. She told Sara not to be intimidated by the presence of a fair-sized audience. Sara said, "Mama, I am like you. It is funny: I perform better when I see an audience that looks intelligent and well-dressed."

Sybille said to Murad, "You see, Murad, she has Norman's and my genes. We both feel the same way."

At nine-thirty, the usher came and escorted them to the auditorium stage. It was large, and the orchestra was set up just behind Sara. When Sara went onto the stage, they stood up and cheered. The curtain was closed, and the music started very softly under the baton of Neil Navarro, a well-respected conductor. The curtain opened, the music picked up, and you could hear Sara's voice blending with the music. When she reached the crescendo, the hall seemed to vibrate, and the large chandeliers seemed to move. It was a powerful rendition. You could have heard a pin drop. At this point, the conductor pointed his baton at Sara, signaling to continue. The original agreement was for Sara to sing only few bars, but she continued and finished the song.

The audience gave her a standing ovation. Charles Burman came up the stage and shook Sara's hand. The audience gave her another standing ovation, shouting, "Encore, encore." She sang few more bars from three more songs, and the program ended. Sara thanked the conductor and the musicians for their excellent work. The conductor brought Sara down to the floor, where all the directors were waiting. She went straight to her husband, Murad. She kissed him, and he congratulated her on her brilliant performance. Her parents hugged her, and her mother told her that she was too good for them.

The music director and other directors came to shake her hand and praise her presentation. Charles Burman told Sybille, "Go with our manager and have lunch. After relaxing, we will get together in the main conference room, where we will present the outcome of the audition."

They all dispersed and came back to the conference room. Charles and other directors sat opposite Sara's party at a large table. Charles Burman spoke. "It has been a long time since we have heard and enjoyed a presentation of this caliber. We thank you for giving us this opportunity to meet you and hear your gentle but strong voice. I have here in my hand four assessment reports from our four directors, and I will read each one.

The first gave Sara ten out of ten, the second and third gave her ten out of ten, and the fourth director marked ten plus. I am puzzled. I will let Joseph Canter explain his reasoning to us."

Joseph explained, "What I mean by ten plus is that Miss Sara Noury is overqualified. She is too good, and our music does not need such a high-priced singer. Therefore, I do not recommend Sara Noury for a background singer."

Murad got up and said, "What I am hearing is that your film is so bad that it does not need an excellent music director or a superb singer. Mr. Joseph Canter, you are forgetting that the film in question is a musical. Such a film has a short life, but the songs are everlasting, and that means your treasury will be collecting for years to come."

The music director commended Murad on his comments. He said, "I must say, Mr. Noury is absolutely right. You can still listen to music from *Oklahoma*. Those were the best singers of their time. In my opinion, musical films are totally depended on their music. I and my three directors completely agree with Murad, and we invite Sara to join us to make a fine, successful musical. As far as contracts and agreements regarding monetary arrangements are concerned, the legal and budget departments are competent enough to deal with it. The first phase of our responsibility is complete, and the next phase will require more effort on our part to provide material, musical scores, music sheets, etc., to Sara and Sybille. We are lucky that Sybille Savera, the world-famous singer, is here to lead us carefully and comfortably. Look, we gave them one day to deliver the songs, and Sara and Sybille came through brilliantly. Am I dreaming?"

Everyone cheered and agreed with Director Charles Burman. He told Sara and Sybille that all the necessary music material would be shipped to them in three to four days by the studio's manager. They would have at least three weeks to finalize the music score. He thanked Sara's group again and told them that their limousine was ready to take them to the airport. Murad told Sara, "I can't leave now. I will wait for the whole contract and financial agreement papers. Signed and sealed, I will bring them with me. Please, you go now. I will take the next flight." They agreed and left for the airport. Murad arrived late at night and went to sleep.

They all met for breakfast in the kitchen. They were very happy for Murad. Norman said, "I was so proud to see Murad going after that director, Joseph Canter. His thinking was so strange, and it did not make any sense. He was looking for a cheaper singer. Boy, Murad, you really nailed him down."

Sara put her arms around him and said, "Papa, he is our hero."

Murad told them, "I am pretty sure that he was trying to push someone else, either for monetary gain or some other advantage. Papa, you are right; it did not make any sense. Anyway, we won. Congratulations to all of us."

After breakfast, he changed into his office clothes. He said, "I have to go and show the agreements and contract to my boss and other experts. Sara, we have the best legal team to handle big contracts. If we do not read every line and paragraph, we could have litigation and unnecessary problems. And there is another angle to it. We know that the music directors have agreed to retain you as the prime singer in the film. The trick is to bring out questions and related discussions to delay the final signature until the point of no return passes. Then you have a chance of getting what you want." Murad said good-bye and left.

After a week, a package arrived from Colombia Pictures complete with all the information related to the film. Charles wrote a letter to Sybille asking her to help Sara practice and, if necessary, modify and experiment. "If you can improve the melody and presentation, you can tape one song at a time and FedEx them to me. We will play and discuss them. I know you and have total confidence in you and Sara. I would like to work as a team with your people. Sybille, I am going to retire next year, and this will be my last musical. For that reason, I do want the best, like Sara. I know Sara and you need to know the story of the film. The songs must represent the feel and emotions of the scene."

Sybille told him that Sara had already asked for the story so that she could bring the correct emotions to the scene. "Sara told me she knew she could make the audience cry or laugh if she knew the scene. We are working on songs and doing well. What we need is the pilot, to fit the right emotion in at the right place. Charles, you know what she did with *Madame Butterfly*.

Charles promised, "As soon as the pilot is available, I will send you a copy. In about sixty days, the first rough cut will be screened in our Hollywood studio, where script writers, songwriters, and music directors along with the primary singer will be invited to first screening. Keep up the good work. I am counting on both of you. Keep well."

Chapter 20

GG BECOME'S PART OF RESEARCH TEAM

One day, Dr. Mark Simpoon called and reminded Sybille and Norm about the International conference on human and animal communication. He told Sybille that the conference would start in two months at the university auditorium. This time, six countries were presenting papers and their own talking birds, like mynahs, big macaws, and south Asian parrots. The subject of human and animal communication had stirred an unusual interest, and some papers were reporting progress in sonic and sub-sonic recordings, thereby giving birth to a human and animal voice communication dictionary. "We would like your and Miss Isabel's involvement if possible," Mark concluded.

Sybille told him that it was not the best time for her because Sara had a contract to sing in an upcoming film. "We are really busy, but I will call Isabel in Madrid. If she can help us out, we may be free during your conference time. Good luck, and let us hope for the best."

Sybille hung up. She talked to Norman and phoned Isabel, who said she would be delighted to take part in the conference. Sybille told her that the university would send her an invitation and a return airline ticket.

Murad was able to finalize Sybille's contract to his satisfaction. All the songs were rehearsed and presented in the New York studio. Charles Burman accepted Sara and Sybille's suggested changes in some songs, and the final presentation was made with a complete orchestra. There was a tremendous feeling of joy and satisfaction in the studio and a sigh of relief for Sara and Sybille. According to Charles, the final acceptance of the film score would be when the songs were integrated with the players on the screen. Charles called Sybille and told her, "I think we have the best songs and a musical score we all can be proud of. I am waiting for a preview of the film, when we will be invited to see the final product, so tell Sara and Norman to be ready to fly to LA next Thursday. Bring Murad as well to enjoy the fruits of labor."

The final showing was screened for the major players, music critics, and the press corps. It was a huge success. *Entertainment News* called it the best musical since *Oklahoma*. The film was released soon after in every large city in the US and Europe. Sara became the number one on *Hit Parade* and became busier than ever.

Sybille called Dr. Simpson and told him that she had some time available and that Isabel would be coming on Friday for the conference. She said, "Mark, you have to send me the program for the session, and Isabel and I would like to have GG and Pita for few days to judge and evaluate their communication skills."

Mark was happy to hear that GG and Pita would get a refresher course. Isabel arrived with her husband. Norman was pleased to have Oskar around while Isabel and Sybille were going around town together. Murad and Sara were on a film promotion tour sponsored by Colombia Pictures. Norman called Karl and asked him to go and see the film with the whole family. The next day, they all went to see the film, and they heard Sara singing in the background.

Mark and his staff brought GG and Pita's little houses to Sybille's place. The two birds were surprised to see Sybille and Isabel, and GG said to Pita, "Look, Pita, my mama Isabel is here. Say hello to Mama Isabel and Sybille."

Isabel went near the houses and said, "It is so nice to see both of you." GG told Isabel that she smelled good, like a garden.

Sybille and Norman took the birds into the studio, where there was a piano. Sybille had asked her cousin Ingrid to bring her cat so that they could go through the communication investigation as it was described in the seminar program.

As soon as Ingrid brought the cat, GG said, "We don't need the cat, Mama Sybille."

The cat started to make funny sounds. Isabel asked GG, "What is the cat saying, Pita?"

GG shouted, "The cat is mad, and she says she will eat us."

Sybille told Ingrid to put the leash on the cat. Sybille said to the birds, "The cat will not bother you now."

Suddenly, GG and Pita barked like dogs, knowing that would scare the cat. She rushed to hide behind her master. GG and Pita started to laugh like humans. Sybille and Isabel burst out laughing while Ingrid picked up her cat and took her in her arms.

Sybille and Isabel continued their training program with GG and Pita. Isabel remarked, "GG's behavior, her perception, and her intelligence are unusually skilled and natural. She still loves her hard candy. I would like to test her memory and knowledge. Let us see what happens. As far as Pita is concerned, she still has to learn a lot before she can be like GG."

Isabel set a teaching program. She bought a world globe that had the capital of every country labeled in red. She planned to test GG's memory by teaching her the capitals of ten countries. Isabel explained to GG and Pita what was being planned. She set the globe on the same table that both birds were sitting on. Isabel spun the globe, and it stopped at India. She pointed at the bold red letters reading "Delhi" and told her that was the capital.

Every time Isabel spun the globe, GG wanted to spin it with her beak. Every time she saw a red word, she and Pita shouted the name of the capital.

In two hours, both birds were able to name four countries and four capitals. It was lunchtime. Isabel told GG to teach Pita what she had learned. She would spin the globe and ask Pita to tell her the capital. If she remembered the capital, GG would give Pita a candy and take one for her.

Sybille and Isabel came back from lunch and asked GG, "Show Mama Sybille the capital of Turkey."

GG turned the globe with her beak and stopped at Turkey. With her beak, she pointed to Ankara. Sybille was impressed with GG's performance, but the object of her research was to confirm that talking birds could understand other voice animals. Sybille explained to Isabel what the study meant by the term "voice animals."

Sybille said, "GG said that she and Pita can understand any animals that make sounds, like dogs, cats, and doves."

Isabel asked, "GG, what about fish?"

She answered, "Fish don't talk. Mark said they talk sub sonically. We don't know subsonic talking."

Sybille told Isabel, "Dr. Mark told me the seminar is going to present sound recordings of dolphins and other aquatic species as well as higher-frequency recordings of some animals like elephants and tigers. Researchers are compiling and cataloging words and sentences with the object of preparing a dictionary. Dr. Mark emphasized that our object is to find translators who are able to clearly talk to researchers and interpret the garbled voices of other animals, like cats, dogs, and chickens. After a reliable technique is established, there will be no limit to our investigation. We are only limited in time and money."

Norman and Isabel were quite impressed with the methodology of achieving a means of understanding and communicating with the so-called voice animals. Isabel and Sybille continued training GG and Pita. The following week, Dr. Simpson took back the gray parrots and prepared them for the opening of the human and animal communication conference.

The second conference featured greater participation from researchers from the European, Asian, and African continents as well as South America. The birds that could speak and understand Spanish, English, and French were amazingly clear and emotionally balanced. At the close of the conference, Dr. Mark Simpson thanked the participants for sharing their experiences and findings. He emphasized that there was still lot of work to be carried out in order to unlock the communication problem. He suggested to the researchers, "There has to be a common link or common thread to the barking of a dog, the purring of a kitten, and the crying of mourning dove. I urge you to seek out funding from wildlife protection institutions to carry on this important mission."

Everyone applauded. The delegates from each institution and from each participating country came and thanked the host, Dr. Simpson, as well as the University for this Initiative. A delegate from Brazil commented, "This has been a project full of fun, amusement, stress relief, and a sense of achievement, all in one." The audience got up and cheered. The conference was over, and everyone went home.

Sara and Murad returned from their film promotion tour after one month. The monetary gain for Sara from Colombia Pictures was substantial. It was the first time for a month that they all sat down for lunch together. Norman told them all what had happened at the conference. "Isabel and Sybille played an important role in proving the importance of African Gray parrots in deciphering dogs' and cats' communication within their species as well as with other animals." Sybille said, "The conference and seminars were attended by representatives from different countries."

As she was talking, the telephone rang. Norman answered. It was Peter Savera. Norman gave the receiver to Sybille, and she said, "Good afternoon, Papa. Is everything all right?"

Peter told her, "Your grandpa Carlos is not well, and he asked me to tell all the children to come to Savera house next Friday. Father said, 'I want to tell them few important things and give them tasks and responsibilities before I lose control of my faculties.' Sybille, please arrange to follow my father's last wish. He is getting weaker by the day. See you soon."

All children and their families from all over the world came. They were invited for lunch, so they were sitting in the main dining room, and everyone was sitting quietly and in a somber mood. After a little while, the nurse wheeled in Grandpa Savera. All the children and grandchildren got up and welcomed him by gently clapping. Peter was standing next to his father. Grandpa Carlos asked for Sybille, and she approached him, gently hugged him, and kissed him. He asked for Sara and Murad, and both walked up to him and kissed him. Peter told Sara to hold his right hand and Murad his left. The photographer was there to record all this. When all the children were around him, he asked his trusted secretary, Nicola, to hand over a manila envelope containing a letter instructing them to get higher education and dedicate their efforts to working for the Savera Corporation.

Each envelope contained a check for the amount equal to their share in the corporation. The biggest check went to Sybille and Sara because of their earnings, which had been deposited in the Savera Corporation. The assistant to Grandpa Savera also announced a restructuring of the corporation, making Oskar Savera the Chief operating officer. Oskar's wife, Isabel, was nominated as the first vice president. Peter Savera and his wife, Andrea, were appointed as advisers and board members of the corporation.

After the business affairs were over, Grandpa asked for a glass of water. He took a sip, cleared his throat, and started to talk to his audience, "As you all are aware, my father, Juan Savera, was the creator of this most successful enterprise. When he passed away, it became harder and harder to continue. The political situation changed, Russia changed, and the Soviet Union broke up, changing the whole dynamics. Today after sharing and handing off my responsibilities, I feel that a big load has been lifted from my shoulders. Thank you."

Sybille and her father, who was the only son of Carlos, were delighted to see him speak in a clear and strong voice. Sybille asked her cousin Oskar, "Do you think this load almost took his life? I am so sorry that his only son, my father, could not share his dilemma. I understand that because of the political situation, the corporation had to diversify or fold."

Oskar and Isabel were not so enchanted with Oskar being named the head of the corporation. Oskar told Sybille, "Grandpa is aware of these facts. Very capable staff began diversifying five years ago. The corporation has invested a large portion of its assets in major US and German companies, giving a big boost to its profit margin. I am quite upbeat."

Sybille kissed her cousin and told him, "Oskar, I know Grandpa has appointed the right man for the job. Good luck. We love you. Isabel, your wife, is my best friend. If you need any moral support, Norman and I are there for you. By the way, Sara and Murad have a new company called 'Saramur Enterprise.' Sara, Murad, and I have come up with a new concept of entertainment. Everyone knows that operas have been around for centuries, and they do not attract young and modern population. There is a reason for that. The story is there, and there is fantastic music written by famous composers, but the dialogue is not in spoken words. It is in boring musical language nobody can understand. We are rewriting *Madame Butterfly*. We will use the famous arias, but the geisha will have a normal love affair with an American hero, like in the movies. There will be a romantic conversation, etc. You see what I mean? We are in the process of converting most popular operas, and we will call them opera stories. Murad is checking legal aspects and copyrights."

Isabel was excited. " Sybille, you have a brilliant idea."

Grandpa asked for Sybille, Norman, Sara, and Murad to meet him in his study. He told them, "The reason I called you is to congratulate you, Sybille and Norman, on Sara's wedding. I like Sara's choice; he is handsome and very smart, just like my favorite little girl, Sara. I am glad for the opportunity to see them before my eyes and mind stop functioning. My son helped me pick out a gift for them. It is one of the best computers available, which Sara and Murad will need to run their Saramur enterprise."

Sara and Murad were so happy that both of them bent down and kissed his bony hands. Grandpa became emotional, and tears of joy were running down his thin face. They all started to cry. The nurse wiped his tears. He pulled himself together; he told them that the car was ordered to take them to the airport at four p.m. They said good-bye, and he said bon voyage.

Oskar, Isabel, Peter, and Grandma Savera were waiting downstairs to say good-bye. Norman's family got into the car and left. Norman said to Sybille, "Did you see how your grandpa was a changed man after handing over the command of his corporation? Sybille, did I ever tell you that I felt the same effect after I gave up the reins of my company?"

Norman and his family slept throughout the flight. They arrived home wide awake and ready to make plans to hire professional writers to convert the most popular operas into opera stories. These stories would become scripts for plays or movies. This was intended to get rid of the elitist attitude of so-called cultured people about operas; an average citizen would be able to discuss operas in society without feeling ignorant or void of culture.

Murad called the university, where one of his childhood friends was a computer instructor. He told him, "Sara's grandfather has given us an IBM computer as a wedding gift. I don't know anyone who has a computer. Can you come over to my house to set the computer up and show me and Sara the basic functions?"

Amir, Murad's computer man, came over that afternoon and, with the help of Norman, set up the computer in the studio. It took him at least an hour to set it up. Murad was on his way home from the office. Norman helped Amir set up and run the computer. Amir told Norman that he would need a separate phone line to get the Internet working. A man from the phone company showed up to install a new line.

When Murad showed up, he was glad to see the computer and Internet working. His friend stayed for dinner and started to show them the workings of the Internet. Norm and Murad were trying to learn from Amir. Sara and Sybille came into the studio. They were amazed at the ability of the computer to find answers to many questions and provide important information not in minutes but in seconds. Amir was answering Murad's questions, and Sara was writing down the answers. It took more than a week to learn the basic functions. Amir came to Murad's place every day to show him how to get quick and accurate information on almost any subject.

Sybille and Sara made a list of the twelve most popular operas with very sad, but interesting, stories. Murad and Amir did background research on each opera. He contacted Joshua Lang, his agent in New York, and asked him to fly out the next day.

In the meantime, Sybille and Norman called their friend Peter Scott, a well-known Canadian writer. Sybille asked him if he had some time for a small project. Sybille asked him, "Peter, could you come tomorrow for breakfast? We would like to discuss a project that needs to be rewritten."

Sybille and Norm had already told Murad and Sara about Peter Scott coming for breakfast. They knew there might be issues with confidentiality, so Murad and Sara had already prepared secrecy documents. If Peter Scott agreed to write twelve opera stories, he would sign these security agreements and contracts, which outlined the monetary compensation and conditions for each story.

Peter arrived the next morning around nine. Norman took him to the dining room, where he met Sara and Murad. He sat in between Sybille and Norman. He kept asking about the secret project, but he was told to eat his breakfast. Only after that would Murad and Sara give him all the information, provided he agreed to take up the challenge.

After breakfast, they moved to the studio. Murad explained to him that there were twelve stories for him to write. Sara said, "We will give you enough material to write the story and dialogue. The stories already exist, but we want to adapt them for our requirements."

They continued to discuss the project. Murad finally asked, "Peter, are you interested in the project?"

Peter answered, "How do you want me to answer without knowing the subject matter? "

Sybille and Norman told him, "If you are interested, Murad will bring the confidentiality papers for you to sign."

Murad brought out the documents, and Peter signed them without hesitation. Sara and Sybille explained to Peter the basic concept and general outlines of their requirements. Their company, Saramur Enterprises, wanted to convert at least twelve operas to spoken language. Sybille and Sara were able to answer all the veteran journalists and writers' questions.

Peter sat back in his chair and said, "Why I did not think about that? It is so simple. You retain the character and the story of the opera, including the music. Now, I am sure that people who hate to go to Operas, like me, will be able to understand and enjoy the conversation between the characters. These stories will retain the heavenly music but replace the boring singing dialogue. People went to operas because it was a cultural thing and the composers were phenomenal; their music was a big attraction. Sybille, can you imagine? When your opera story of *Madame Butterfly* comes out with the original music score, you will kill the opera market."

Sybille said, "Peter, we are not there to kill the opera market. We are trying to make opera palatable to others. The opera market will still be there for elitists to show off their formal gowns and tuxedos. Don't forget, I was a top opera singer in my younger days."

Sybille and Sara told Peter, "If you want to start writing, we will have the package ready for you a week from today."

Peter told them, "The sooner I get it, the sooner I can start. I am very curious to finish one and let you be the judge."

As he was walking out of the studio, he saw the computer. He said to Murad, "Is this what I think it is? Boy, it seems to have everything. I see it has a printer, too."

Murad was pleasantly surprised. He asked, "Peter, have you used a computer in your work? Would it be faster than writing manually?"

Peter said, "Murad, sure. My last customer provided me an office with an IBM in their facility. Believe you me; I was able to write all their manuscripts in less than half the time. Not only that, but the computer corrected spelling mistakes, grammar, and the structure of phrases. It printed nice and clean pages, numbered them, and even gave the number of written words per manuscript. They gave me a bonus because their editing department had such an easy time."

He turned to Sybille and Norm and asked them, "Do you want me to use your computer? I will give you a good deal, and it will save me and you lots of time. Arthritis is bothering my hands; I am not so young anymore."

Sybille looked at Norman, Sara, and Murad. They said, "Why not?"

Just before he was about to leave, he asked Sybille, "You think I can come at nine-thirty for breakfast?"

She said, "All right, but don't make a habit of it. I know you smoke, and that is not allowed here."

Peter told her, "Not to worry about that. I promised my dying wife that I will quit today if she would promise to live another day."

They all felt sorry for him. He left quietly.

Peter Scott came at exactly nine-thirty the next day and was invited into the kitchen for breakfast. He looked a lot better, not so depressed and more cheerful. Sybille gave him a folder marked in bold letters *"Madame Butterfly* Story," containing the story and singing dialogue. Peter Scott had done a lot of work with film producers and writers; he could visualize the total picture in his mind.

It took Peter two weeks to write the story with dialogue. His written words were very descriptive. The romance between the American and Madame Butterfly was full of love and joy. Peter was a master at describing love, desire, and passion. When he finished the first draft of the story, he gave a copy to each member of the family to comment on and criticize. Sybille corrected Peter's work and suggested revisions. Sara seemed happy with what Peter had written. It took another week to finalize the story and the script.

Murad and Sara picked up the agent, Joseph Jordon, from the airport and brought him to the house. After a little refreshment, they all went to the studio. Murad gave the security and secrecy papers to Joseph, and he signed without any hesitation. They were quite interested to see Joseph's reaction to the idea. Since Sybille was the opera expert, she tried to explain the object and the end product of this project. After asking many questions, he asked, "Are you sure that no one has done this conversion? It looks so logical, with huge marketing possibilities in movies and theater. I think you have hit the jackpot. Now, have you got any opera stories ready to show?"

Sybille gave him the folder. Joseph was so excited that he wanted to make a call to Colombia Pictures vice president Kevin Hagar immediately. His secretary answered. She told him that Mr. Hagar would be in at nine-thirty. Joseph was confused until Murad reminded him that there was a three-hour time difference between Toronto and LA.

Joseph said, "Sybille, I am so charged up with your new discovery that I forgot the time difference."

Murad, Sybille, and Sara continued to discuss the project. Joseph said, "*Madame Butterfly* may not be the best story to convert, and I think it was already written by an American author, so the dialogue is already there. I see you have a computer. Let us turn to the Internet and find out everything about the opera."

Joseph researched the history of *Madame Butterfly*. Its author, John Luther Long, originally published the story in a newspaper. Puccini made the story into an opera in 1898. Of course, the addition of beautiful music by Puccini made it famous. It played almost in every city in Europe. Murad and the family were disappointed in their selection of *Madame Butterfly* as the first opera to convert into a story production.

Peter showed up for work late. Sybille told Joseph and Peter along with the rest of the gang to come to the living room, where they held an emergency meeting. She broke the news to Peter about the selection of *Madam Butterfly*, revealing that it had already been a published story before Giacomo Puccini converted it into an opera in 1898.

Peter's jaw dropped. He said, "I wish I had checked the computer before starting to write." Peter went through the list of operas that were to be adopted for conversion. He identified the author, composer, and the story with singing dialogues for each. Peter and Sybille selected eleven operas that were suitable for conversion. Sybille told Peter, "Remember, we are not going to make any changes in the music or songs, and we are not going to make drastic changes even in the singing dialogue, except to remove the music and write spoken words that come close to the sung ones. However, nothing stops us from refining the dialogue to achieve a meaningful and understandable conversation. We will let the music director decide what music goes with the situation."

Sybille and Sara promised to help Peter by going through his completed work every night.

A few weeks later, Murad called Joseph and told him that there were three new converted operas that had been checked and finalized for discussion. Joseph was very enthusiastic and told Murad, "Colombia Pictures wants us to go to LA and make a presentation using at least three selected operas. The production and music directors want us to play the beginning and the end of the old operas. After that, they want us to present the same three, in converted form."

Murad replied, "There is no problem in presenting the beginning and the end of the operas. We will act out the scenes by deleting the sung words and replacing them with spoken words along with light background music. I will discuss this with Sybille and Sara. Come to think of it, Sybille knows a filmmaker who could take the existing VCR of the old opera, delete the singing words, and insert the spoken words with chosen music playing in the background. Let me see how quickly it can be done."

Murad talked to Sybille, who said, "Norman, do you remember the man who taped operas and did all kinds of trick photography, changed voices, and inserted jokes?"

Norman thought for a while, and a name popped up in his mind: Edward Brown. Norman remembered him as an expert on VCR making. He modified images and dubbed videos with strange voices. He looked in his files but could not find Edward's contact information. Sybille came up with his last address and phone number. She called him. Norman and Sybille were glad to find him. Norman explained to him the situation. He asked Ed, "Would it be possible for you to come over to discuss the project?"

His answer was, "I could see you in the afternoon, say at two o'clock."

Edward Brown came over that afternoon. Sybille, Sara, and Norman took him to the studio, where Peter was working on the computer. Norman introduced Ed to Peter. They sat down. Sybille explained to Edward the situation. Edward told to Sybille and Norman, "I think I can help you. Using your computer, we can isolate dialogues that belong to the sections of the opera for presentation. Also, we will need at least two male and female voices to say the dialogues involved in the required sections. Sybille, you can read the dialogue that Peter will print out. When we do a drama on the radio, one actor reads her part, the other player reads his part, and then I can do the rest. Believe me; this kind of production is being done routinely."

Peter told Ed, "I can give you dialogue for those sections—no problem."

The whole team spent almost two weeks writing and rewriting the three operas and coming up with the music scores. They rehearsed again and again. Finally, Edward Brown asked Sara to sing arias from the beginning and end of the operas. Ed recorded those live on his machine and synchronized the dialogue with Sara's live singing. Edward showed both the old operas and the converted pieces. Everyone was stunned to see and hear the converted operas. They were easy to understand, and the main arias sung by Sara added a powerful combination of clean and smooth listening.

When Murad was back from office, he was received by Sara with hugs and smiles. She told him, "We did it. Do you want to listen and compare the new version with the old one?"

They all listened again, and Murad could not wait to call Joseph Jordon. He told him, "Joseph, we are ready. It is unbelievable what all these people have achieved in two weeks. Sara, Sybille, and Norm got the right people who knew what they were doing, so call your friends in LA and tell them we will be there on Sunday, for a ten o'clock meeting on Monday. By the way, Joseph, you come here on Saturday and judge for yourself. We all can fly from Toronto."

Joseph was thrilled and told Murad, "I can't wait till Saturday."

Murad, Norman, Sybille, and Sara were all busy organizing paperwork, VCR tapes, and other necessary items related to the presentation. Both Peter and Edward helped in rehearsing and more rehearsing until Murad and Sybille were satisfied and felt confident. On Saturday, Murad picked up Joseph from the airport. They all gathered in the studio and went through the rehearsal.

Joseph said, "Boy, I cannot believe you were able to do that in such a short time and so efficiently."

The next morning, they all left for Colombia Pictures in Los Angeles. Sara and Sybille were tired and dozed off on the way while Murad, Norman, and Joseph were discussing the prospects of Colombia Pictures going into totally unknown territory.

Joseph said, "There is one thing for sure. If they sign an exclusive deal, they could franchise drama deals and at the same time make films out of these operas. Murad, just imagine. They could have twenty-five to thirty-five movies. They won't have to pay movie writers, song writers, or music directors. I think you will need a music director to direct the orchestra if you want Sara and Sybille to sing the arias."

Murad said, "We want both Sara and Sybille to sing when there is a need for female opera singers. This is where we can cash in more. Let's face it: where could they find better, more experienced opera singers?"

The plane touched down. Murad and Joseph went down to collect the baggage. When they came out of the terminal, Colombia Picture's limousine was waiting. Everyone climbed in, and the limousine took them to a multistory Colombia Pictures guesthouse situated close to the studio. It was already two p.m.; they went down to the restaurant and had their lunch. Joseph Jordon made a call to his counterpart in the studio office. The secretary picked up the phone and gave him the details of the next day's meeting. She told Joseph that the limousine would pick them up at ten a.m. and bring them down to the director's hall for a meeting at eleven. This was the corporation's head office and was the most up-to-date studio in the industry.

When they arrived the next morning they saw that the offices were spick and span, giving the impression of a very successful corporation. The walls were decorated with scenes from the company's most outstanding movies and musicals. On the next wall, pictures of presidents and directors were hung meticulously. The boardroom was furnished with a large table and comfortable red velvet chairs.

They were received by the secretary of the board. They sat down, and the chairman arrived along with the other members. Joseph Jordon introduced Sybille, saying, "I am sure the board knows Miss Rockville, the past diva of the opera world. Her daughter, Miss Sara Noury, is the winner of the recent Queen Elizabeth international music award. Here is Mr. Murad Noury, legal representative of Saramur Entertainment, and, finally, the internationally recognized artist Norman Rockville."

The directors introduced themselves. Joseph told the directors, "We are here to demonstrate the old versions of three popular operas, and then you will witness a converted version of the same operas. The arias in the new versions are sung by none other than Sybille and Sara. Now, we are anxious to present a new dimension in the operatic field, opening the gates of heavenly music and stories to all." They were all led to a smaller studio designed to make such presentations. The watching and discussing took longer than expected. They all were there in the presentation room for two hours, and the board members were so impressed that they could not believe what a pleasant change there was from most of the presentations they saw. The presentation sold the project. Murad cautioned the directors to keep the project secret until the rest of the twenty-two operas had been legally protected.

The production director and others told him, "We cannot wait too long. It is a revolutionary idea, and we want to take advantage of it now."

Murad suggested that their legal team work with him to expedite the situation. They all agreed to sign the contract soon and release the three opera stories immediately.

It was agreed that the Colombia Pictures legal team would meet at the Royal York hotel in Toronto on next Thursday at ten a.m.

The trip to Colombia was so successful that Murad, Sara, Sybille, and Norm decided to have a party to celebrate. They invited Karl and his family along with other relatives and friends to join them on the next weekend. Norman invited Ed Brown and Peter Scott, too.

Sara said to Norman, "Papa, you know, we will need jackets for each opera to package these VCRs. If you would design these jackets with your signature, I would be thrilled."

Sybille agreed. She said, "Oh Norman, could you, please?"

Norman agreed. The next day, he contacted his artist Jamal to come over and give him a helping hand in creating designs for twelve jackets.

Norman told him, "It may take me couple of weeks to sketch the designs."

Norman and Sybille received guests to celebrate the success of their famous opera stories. Although they had signed lucrative contracts with Colombia Pictures, this was not just a monetary success; it was a technical and cultural achievement. Sybille and Sara explained to the Canadian broadcasting media that in the old age, operas were watched and enjoyed by the rich and famous, who tried to create an exclusive hold on opera culture. It was the singing dialogue that the opera haters neither understood nor liked. Sara told reporters that their company had rewritten the dialogue in normal conversational language and removed the boring music that accompanied the dialogue without changing the character of the opera.

Sybille said, "I have to tell you, I have been an opera diva for years, and when I saw the new version, I liked it better than the old one."

Peter Scott was very, very happy when he learned that the converted opera story had become a big success. He was more determined than ever to complete the project.

Murad came back from the legal office of Colombia Pictures and sat down with the family. He said, "Papa Norman, we have finally signed the contract and legal agreements. I have to tell you, my boss, Josh Duval, the most experienced attorney in the field of entertainment, got what he wanted. At one point, he told them, 'Listen, if you guys don't play a fair game, we can go somewhere else. Don't forget, this project is innovative, totally copyrighted, and has the best international opera singers. No one else can have what we have.' He told them, 'We are going out for half an hour. In the meantime, you discuss this with your decision makers, and then we will take it from there.' We left and came back after exactly half an hour. The legal team signed the contract without changing one word."

Murad addressed Sara and Sybille, "This contract has been the toughest challenge, not only for me but for all our legal team. This is going to be one of the most lucrative contracts for our corporation."

In the meantime, Peter Scott was inspired by the success of his work, and that was driving him to finish the project as early as he could.

The production was scheduled to begin three months later. Actors and actresses were chosen, stages were built, and scenes were created. Everyone in California was talking about the project with anticipation. The studio in New York sent tapes and information related to all three opera stories, which they called new wave operas.

Sybille and Sara, along with their spouses, received a lovely invitation to attend the inauguration of *Carmen*. Colombia Pictures started a huge ad campaign advertising the new wave opera. The ads appeared on TV, on the radio, and in newspapers and entertainment papers. There were articles written explaining the reason for the popularity of the concept. Of course, some critics played down the idea and complained that the drive of Colombia Pictures to make more money was destroying cultural icons.

Other experts on culture praised the introduction of the new wave operas, calling the idea an achievement that would bring culture to the masses. Sybille and other opera artists gave a statement to the press saying, "We have deprived a great number of people from enjoying the gift of music and comprehensible dramas. It is about time for everyone to enjoy these artistic masterpieces."

When Sara and her family flew to the first screening at the Colombia Pictures, studio, they were treated as royalty. The part held for the inaugural showing featured so much glamour and fanfare that it boggled the mind. The company's money supply seemed to be endless. Sybille and Sara were stars of the show and were escorted by the president and his directors. Before the screening began, opera singers from the Metropolitan Opera came on stage and sang. Charles Burman asked Sara if she would sing an aria from *Madame Butterfly*. She looked at her mother and Murad. Both said yes.

Charles held Sara's hand and escorted her to the stage. He told the audience, "This is our upcoming singing star. Whatever and whenever she sings, it sends a chill through your spine. She is not supposed to be singing here today, but I could not resist. I went and asked her to sing my favorite aria, and her mother and husband said yes, so here is my Sara."

She looked at the orchestra. The conductor waved at her, and the music began. Sara began singing. The auditorium was silent. When she reached the crescendo, the walls and chandeliers seemed to dance. Her voice was powerful and magnetic, yet melodious. When the music stopped, the audience went wild. It stood up and applauded at least for five minutes. Sara's family kept standing until the conductor brought her down to her mother.

Other opera singers delighted the audience, and finally the president of Colombia Pictures, Serco Rossi, came to the podium and addressed the audience. "Welcome to this special screening of the famous opera *Carmen*. The unusual and interesting thing about this production is that I can sit through the story and enjoy it. I remember when I was young; my parents dragged me to the opera in Milan. I could not stand it, could not understand it, and hated the dialogue. I was not alone. All my schoolmates had the same feeling. Two days ago was the first time I sat through an entire opera and enjoyed it. So if you hated the opera as much as I did, here is a treat for you. Enjoy it."

When the show was on, there was a whole lot of interest. Everyone seemed emotionally and physically involved during the show, and every individual was awake. During the time when Sara's voice was thundering, there was pin-drop silence. When the show was over, the audience was on their feet and genuinely showing their appreciation. At the end of the show, the producer, production director, production managers, and vice presidents of different departments gave recognition to all the technical and non-technical participants involved in bringing the show to life. There were important shareholders among the audience. At the end of the show, the company's officials received a market report from their brokers. The word was that Colombia Picture's stock was up just because the new venture was predicted to enhance the prestige and income of the company.

Sybille's family was surrounded by the top brass of the organization; Sara had become the darling of the movie company. Producers from MGM and other large organizations were inviting her to visit their studios. Murad was always by her side to guide and advise her whenever she needed him. While they were about to leave, the art director came to see Norman Rockville and gave him three framed copies of his work that he had done to adorn the VCR jackets. The art director asked him if he would be kind enough to sign few more copies, and Norman obliged.

When Norman looked at Sybille, he saw that she was really tired. He had noticed recently that whenever she went to functions as important and as big as this one, she got exhausted. When Sybille told Sara that she was exhausted, her daughter Sara's answer was always the same: "Ma, you will be seventy-two next month. When we go to our hotel, I will take you for a nice, gentle massage and herbal bath. You always agree to do that but end up in bed, fast asleep."

When they arrived at the hotel, it was eleven p.m., and both Norman and Sybille were fast asleep in a very short time. Murad escorted Sara to their room. She looked tired and sleepy. They went to sleep without any problem.

The next day, Sybille's family flew home. Sybille and Norman were still tired, and when everyone sat down in the kitchen's eating area, the housekeeper and Sybille's personal helper saw that Sybille needed help. She told her, "Finish your dinner, and later I will give you a foot and leg massage."

Sybille went to rest until she felt better. She told Norman, "I don't think I can keep going far away for so many days, attending meetings and parties. Norman, why do I get so tired? Do you get tired too, like I do?"

Norman told her, "I do not get as tired, Sybille, but you are right. We forget that we did a lot more than what our children are doing. Our time to run, jump, and love has passed. It is normal; it is a phase everyone has to go through. Look at your grandfather, Carlos Savera. He is in his last hours or even moments. My darling Sybille, we had a wonderful life. Just think we both reached heights many can only wish for. But Sybille, I know there is one thing that we do not have that almost everyone has: a baby, a grandchild."

Sybille almost jumped with joy, just thinking about it. She said, "I felt there was something missing. We have everything, and I mean everything, but a beautiful baby. But we cannot tell Sara and Murad that."

Norman thought for a moment and said, "I bet you they are thinking about that now, too. Sara also has an internal clock. Both are smart and are very loving."

Another month passed. The new wave operas seemed to have worldwide appeal. The success of Sara and Sybille's records, their public appearances, and more new wave opera releases made more and more money. Murad, in the meantime, started his own law firm and attracted top lawyers in the business to join him.

One day, Sybille's father in Madrid called and told her that her grandfather was very ill. Peter said, "My father achieved a lot in his life. His days on this earth are an anticlimax. He was so busy. And don't get me wrong; he enjoyed being controlling and creating wealth in his prime. The anticlimax crept in slowly and eventually made him bedridden. Luckily, his mind is not following his body. Sybille, I hope Sara is going to have a boy to carry on the Savera name."

Sara interrupted her grandfather. "Grandpa, I am not Savera. I am Nouri, married to Murad."

Peter admitted, "Yes, Sara, you are right. I am always thinking that all my children, married or not married, are Savera. I think I am getting paranoid. I am the last one." Sybille reminded him. "Papa, you are not the last one; Oskar is. Maybe we will find more Saveras. Murad will work on it."

Peter changed the subject. He told Sybille, "We would love to see you and your family. Come with Sara and her husband. If you all agree, we all can go to Majorca. Sara and Murad were supposed to go there, but they never did. I do not know what happened. I am expecting you and your family to be here the day after tomorrow. Good night." Sybille got off the phone and told her family about her grandpa's grave condition. Norman phoned his travel agent to book an early flight to Madrid and arranged the necessary transport arrangements.

Early the next morning, Norman, Sybille, Sara, and Murad were sitting at the table. The smell of pancakes was in the air. Suddenly, Sara got up and ran toward the bathroom. Murad was worried. Sybille went in and brought Sara back and announced to everyone, "She is all right. She did not throw up. May be she is tired."

Sara was becoming stronger. Two months passed. Sara had a good appetite and started to feel as if she was putting on too much weight her mother was sure Sara was pregnant.

Sara started to cry. Happiness gripped everyone. Murad was thanking God silently. Sara asked her mother, "Mama, is it true?"

Murad was so happy that he picked up Sara and danced around. Sybille told Murad, "Do not do that. She could get dizzy and fall."

It was wonderful news. Norman called his friend Dr. Chen and gave him the good news. Dr. Chen came to see Sara and her family, and he brought his wife, Lily, who was a practicing gynecologist.

Norman told Murad, "You know, it is like a miracle. Things happen to us at the right time, as if it were prescribed and written. You know, the other day Sybille's father called and told us that Grandfather Savera was very ill. He told Sybille that he, Peter Savera, was the last male member of the Savera clan. The only hope we now have is that if Sara has a baby boy, the Savera name can continue. Can you imagine? Your son could save the future Savera generations."

Sybille said, "I don't think it is right. Sara's children's name is Noury, not Savera. What about Oskar? He is a Savera too."

The next morning, Norman's family left for Madrid. Dr. Lily Chen had given Sara medication to deal with any pregnancy-related problems. When they arrived in Madrid, they were picked up and brought to the Savera house. The house was in a somber mood. Grandpa Carlos Savera lay in his bed as if he was in a coma. Sara stayed at home with Murad and Grandma Savera. All the family was aware of Sara's condition. The servants looked after Sara. It seemed that the Savera family members knew the situation and were silently praying for a boy.

Sara and Murad suddenly became the saviors of the clan. They were treated like royalty. The next day, everything was back to normal, and arrangements were being made to take the Norman Rockville family to Majorca. Sara and Murad were finally able to stay in Majorca. They were given the honeymoon suite. Murad was worried for Sara, knowing that she was expecting.

Peter, Andrea, and Sybille's family were in a larger complex facing the ocean. It was the first time in a long time that Sybille had felt so close to her father. He had a feeling of comfort and unusual internal happiness that he had never recovered after his wife Anna's devastating murder. His granddaughter Sara was standing in front of him. He had never looked at her so closely. Even if he was close by, his mind had been far away. He looked at Sara, and he could not believe how beautiful she was. All her fame and fortune flashed in front of him. Peter remembered very well what his grandfather had told him before he fell very ill and had become bedridden: "My boy, your mother told me that Sara, your granddaughter, is expecting. It is big news. I hope she will have a boy to carry the name of Savera."

Peter replied, "Papa she is married outside the Savera family. How could her son carry on the Savera name?"

Grandpa thought for a while and said, "You are right, my son. It is possible that they could use Savera as a middle name." Those were his last words before he went into a coma situation. He was so concerned about the Savera name disappearing after Oskar and Peter were gone. After that, Peter would be the chief of the Savera clan. That it was his responsibility to keep the clan informed and give its members a sense of pride and belonging.

When he finished replaying his memories, he saw that Sara was still standing before him. He took her arm and gently made her sit next to him. All the memories of lovely little Sybille came back to him, and he heard Anna's voice saying, "Be careful, Peter." He tried to fight his small tears. Sara saw that, wiped his tears, held his hand, and kissed him. He felt good. Sybille was not far away. Andrea moved to get up from the sofa and gave Sybille a place close to her father. Sybille suddenly saw Andrea as an angel who, in spite of Peter's devotion to his past wife, Anna, did not stop serving and loving Peter.

Murad came and told Sara, "Come and see the sun going down. It is so beautiful."

They all went to the balcony and enjoyed the moment. It was about time to go to the dining room; they went to their rooms and got ready for dinner.

Murad and Sara were admiring the Mediterranean architecture and the bright blue and yellow colors. They were directed to their large table. As they were walking, a handsome older couple came and stood right in front of Peter. He looked up and recognized the couple. Peter said, "How wonderful to see both of you here after fifty years. I am sorry, but I've forgotten your name."

Sybille reminded Peter, "Papa, they are the famous Spanish tennis stars, Nazareth and Estefan."

Peter was delighted. He told Sara, "Anna and me played tennis against them during our honeymoon. They were so good that it was almost impossible to have a normal game. I remember, Sybille, your mother, Anna, was laughing all the time. We, of course, could not even see the ball when they served. Did you know, Sybille, that year they represented Spain at the Olympics?" Peter introduced Andrea, Norman, and Murad.

Nazareth told Peter, "We know Sybille and Sara. They are international celebrities. I always loved Sybille's singing, and now recently, Sara has become a sensation and the darling of the younger generation."

Peter and family were enjoying each other's company. Sara told her grandpa that she felt tired and would like to go to her room. Murad and Sara said good night and left. Three days passed, and they all left for the Savera house. The next day, Sybille, Norman, Sara, and Murad all left for Toronto. Before leaving the Savera house, Murad promised Grandpa Peter that he and his office would search to see if there were any other Savera family members living in any part of Europe. He told Peter that his legal team was always searching for relatives to settle inheritances. He told Grandpa Savera they often found relatives in strange places.

As time passed, Sara got tired more easily and needed more rest. Often, Murad jokingly told her, "Finally, you are getting chubby. You look so radiant and lovely."

Dr. Chen and his wife came to see and examine Sara. After a complete and thorough exam, they told Norman, "Norm, I am pretty sure Sara is going to have twins."

Sybille jumped. She said, "Twins? You mean she is going to have two babies? No wonder she is tired."

Norman asked Dr. Chen, "Can we now determine sex of the babies at this stage?"

Dr. Chen told him, "We have a Swedish machine that can show you the sex of the babies as early as three months. If you bring Sara to our clinic, we can get the results very soon."

SARA IS EXPECTING TWIN BABY BOYS

The next day, Norman took Sara, Sybille, and Murad to Dr. Chen's clinic. They were all taken to the examination room. Everyone waited anxiously as the doctor performed the test. Suddenly, they saw two male organs. Sybille and Norman shouted, "Look at that—two boys!"

Murad kissed Sara. "You have two boys, Sara. Is it not wonderful?"

Sara said, "I know it is nice having boys, but it would have been nicer if there was one boy and one girl." The test was over, and they went home.

Sybille went to Norman's studio, where she found Norman working on architectural drawings. There were more drawings spread on his large desk. The drawings appeared to be of a beautiful mansion. Norman saw that Sybille was a bit perplexed. She looked at him and asked him,

"Norman, are you working on another project for someone? It looks like a lovely mansion."

Norman said, "Oh, I am glad you found these. I have been working on a house design. This house is too small, and now we are going to have two babies coming in few months. Sybille, if we want Sara, Murad, and the babies close to us, I need to design a house that is architecturally and artistically appealing and that offers independent living under the same roof. Tell me, how could anyone refuse such an offer? If they want to move away, Sybille, I do not know if I could take it. It will break my heart. I have already bought a beautiful piece of land in this area. I have been working on this project for about six months with a world-renowned architect friend, Amoco Onazava. Maybe you know her. We have designed a house that looks like a single mansion from outside but has two separate residences inside. It is suitable for the parents and includes a nursery for the babies and two apartments—one for Nanny and the other for a housekeeper. We have added an apartment for their guests. You should see the office Amoco designed. Murad will love it. Sybille, we have money, so why not keep everyone happy? I want everyone, including Ingrid and Karl, to get together tomorrow at ten a.m. in the living room. I will make a presentation, showing the complete design. Amoco will be there, too. I have prepared sketches of all the rooms. Not only that, but we will have the whole house fitted with suitable furnishings and decorated by none other than Adam Ashcraft. I am sure you will like it."

Sybille was getting excited and could not wait to see the details. She asked, "When is this mansion going to be ready?"

Norman told her that the plan was to move in August, just before the babies were born. She was anxious for the presentation, but Norman warned her not to tell anyone yet. He wanted to see the expressions on their faces and see whether they liked the idea.

The next day, everyone came to the meeting. Norman introduced his team, architect Amoco Onazava; Adam Ashcraft, the decorating master; and his drafters. Norman said, "We have been working on a large house design to be built and ready before the babies arrive. This house, if I may say so, is a masterpiece of architecture, with an aesthetic sense of fine lines and gentle curves that will become a standard in house design." Norman asked Amoco to present the architectural aspects.

She pointed out the special design aspect of multifamily living under one roof. Norman got up and pointed out the artistic touches, using slides of every location. Next, Adam showed slides of the bare house before furnishings and decorations and then of the finished product. After the presentation, Sara was so happy; she rushed to hug her father. Murad was stunned to see how much work and how many hours had been spent on the project without anyone else's knowledge. He admitted that the present accommodation had been a source of anxiety and concern. As the time was advancing, the thought of moving his family with new babies was troubling him.

He told Norman, "Papa, today you have solved our problem."

Sybille and Karl admired Norman's ability to quietly present wonderful and practical results. They all thanked Onazava and the decorator, Adam. Norman announced that the ground-breaking would take place early the next morning.

Chapter 21

SEARCH FOR OTHER SAVERA MEMBERS

Carlos Savera was getting better but was very frail. One day Sybille called. Grandpa Savera answered and said, "Sybille, I am glad you called. There is something that is very disturbing. Did you know that there is only one male member of Savera left after your father, Peter, and I are gone? We know Oscar is our last Savera member; after him Savera family will cease to exist, unless he has a son."

Sybille was shocked to learn that. "Grandpa, I never thought that Savera name would disappear. I do not think Oskar and Isabel can have any more babies. Isabel has passed that stage. Grandpa, I remember Papa once mentioned a cousin Savera living somewhere in Portugal."

Grandpa Carlos remembered and said, "Sybille, you are right. Papa Juan Savera had talked about a cousin named Jose, who did not like Communism and Soviet policy. He broke away and left Spain. He was a graduate of medical school in Barcelona. Papa Savera told me that he, Jose Savera, joined Antonio Salazar's party and married his niece. He broke all ties with us and because of Salazar's right-wing policy. We lost contact with him."

Sybille said, "Grandpa, you know Murad, Sara's husband? His legal firm is involved in searching and locating people. Maybe his agents can locate Cousin Jose and his family in Portugal. He must be a well-known figure if he was in Salazar's party. After all, he was a doctor and graduated from Barcelona. Murad's men will find out if he has children or even grandchildren and maybe some male members in his family."

Carlos was happy to know that there was a possibility of finding a male Savera. Sybille told the story to Norman, her husband. Norman suddenly realized that he was also the last member of Rockville name. He said to Sybille, "Did you know that we are in the same boat?"

Sybille was shocked again. "I wish we'd known all this a long time ago, when we could have had a boy. I wonder how many families are in this situation." Sybille discussed this subject at the dinner table and asked Murad to do the research. Sybille provided all the background information to Murad. It took about two weeks before he located a Savera family in Lisbon, Portugal.

Murad sent two agents to confirm the relatives' identities and relationship with the present Savera family. He also told them to talk to Mr. Stephan Savera and tell him that Murad Noury, the husband of Sara, would call him tomorrow evening. He instructed them to get their home phone number and full address. The agents called Murad and gave him the phone number and address. The next evening, Murad called and talked to Stephan, Stephan was delighted to receive Murad's call.

He said, "I understand you will be paying us a visit soon. When do you think we will see you?"

Murad replied, "If I can get a flight tomorrow early morning, I will be there for lunch."

Stephan got Murad's flight number and promised to meet him at the airport. All members of Stephan's family met Murad and greeted him. Stephan and Suzan hugged him, and the boys were happy to shake his hand. Harry told him, "We have seen you on TV with Sara a few times." They brought him home.

Murad told Stephan and Suzan, "You have a lovely home and a beautiful garden." They went in. Murad refreshed himself and sat down. Soon it was lunchtime; the meal was delicious. After lunch, Suzan suggested that they move into the drawing room, where it was more comfortable. Dessert and coffee were served. Murad told Suzan and Stephan that Carlos Savera, the head of Savera family, had been ill for some time and was under doctor's care. Murad asked Stephan, "We have heard many versions of stories and nothing from people who have the real facts. Could you tell me a little about you and your father?"

Stephan answered, "Everything I know about my father is from my mother. She was a charming, very patient, and a gentle woman. I will tell you the shorter version. She told me that my father was an impatient, angry man. He was a long-time friend of Antonio Salazar. When they were in high school together, they were great friends and got heavily involved in a right-wing extremist party. This may have been a backlash from the Juan Savera Communist relationship. He continued his medical studies in Barcelona but he visited Salazar on weekends. In the meantime, Antonio Salazar, being a smart man, reached the top and was elected a president of the party. He was a dedicated Royalist and eventually became the president of Portugal and the territories. My father was already a full-fledged doctor when Salazar became the president, he asked my father to become his personal physician and he accepted it. According to my mother, I was born when Portugal was in its glory; the colonies were responsible for the prosperity in Portugal that gave him more power. During this time, my sister was born. Unfortunately, she was born three months premature. This caused a great concern and sadness for my mother. This was a very painful experience for her.

"Years passed. My sister was doing well. I was in a high school. GG had captured the hearts of young and old on TV. Sybille Savera had become an icon, and the Savera name was most of the time in the news. My friends were always asking me if I was related to Sybille. I did not know what to say, because I was not sure. It started to bother me, so I went to my mother and asked her. She told me, 'Yes, you are a very close cousin of Sybille and of the Madrid Saveras. Your father broke away from the patriarch, who is his first cousin. He had a huge argument with him because they were Communist and was selling Soviet arms to South American countries. You know your father has a bad temper. He walked out from the House of Savera, promising never to return. I am warning you never to mention the Madrid Saveras in front of your father.' My mother was right; I was really afraid of him."

Murad said, "I am sure you are tired. You should rest." Murad looked at Suzan. He asked her, "Could you tell me when and where you and Stephan met?"

Suzan came closer and sat down in the armchair. She said, "It was a long time ago. Stephan was a student at King Memorial Medical Institute. He was tall and handsome. I met him when he was almost at the end of his studies. He and his Spanish friend came to a charitable dance. It was a lovely hall in the hospital auditorium. His friend had his lady friend. She was a nurse, like me, and we knew each other. She introduced me to Stephan. I liked him immediately His mannerism, his demeanor gave me an impression that he came from a very classy family. We were very much impressed with each other, and we exchanged phone numbers.

He did not care too much for dances. We went to museums, parks, and cinema instead.

"He came to do his internship in my hospital. It was easier to be together. His living quarters were here. We were passionately in love, and graduation time came. I could sense that there was something bothering him. Finally, I asked him, 'You seem so disturbed and lost. I have never seen you like this. Would you like to share your concern or problem?' He smiled and said, 'I am glad you asked. You know how much I love you, and I know you love me too. I would like to marry you before I leave for Portugal. My father is a very strict and hot-tempered man. I was always afraid of him. I know he will be there at the airport with my mother to receive me. I don't know, when he sees you with me, how he will react. I have not been able to sleep for one week.' I was really sad and started to cry. I said, 'Stephen, I am sorry I am the cause of your problem.' My eyes were filled with tears. Stephan rushed to me and wiped my tears. We got married without telling his father but had the blessing of his mother. When Stephan and I arrived at Lisbon airport, his father and mother were there. He seemed not be upset, and there was not a hint of anger towards us."

Stephan got up from his chair and came forward and told Murad, "It was amazing. I could not believe my ears. He said, 'My son, congratulations for bringing a charming daughter-in-law. At this moment, Suzan thanked him, bent over, and kissed both of them. Both my mother and father could not help but embrace Suzan and me. In a week's time my father called his friend President Salazar and told him, 'Antonio, my son has come back from England with a medical degree and a lovely bride. I am planning a reception next Saturday, and Mr. President, your presence at the reception will give us a joy and honor.' The reception was held at the president's hall. It was a memorable day. The president came and stayed only for a short period and left. When my mother found out that Suzan was pregnant with twins, she was delighted."

Murad asked Suzan, "Were you surprised that your father-in-law gave you a reception and presented you to the president, who attended your reception?"

Suzan replied, "Murad, the moment we arrived at the airport, I knew that he was happy and proud of his son. With the news that he was going to be a grandfather of not one but two boys, it was a big change in his and my mother-in-law's life."

Stephan told Murad, "It was an amazing scene—the birth of the boys took place at my parents' mansion. The room where Suzan gave birth had one midwife and one nurse, and a senior gynecologist with his assistant. All the necessary equipment was brought from the hospital. The twins were born in the afternoon. There was a big celebration. My father and mother were overjoyed. The boys were named Henry and Harry. I was happy and could not believe how everything was filled with just pure love and happiness.

"Life was pleasant for everyone. Time was flying, children were growing, and I was in heaven. My father remarked once, 'Son, you are the most happy father I have ever seen.' Now my sons are twenty-four years old. After graduating from university in Lisbon, both boys wanted to join the armed forces. Their desire to join the forces came because I served as a medical doctor with a rank of captain in the Portuguese air force medical core. The two boys grew up in the armed forces environment. We had a big circle of friends and life was pleasant. Now I am retired from the air force and am in the process of planning our civilian life. The boys received their university degrees at the convocation only few weeks ago."

Murad thanked both Suzan and Stephan for such a heartwarming story. He asked them if he could call Sybille and give her the good news, as everyone was waiting to hear from him. He called Sybille.

Sara picked up the phone and said to him, "Oh, I am glad you called. Ma is waiting to hear from you. How is it going?"

He told her, "Oh, Sara, these are wonderful people. Is your ma there?" He told Sybille that he would arrange a three-way telephone conversation between Madrid, her, and Stephan's family. "Can you call Papa Peter to be ready to take the call?"

Sybille did as he asked, and then she asked Peter to give the news to Grandpa Carlos. Peter went to see Grandpa Carlos. He was lying in his large bed. Peter went close and gently put his hand on his shoulder. He opened his eyes. Peter said, "Father, we have good news. Murad is in Lisbon right now. He's been at Jose's house since this morning. He has been talking to his son, Stephan, his wife, and his twin twenty-four-year-old sons."

Peter's father came alive. He sat up and said, "Wonderful news. Congratulations are in order." Grandfather was happy and relieved; the news spread in the Savera house, and everyone was delighted. Peter Savera and Sybille decided to call Stephan Savera in Lisbon. Murad made a special arrangement with the telephone company for a three-way communication between Toronto, Madrid, and Lisbon through an operator. The operator was able to get Lisbon and told Peter, "Sir, the bell is ringing. Go ahead and take over." Stephan answered the phone.

Peter said, "Stephan, this is your cousin Peter, in Madrid, and Sybille, my daughter, is on the line from Toronto."

Sybille spoke, "Good evening, Stephan. I am Sybille. It is so good to talk to you."

Stephan said, "The pleasure is ours. We always hoped and wished to meet Grandpa Carlos's family. My wife and children know and love Sara and Sybille. They will not miss them or their performance when they know that they are going to be on television. I did not tell them about the background of our family until my father died a few years ago. Henry and Harry could not believe that one day we would meet not only more cousins but their favorite GG. Now we can talk in front of my mother openly about our extended family in Madrid without any hesitation. Immediately after our wedding in London, I had told Suzan about Sara and Sybille being our close relatives, but I had warned her about my father's anger and dislike of the Saveras in Madrid. I told her not to mention the Madrid Saveras or the extended family in front of my father. Suzan and I noticed a big change in my father's disposition. He was lot happier and at ease. When I setup my medical practice in Lisbon, I found him relaxed, happy, and proud. I could tell, although it was hard for him to show his affection. At that time, I had told my mother, 'Ma, I think if Dad continues to live in stress and anger, the way he has been living, he will not live too long. I can assure you; he will end up with a severe stroke and die.' Unfortunately that is what happened.

"Now my father was gone, and my children, Henry and Harry, were getting older. I saw my friends and their fathers playing, laughing, and just being happy together. I missed that. I never saw my father kissing or showing affection to my mother. From that moment on, I decided that when I had a family, I would play, hug, and kiss them in private and public. I want my wife and children to know that we are a loving family. After my father passed away, the house was stress-free, and watching television or playing outside was a joy and fun. Unfortunately, my mother passed away one year after my father's death. Sybille and Peter, can you imagine—there is someone up there working and planning. Here is my wife. Suzan is dying to talk to you."

Suzan said, "Cousin Sybille, what a delight it is to talk to you." They continued talking for a while. Suzan told Sybille, "The boys want to talk to you."

They told her that they had been watching GG and Sara's singing. They said good-bye to Sybille and gave the phone to Stephan.

Sybille told Stephan, "We and the rest of Savera clan are anxious to see all of you."

Stephan told Peter and Sybille, "It is a strange coincidence; we were sitting at the dining table and planning to go on a holiday outside Portugal. Now we know where we will be going. We will be flying to the Savera house in Madrid."

Peter burst out laughing and yelled, "Bravo!" Peter asked Stephan, "When do you think your trip will start?"

Suzan came to the phone and said, "We plan to take Iberia Airlines. There is one flight leaving Lisbon airport at seven-thirty a.m. tomorrow and arriving at nine-forty a.m. at Madrid International. Peter, one second—Stephan wants to say something."

Stephan said, "Peter and Sybille, you know I have a younger sister. Unfortunately she will not be able to come. I was talking to her doctor, and he told me that her condition is not good. She cannot even get out of her bed."

Sybille told Stephan, "Please give our regards to her and tell her that we will miss her. I hope we will see her one day."

Stephan and Suzan thanked Peter and Sybille for bringing them together. "See you soon. Good-bye until we meet."

Chapter 22

Savera family arrives from Portugal

The day arrived when Stephan, Suzan, and the kids got up early in the morning. Naomi, the housekeeper, set the table for breakfast and called everyone to have breakfast. Naomi's husband helped outside and took care of the old white Mercedes that Stephan's father had bought for the family. George, the driver, prepared the car while the family was having their breakfast.

They all came out to the portico, where the car was parked just outside the door. George had secured the suitcases in the large trunk. Everything was ready. Stephan and the family got in the car. George got into the driver's seat, and they said good-bye to Naomi. In few minutes, the car sped away to the airport.

After talking to Stephan and Suzan, Peter got together with his father and Oskar. Peter gave them the good news. He said, "Papa, Stephan, his wife, and two children, Henry and Harry, are flying next Saturday and will land at Madrid International at nine-thirty in the morning. Oskar, we must organize a welcome party to receive them at the airport."

Carlos sat up in his bed and came alive when he heard the news about the Saveras coming from Portugal. He turned to Oskar and told him to call a meeting with the manager, Bernard. He told Peter, "Call Sybille and ask her to bring the whole family, including Sara and Murad with their children. They should be here in two days. That will be Thursday, before Stephan's family arrives. Peter, call Sybille now, and Oskar, you go and arrange a meeting with Bernard. Go now." Carlos got a little bit too excited and wanted to rest.

The Savera house was looking happy, outside and inside.

Peter, Oskar, Andrea, and others went to receive Sybille, Norman,

Murad, and Sara with the babies. The limousine picked them up and they arrived home. It was four in the afternoon, and after having refreshment, Sybille and her party went to see Grandpa Carlos He was enjoying the little great-great-grandchildren. He sat in his bed, as his wife picked up the babies, one by one, and placed them in Carlos's big bed. The House of Savera was filling up with more members of the family. Peter made sure that every Savera or those related to a Savera was there.

The day arrived when the long-lost cousins from Lisbon were arriving at Madrid airport. The airport lounge was filled with Saveras in anticipation of Stephan, Suzan, and the boys, Henry and Harry's, arrival. The airport manager had made special arrangements to accommodate so many guests. The flight 707 touched down, and as the newfound Saveras approached the terminal, there were shouts of welcome, and the crowd burst out singing Spain's national anthem. The guests were showered with flowers, and two little girls stepped forward and gave roses to Suzan and Stephan. Then two little boys came forward and gave flowers to Henry and Harry. Stephan and Suzan were overwhelmed; Henry and Harry were enjoying the attention of younger boys and young girls. They all got into the limousines. Stephan and Suzan sat with Peter, Sybille, and Oskar. There were mothers, grandmothers, and great-grandmothers waiting in the living room, along with Sara and Murad. It was nice; everyone greeted them and hugged newfound Saveras. It was a pleasant and lively scene.

Two days were spent in getting to know each other. Everyone loved Sara's boys. Suzan exchanged her experiences with her twin boys, and Sara told her stories. Suzan told Sara how much she and the boys loved her and Sybille's singing. She asked Sara, "You think we will have an opportunity to hear you and your mother's voices?"

Sara told her, "I think Mama has planned a concert at the university where Mama and I will sing. We are doing it for a charity to collect money for underprivileged children and to celebrate your visit."

Stephan spent time with Grandpa Carlos, Peter, and Oscar. One could see that the whole clan was at peace and relaxed. Henry and Harry were surrounded by younger boys and girls.

Sybille drove Stephan and his family, showing them downtown. They passed by the university and saw a big billboard, announcing the concert, which was presented by none other than Diva Sybille and daughter Sara. The boys and Suzan were excited and eager to attend the concert. Sara told them that they would leave for the concert tomorrow evening at four.

The next day, they left for the concert hall. They entered the backstage. The boys, Suzan, and Stephan had never been backstage in a theater. They were surprised to see all the elaborate arrangement that goes into making a concert. Suzan and her family were taken to the front seats in the hall, while Sybille and Sara went to the dressing room to get ready for the show. The curtain opened; the house was full. The chairman of charity came to the microphone and thanked the two international stars for their dedication and help in raising funds to help underprivileged children. He thanked the audience for their support as well.

The show began with Sara, singing numbers from her latest album. The audience went wild when she sang, "Let us fly above the clouds of hate and war." The next item was a duet by Sybille and Sara—arias from the operas *La Boehme* and *Madame Butterfly*. The hall was electrified. The audience was standing, clapping, and shouting, "Bravo! Bravo!" The Savera boys, Suzan, and even Stephan just could not believe their ears and eyes at what a live concert could do to the atmosphere in the place; it could never be duplicated on radio or television. After the concert, they were taken backstage. Henry and Harry, Suzan, and Stephan were really thrilled. They all hugged and kissed Sybille and Sara. Soon, the Saveras' manager escorted Sybille and Suzan's families to the waiting limousine. Henry and Harry constantly talked about the concert.

Harry asked his father, "Dad, so what do you think about the concert?"

Suzan said, "Harry, do not bother him you know your father never liked operas."

Stephan was annoyed and said, "Suzan, Harry was asking me, not you. If you really want to know, Harry, I did like today. It has a lot to do with the singers."

Sara and Sybille were sitting next to him, and they kissed him. Sybille said, "Sara, I think Stephan needs to see few more opera concerts, and he will enjoy many hot operas." They arrived home. Sara took Suzan's hand and went inside, while Sybille took Stephan's arm, and they all went in. Almost one week passed. Sybille and Sara informed Stephan and Suzan, "Since you are on holiday, our husbands want you all to come with us to Toronto. We promise you will like it, and we will enjoy your company. You are lucky Sara and I am free for the whole week. Murad will be busy at the courts. Stephan, don't say no, because we already have your plane tickets." They, Sybille and Sara's families, along with Stephan's family left the House of Savera the next day for Toronto, with a big fanfare. Almost all the Savera clan was there at the airport to bid them farewell.

They arrived at Toronto International Airport and were driven to Norman's family home. Toronto weather, compared to Madrid, was cooler and pleasant. Trees were green and flowers were in bloom. As soon as they reached home, the boys were thirsty, so they all sat down in the family room and enjoyed a cold drink. Henry and Harry were eager to see GG. Henry asked Sybille, "Aunty Sybille, would it be possible to go and see GG?"

She told him that she had to call Dr. Simpson at the university and ask him if it was all right to visit GG. Dr. Simpson told Sybille, "I know she would love to see you, even now, when she is getting older. It is too late today, but if you and your nephews come tomorrow at ten in the morning, we will prepare her for your visit."

Sybille told the boys that they all would visit GG tomorrow at ten in the morning. In the meantime, they had some refreshments, and Norman took them to visit his studio. They all loved and admired his studio. Stephan's family was overwhelmed. Suzan said, "Norman, all these things—don't they belong to a museum?"

Norm replied, "Suzan, they are my creations, and they are new."

Stephan told Norman that art deco was very much in demand in Europe; He remembered he'd seen an auction on television. "I saw that an armoire almost like that one, or similar, went for fifty thousand pounds. It was by a French artist and was made in 1926."

Dinnertime came, and everyone was asked to wash hands and come to the table. They had their dinner. Sara brought her twin boys. Henry and Harry were having fun playing with them.

Henry and Harry woke up early and were having their breakfast in the dining room, waiting for Sybille. She came with Stephan and Suzan. The boys were surprised to see their parents going with them. They all arrived at Dr. Simpson's office. Sybille introduced Suzan, Stephan, and the boys to Dr. Simpson, and she told him that her cousins were visiting from Lisbon.

Dr. Simpson took them to the bird sanctuary and told them that GG was not the same. She was getting older, but she still remembered some songs from her shows. He told the boys that she belonged to the African Gray parrot family. "They can easily live to be seventy-five years old. GG was checked last week by our veterinarian. His report said that GG, who is almost seventy-five years old, was doing really well."

They arrived at the sanctuary. Sybille approached the large cage. GG woke up. "Oh, Mama, you came. I missed you."

Sybille told her that she missed her too. She said, "Look, GG, I brought my cousins to meet you. See Henry and Harry? They came to meet you from far away. Can you say hallo to them?"

GG said, "Hello, Harry. Harry, how are you? Mama, I love you. Good-bye, Mama. I have to rest now. Good-bye, Harry, Harry." She closed her eyes and lay down on her little blanket. Sybille and Suzan were wiping their tears. Mark Simpson took Suzan and Sybille's arms and led them away to their car. Sybille and Suzan were sad. Sybille started to drive Nobody talked till they reached the Savera house.

They entered the house. Sara and Norman were waiting for them. Sara and Norm saw Sybille's face. They knew she was crying. Norm and Sara hugged both of them. They took them to the living room, and a girl brought orange juice for everyone.

Sara asked her mother, "Mama, why were you and Suzan crying?"

Sybille told Sara that poor GG looked so tired and exhausted, and it was the way she said "I missed you, Mama."

Three days passed, Sybille did not hear from Mark, so she called him.

He answered, "I am sorry, Sybille. I should have called. You know GG is not doing better. She seems to be hallucinating. She talks in her sleep. A few times I heard her calling you. If you want to come next week, we will be free, and your guests will be gone."

Sybille was hoping that GG might live for few more months. She told Mark that she will be there in one week. Sybille phoned her father again. "Papa, Sara is a bit disappointed that you and Andrea have not come to see our new house and her beautiful babies yet. They will be one month old next Sunday. I know you saw them at the Savera house, when Stephan and his family were there. You should see. The boys they named Danish and Zane are growing. I want you to enjoy them before they are older. They are so cute. They weighed seven and a half pounds each. Murad's parents visited and stayed for one week. Papa, we are in our new mansion, with a smaller section for us and the larger section for Sara's family. Papa, the house is really unique. It has state-of-the-art everything. You will not believe it when you visit Norman's studio. Oh, it is superb. I feel like staying there all the time. The walls are pastel green with a slight hint of misty pink—very soothing to the eyes and mind. You should see the ceiling of the studio. It is some kind of glass that becomes light gray to dark gray, depending on the intensity of the sun. If the skies are gray, the ceiling becomes sunny, and it looks as if the sun is shining outside. It tries to create a pleasant mood. What a lovely feeling. It certainly keeps your depression away. So, when are you coming with Mother Andrea?"

Peter promised to be in Toronto on Sunday. All the family was awaiting his arrival. When Sunday came, Sybille, Sara, and Murad went to pick them up. When they arrived at the newly built mansion, Peter and Andrea could not believe the size of the place. It had six garages, and the driveways had built-in heating systems and lighted channels built in quartz glass. When a car approached the house, the driveway would light up the area.

Peter could not help saying to Norman, "You certainly have raised the standard of house design and architecture. By the way, where are Sara and the babies?"

Sybille took Peter and Andrea to the Sara and Murad section of the house. Sara and Murad came running to meet them. Sara had Zane in her arms, and Murad had Danish in his arms. They were beautiful children. Peter kissed them and gave each of them a golden spoon, which of course Sara took for safekeeping. Sara asked her grandfather if he liked his first pair of great-grandchildren. He answered, "Like them? I love them."

Andrea stayed behind to be with the children, and Norman brought Peter back to Sybille.

The next evening, there was a big gathering of music directors, producers, and friends to celebrate the release of Sara's album by Colombia Recordings. Her song, "Let Us Fly above the Clouds Full of Hate and War," became number two on the hit parade.

The evening ended with Sara and Sybille singing songs from Sara's album. Norman was there with his architect friend, Onazava.

GG DIES IN HER SLEEP

In the meantime, the university in Toronto had issued a report of its latest results on human and animal communication. It was very optimistic in predicting that the international team in the near future was going to release very important discoveries.

Sybille, Sara, and Norman were enjoying Sara's twin babies. The telephone rang, and Sybille answered the phone. It was Mark Simpson. "Oh, how are you, Mark? How is GG?"

Mark replied, "I am okay. It is GG. Lately, she seems to be hallucinating and talking in her sleep. Sometimes she sings. The other day, she was dreaming of you and calling 'Mama Sybille.' I have called a veterinarian. He looked at her and told me it is just old age. I think I would like to bring her to you. If she has to die, she should be with her loved ones."

At this point, Sybille was sad and crying. Norman, after hearing about GG's condition, told Sybille that they would go tomorrow to pick up GG and bring her home. The next morning, when they arrived at Mark's office, Sybille told him, "We are going to take GG home. Hopefully, she will feel better there."

Mark replied, "Sorry, it is too late. She died in her sleep last night."

About the Author

Ash Jafri was born in 1925 in India, the famigrated to Pakistan in 1947. He went to England in 1950, upon his return, he joined Royal Pakistan Airforce as a cadet and was sent to Florida, USA in 52 for fighter pilot's training, returned to Pakistan, served and left for Canada as an immigrant in 55. He joined University and graduated in 60, married a Venetian Tecla Mel, they had 2 children, Fabia and Danish. Ash joined Bell Northern Research where he was applauded for his work on Metal whiskers, later he joined Litton Systems working on Cruise Missile project. He worked on various businesses and chemical formulations. Florida condo gave them a good and relaxed life to write stories. This is his first book titled "HOUSE OF SAVERA"

CPSIA information can be obtained at www.ICGtesting.com
Printed in the USA
LVOW050753021012

301066LV00001B/1/P

9 781477 264003